Also by J. R. Ward

Dark Lover
Lover Eternal

LOVER AWAKENED

*A Novel of the Black
Dagger Brotherhood*

J. R. Ward

A SIGNET ECLIPSE BOOK

SIGNET ECLIPSE
Published by New American Library, a division of
Penguin Group (USA) Inc., 375 Hudson Street,
New York, New York 10014, USA
Penguin Group (Canada), 90 Eglinton Avenue East, Suite 700, Toronto,
Ontario M4P 2Y3, Canada (a division of Pearson Penguin Canada Inc.)
Penguin Books Ltd., 80 Strand, London WC2R 0RL, England
Penguin Ireland, 25 St. Stephen's Green, Dublin 2,
Ireland (a division of Penguin Books Ltd.)
Penguin Group (Australia), 250 Camberwell Road, Camberwell, Victoria 3124,
Australia (a division of Pearson Australia Group Pty. Ltd.)
Penguin Books India Pvt. Ltd., 11 Community Centre, Panchsheel Park,
New Delhi - 110 017, India
Penguin Group (NZ), cnr Airborne and Rosedale Roads, Albany,
Auckland 1310, New Zealand (a division of Pearson New Zealand Ltd.)
Penguin Books (South Africa) (Pty.) Ltd., 24 Sturdee Avenue,
Rosebank, Johannesburg 2196, South Africa

Penguin Books Ltd., Registered Offices:
80 Strand, London WC2R 0RL, England

First published by Signet Eclipse, an imprint of New American Library,
a division of Penguin Group (USA) Inc.

First Printing, September 2006
10   9   8   7   6   5   4   3   2   1

Dedicated to: *You.*
There will never be another like you.
For me . . . you are the one.
Yeah, I don't have enough words for this. . . .

Acknowledgments

With immense gratitude to the readers
of the Black Dagger Brotherhood
and a shout-out to the Cellies.

Thank you so very much:
Karen Solem, Kara Cesare, Claire Zion,
Kara Welsh, Rose Hilliard.

Thank you to the best dental teams in the world:
Robert N. Mann, D.M.D., and Ann Blair
Scott A. Norton, D.M.D., M.S.D., and Kelly Eichler
and their incomparable staffs.

As always with thanks to my Executive Committee:
Sue Grafton, Dr. Jessica Andersen, Betsey Vaughan.

With love to my family.

Glossary of Terms and Proper Nouns

ahvenge (v.) Act of mortal retribution, carried out typically by a male loved one.

Black Dagger Brotherhood (pr. n.) Highly trained vampire warriors who protect their species against the Lessening Society. As a result of selective breeding within the race, Brothers possess immense physical and mental strength as well as rapid healing capabilities. They are not siblings (for the most part), and are inducted into the Brotherhood upon nomination by the Brothers. Aggressive, self-reliant, and secretive by nature, they exist apart from civilians, having little contact with members of the other classes except when they need to feed. They are the subjects of legend and the objects of reverence within the vampire world. They may be killed only by the most serious of wounds (e.g., a gunshot or stab to the heart, etc.).

blood slave (n.) Male or female vampire who has been subjugated to serve the blood needs of another. The practice of keeping blood slaves has largely been discontinued, though it has not been outlawed.

the Chosen (n.) Female vampires who have been bred to serve the Scribe Virgin. They are considered members of the aristocracy, though they are spiritually rather than temporally focused. They have little or no interaction with males, but can be mated to Brothers at the Scribe Virgin's direction to propagate their class. They have the ability to prognosticate. In the past, they were used to meet the blood needs of unmated members of the Brotherhood, but that practice has been abandoned by the Brothers.

cohntehst (n.) Conflict between two males competing for the right to be a female's mate.

doggen (n.) Member of the servant class within the vampire world. *Doggen* have old, conservative traditions about service to their superiors, following a formal code of dress and behavior. They are able to go out during the day, but they age relatively quickly. Life expectancy is approximately five hundred years.

the Fade (pr. n.) Nontemporal realm where the dead reunite with their loved ones and pass eternity.

First Family (pr. n.) The king and queen of the vampires, and any children they may have.

ghardian (n.) Custodian of an individual. There are varying degrees of *ghardians,* with the most powerful being that of a *sehcluded* female.

glymera (n.) The social core of the aristocracy, roughly equivalent to Regency England's ton.

hellren (n.) Male vampire who has been mated to a female. Males may take more than one female as mate.

leelan (adj.) A term of endearment loosely translated as "dearest one."

Lessening Society (pr. n.) Order of slayers convened by the Omega for the purpose of eradicating the vampire species.

lesser (n.) De-souled human who targets vampires for extermination as a member of the Lessening Society. *Lessers* must be stabbed through the chest in order to be killed; otherwise they are ageless. They do not eat or drink and are impotent. Over time, their hair, skin, and irises lose pigmentation until they are blond, blushless, and pale-eyed. They smell like baby powder. Inducted into the society by the Omega, they retain a ceramic jar thereafter into which their heart was placed after it was removed.

mahmen (n.) Mother. Used both as an identifier and a term of affection.

nalla (adj.) A term of endearment meaning "beloved."

needing period (n.) Female vampire's time of fertility, generally lasting for two days and accompanied by intense sexual cravings. Occurs approximately five years after a female's transition and then once a decade thereafter. All males respond to some degree if they are around a female in her need. It can be a dangerous time, with conflicts and fights breaking out between competing males, particularly if the female is not mated.

the Omega (pr. n.) Malevolent, mystical figure who has targeted the vampires for extinction out of resentment directed toward the Scribe Virgin. Exists in a nontemporal realm and has extensive powers, though not the power of creation.

princeps (n.) Highest level of the vampire aristocracy, second only to members of the First Family or the Scribe Virgin's Chosen. Must be born to the title; it may not be conferred.

pyrocant (n.) Refers to a critical weakness in an individual. The weakness can be internal, such as an addiction, or external, such as a lover.

rythe (n.) Ritual manner of assuaging honor granted by one who has offended another. If accepted, the offended chooses a weapon and strikes the offender, who presents him- or herself without defenses.

the Scribe Virgin (pr. n.) Mystical force who is counselor to the king as well as the keeper of vampire archives and the dispenser of privileges. Exists in a nontemporal realm and has extensive powers. Capable of a single act of creation, which she expended to bring the vampires into existence.

sehclusion (n.) Status conferred by the king upon a female of the aristocracy as a result of a petition by the female's family. Places the female under the sole direction of her *ghardian*, typically the eldest male in her household. Her *ghardian* then has the legal right to determine all aspects of her life, restricting at will any and all interactions she has with the world.

shellan (n.) Female vampire who has been mated to a male. Females generally do not take more than one mate due to the highly territorial nature of bonded males.

symphath (n.) Species within the vampire race characterized by the ability and desire to manipulate emotions in others (for the purposes of an energy exchange), among other traits. Historically, they have been discriminated against and during certain eras hunted by vampires. They are near to extinction.

tahlly (adj.) A term of endearment loosely translated as "darling."

the Tomb (pr. n.) Sacred vault of the Black Dagger Brotherhood. Used as a ceremonial site as well as a storage facility for the jars of *lessers*. Ceremonies performed there include inductions, funerals, and disciplinary actions against Brothers. No one may enter except for members of the Brotherhood, the Scribe Virgin, or candidates for induction.

transition (n.) Critical moment in a vampire's life when he or she transforms into an adult. Thereafter, they must drink the blood of the opposite sex to survive and are unable to withstand sunlight. Occurs generally in the mid-twenties. Some vampires do not survive their transitions, males in particular.

Prior to their transitions, vampires are physically weak, sexually unaware and unresponsive, and unable to dematerialize.

vampire (n.) Member of a species separate from that of Homo sapiens. Vampires must drink the blood of the opposite sex to survive. Human blood will keep them alive, though the strength does not last long. Following their transitions, which occur in their mid-twenties, they are unable to go out into sunlight and must feed from the vein regularly. Vampires cannot "convert" humans through a bite or transfer of blood, though they are in rare cases able to breed with the other species. Vampires can dematerialize at will, though they must be able to calm themselves and concentrate to do so and may not carry anything heavy with them. They are able to strip the memories of humans, provided such memories are short-term. Some vampires are able to read minds. Life expectancy is upward of a thousand years, or in some cases even longer.

wahlker (n.) An individual who has died and returned to the living from the Fade. They are accorded great respect and are revered for their travails.

whard (n.) Equivalent of a godfather or godmother to an individual.

Chapter One

"Goddamn it, Zsadist! Don't jump—"

Phury's voice barely carried over the sound of the car crash in front of them. And didn't stop his twin from leaping free of the Escalade while the thing was going fifty miles an hour.

"V, he's out! One-eighty us!"

Phury's shoulder slammed against the window as Vishous sent the SUV into a controlled skid. The headlights swung around and caught Z rolling on the snow-covered asphalt in a ball. Split second later he sprang to his feet and hauled ass, gunning for the steaming, crumpled sedan that now had a pine tree for a hood ornament.

Phury kept an eye on his twin and went for his seat belt. The *lessers* they'd chased out to Caldwell's rural edges might have just had their ride screwed by the laws of physics, but that didn't mean they were out of commission. Those undead bastards were durable.

As the Escalade heaved to a stop, Phury popped his door while going for his Beretta. No telling how many *lessers* were in the car or what kind of munitions they had. The vampire race's enemies traveled in packs and were always armed— *Holy hell!* Three of the pale-haired slayers got out, and only the driver looked wobbly.

The goat-fuck odds didn't slow Z down. Suicidal maniac

that he was, he headed right for the undead triangle with nothing but a black dagger in his hand.

Phury tore across the road, hearing Vishous pound it out behind him. Except they weren't needed.

As silent flurries swirled in the air, and the sweet smell of pine mingled with leaking gas from the busted car, Z took down all three *lessers* with just the knife. He sliced the tendons behind their knees so they couldn't run, broke their arms so they couldn't fight back, and dragged them across the ground until they were lined up like gruesome dolls.

Took four and a half minutes tops, including stripping them of their IDs. Then Zsadist paused to catch his breath. As he looked down at the oil spill of black blood smudged across the white snow, steam rose from his shoulders, a curiously gentle mist teased by the cold wind.

Phury holstered the Beretta on his hip and felt nauseous, like he'd hammered a six-pack of bacon grease. Rubbing his sternum, he looked left, then right. Route 22 was dead quiet this time of night and this far outside of Caldwell proper. Human witnesses were unlikely. Deer didn't count.

He knew what was coming next. Knew better than to try to stop it.

Zsadist knelt down over one of the *lessers*, his scarred face distorted with hatred, his ruined upper lip curled back, his fangs long as a tiger's. With his skull-trimmed hair and the hollows under his cheekbones, he looked like the Grim Reaper; and like death, he was comfortable working in the cold. Wearing only a black turtleneck and loose black pants, he was more armed than dressed: The Black Dagger Brotherhood's signature blade holster crisscrossed over his chest, and two more knives were strapped on his thighs. He also sported a gun belt with two SIG Sauers.

Not that he ever used the nine-millimeters, though. He liked to get personal when he killed. Actually, it was the only time he ever got close to anyone.

Z grabbed the *lesser* by the lapels of its leather jacket and jerked the slayer's torso off the ground, getting mouth-to-mouth tight.

"Where is the female?" When there was no answer other than an evil laugh, Z coldcocked the slayer. The crack echoed through the trees, a stark sound like a branch snapping in half. *"Where is the female?"*

The slayer's mocking grin jacked Z's rage so high he became his own arctic circle. The air around his body grew magnetically charged and colder than the night. Snowflakes no longer fell anywhere near him, as if they disintegrated in the force of his anger.

Phury heard a soft rasp and glanced over his shoulder. Vishous was lighting up a hand-rolled, the tattoos around his left temple and the goatee around his mouth getting highlighted in the orange glow.

At the sound of another fist pop, V took a deep drag and shifted his diamond eyes over. "You okay there, Phury?"

No, he wasn't. Z's savage nature had always been the stuff of a morality tale, but lately he'd become so violent he was hard to watch in action. The bottomless, soulless pit of him had been on a rampage ever since Bella had been abducted by the *lessers.*

And still they hadn't found her. The Brothers had no leads, no info, no nothing. Even with Z's hard-core questioning.

Phury was a mess about the abduction. He hadn't known Bella for long, but she'd been so lovely, a female of worth from the highest level of aristocracy within the race. Though to him she'd been more than her lineage. So much more. She'd reached beyond his vow of celibacy to the male beneath the discipline, stirring up something deep. He was as desperate as Zsadist to find her, but after six weeks, he'd lost faith that she'd survived. The *lessers* were torturing vampires for information on the Brotherhood, and like all civilians, she'd known little about the Brothers. Surely she would have been killed by now.

His only hope was that she hadn't endured days and days of hell before she went unto the Fade.

"What did you do with the female?" Zsadist growled to the next slayer. When all that came back at him was a "Fuck you," Z pulled a Tyson and bit the bastard.

Why Zsadist cared about a missing civilian female, no one in the Brotherhood could understand. He was known for his misogyny . . . hell, he was feared for it. Why Bella mattered to him was anyone's guess. Then again, no one, not even Phury, as his twin, could predict the male's reactions.

While echoes of Z's brutal work cut through the isolation of the forest, Phury felt himself cracking under the interrogation even as the *lessers* stayed strong and gave up no information.

"I don't know how much more of this I can take," he said under his breath.

Zsadist was the only thing he had in his life other than the Brotherhood's mission to protect the race against the *lessers*. Every day Phury slept alone, if he slept at all. Food gave him little pleasure. Females were out because of his celibacy. And every second he was worried about what Zsadist would pull next and who would get hurt in the process. He felt like he was dying from a thousand cuts, slowly bleeding out. A target by proxy for all his twin's murderous intent.

V reached out with a gloved hand and clasped Phury's throat. "Look at me, my man."

Phury glanced over and cringed. The brother's left eye, the one with the tattoos around it, dilated until there was nothing but a black void.

"Vishous, no . . . I don't . . ." *Shit.* He didn't need to hear about the future right now. Didn't know how he would handle the fact that things were only going to get worse.

"The snow falls slowly tonight," V said, rubbing his thumb back and forth over a thick jugular vein.

Phury blinked as an odd calm came over him, his heart slowing to the rhythm of his brother's thumb. "What?"

"The snow . . . it falls so slowly."

"Yes . . . yes, it does."

"And we've had a lot of snow this year, haven't we?"

"Uh . . . yes."

"Yeah . . . lot of snow, and there's going to be more. Tonight. Tomorrow. Next month. Next year. The stuff comes when it comes and falls where it will."

"That's right," Phury said softly. "There's no stopping it."

"Not unless you're the ground." The thumb stopped. "My brother, you don't look like the earth to me. You're not stopping him. Ever."

A series of pops and flashes broke out as Z stabbed the *lessers* in the chest and the bodies disintegrated. Then there was only the hiss from the shattered car's radiator and the heavy pump of Z's breathing.

Like a wraith he rose from the blackened ground, the blood of *lessers* streaking his face and his forearms. His aura was a shimmering haze of violence that warped the scenery behind him, the forest beyond him wavy and indistinct where it bracketed his body.

"I'm going downtown," he said, wiping his blade on his thigh, "to look for more."

Right before Mr. O went back out hunting for vampires, he released the clip from his nine-millimeter Smith & Wesson and eyed the inside of the barrel. The gun was overdue for a cleaning, and so was his Glock. He had other shit he wanted to do, but only an idiot let his heat degrade. Hell, *lessers* had to be on top of their weapons. The Black Dagger Brotherhood was not the kind of target you wanted to get sloppy with.

He walked across the persuasion center, making a little detour around the autopsy table they used for their work. The one-room layout had no insulation and a dirt floor, but because there were no windows, the wind was mostly kept out. There was a cot that he slept on. A shower. No toilet or kitchen because *lessers* didn't eat. Place still smelled of fresh boards, because they'd built it only a month and a half ago. Also smelled of the kerosene heater they used to warm it up.

The only finished fixture was the shelving that ran from dirt to rafters down one whole forty-foot-long wall. Their tools were laid out, nice and neat, on the various levels: knives, vises, pliers, hammers, Sawzalls. If something could rip a scream out of a throat, they had it.

But the place wasn't just for torture; it was also used for storage. Keeping vampires over time was a challenge, because they could poof! on you if they were able to calm themselves and concentrate. Steel prevented them from pulling the disappearing act, but a cell with bars wouldn't have sheltered the things from sunlight, and building a solid-steel room was impractical. What worked nicely, though, was a corrugated-metal sewer pipe set vertically into the ground. Or three of them, as the case was.

O was so tempted to go over to the storage units, except he knew that if he did he wouldn't make it back out into the field, and he had quotas to meet. Being the *Fore-lesser*'s second in command gave him some extra benes, like having the run of this place. But if he was going to protect his privacy, he had to dial in an adequate performance.

Which meant taking care of his weapons, even when he'd rather be doing other things. He pushed a first-aid kit out of the way, grabbed the gun cleaning box, and pulled a stool over to the autopsy table.

The only door in the place swung open without a knock. O glared over his shoulder, but when he saw who it was, he forced the pissed-off expression to bleed out of his puss. Mr. X was not welcome, but the Lessening Society's tough-ass in charge could hardly be denied. If only for reasons of self-preservation.

Standing under a bald lightbulb, the *Fore-lesser* was not a good opponent if you were looking to stay in one piece. At six foot four, he was built like a car: square and hard. And like all members of the Society who were long past their initiation, he was paled-out. His white skin never blushed and didn't get windburned. His hair was the color of a spider's web. Eyes were the light gray of an overcast sky and just as glowless and flat.

With a casual stroll, Mr. X started looking around the place, not measuring the order of objects, but searching. "I was told you just got another one."

O put the cleaning rod down and counted the weapons he had on his body. Throwing knife at his right thigh. Glock at the small of his back. He wished he had more. "I picked him up downtown about forty-five minutes ago outside of Zero-Sum. He's in one of the holes, coming around."

"Good work."

"I'm planning on going out again. Right now."

"Are you?" Mr. X paused in front of the shelving and picked up a serrated hunting knife. "You know, I've heard something that's pretty goddamned alarming."

O kept his yap shut and moved his hand onto his thigh, closer to the butt of his blade.

"Not going to ask me what it is?" the *Fore-lesser* said as he walked over to the three storage units in the earth. "Maybe that's because you already know the secret."

O palmed his knife as Mr. X lingered over the mesh metal plates that covered the tops of the sewer pipes. He didn't give a shit about the first two captives. The third was no one's business but his.

"No vacancies, Mr. O?" The tip of Mr. X's combat boot nudged at one of the sets of ropes that disappeared down into each of the holes. "I thought you killed off two after they had nothing worthwhile to say."

"I did."

"So with the civilian you caught tonight, there should be one empty pipe. Instead, you're jam-packed."

"I caught another."

"When?"

"Last night."

"You are lying." Mr. X kicked off the mesh cover of the third unit.

O's first impulse was to surge to his feet, take two running strides, and punch his knife into Mr. X's throat. But he wouldn't make it that far. The *Fore-lesser* had a nifty trick of freezing his subordinates in place. All he had to do was look at you.

So O stayed put, shaking from the effort of keeping his ass on the stool.

Mr. X took a penlight out of his pocket, clicked it on, and angled the beam into the hole. As a muffled squeak came out, his eyes peeled wide. "*Jesus Christ,* it really is a female! Why the hell wasn't I told?"

O slowly rose to his feet, letting the knife hang by his thigh in the folds of his cargo pants. His grip on the handle was steady, sure. "She's new," he said.

"That's not what I hear."

In quick strides, Mr. X went to the bathroom and threw back the clear plastic shower curtain. With a curse, he kicked the bottles of girlie shampoo and baby oil that were lined up in the corner. Then he marched over to the ammunition supply closet and pulled out the ice chest that was hidden behind it. He upended the thing so the food inside hit the floor. As *lessers* didn't chew and swallow, that was as clear a confession as any.

Mr. X's pale face was furious. "You've been keeping a *pet,* haven't you?"

O considered his plausible denials while he measured the distance between them. "She's valuable. I use her in my interrogations."

"How?"

"Males of the species don't like to see a female hurt. She's an inducement."

Mr. X's eyes narrowed. "Why didn't you tell me about her?"

"This is my center. You gave it to me to run as I want." And when he found the fucker who'd squealed, he was going to peel the bastard's skin off in strips. "I take care of business here, and you know it. How I do the job shouldn't matter to you."

"I should have been told." Abruptly, Mr. X went still. "You thinking of doing something with that knife in your hand, son?"

Yeah, Dad, as a matter of fact I am. "Am I in charge here or not?"

As Mr. X shifted his weight onto the balls of his feet, O primed for a collision.

Except his cell phone went off. The first ring was shrill in the tense air, like a scream. The second seemed less of an intrusion. The third was no BFD.

As their head-on got derailed, it dawned on O that he wasn't thinking clearly. He was a big guy and a damn good fighter, but he was no match for Mr. X's tricks. And if O got himself injured or killed, who would take care of his wife?

"Answer it," Mr. X commanded. "And put it on speaker-phone."

The news was from another Prime. Three *lessers* had been eliminated at the side of the road only two miles away. Their car had been found wrapped around a tree trunk, and the burn spots of their disintegrations had scorched the snow.

Son of a bitch. The Black Dagger Brotherhood. *Again.*

As O ended the call, Mr. X said, "Look, do you want to fight with me or do you want to go to work? One way will get you killed for sure and right now. It's your choice."

"Am I in charge here?"

"As long as you get me what I need."

"I've been bringing plenty of civilians in here."

"But it's not like they're saying much."

O went over and slid the mesh top back on the third hole, making sure he could see Mr. X the whole time. Then he put his combat boot on the cover and met the *Fore-lesser* in the eye.

"I can't help it if the Brotherhood keeps themselves secret from their own species."

"Maybe you just need to focus a little harder."

Do not tell him to fuck off, O thought. *Fail this test of wills and your female is dog food.*

As O tried to rein in his temper, Mr. X smiled. "Your re-straint would be more admirable if it weren't the only appro-priate response. Now about tonight. The Brothers will go for the jars of those slayers they wiped out. Get over to Mr. H's house ASAP and get his. I'll assign someone to A's place, and I'll cover D's myself."

Mr. X paused at the door. "About that female. If you use her as a tool, that's fine. But if you're keeping her for any other reason, we've got a problem. You go soft and I'll feed you to the Omega piece by piece."

O didn't even shudder. He'd lived through the Omega's tortures once, and he figured he could do it again. For his woman he would go through anything.

"Now, what do you say to me?" the *Fore-lesser* demanded.

"Yes, sensei."

As O waited for Mr. X's car to get gone, his heart was going off like a nail gun. He wanted to take his woman out and feel her against him, except then he'd never leave. To try and calm himself, he quickly cleaned his S&W and armed up. It didn't really help, but at least his hands had stopped shaking by the time he was through.

On his way to the door he picked up the keys to his truck and engaged the motion detector over the third hole. That techno prop was a real ass-saver. If the infrared laser was broken, a triangulated gun system would go off, and whoever got curious would have a serious case of the leaks.

O hesitated before leaving. God, he wanted to hold her. The thought of losing his woman, even in the hypothetical, made him mental. That female vampire . . . she was his reason for living now. Not the Society. Not the killing.

"I'm going out, wife, so be good." He waited. "I'll come back soon and then we'll wash you." When there was no answer, he said, "Wife?"

O swallowed compulsively. Even though he told himself he should be a man, he couldn't make himself leave without hearing her voice.

"Don't send me out with no good-bye."

Silence.

Pain seeped into his heart, making the love he felt for her soar. He took a deep breath, the delicious weight of despair settling into his chest. He'd thought he'd known love before he'd become a *lesser.* He'd thought that Jennifer, the woman he'd fucked and fought with for years, had been special. But he'd been such a naive fool. Now he knew what passion really was. His captive female was the burning pain that made him feel like a man again. She was the soul that replaced the one he'd given to the Omega. Through her he lived, though he was undead.

"I'll be back as soon as I can, wife."

Bella sagged inside the hole as she heard the door shut. The fact that the *lesser* was going out off-kilter because she hadn't answered him pleased her. So the madness was complete now, wasn't it?

Funny that this insanity was the death that awaited her. From the moment she'd woken up in the pipe however many weeks ago, she'd assumed her demise was going to be of the conventional, broken-body variety. But no, hers was the death of self. As her body lingered in relative health, the inside of her was no longer living.

The psychosis had taken its time getting a hold on her, and like corporeal illness, there had been stages. At first she'd been too petrified to think of anything except how the torture would feel. But then days passed and nothing like that happened. Yes, the *lesser* struck her, and his eyes on her body were revolting, but he didn't do to her what he did to others of her species. Nor did he rape her.

In response, her thoughts had gradually shifted, her spirits reviving as she'd grown hopeful that she'd be rescued. This phoenix period had lasted longer. A whole week, maybe, though it was hard to measure the passage of days.

But then she'd begun the irreversible slide, and what had sucked her down was the *lesser* himself. It had taken her a while to realize it, but she had a bizarre power over her captor, and after some time had passed, she'd started using it. At first she pushed him to test boundaries. Later she tormented him for no other reason than that she hated him and wanted to make him hurt.

For some reason the *lesser* who had taken her . . . loved her. With all his heart. He yelled at her sometimes, and he did terrify her when he was in one of his moods, but the harder she was on him, the better he treated her. When she withheld her eyes from him, he'd go into a tailspin of anxiety. When he brought her gifts and she refused them, he wept. With increasing fervor, he worried over her and begged for her attention and curled up against her, and when she shut him out, he crumbled.

Toying with his emotions was her whole, hateful world, and the cruelty that fed her was killing her. Once she'd been a living thing, a daughter, a sister . . . a *someone*. . . . Now she was hardening, setting like concrete in the midst of her night-mare. Embalmed.

Dear Virgin in the Fade, she knew he wasn't ever going to let her go. And sure as if he'd killed her outright, he'd taken her future. All she had now was just this god-awful, infinite present. With him.

Panic, an emotion she hadn't felt for a while, surged into her chest.

Desperate to go back to the numbness, she concentrated on how cold it was in the earth. The *lesser* kept her dressed in clothes he had taken from her own drawers and closet, and she was insulated by long johns and fleeces and warm socks and boots. Except, even with all that, the chill was relentless, sneaking through the layers, burrowing into her bones, turn-ing her marrow into an icy slush.

Her thoughts shifted to her farmhouse, where she had lived for such a short time. She remembered the cheery fires she'd made herself in the hearth in the living room and the happi-ness she'd felt to be on her own. . . . These were bad visions, bad memories. They reminded her of her old life, of her mother . . . of her brother.

God, Rehvenge. Rehv had driven her crazy with all his domineering behavior, but he'd been right. If she'd stayed with the family, she never would have met Mary, the human who had lived next door. And she never would have crossed the meadow between their houses that night to make sure everything was okay. And she never would have run into the *lesser* . . . so she never would have ended up both dead and breathing.

She wondered how long her brother had looked for her. Had he given up by now? Probably. Not even Rehv could keep going for so long without hope.

She bet he'd looked for her, but she was glad in a way that he hadn't found her. Although he was a highly aggressive male, he was a civilian, and liable to get hurt if he came to res-cue her. Those *lessers* were strong. Cruel and powerful. No, to get her back it would take something equal to the monster that held her.

An image of Zsadist came to mind, clear as a photograph. She saw his savage black eyes. The scar that ran down his face and distorted his upper lip. The tattooed blood-slave bands around his throat and wrists. She remembered the whip marks on his back. And the piercings that hung from his nipples. And his muscled, too-lean body.

She thought of his vicious, uncompromising will and all of his high-test hatred. He was terrifying, a horror of her species. Ruined, not broken, in the words of his twin. But that was what would have made him such a good savior. He alone was a match for the *lesser* who'd taken her. Zsadist's kind of brutality was probably the only thing that could have gotten her out, though she knew better than to think that he'd ever try to find her. She was just some civilian whom he'd met twice.

And the second time, he'd made her swear she would never come near him again.

Fear closed in on her, and she tried to bridle the emotion by telling herself that Rehvenge was still searching for her. And that he would call upon the Brotherhood if he found any clues as to where she was. Then maybe Zsadist would come after her, because he was required to, as part of his job.

"Hello? Hello? Is anyone there?" The shaky male voice was muted, the tone tinny.

It was the newest captive, she thought. They always tried to reach out in the beginning.

Bella cleared her throat. "I am . . . here."

There was a pause. "Oh, my God . . . are you the female that was taken? Are you . . . Bella?"

Hearing her name was a shock. Hell, the *lesser* had been calling her *wife* for so long, she'd almost forgotten she'd gone by something else. "Yes . . . yes, I am."

"You're still alive."

Well, her heart was still beating, at any rate. "Do I know you?"

"I-I went to your funeral. With my parents, Ralstam and Jilling."

Bella started to tremble. Her mother and her brother . . . had put her to rest. But then, of course they would have. Her

mother was deeply religious, a great believer in the Old Traditions. Once she was convinced her daughter was dead, she
would have insisted on the proper ceremony so that Bella
could enter the Fade.

Oh . . . God. Thinking they'd given up and knowing they
had were two such different things. No one was coming after
her. Ever.

She heard something weird. And realized she was sobbing.

"I'm going to escape," the male said with force. "And I'll
take you with me."

Bella let her knees give out, and she slid down the ribbed
wall of the pipe until she was lodged at the bottom. Now she
really was dead, wasn't she? Dead and buried.

How horribly appropriate that she was stuck in the earth.

Chapter Two

Zsadist's shitkickers carried him through an alley off Trade Street, the heavy soles stomping apart frozen slush puddles and crushing through the icy ripples of tire treads. It was pitch-dark, because there were no windows in the brick buildings on either side of him and the clouds had shut out the moon. Yet as he walked alone, his night vision was perfect, penetrating everything. Just like his rage.

Black blood. What he needed was more black blood. He needed it on his hands and kicking up into his face and splattering onto his clothes. He needed oceans of it to run onto the ground and seep into the earth. To honor Bella's memory, he would make the slayers bleed, each death his offering to her.

He knew she no longer lived, knew in his heart she must have been killed in a gruesome way. So why did he always start off asking those bastards where she was? Hell, he didn't know. It was just the first thing that came out of his mouth, no matter how many times he told himself she was gone.

And he was going to keep asking those fuckers questions. He wanted to know the *where* and *how* and *with what* they'd gotten her. The information would only eat at him, but he needed to know. *Had* to know. And one of them was going to talk eventually.

Z stopped. Sniffed the air. Prayed for the sweet smell of

baby powder to drift into his nose. Goddamn it, he couldn't stand this . . . not knowing any longer.

But then he laughed in a nasty crack. Yeah, the hell he couldn't take it. Thanks to his hundred years of careful training with the Mistress, there was no level of shit he hadn't survived. Physical pain, mental anguish, cringing depths of humiliation and degradation, hopelessness, helplessness: *Been there, sweated that.*

So he could survive this.

He looked up at the sky, and as his head shifted back he swayed. With a quick hand he steadied himself against a Dumpster, then took a deep breath and waited to see if the drunken sensation passed. No luck.

Feeding time. Again.

Cursing, he hoped he could squeeze out another night or two. Sure, he'd been dragging his body around by force of will the last couple of weeks, but that was nothing unusual. And tonight he just didn't want to deal with the bloodlust.

Come on, come on . . . focus, asshole.

He forced himself to keep going, stalking the downtown alleys, weaving in and out of the dangerous urban maze of Caldwell, New York's club and drug scene.

By three A.M., he was so blood-hungry he felt stoned, and that was the only reason he gave in. He couldn't stomach the disassociation, the numbness in his body. It reminded him too much of the opium stupors he'd been forced into as a blood slave.

Walking as quickly as he could, he headed for ZeroSum, the Brotherhood's current downtown hangout. The bouncers let him bypass the wait line, easy access being one of the perks of folks who dropped the kind of cash the Brothers did. Hell, Phury's red smoke habit alone was worth a couple grand a month, and V and Butch only liked the buzz that came from top-shelf booze. Then there were Z's own regular purchases.

The club was hot and dark inside, a kind of humid, tropical cave with techno music twirling in the air. Humans crowded the dance floor, sucking on lollipop rings, guzzling water, sweating while they moved with pulsing pastel lasers.

All around, bodies were up against the walls, paired off or in triplicate, writhing, touching.

Z headed for the VIP lounge, and the human horde gave way before him, parting like velvet cloth torn open. Though high on X and coke, those overheated bodies still had enough survival instinct to spot him as a coffin waiting to happen.

In the way back, a bouncer with a buzz cut let him into the best real estate in the club. Here, in relative quiet, twenty tables with banquet seating were spaced far apart, with only the black marble tops spotlit from the ceiling. The Brotherhood's booth was right by the fire exit, and he wasn't surprised to see Vishous and Butch there with shot glasses in front of them. Phury's martini glass was sitting all alone.

The two roommates didn't look glad to see him. No . . . they seemed resigned to his arrival, like they'd been hoping to take a load off and he'd just thrown them both an engine block.

"Where is he?" Z asked, nodding at his twin's martini.

"Making a red smoke buy in the back," Butch said. "Ran out of O-Zs."

Z sat down on the left and leaned back, taking himself out of the light falling on the glossy table. As he glanced around, he recognized the faces of meaningless strangers. The VIP section had a hardcore of regulars, but none of the big spenders interacted much beyond their tight groups. In fact, the whole club was permeated by a "don't ask, don't tell" vibe, which was one of the reasons the Brothers came here. Even though ZeroSum was owned by a vampire, they needed to keep a low profile about who they were.

Over the last century or so, the Black Dagger Brotherhood had become secretive about their identities within the race. There were rumors, of course, and civilians knew a few of their names, but everything was kept on the QT. The subterfuge had started when the race had fragmented about a century ago and tragically, trust had become an issue within the species. But now, though, there was another reason. The *lessers* were torturing civilians for information on the Brotherhood, so it was imperative to keep on the down-low.

As a result, the few vampires who worked this club weren't sure the big males in leather who sucked back drinks and dropped bills were Black Dagger members. And fortunately, social custom, if not the way the Brothers looked, prevented questions.

Zsadist shifted in the booth, impatient. He hated the club; he really did. Hated having so many bodies so close to his. Hated the noise. The smells.

In a chatty tangle, a trio of human females approached the Brothers' table. The three of them were working tonight, though what they were serving up didn't fit in a glass. These were your typical high-class hookers: hair extensions, fake breasts, faces molded by plastic surgeons, clothes out of a spray can. There were a lot of their kind of movable feast in the club, particularly in the VIP section. The Reverend, who owned and ran ZeroSum, believed in product diversification as a business strategy, offering their bodies as well as the alcohol and the drugs. The vampire also loaned money and had a team of bookies and did God knew what else from his back office in service to his mostly human clientele.

As the three prostitutes smiled and talked, they presented themselves for a buy. But none of them were what Z was looking for, and V and Butch didn't pick them up either. Two minutes later, the women headed off to the next booth.

Z was goddamned hungry, but he had one nonnegotiable when it came to feeding.

"Hey, daddies," another woman said. "Any of you looking for some company?"

He glanced up. This human female had a hard face to match her hard body. Clothes were black leather. Eyes were glassy. Hair was short.

Fucking perfect.

Z put his hand into the pool of light on the table, lifted two fingers, then rapped twice on the marble with his knuckles. As Butch and V started shifting in the seat, their tension annoyed him.

The female smiled. "Well, all right."

Zsadist leaned forward and uncoiled to his full height, his

face becoming illuminated by the spotlight. The whore's expression froze solid as she took a step back.

At that moment Phury came out of a door to the left, his spectacular mane of hair reflecting the shifting lights. Right behind him was a hard-ass male vampire with a mohawk: the Reverend.

As the two came up to the table, the owner of the club smiled tightly. Eyes the color of amethysts missed nothing about the prostitute's hesitation. "Evening, gentlemen. You going somewhere, Lisa?"

Lisa's bravado came back with a vengeance. "Wherever he wants, boss."

"Right answer."

Enough with the yakkies, Z thought. "Outside. Now."

He pushed open the fire door and followed her into the alley behind the club. The December wind blew through the loose jacket he'd put on to cover his weapons, but he didn't care about the cold, and neither did Lisa. Even though the icy gusts teased her cropped hair and she was close to naked, she faced him without shivering, chin up.

Now that she'd committed herself, she was ready for him. A real professional.

"We do it here," he said, stepping into the shadows. He took two one-hundred-dollar bills from his pocket and held them out. Her fingers crushed them before she disappeared the cash into her leather skirt.

"How do you want it?" she asked, sidling up to him, reaching for his shoulders.

He spun her around to the brick wall, face-first. "I do the touching. Not you."

Her body tensed and her fear tingled in his nose, a sulfurous sting. But her voice was strong. "Watch it, asshole. I come back with bruises and he'll hunt you down like an animal."

"Don't worry. You're going to walk away from this just fine."

But she was still scared. And he was blessedly numb to the emotion.

Usually fright in a female was the only thing that could turn him on, the only way the *it* in his pants would get hard. Lately, though, the trigger wasn't working, which was just fine with him. He despised the response of that thing behind his zipper, and because most females were scared shitless of him, the *it* got aroused a hell of a lot more often than he wanted. Not at all would have been better. Shit, he was probably the only male on the planet who wanted to be impotent.

"Tilt your head to the side," he said. "Ear to your shoulder."

Slowly she complied, exposing her neck to him. This was why he'd chosen her. Short hair meant he wouldn't have to touch anything to clear his way. He hated having to put his hands on them anywhere.

As he stared at her throat, his thirst rose and his fangs elongated. God, he was dry enough to drain her.

"What are you going to do?" she snapped. "Bite me?"

"Yeah."

He struck quickly and held her in place as she thrashed. To make it easier on her, he calmed her with his mind, relaxing her, giving her a kind of high she was no doubt very familiar with. While she settled down, he swallowed as much as he could without gagging, tasting the coke and alcohol in her blood as well as the antibiotics she was on.

When he was finished, he licked the puncture marks so the healing process would get its groove on and she wouldn't bleed out. Then he popped her collar to hide the bite, cleaned himself from her memory, and sent her back into the club.

Alone again, he sagged against the bricks. Human blood was so weak, it barely got him what he needed, but he wasn't about to drink from females of his own species. Not again. Ever.

He looked up at the sky. The clouds that had brought the flurries earlier were gone, and between the buildings he could see a slice of the clear pincushion of stars. The constellations told him he had only two hours left to be out.

When he had the strength, he closed his eyes and dematerialized to the only place he wanted to be.

Thank God there was still enough time to go there. To be there.

Chapter Three

John Matthew moaned and rolled over in his bed onto his back.

The woman followed his lead, her naked breasts pressing down on his broad, bare chest. With an erotic smile, she reached down between his legs and found his heavy ache. He kicked his head back and moaned as she stood his erection up and sat down on it. While he gripped her knees, she fell into a good, slow ride.

Oh, yeah . . .

With one hand she played with herself; with the other she tantalized him, sweeping her palm over her breasts and up to her neck, taking her long, platinum blond hair with her as she went. Her hand moved higher to her face, and then her arm was over her head, a graceful arc of flesh and bone. She arched back and her breasts pushed out, the hard tips distended, rosy. Her skin was so pale it looked like fresh snow.

"Warrior," she said, grinding. "Can you handle this?"

Handle it? Damn straight, he could. And just so they were clear on who was handling what, he grabbed her thighs and thrust his hips up until she cried out.

When he retreated, she smiled down at him, working against him faster and faster. She was slick and she was tight, and his erection was in heaven.

"Warrior, can you handle this?" Her voice was deeper now from the exertion.

"Hell, yeah," he growled. Man, the second he came, he was going to flip her over and pound into her all over again.

"Can you handle this?" She pumped even harder, milking him. With her arm still over her head, she was riding him like a bull, bucking against him.

This was *great* sex . . . awesome, incredible, great—

Her words began to warp, distort . . . fall below the register of a female. "Can you handle this?"

John felt a chill. Something was off here. Something was way off. . . .

"Can you handle this? Can you handle this?" Suddenly a man's voice was coming out of her throat, a man's voice was sneering at him. *"Can you can handle this?"*

John struggled to throw her off, but she was clamped on to him, and the fucking wouldn't stop.

"Do you think you can handle this? Do-you-think-you-can-handle-this? *Doyouthinkyoucanhandlethis?*" The male voice was screaming now, roaring out of the female's face.

The knife came at John from over her head—only she was a man now, a man with white skin and pale hair and eyes the color of fog. As the blade flashed silver, John reached up to block it, but his arm wasn't heavy with muscle anymore. It was thin, emaciated.

"Can you handle this, warrior?"

With a graceful slice, the dagger landed square in the middle of his chest. A blazing pain lit off from where it penetrated him, the violent burning sluicing through his body, ricocheting around inside of his skin until he was alive with agony. He gasped for breath and choked on his own blood, choked and gagged until he could get nothing into his lungs. Flailing around, he fought against the death that was coming for him—

"John! John! Wake up!"

His eyes popped wide. His first thought was that his face hurt, though he had no idea why, because he'd been stabbed in the chest. Then he realized his mouth was stretched open, accommodating what would have been a scream if he'd been born with a voice box. As it was, all he was doing was letting out a steady stream of air.

Then he felt the hands . . . hands were pinning his arms. Terror returned, and in what was for him an awesome surge, he threw his little body off the bed. He landed face-first, his cheek skidding on the low-napped carpet.

"John! It's me, Wellsie."

Reality came back at the sound of the name, shaking him free of the hysteria like a slap.

Oh, God . . . It was okay. He was okay. He was alive.

He launched himself into Wellsie's arms and buried his face in her long red hair.

"It's all right." She pulled him into her lap and stroked his back. "You're home. You're safe."

Home. Safe. Yes, after only six weeks this was home . . . the first he'd ever had after growing up in Our Lady's orphanage and then living in hovels since he was sixteen. Wellsie and Tohrment's was home.

And he wasn't just safe here; he was understood. Hell, he'd learned the truth about himself. Until Tohrment had come and found him, he hadn't known why he'd always been different from other people or why he was so scrawny and weak. But male vampires were like that before they went through the transition. Even Tohr, who was a full-fledged member of the Black Dagger Brotherhood, had apparently been small.

Wellsie tilted John's head up. "Can you tell me what it was?"

He shook his head and burrowed deeper into her, holding on to her so hard he was surprised she could still breathe.

Zsadist materialized in front of Bella's farmhouse and cursed. Someone had been in the place again. There were fresh tire tracks through the powdered snow in the driveway and footprints to the door. *Ah, shit* . . . There were a lot of footprints, so many back and forth to whatever car had been parked there that it looked as if things were being moved out.

This made him anxious, like little bits of her were disappearing.

Holy hell. If her family dismantled the house, he didn't know where he would go to be with her anymore.

With a hard eye, he stared at the front porch and the long windows of the living room. Maybe he should pack up some of her stuff for himself. It would be a bastard thing to do, but then, he wasn't above being a thief.

Once again, he wondered about her family. He knew they were aristocrats of the highest social order, but that was about it, and he didn't want to meet them to find out more. Even on his best day, he was shit-awful with people, but the situation with Bella made him dangerous, not just nasty. No, Tohrment was the liaison with her blood ties, and Z was always careful not to run into them.

He went around the back of the house, entered through the kitchen, and turned off the security alarm. As he did every night, he checked on her fish first. Flakes of food were scattered across the top of the water, evidence that someone had already taken care of them. He was pissed off that he'd been robbed of the opportunity.

Truth was, he thought of her house as his space now. He'd cleaned it up after she'd been abducted. He'd watered the plants and taken care of the fish. He'd walked the floors and the stairs and stared out of the windows and sat on every chair and sofa and bed. Hell, he'd already decided to buy the damn thing when her family sold it. Though he'd never had a house before or many personal possessions, these walls and this roof and the shit sheltered inside—he would own it all. A shrine to her.

Z made a quick trip through the house, cataloging the things that had been removed. It wasn't much. A painting and a silver dish from the living room and a mirror from the front hall. He was curious why those particular objects had been chosen and wanted them back where they belonged.

As he came into the kitchen again, he pictured the room after she'd been abducted, all the blood, the glass shards, the busted chairs and china. His eyes went down to a black streak of rubber on the pine floor. He could guess how it had been made. Bella struggling against the *lesser,* being dragged, the sole of her shoe squeaking as it left a trail.

Anger crawled around his chest on all fours until he was panting from the ugly, familiar feeling. Except . . . Christ, the whole thing didn't make sense: him searching for her and obsessing over her shit and walking around her house. They hadn't been friends. Hell, they hadn't even been acquaintances. And he hadn't been nice to her on the two occasions he'd met her.

Man, he regretted that. During those few moments he'd had with her, he wished he hadn't been so . . . Well, not throwing up after he'd found out she was aroused by him would have been a good fricking start. Except there'd been no way to suck back the response. No female other than that sick bitch mistress of his had ever been wet for him, so he sure as hell didn't associate slick female flesh with anything good.

As he remembered Bella being up against his body, he still wondered why she'd wanted to lay with him. His face was a goddamned mess. His body wasn't much better, at least not on the back. And his reputation made Jack the Ripper look like a Boy Scout. Damn it, he was angry at everyone and everything all the time. She'd been beautiful and soft and kind, a regal, aristocratic female from a privileged background.

Oh, but their contradictions had been the point, hadn't they? He'd been the change-of-pace male for her. The walk on the wild side. The savage creature who would shock her out of her nice little life for an hour or two. And even though it had hurt to be reduced to precisely what he was, he'd still thought she was . . . lovely.

From behind him, he heard a grandfather clock start to chime. Five o'clock.

The front door to the house opened with a creak.

In a soundless rush, Z unsheathed a black dagger from his chest and flattened himself against the wall. He angled his head so he had a view down the hall to the foyer.

Butch held up his hands as he walked inside. "Just me, Z."

Zsadist lowered the blade, then put it back in its holster.

The former homicide detective was an anomaly in their

world, the only human who'd ever been let into the Brotherhood's inner circle. Butch was V's roommate, Rhage's lifting partner in the gym, Phury's clothes-whore buddy. And for reasons of his own, he was obsessed with Bella's abduction, so he had some shit in common with Z, too.

"What up, cop?"

"You heading back to the compound?" The guy's question might have been framed as an inquiry, but it was more like a suggestion.

"Not right now."

"Close to daylight."

Whatever. "Phury send you for me?"

"My choice. When you didn't come back from what you paid for, I figured you might end up here."

Z crossed his arms over his chest. "You worried I killed that female I took into the alley?"

"Nope. Saw her working the club before I left."

"So why am I looking at you right now?"

As the male glanced down like he was putting words together in his head, his weight moved back and forth in those expensive loafers he liked. Then he unbuttoned his fancy black cashmere coat.

Ah . . . so Butch was a messenger. "Spit it out, cop."

The human rubbed his thumb over his eyebrow. "You know Tohr's been talking to Bella's family, right? And that her brother's a real hothead? Well, he knows someone's coming in here. He can tell because of the security system. Every time it's shut off or turned on, he gets a signal. He wants the visits to stop, Z."

Zsadist bared his fangs. "Tough."

"He's going to put up guards."

"Why the hell does he care?"

"Come on, man, it's his sister's place."

Son of a bitch. "I want to buy the house."

"That's a no-go, Z. Tohr said the family's not putting it on the market anytime soon. They want to keep it."

Z ground his molars for a moment. "Cop, do yourself a favor and get out of here."

"Rather drive you home. Damn close to daybreak."

"Yeah, I really need a human telling me that."

Butch cursed on an exhale. "Fine, go crispy if you want. Just don't come back here again. Her family's been through enough."

As soon as the front door shut, Z felt a flush come over his body, like someone had wrapped him up tight in an electric blanket and cranked the dial. Sweat broke out on his face and his chest, and his stomach rolled. He lifted his hands. The palms were wet and the fingers sported a fine tremble.

Physiological signs of stress, he thought.

He was clearly having an emotional reaction, although damned if he knew what it was. All he picked up on were the ancillary symptoms. Inside of himself there was nothing, no feeling that he could identify.

He looked around and wanted to set fire to the farmhouse, just burn the thing down to the ground so no one could have it. Better that than knowing he couldn't go in anymore.

Trouble was, torching her place was like hurting her.

So if he couldn't leave a pile of ashes behind, he wanted to take something. As he thought about what he could carry with him and still dematerialize, he put his hand up to the slender chain stretched tight around his throat.

The necklace with its tiny inset diamonds was hers. He'd found the thing in the rubble the night after she'd been abducted, on the terra-cotta floor under her kitchen table. He'd cleaned her blood off of it, fixed the broken clasp, and had worn it ever since.

And diamonds were eternal, weren't they? They lasted forever. Just like his memories of her.

Before Zsadist left, he took one last look at the fish tank. The food was almost gone now, snipped off the surface by little gaping mouths, mouths that came at it from the underside.

John didn't know how long he stayed in Wellsie's arms, but it took him a while to get back to reality. When he finally pulled back, she smiled at him.

"Sure you don't want to tell me about the nightmare?"

John's hands started moving, and she stared at them hard because she was just learning American Sign Language. He knew he was going too fast, so he leaned over and picked up one of his pads and a pen from the bedside table.

It was nothing. I'm okay now. Thanks for waking me up, though.

"You want to go back to bed?"

He nodded. It seemed as if he'd done nothing except sleep and eat for the last month and a half, but there was no end to his hunger or his exhaustion. Then again, he had twenty-three years of starvation and insomnia to make up for.

He slid between the sheets, and then Wellsie eased down beside him. Her pregnancy didn't show that much if she was standing, but when she was sitting there was a subtle swell under her loose shirt.

"You want me to put the light on in your bathroom?"

He shook his head. That would only make him feel more like a pansy, and right now his ego had pretty much taken all the shriveling up it could handle.

"I'm just going to be at my desk in the study, okay?"

As she left, he felt bad that he was kind of relieved, but with the panic gone he was ashamed of himself. A man didn't act like he had just now. A man would have fought the pale-haired demon in the dream and won. And even if he'd been terrified, a man wouldn't have cowered and shook like a five-year-old when he woke up.

Then again, John wasn't a man. At least not yet. Tohr had said the change wouldn't come to him until he was closer to twenty-five, and he couldn't wait for the next two years to pass. Because even though he now understood why he was only five feet, six inches tall and 112 pounds, it was still tough. He hated facing his bony body every day in the mirror. Hated wearing boy-sized clothes though he could legally drive and vote and drink. Cringed at the fact that he'd never had an erection, even when he woke up from one of his erotic dreams. And he'd never even kissed a woman, either.

No, he just didn't feel like much in the masculine department all the way around. Especially given what had happened to him almost a year ago. God, the anniversary of that attack was coming up, wasn't it? With a wince he tried not to think of that dirty stairwell or the man who'd held a knife to his throat or those horrible moments when something irretrievable had been taken from him: His innocence violated, gone forever.

Forcing his mind out of that tailspin, he told himself that at least he was no longer hopeless. Sometime soon he would change into a man.

Itchy from thinking about the future, he threw the covers off and went to his closet. As he opened the double doors, he was still unused to the display. He'd never owned this many pants and shirts and fleeces in his whole life, but here they were, so fresh and new . . . all their zippers working, no buttons missing, no fraying, no tears at the seams. He even had a pair of Nike Air Shox.

He took out a fleece and pulled it on, then pushed his spindly legs into a pair of khakis. In the bathroom he washed his hands and face and combed his dark hair. Then he headed for the kitchen, walking through rooms that had clean, modern lines but were decorated with Italian Renaissance furniture, textiles, and art. He stopped when he heard Wellsie's voice coming out of the study.

". . . some kind of nightmare. I mean, Tohr, he was terrified. . . . No, he fudged when I asked him what it was, and I didn't press. I think it's time he sees Havers. Yes . . . Uh-huh. He should meet Wrath first. Okay. I love you, my *hellren*. What? God, Tohr, I feel the same way. I don't know how we ever lived without him. He is such a blessing."

John leaned against the wall in the hall and closed his eyes. Funny, he felt the same way about them.

Chapter Four

It was hours later, or at least it seemed like hours, when Bella awoke to the sound of the mesh plate sliding back. The sweet smell of the *lesser* drifted down to her, overpowering the pungent, damp earth.

"Hello, wife." The harness around her torso tightened as he lifted her out.

One look into his pale brown eyes and she knew now was not the time to push any limits. He was wired, his smile way too excited. And unbalanced was not good with him.

Just as her feet hit the floor, he jerked the harness so she fell against him. "I said hello, *wife*."

"Hello, David."

He closed his eyes. He loved it when she said his name. "I have something for you."

He left the straps on her and led her over to the stainless-steel table in the center of the room. When he handcuffed her to the thing, she knew it must be dark out still. He got lax about restraining her only during the day, when she couldn't run.

The *lesser* went out the door and left it open wide. Shuffling and grunting noises followed, and then he came back dragging a groggy civilian vampire. The male's head rolled on his shoulders as if it were on a loose hinge, his feet trailing behind at the toes. He was dressed in what had been nice black slacks and a cashmere sweater, but now the clothes were torn and wet and blood-marked.

With a moan choking in her throat, Bella backed away until her tether prevented her from going any farther. She couldn't watch the torture; she just couldn't.

The *lesser* muscled the male over to the table and laid him out flat on it. Chains were looped with efficiency around his wrists and ankles, and the links were secured with metal clips. As soon as the civilian's hazy eyes latched on to the shelves with the tools, he began to panic. He pulled against his steel binds, making them rattle against the metal table.

Bella met the vampire's blue eyes. He was terrified, and she wanted to reassure him, but she knew that wasn't smart. The *lesser* was watching her reaction, waiting.

And then he took out a knife.

The vampire on the table screamed as the slayer leaned over him. But all David did was yank up the male's sweater and slit it open, exposing his chest and throat.

Though Bella tried to fight it, bloodlust stirred in her gut. It had been a long time since she'd fed, maybe months, and all the stress she'd been under meant her body needed badly what only drinking from the opposite sex could give her.

The *lesser* took her arm and pulled her around, the handcuff sliding down the table's rail with her.

"I figured you must be thirsty by now." The slayer reached out and rubbed her mouth with his thumb. "So I got this for you to feed from."

Her eyes rounded.

"That's right. He's just for you. A present. He's fresh, young. Better than the two I have in the holes now. And we can keep him as long as he serves you." The *lesser* pushed her upper lip off her teeth. "Goddamn . . . look at those fangs getting longer. Hungry, aren't you, wife?"

His hand clamped on the back of her neck and he kissed her, licking at her with his tongue. Somehow she kept her gag reflex down until he lifted his head.

"I've always wondered what this looks like," he said, eyes

roaming around her face. "Is it going to turn me on? I'm not sure whether I want it to or not. I think I like you pure. But you've got to do this, right? Or you're going to die."

He pushed her head down toward the male's throat. When she resisted, the *lesser* laughed softly and spoke into her ear.

"That's my girl. If you'd gone willingly to him, I think I would've beaten you out of jealousy." He stroked her hair with his free hand. "Now drink."

Bella looked into the vampire's eyes. *Oh, God . . .*

The male had stopped struggling and was staring up at her, his eyes about to pop out of his skull. Hungry though she was, she couldn't bear the idea of taking from him.

The *lesser* gripped her neck hard, and his voice got nasty. "You better drink from him. I went to a lot of fucking trouble to get this for you."

She opened her mouth, her tongue like sandpaper from the thirst. "No . . ."

The *lesser* put the knife up to her eyes. "One way or the other he's going to bleed in the next minute and a half. If I go to work on him, he's not going to last long. So maybe you want to try, *wife?*"

Tears speared her eyes at the violation she would perpetrate.

"I'm so sorry," she whispered to the chained male.

Her head was yanked back, and the *lesser*'s palm came at her face from the left. The slap snapped her upper body around, and the slayer grabbed a chunk of her hair to keep her from falling. He pulled hard, arching her against him. She had no idea where the knife he'd had went.

"You do not apologize to that." He clapped his hand on her chin, digging his fingertips into the hollows under her cheekbones. "I'm the only one you worry about. We clear? I said, *are we clear?*"

"Yes," she gasped.

"Yes, what?"

"Yes, David."

He took her free arm and bent it behind her back. Pain shot into her shoulder. "Tell me you love me."

From out of nowhere, anger lit off a firestorm in her chest. She would *never* say that word to him. *Never.*

"Tell me you love me," he yelled, blasting the demand into her face.

Her eyes flashed and she bared her fangs. The instant she did his excitement shot out of control, his body starting to tremble, his breath falling into a fast pant. He was instantly primed to fight her, aroused for the battle, ready as if he were erect for sex. This was the part of the relationship he lived for. He *loved* to fight her. Had told her that his former woman hadn't been as strong as she was, hadn't been able to last as long before passing out.

"Tell me you love me."

"I. Despise. You."

As he lifted his hand and made a fist out of it, she glared up at him, steady, calm, ready to take the hit. They stayed like that for a long time, their bodies suspended in twins arcs like a heart, tied by the strings of violence that ran between them. In the background the civilian male on the table whimpered.

Suddenly the *lesser*'s arms shot around her and he buried his face in her neck. "I love you," he said. "I love you so much. . . . I can't live without you—"

"Holy shit," someone said.

The *lesser* and Bella both looked to the voice. The persuasion center's door was wide-open and a pale-haired slayer was stopped dead in its jamb.

The guy started laughing and then said the three words that triggered everything that followed: "I'm gonna tell."

David went after the other *lesser* at a dead run, chasing him outside.

Bella didn't hesitate as the first cracks of the fight rang out. She went to work on the chains that bound the civilian's right wrist, flipping the clips free, unraveling the links. Neither of them said a word as she freed his hand and then started on his right ankle. As soon as he could, the male worked as fast as she did, frantically stripping the left side of himself. The second he was free, he popped off the table and looked at the steel handcuffs that tied her.

"You can't save me," she said. "He has the only keys."

"I can't believe you're still alive. I heard about you—"

"Go, go on—"

"He'll kill you."

"No, he won't." He was just going to make her wish she were dead. "*Go!* That fight isn't going to last forever."

"I'll come back for you."

"Just get home." When he opened his mouth, she said, "Shut the hell up and focus. If you can, tell my family I'm not dead. *Go!*"

The male had tears in his eyes as he closed them. He took two long breaths . . . and dematerialized.

Bella started shaking so badly she fell down on the floor, her arm stretching over her head from where it was hand-cuffed to the table.

The noises of the fight outside abruptly stopped. There was a silence and then a flash of light and a popping sound. She knew without a doubt that her *lesser* had won.

Oh, God . . . This was going to be bad. This was going to be a very, very bad day.

Zsadist stood on Bella's snow-covered lawn until the last possible moment, and then he dematerialized to the dreary, Gothic monster the Brotherhood all lived in. The mansion looked like something out of a horror movie, all gargoyles and shadows and leaded-glass windows. In front of the mountain of stone there was a courtyard full of cars, as well as a gate-house that was Butch and V's crash pad. A twenty-foot-tall wall encased the compound, and there was a double-gated entry as well as a number of nasty surprises set up to deter unwanted visitors.

Z walked over to the main house's steel-cored doors and opened one side of them. Stepping into the vestibule, he punched in a code on a keypad and was granted access immediately. He grimaced as he emerged into the foyer. The soaring space with its jewel-toned colors and its gold leafing and its wild, mosaic floor was like that crowded bar: too much stimulation.

To his right, he heard the sounds of a full dining room: the soft clinking of silver on china, indistinct words from Beth, a chuckle from Wrath . . . then Rhage's bass voice cutting in. There was a pause, probably because Hollywood was making a face, and then everyone's laughter mingled, spilling out like gleaming marbles across a clean floor.

He wasn't interested in tangling with his brothers, much less eating with them. They'd all know by now that he'd been booted from Bella's house like a felon for marking too much time there. Few secrets got kept within the Brotherhood.

Z hit the grand staircase, taking the steps two at a time. The faster he went the more muted the meal's noises became, and the quiet suited him. At the top of the stairs he headed left and then went down a long hallway marked by Greco-Roman statuary. The marble athletes and warriors were illuminated by recessed lighting, their white marble arms and legs and chests forming a pattern against the bloodred wall. If you walked fast enough, it was like going by pedestrians when you were in a car, the rhythm of the statues' bodies animating what in fact did not move.

The room he slept in was at the end of the corridor, and as he opened the door he hit a wall of cold. He never turned on the heat or the air-conditioning, just like he never slept in the bed or used the phone or put anything in the antique bureaus. The closet was the only thing he needed, and he went there to disarm. His weapons and ammo were kept in the fireproof cabinet in the back, and his four shirts and three sets of leathers hung closely together. With nothing much in the walk-in, he often thought of bones as he went inside, all the empty hangers and brass rods looking spindly and fragile.

He stripped and showered. He was hungry for food, but he liked to keep himself that way. The pang of starvation, the dry yearning of thirst . . . these denials that were within his control always eased him. Hell, if he could pull off not sleeping, he'd take that away from himself, too. And the goddamned bloodlust . . .

He wanted to be clean. On the inside.

When he got out of the shower he ran a buzz razor over his head to keep his hair tight to his skull and then did a quick shave. Naked, chilled, logy from the feeding, he went over to his pallet on the floor. As he stood above the two folded blankets that offered as much cushioning as a pair of Band-Aids, he thought of Bella's bed. Hers had been queen-sized and all white. White pillowcases and sheets, big, white Wonder bread comforter, a white poodlelike throw at the foot of it.

He'd lain on her bed. Often. Had liked to think he could smell her in it. Sometimes he'd even rolled around on top, the softness giving way under his hard body. It was almost as if she had touched him then, and better than if she actually had. He couldn't stand to have anyone put their hands to him . . . though he wished he'd let Bella find a piece of his flesh just once. With her, he might have been able to handle it.

His eyes shifted to the skull that sat on the floor next to the pallet. The eye sockets were black holes, and he pictured the iris-and-pupil combination that had once stared out at him. Between the teeth there was a strip of black leather about two inches wide. Traditionally words of devotion to the deceased were inscribed on it, but the strap these jaws bit down on was blank.

As he lay down, he put his head next to the thing and the past came back, the year 1802. . . .

The slave came partially awake. He was flat on his back and he ached all over, though he couldn't think of why . . . until he remembered going into his transition the night before. For hours he'd been crippled by the pain of his muscles sprouting, his bones thickening, his body transforming into something huge.

Strange . . . verily, his neck and his wrists hurt in a differing way.

He opened his eyes. The ceiling was far above him and marked with thin black bars inset into stone. When he turned his head, he saw an oak door with more bars running vertically down its thick planks. On the wall, too, there were strips of steel . . . In the dungeon. He was in the dungeon, but why? And he'd best get to his duties before . . .

He tried to sit up, but his forearms and shins were pinned down. Eyes going wide, he jerked—

"Mind y'self!" It was the blacksmith. And he was tattooing black bands on the slave's drinking points.

Oh, dear Virgin in the Fade, no. Not this . . .

The slave fought against the holds, and the other male looked up, annoyed. "Settle! I'll not be whipped for a fault that'd be not mine own."

"I beg of you . . ." The slave's voice didn't sound right. It was too deep. "Have mercy."

He heard a soft, female laugh. The Mistress of the household had entered the cell, her long gown of white silk trailing behind her on the stone floor, her blond hair down around her shoulders.

The slave dropped his eyes as was appropriate and realized he was wholly unclothed. Flushing, embarrassed, he wished he were covered.

"You wake," she said, approaching him.

He couldn't fathom why she had come to see one of such lowly station as himself. He was a mere kitchen boy, someone beneath even the maids who cleaned her privy quarters.

"Look at me," the Mistress commanded.

He did as he was told, though it went against everything he'd ever known. He had never been allowed to meet her stare before.

What he saw in it was a shock. She was looking at him in a way no female had ever regarded him. Greed marked the refined bones of her face, her dark gaze glowing with some kind of intent he couldn't discern.

"Yellow eyes," she murmured. "How rare. How beautiful."

Her hand landed on the slave's bare thigh. He twitched at the contact, feeling uneasy. This was wrong, he thought. She shouldn't be touching him there.

"What a magnificent surprise you've presented. Rest

assured, I have fed well the one who brought you to my attention."

"Mistress . . . I would beg you to let me go to work."

"Oh, you will." Her hand drifted across the juncture of his pelvis, where his thighs met his hips. He jumped and heard the blacksmith's soft curse. "And what a boon for me. My blood slave fell prey to an unfortunate accident this day. As soon as his quarters are renewed, you shall be moved into them."

The slave lost his breath. He'd known of the male she'd kept locked up, for he'd brought food to the cell. Sometimes, as he'd left the tray with the guards, he'd heard strange sounds coming out from behind the heavy door. . . .

His fear must have registered on the Mistress, because she leaned over him, getting close enough so he could smell her perfumed skin. She laughed softly, as if she had taken a taste of his fright and the dish had pleased her.

"In truth, I cannot wait to have you." As she turned to leave, she glared at the blacksmith. "Mind what I said or I shall have you sent unto the dawn. Not one misstep with that needle. His skin is far too perfect to mar."

The tattooing was finished soon thereafter, and the blacksmith took the one candle with him, leaving the slave tied down on the table in the darkness.

He shook from despair and horror as his new station became real. He was now the lowest of the low, kept alive solely to feed another . . . and only the Virgin knew what else awaited him.

It was a long while before the door opened again and candlelight showed him that his future had arrived: the Mistress in a black robe with two males known for their love of their own sex.

"Cleanse him for me," she ordered.

The Mistress watched as the slave was washed and oiled, and she moved around his body as the candlelight did, ever shifting, never still. The slave trembled, hating the sensation of the males' hands on his face, his chest, his privates. He

*was fearful that one or both would try to take him in an un-
holy way.*

*When they were finished, the taller of them said, "Shall
we attempt him for you, Mistress?"*

"I shall keep him for myself this night."

*She dropped her robe and lithely got up onto the table,
straddling the slave. Her hands sought his private flesh, and
as she stroked him he was aware of the other males taking
themselves in hand. When the slave remained flaccid, she
covered him with her lips. The sounds in the room were horrific, the moans of the males and the Mistress's mouth sucking and smacking.*

*The humiliation was complete as the slave started to cry,
tears seeping out of the corners of his eyes, falling down his
temples, landing in his ears. He had never been touched between his legs before. As a pretransition male, his body had
not been ready for or capable of mating, though that hadn't
kept him from looking forward to someday being with a female. He'd always imagined that the joining would be wondrous, for in the slave quarters he had seen the pleasure act
on occasion.*

*But now . . . to have the intimacy happening in this way,
he was ashamed that he had dared to want something.*

*Abruptly, the Mistress released him and slapped him
across the face. The palm print stung on his cheek as she got
off the table.*

*"Bring me the salve," she snapped. "That thing of his
knows not its function."*

*One of the males came forward to the table with a small
pot. The slave felt someone put a slippery hand on him, he
wasn't sure who, and then there was a burning sensation. As
a curious weight settled in his groin, he felt something shift
on his thigh and then slowly move across his stomach.*

"Oh . . . good Virgin in the Fade," one of the males said.

*"Such size," the other breathed. "He would o'er-spill the
depths of a well."*

*The Mistress's voice was likewise amazed. "'Tis enor-
mous."*

The slave lifted his head. There was a mighty swollen thing lying on his belly, the likes of which he had never seen before.

He lay back down against the table as the Mistress mounted his hips. This time he felt something engulf him, something wet. He put his head up again. She was astride him and he was . . . inside of her body. She moved against him, pumping up and down, panting. He was dimly aware that the other males in the room were moaning again, the guttural sounds growing louder as she moved faster and faster. And then there were shouts, hers, theirs.

The Mistress collapsed against the slave's chest. While she still breathed heavily, she said, "Hold his head down."

One of the males put a palm on the slave's forehead and then stroked the slave's hair with his free hand. "So lovely. So soft. And look at all the colors."

The Mistress buried her face in the slave's neck and bit him. He cried out at the sting and the taking. He'd seen males and females drink from one another before, and it had always seemed . . . right. But this hurt and made him dizzy, and the harder she pulled at his vein, the more light-headed he became.

He must have passed out, because when he woke up she was lifting her head and licking her lips. She climbed off him, robed herself, and the three of them left him alone in the dark. Moments later guards whom he recognized entered.

The other males refused to look upon him, though he had been on friendly terms with them before because he had rendered them their ale. Now, though, they kept their eyes averted and didn't speak. As he glanced down at his body, he was ashamed that whatever salve had been put on him was still working, that his private staff was still stiff and thick.

The gloss on it nauseated him.

He desperately wanted to tell the males that it wasn't his fault, that he was trying to will the flesh down, but he was too mortified to speak as the guards released his arms and ankles from the table. When he stood up he sagged, because he'd been stretched out flat on his back for hours and was only a day past his transition. No one helped him as he struggled to stay upright, and he knew it was because they didn't want to touch him, didn't want to be near him now. He went to cover himself, but they shackled him in a practiced manner so he didn't have a free hand.

The shame got worse as he had to walk down the hall. He could feel the heavy weight at his hips bouncing with his footfalls, bobbing obscenely. Tears welled and slid down his cheeks, and one of the guards snorted with disgust.

The slave was taken to a different part of the castle, to another solid-walled room with inlaid steel bars. This one had a bed platform and a proper chamber pot and a rug and torches set high up on the walls. As he was brought in, so were food and water, the victuals left by a fellow kitchen boy he'd known all of his life. The pretransition male also refused to look at him.

The slave's hands were released and he was locked in.

Bereft and trembling, he went over to a corner and sat on the floor. He cradled his body gently, for no one else would, and tried to be kind to this newly transitioned form of his . . . a form that had been used in a way that was so wrong.

As he rocked back and forth, he worried for his future. He'd never had any rights, any learning, any identity. But at least before he'd been free to move around. And his body and his blood had been his own.

The remembered sensation of those hands on his skin brought up a wave of nausea. He looked down at his privates and realized he could still smell the Mistress on himself. He wondered how long the swelling would last.

And what would happen when she came back for him.

Zsadist rubbed his face and rolled over. She'd come back for him, all right. And she'd never come alone.

He closed his eyes against the recollections and tried to will himself to sleep. The last thing that flashed through his mind was a picture of Bella's farmhouse in its snow-covered meadow.

God, that place was so very empty, deserted though it was

filled with things. With Bella's disappearance it had been
stripped of its most important function: Though it was still a
sound structure and capable of keeping out wind and weather
and strangers, it was no longer a home.

Soulless.

In a way, her farmhouse was just like him.

Chapter Five

Dawn had arrived by the time Butch O'Neal pulled the Escalade into the courtyard. As he got out, he could hear G-Unit bumping at the Pit, so he knew his roommate was in. V had to have his rap music; the shit was like air to him. Said those bass beats helped keep the intrusions of other people's thoughts down to a manageable level.

Butch walked over to the door and punched in a code. A lock popped and he stepped into a vestibule, where he did another check-in. Vampires were big on double door systems. That way you never worried about someone flooding your house with sunlight, because one of the buggers was always closed.

The gatehouse, a.k.a. the Pit, was nothing too fancy, just a living room, galley kitchen, and two bed/bath combos. But he liked it, and he liked the vampire he lived with. He and his roomie were tight as . . . well, brothers.

As he walked into the main room, the black leather couches were empty, but SportsCenter was on the plasma-screen TV, and the chocolaty scent of red smoke was all around. So Phury was in the house, or had just left.

"Hello, Lucy," Butch called out.

The two Brothers came from the back. Both were still dressed in their fighting clothes, the leathers and the shit-kickers making them look exactly like the killers they were.

"You seem tired, cop," Vishous said.

"Actually, I feel strung out."

Butch eyed the blunt at Phury's mouth. Even though he'd put his drugging days long behind him, tonight he almost caved and asked for a hit of that red smoke. Thing was, he already had two addictions so he was kind of busy.

Yeah, sucking back Scotch and pining after a female vampire who didn't want him were about all he had time for. Besides, there was no reason to screw with a system that worked. The lovelorn crap fueled the boozing, and whenever he was drunk, he missed Marissa even more, so then he'd want to do another shot. . . . And there you had it. One hell of a merrygo-round. Even made the room spin, too.

"You talk to Z?" Phury asked.

Butch stripped off his cashmere coat and hung it in the closet. "Yeah. He wasn't happy."

"Is he going to stay away from there?"

"I think so. Well, assuming he didn't burn the place down after he kicked me out. He had that special little twinkle in his eye as I left. You know, the one that makes your balls get tight when you're standing next to him?"

Phury dragged a hand through his outrageous hair. The stuff fell down past his shoulders, all blond and red and brown waves. He was a handsome Joe without it; with that mane, he was . . . okay, fine, the brother was beautiful. Not that Butch went that way, but the guy was better-looking than a lot of women. Dressed better than most of the ladies, too, when he wasn't in his ass-kicking clothes.

Man, it was a good thing he fought like a nasty bastard or he might have been taken for a nancy.

Phury sucked in a deep breath. "Thanks for dealing with—"

A phone rang on a desk full of computer equipment.

"Outside line," V murmured, going over to his IT command center.

Vishous was the resident computer genius in the Brotherhood—actually, he was the resident genius on everything—and he was in charge of communications and security at the compound. He ran it all from the Four Toys, as he called his quartet of PCs.

Toys . . . yeah, right. Butch didn't know jack about computers, but if those suckers were toys, then they were in the Department of Defense's playground, too.

While V waited for the call to dump into voice mail, Butch glanced at Phury. "So, have I shown you my new Marc Jacobs suit?"

"Did that come in already?"

"Yeah, Fritz brought it over earlier and fitted it."

"Sweet."

As they went back to the bedrooms, Butch had to laugh. He was as guilty as Phury when it came to being a metrosexual thread humper. Funny, he hadn't given a shit about his clothes when he'd been a cop. Now that he was with the Brothers, he was working his walk in haute couture and loving it. So, like Phury, he was lucky he fought dirty.

The Brother was fondling yards of fine black wool on a hanger and making appropriate "ahhhing" sounds when V came in.

"Bella's alive."

Butch and Phury whipped their heads around as the suit landed on the floor in a heap.

"Civilian male was abducted from the alley behind Zero-Sum tonight and taken to a place way out in the woods for the purpose of feeding Bella. He saw her. Talked with her. Somehow she let him go."

"Tell me he can find the place again," Butch breathed, aware of a suffocating urgency. And he wasn't the only one on instant alert. Phury looked so intense he didn't seem capable of speech.

"Yeah. He marked his way out, dematerializing two hundred yards at a time until he reached Route 22. He's e-mailing me the trail on a map. Damn smart for a civilian."

Butch ran out to the living room, heading for his coat and the keys to the Escalade. He hadn't taken off his holster, so his Glock was still strapped under his arm.

Except V got between him and the door. "Where you going, my man?"

"Has that map come through your e-mail yet?"

"Stop."

Butch glared at his roommate. "You can't go out during the day. I can. Why the hell should we wait?"

"Cop"—V's voice grew soft—"this is Brotherhood business. You're not going in on this."

Butch stalled. *Ah, yes, shut down again.*

Sure, he could work around their periphery, do some crime scene analysis, get his gray matter churning over tactical problems. But when the fighting started, the Brothers always kept him off the field.

"Goddamn it, V—"

"No. You're not handling this. Forget it."

It was two hours later before Phury had enough information to go to his twin's room. He figured there was no point in getting Zsadist agitated with a half-story, and it had taken a while for the plan to jell.

When he knocked and there wasn't an answer, he stepped inside and winced. The room was cold as a meat locker.

"Zsadist?"

Z lay on a couple of folded blankets in the far corner, his naked body drawn up tightly against the chill in the room. There was a sumptuous bed not more than ten feet away from him, but it had never been used. Z slept on the floor always, no matter where he had lived.

Phury walked over and knelt down beside his twin. He wasn't going to touch the male, especially when he would be caught unaware. Z was likely to come to on the attack.

My God, Phury thought. Asleep like this, all his anger banked, Z was almost frail.

Hell, take back the *almost.* Zsadist had always been so damned thin, so terribly lean. Now, though, he was just big bones and veins. When had this happened? *Christ,* back during Rhage's *rythe,* they'd all been naked in the Tomb, and Z certainly hadn't looked like a skeleton. That had been only about six weeks ago.

Right before Bella's abduction . . .

"Zsadist? Wake up, my brother."

Z stirred, black eyes opening slowly. Usually he came awake in a rush and at the slightest noise, but he'd fed, so he was sluggish.

"She's been found," Phury said. "Bella's been found. She was alive as of early this morning."

Z blinked a couple of times, as if he weren't sure whether he was dreaming. Then he hefted his torso off the pallet. His nipple rings caught the light from the hall while he rubbed his face.

"What did you say?" he asked in a gravel voice.

"We have a bead on where Bella is. And confirmation that she's alive."

Z grew more alert, his consciousness moving like a train, gathering speed, creating power with its momentum. With every second the force of him was coming back, the vicious vitality surging until he no longer looked weak at all.

"Where is she?" he demanded.

"In a one-room house in the woods. A civilian male got loose because she helped him escape."

Z sprang to his feet, landing in a lithe punch to the floor. "How do I get to her?"

"The male who escaped e-mailed V the directions. But—"

Z headed for his closet. "Get a map for me."

"It's noontime, my brother."

Z stopped. Abruptly, a blast of cold came out of his body, making the temperature of the room feel balmy. And those black eyes were dangerous as hammer claws when they flashed over his shoulder.

"So send the cop. Send Butch."

"Tohr won't let him—"

"*Fuck that!* The human goes."

"Zsadist—stop. Think. Butch wouldn't have any backup, and there could be multiple *lessers* at the location. You want to risk her getting killed in a botched rescue attempt?"

"The cop can handle himself."

"He's good, but he's only a human. We can't send him in there."

Z bared his fangs. "Maybe Tohr is more worried the guy will get pinched and squeal about us on one of their tables."

"Come on, Z, Butch knows shit. He knows a lot of shit about us. So of course that's part of it."

"But if she helped a captive escape, what the hell do you think those *lessers* are doing to her right now!"

"If a pack of us go at sundown, we're more likely to get her out alive. You know that. We have to wait."

Z stood there naked, breathing deeply, his eyes narrow slits of rank hatred. When he finally spoke, his voice was a nasty growl.

"Tohr better pray to God she's still alive when I find her tonight. Or I will have his fucking head, brother or no brother."

Phury shifted his eyes to the skull on the floor, thinking that Z had already proven how good he was at decapitation.

"Did you hear me, brother?" the male snapped.

Phury nodded. Man, he had a bad feeling about how this was going to play out. He really did.

Chapter Six

As O drove his F-150 truck along Route 22, the waning four-o'clock sun stung his eyes and he felt as if he were hungover. Yeah . . . along with the headache, he had the same body crawls he used to get after a night of boozing, the little tremors flickering just under his skin like worms.

The long line of regret he was towing behind him also reminded him of his drinking days. Like when he'd woken up next to an ugly woman he despised, but had fucked anyway. The whole thing was just like that . . . only much, much worse.

He shifted his hands on the steering wheel. His knuckles were busted open and he knew he had scratches on his neck. As images of the day blinded him, his stomach heaved. He was disgusted by the things he'd done to his woman.

Well, *now* he was disgusted. When he'd been doing them . . . he'd been righteous.

Christ, he should have been more careful. She was a living thing, after all. . . . Shit, what if he'd gone too far? *Oh, man* . . . He should never have let himself do those things. The trouble was, as soon as he'd seen that she'd freed the male he'd brought her, he'd lost it. Just splintered into shrapnel that had torn right through her.

He lifted his foot from the gas. He wanted to go back and

take her out of her pipe and reassure himself that she was still breathing. Except there wasn't enough time before the meeting of the Primes started.

As he stomped on the accelerator, he knew he wouldn't be able to leave her once he saw her anyway, and then the *Fore-lesser* would come looking for him. And that would be a problem. The persuasion center was a mess. *Goddamn it . . .*

O slowed and wrenched the wheel to the right, the truck lurching off Route 22 onto a one-lane dirt road.

Mr. X's cabin, also the Lessening Society's HQ, was smack in the middle of a seventy-five-acre forest, completely isolated. The place was nothing more than a small log setup with a dark green shingled roof and an outbuilding about half the size behind it. As O pulled up, there were seven cars and trucks parked in a loose configuration, all of them domestic, most of them at least four years old.

O walked inside the cabin and saw he was the last to show. Ten other Primes were packed into the shallow interior space, their pale faces grim, their bodies broad and heavy with muscle. These were the Lessening Society's strongest men, the ones who had been in it the longest. O was the only exception when it came to time served. He had just three years since his induction, and none of them liked him because he was new.

Not that they got a vote. He was as tough as any Prime and had proved it. *Jealous fuckers . . .* Man, he was never going to be like them, just cattle for the Omega. He couldn't believe the idiots prided themselves on their paling out over time and losing their identities. He fought against the fading. He colored his hair to keep it the dark brown it had always been, and he dreaded the gradual lightening of his irises. He did not want to look like them.

"You're late," Mr. X said. The *Fore-lesser* leaned back against a refrigerator that wasn't plugged in, his pale eyes latching onto the scratches all over O's neck. "Been fighting?"

"You know how those Brothers are." O found a place to stand across the way. Though he nodded to his partner, U, he didn't acknowledge anyone else.

The *Fore-lesser* continued to look at him. "Has anyone seen Mr. M?"

Fuck, O thought. That *lesser* he'd taken out for walking in on him and his wife would have to be accounted for.

"O? You got something to say?"

From the left, U spoke up. "I saw M. Right before dawn. Fighting with a Brother downtown."

As Mr. X shifted his stare to the left, O was cold-shit shocked at the lie.

"You saw him with your own eyes?"

The other *lesser*'s voice was steady. "Yeah. I did."

"Any chance you're protecting O?"

Wasn't that the question to ask? *Lessers* were cutthroats, always jockeying with one another for position. Even among partners there was little loyalty.

"U?"

The guy's pale head went back and forth. "He's on his own. Why would I risk my skin for his?"

Clearly that was some logic Mr. X felt he could trust, because he went on with the meeting. After the quotas for kill and capture were assigned, the group broke up.

O went over to his partner. "I have to go back to the center for a minute before we go out. I want you to follow me."

He had to find out why U had saved his ass, and he wasn't worried about the other *lesser* seeing the shape the place had been left in. U wouldn't cause trouble. He wasn't particularly aggressive or an independent thinker, more operator than innovator.

Which made it even more weird that he'd taken the initiative he had.

Zsadist stared at the grandfather clock in the mansion's foyer. By the position of the hands he knew he had eight minutes before the sun was officially down. Thank God it was winter and the nights were long.

He eyed the double doors and knew just where he was going as soon as he could get through them. He'd memorized the location the civilian male had given them. Was going to dematerialize and be there in the blink of an eye.

Seven minutes.

It would be better to wait until the sky was all dark, but fuck that. The instant that godforsaken fireball slipped over the edge of the horizon, he was out. To hell with it if he ended up with a bitch of a tan.

Six minutes.

He rechecked the daggers on his chest. Took the SIG Sauer out of the holster at his right hip and ran through it one more time, then did the same for the one that was on the left. He felt for the throwing knife at the small of his back and the six-inch blade he had on his thigh.

Five minutes.

Z cocked his head to the side, cracking his neck to loosen it up.

Four minutes.

Fuck this. He was going now—

"You'll fry," Phury said from behind him.

Z closed his eyes. His impulse was to lash out, and the urge grew irresistible as Phury kept talking.

"Z, my man, how're you going to help her if you fall flat on your face and start steaming?"

"Do you get off being a buzz kill? Or does it just come natural?" As Z glared over his shoulder, he had a sudden memory of that one night Bella had come to the mansion. Phury had seemed so taken by her, and Z remembered the two of them standing together and talking, right where his boots were planted now. He'd watched them from the shadows, wanting her as she'd smiled and laughed with his twin.

Z's voice got sharper. "I'd think you'd want to get her back, being that she was all into you and shit, thinking you were handsome. Or . . . maybe you want her to stay gone because of that. Did your vow of celibacy get shaken, my brother?"

As Phury winced, Z's instinct for weakness jumped into the opening. "We all saw you checking her out that night she came here. You were looking, weren't you? Yeah, you were, and not just at her face. Did you wonder how she'd feel underneath you? Did you get all nervous about breaking that no-sex promise to yourself?"

Phury's mouth thinned into a slash, and Z hoped the male's response was a nasty one. He wanted something hard to come back at him. Maybe they could even go at it for the remaining three minutes.

But there was only silence.

"Nothing to say to me?" Z glanced at the clock. "Just as well. It's time to go—"

"I bleed for her. The same as you do."

Z looked back at his twin, witnessing the pain on the male's face from a long distance, as if he were staring through a pair of binoculars. He had a passing thought that he should feel something, some kind of shame or sorrow for forcing Phury to give up that intimate, sad revelation.

Without a word, Zsadist dematerialized.

He triangulated his reappearance to a wooded area about one hundred yards away from where the civilian male said he'd escaped from. As Z took form, the fading light in the sky blinded him and made him feel like he'd volunteered for an acid facial. He ignored the burning and headed in a northeasterly direction, jogging over the snow-covered ground.

And then there it was, in the middle of the woods, about a hundred feet from a stream: a single-story houselike structure with a black Ford F-150 and a nondescript silver Taurus parked off to one side. Z sidled up to the structure, staying behind the trunks of pine trees, moving quietly in the snow as he worked the building's periphery. It had no windows and only one door. Through the thin walls he could hear movement, talking.

He took out one of his SIGs, flipped off the safety, and considered his options. Dematerializing inside was a dumb move, because he didn't know the interior layout. And his only other alternative, though satisfying, wasn't that strategic either: Kicking the door down and going in shooting was damn appealing, but as suicidal as he was, he wasn't going to risk Bella's life by lighting the place up.

Except then, miracle of miracles, a *lesser* came out of the building, the door shutting with a smack. Moments later a second one followed, and then there was the *beep-beep* of a security alarm activating.

Z's first instinct was to shoot them both in the head, but he held his finger to the side of the trigger. If the slayers had re-activated the alarm, there was a good chance no one else was in-house, and his chances of getting Bella out had just improved. But what if that was SOP on exit regardless of whether the place was empty? Then all he'd do is announce his presence and set off a shit storm.

He watched the two *lessers* as they got in the truck. One had brown hair, which usually meant the slayer was a new recruit, but this guy didn't act like a FNG: He was sure in his boots and doing the talking. His pale-haired buddy was the one sporting the bobble-head nod.

The engine started up and the truck backed around, packing the snow under its tires. Without headlights, the F-150 headed down a barely-there lane through the trees.

Letting those two bastards drive off into the sunset was an exercise in bondage, with Z turning the large muscles of his body into iron ropes over his bones. It was either that or he'd be on the truck's hood, smashing his fist through the windshield, pulling the SOBs out by their hair so he could bite them.

As the sound of the truck faded, Z listened hard to the silence that followed. When he heard nothing, he went back to wanting to blast through the door, but he thought about the alarm and checked his watch. V would be on site in about a minute and a half.

It would kill him. But he would wait.

While he twitched in his shitkickers, he became aware of a smell, something. . . . He sniffed the air. There was propane around, somewhere close. Probably feeding that generator around the back. And kerosene from a heater. But there was something else, some kind of smoky, burning . . . He looked at his hands, wondering if he was on fire and hadn't noticed. No.

What the hell?

His bones went cold as he realized what it was. His boots were planted in the middle of a scorched patch of earth, one about the size of a body. Something had been incinerated right where he was standing—within the last twelve hours, by the scent of it.

Oh . . . God. Had they left her out for the sun?

Z eased down on his haunches, putting his free hand on the withered ground. He imagined Bella lying there when the sun came out, imagined her feeling ten thousand times more pain than he had as he'd just materialized.

The blackened spot got blurry.

He scrubbed his face and then stared at his palm. There was wetness on it. Tears?

He searched his chest for what he was feeling, but all that came to him was information about his body. His torso was swaying because his muscles were weak. He was light-headed and vaguely nauseous. But that was it. There were no emotions for him.

He rubbed his sternum and was about to do another sweep with his hands when a pair of shitkickers came into his line of sight.

He looked up into Phury's face. The thing was a mask, all frozen and pasty.

"Was it her?" he croaked, kneeling down.

Z lurched backward, just barely managing to keep his gun out of the snow. He couldn't be anywhere near someone right now, especially Phury.

In a messy scramble, he got to his feet. "Vishous here yet?"

"Right behind you, my brother," V whispered.

"There's . . ." He cleared his throat. Rubbed his face on his forearm. "There's a security alarm. I think the place is clear, because two slayers just left, but I'm not sure."

"I'm on the alarm."

Z caught a number of scents all of a sudden and glanced behind him. The whole of the Brotherhood was there, even Wrath, who as king was not supposed to be in the field. They were all armed. They had all come to get her back.

The group lined up flat against the house as V used a pick on the door lock. His Glock went in first. When there was no reaction, he slipped inside and closed himself in. A moment later there was one long beep. He opened the door.

"Good to go."

Z rushed forward, practically mowing down the male.

His eyes penetrated the dim corners of the single room. The place was a mess, with shit scattered all over the floor. Clothes . . . knives and handcuffs and . . . shampoo bottles? And what the fuck was that? God, a disemboweled first-aid kit, its gauze and tape bleeding out of the ruined lid. The thing looked like it had been stomped on until it had opened.

Heart pounding in his chest, sweat blooming all over him, he looked for Bella and saw only inanimate objects: A wall of shelving that held nightmarish instruments. A cot. A fireproof metal closet the size of a car. An autopsy table with four sets of steel chains hanging off its corners . . . and blood smudged on its smooth surface.

Random thoughts fired through Z's brain. She was dead. That burned oval proved it. Except what if that had just been another captive? What if she'd been moved or something?

As his brothers hung back, like they knew better than to get in his way, Z went over to the fireproof closet, keeping his gun in hand. He wrenched the doors off, just grabbed onto the metal panels and bent them until the hinges broke. He tossed the heavy sections away, hearing them clatter and bang.

Guns. Ammunition. Plastic explosives.

The arsenal of their enemies.

He went into the bathroom. Nothing but a stall shower and a bucket with a toilet seat on it.

"She's not here, my brother," Phury said.

In a fit of rage Z launched himself at the autopsy table, picking it up with one hand and throwing it into a wall. In midflight, a length of chain came back at him, catching him in the shoulder, nailing him to the bone.

And then he heard it. A soft whimpering sound.

His head snapped around to the left.

In the corner, on the ground, there were three cylindrical metal lips protruding from the earth, and they were capped by mesh plates that were the dark brown color of the dirt floor. Which explained why he hadn't noticed them.

He went over and kicked off one of the covers. The whimpering got louder.

Suddenly light-headed, he fell to his knees. "Bella?"

Gibberish rose from the earth to answer him, and he dropped his gun. How was he going to . . . ? Ropes—there were ropes coming out of what looked like a sewer pipe. He grabbed onto them and pulled gently.

What emerged was a dirty, bloody male, about ten years out of his transition. The civilian was naked and shivering, his lips blue, his eyes rolling around.

Z dragged him free, and Rhage wrapped his leather trench coat around the male.

"Get him out of here," someone said as Hollywood sliced the ropes.

"Can you dematerialize?" another brother asked the male.

Z paid no attention to the conversation. He went for the next hole, but there were no ropes leading down into it, and his nose detected no scent. The thing was empty.

He was stepping over to the third when the captive yelled, "No! Th-that one's booby-trapped!"

Z froze. "How?"

Through chattering teeth, the civilian said, "I d-don't know. I just heard the *l-lesser* warn one of his m-men about it."

Before Z could ask, Rhage started walking the room. "Got a gun over here. Business end pointed in that direction." There were the sounds of metal clicks and shifting. "It's not armed. Anymore."

Z looked above the hole. Mounted on the exposed rafters of the roof, about fifteen feet from the floor, was a small device. "V, what have we got up there?"

"Laser eye. You break it, it probably triggers the—"

"Hold up," Rhage said. "I got another gun to empty out here."

V stroked his goatee. "There must be a remote-control activator, although the guy probably took it with him. That's what I would do." He squinted up at the ceiling. "That particular model runs on lithium batteries. So it's not like we could kill the generator to turn it off. And they're tricky to disarm."

Z glanced around for something he could use to push the plate off and thought of the bathroom. He went inside, whipped the shower curtain down, and brought the pole it had hung from back.

"Everyone clear out."

Rhage spoke sharply. "Z, man, I don't know that I've found all the—"

"Take the civilian with you." When no one moved, he cursed. "We don't have time to fuck around, and if someone's getting shot it's going to be me. Jesus Christ, will you brothers *leave?*"

When the place was cleared out, Z approached the hole. Standing with his back to one of the guns that had been removed, so that he would have been in its line of fire, he nudged the cover off with the pole. A gunshot rang out with a popping sound.

Z caught the slug in his left calf. The searing impact brought him down on one knee, but he ignored it and dragged himself to the neck of the pipe. He took hold of the ropes that led down into the earth and began to pull.

The first thing he saw was her hair. Bella's long, beautiful mahogany hair was all around her, a veil over her face and shoulders.

He sagged and lost his vision, partly passing out, but even through the full-body wobble, he kept pulling. Abruptly the effort became easier . . . because there were hands helping him . . . other hands on the rope, other hands laying her gently on the floor.

Dressed in a sheer nightgown that was stained with her blood, she wasn't moving, but she was breathing. He carefully pushed her hair back from her face. . . .

Zsadist's blood pressure took a nosedive. "Oh, sweet Jesus . . . oh, sweet Jesus . . . oh, sweet—"

"What did they do . . ." Whoever had spoken couldn't find the words to finish.

Throats cleared. A couple of coughs were smothered. Or maybe they were gags.

Z gathered her in his arms and just . . . hugged her. He had to get her out, but he couldn't move for what had been done to her. Blinking, dizzy, screaming inside, he rocked her gently back and forth. Words fell from his mouth, lamentations for her in the Old Language.

Phury sank down to his knees. "Zsadist? We have to take her away from here."

Focus came to Z in a rush, and suddenly all he could think about was moving her to the mansion. He sliced the harness off her torso, then struggled to his feet with her in his arms. When he tried to walk, his left leg gave out and he stumbled. For a split second he couldn't think of why.

"Let me take her," Phury said, putting out his hands. "You've been shot."

Zsadist shook his head and brushed by his twin, limping.

He took Bella out to the Taurus that was still parked in front of the building. Holding her against his chest, he broke the driver's-side window with his fist, then craned his arm inside and unlocked everything while the alarm went crazy. Opening the rear door, he leaned down and put her on the seat. When he bent her legs slightly to make them fit, the nightgown rode up and he winced. She had bruises. A lot of them.

As the alarm ran out of steam, he said, "Someone give me a jacket."

The second he held his hand out behind him, leather hit his palm. He draped her carefully in what he realized was Phury's coat, and then he shut her in and got behind the wheel.

The last thing he heard was a command from Wrath. "V, get out that hand of yours. This place needs to be torched."

Reaching under the dash, Z hot-wired the sedan and sped from the scene like a bat out of hell.

O pulled his truck over to the curb on a dark section of Tenth Street. "I still don't get why you lied."

"If you got yourself sent home to the Omega, where would that leave us? You're one of the strongest slayers we've got."

O glanced over with distaste. "You're such a company man, aren't you?"

"I take pride in our work."

"How nineteen-fifties, Howdy Doody of you."

"Yeah, and that shit saved your ass, so be grateful."

Whatever. He had better things to worry about than U's gung ho pep rally crap.

He and U got out of the truck. ZeroSum and Screamer's and Snuff'd were down a couple blocks, and though it was cold, there were lines waiting to get into the clubs. Some of the shivering masses were undoubtedly vampires, and even if they weren't, the night would be busy. There were always fights with the Brothers to get down with.

O hit the security alarm, stuffed the keys into his pocket . . . and stopped dead in the middle of Tenth Street. He literally couldn't move.

His wife . . . Jesus, his wife really hadn't looked well when he'd left with U.

O grabbed the front of his black turtleneck, feeling like he couldn't breathe. He didn't care about the pain she was enduring; she'd brought that on herself. But he couldn't bear it if she died, if she left him. . . . What if she was dying right now?

"What's the matter?" U asked.

O fished around for the car keys, anxiety sizzling in his veins. "I've got to go."

"You're bailing? We missed quota last night—"

"I just have to go back to the center for a sec. L's over on Fifth Street hunting. Hang with him. I'll find you in thirty."

O didn't wait for an answer. He hopped in the truck and sped out of town, taking Route 22 through Caldwell's rural sprawl. He was about fifteen minutes away from the persuasion center when he saw the flashing tangle of a cop car convention up ahead. He cursed and hit the brakes, hoping it was just an accident.

But no, in the intervening time since he'd left, the goddamned police had set up another one of their intoxication checkpoints. Two squad cars were parked on either side of Route 22, and orange cones and flares ran up the middle of the road. On the right, there was a reflective sign announcing the Caldwell Police Department's Safety First program.

Holy Christ, like they had to do this here? In the middle of nowhere? Why weren't they downtown, near the bars? Then again, people from the shit burg next to Caldwell did have to drive home after club-hopping in the big city. . . .

There was one car in front of him, a minivan, and O drummed his fingers on top of the steering wheel. He had half a mind to pull out his Smith & Wesson and pop both the cop and the driver to their royal reward. Just for slowing him up.

A car approached from the opposite direction, and O looked across the road. The unremarkable Ford Taurus stopped with a little squeak of the brakes, its headlights milky and dim.

Man, those lame-ass cars were a dime a dozen, but that was why U had chosen the make and model for his own ride. Fitting in with the general human population was critical to keeping the war with the vampires secret.

As the policeman approached the POS, O thought it was weird that the driver's window was already down on a cold night like this. Then he got a gander at the guy behind the wheel. *Holy shit.* Bastard had a scar as thick as a finger running down his face. And a gauge in his earlobe. Maybe the car was stolen.

The cop obviously had the same idea, because his hand was on the butt of his gun as he bent over to address the driver. And the shit really went down when the badge trained his flashlight into the backseat. Abruptly his body jerked like he'd been nailed between the eyes, and he reached for his shoulder, going for what was probably his transmitter. Except the driver stuck his head out the window and stared up at the officer. There was a frozen moment between them.

Then the policeman dropped his arm and casually waved the Taurus through without even checking the driver's ID.

O glared at the cop doing duty on O's side of the road. The fucker was still detaining the soccer-mom special in front like the minivan was full of drug dealers. Meanwhile, the guy's buddy across the way was letting what looked like a serial killer go through without so much as a *hi-how-are-ya.* It was like getting in the wrong lane at a tollbooth.

Finally O pulled up. He was as civil as he could be, and a couple minutes later he was hitting the gas. He'd gone about five miles when a brilliant flash of light broke out over the landscape to the right. About where the persuasion center was.

He thought of the kerosene heater. The one that leaked.

O floored the accelerator. His woman was stuck in the ground. . . . If there was a fire . . .

He cut into the forest and sped under the pine trees, bumping up and down, his head smacking the roof while he tried to hang onto the steering wheel. He reassured himself that up ahead there was no orange glow from a blaze. If there had been an explosion, there would be flames, smoke. . . .

His headlights swung around. The persuasion center was gone. Eliminated. Ash.

O punched into the brake to keep the truck from smashing into a tree. Then he looked around the forest to make sure he was in the right place. When it was clear he was, he leaped out and threw himself to the ground.

Grabbing handfuls of dust, he waded around in the residue until the shit got in his nose and his mouth and covered his body like a robe. He found bits of melted metal, but nothing larger than his palm.

Through the roaring in his mind, he remembered seeing this odd ghostly powder before.

O tilted his head back and hurled his voice to the heavens. He had no idea what left his mouth. All he knew was that the Brotherhood had done this. Because the same thing had happened to the *lessers'* martial-arts academy six months ago.

Dust . . . ashes . . . gone. And they had taken his wife.

Oh, God . . . Had she been alive when they'd found her? Or had they taken her body with them? Was she dead?

This was his fault; this was all his fault. He'd been so hellbent on punishing her, he'd missed the implications of that civilian getting loose. The male had gone to the Brotherhood and told them where she was, and they had come at the first shades of night and taken her away.

O wiped desperate tears out of his eyes. And then he

stopped breathing. He swiveled his head around, taking in the landscape. U's silver Ford Taurus was gone.

The checkpoint. The fucking checkpoint. That scary-ass man behind the wheel had in fact been no man at all. He'd been a member of the Black Dagger Brotherhood. Had to be. And O's wife had been in the back, either barely breathing or dead. That was why the cop had freaked out. He'd seen her as he'd looked into the rear of the car, but the Brother had brainwashed him into letting the Taurus through.

O lurched into the truck and hammered the accelerator, driving east, heading for U's place.

The Taurus had a LoJack system.

Which meant with the right computer equipment, he could find that POS anywhere.

Chapter Seven

Bella had some vague thought that she was in a car. Except how was that possible? She must be hallucinating.

No . . . it really sounded like a car, with that steady hum of an engine. And it felt like a car, a subtle vibration that at times condensed into a bump as something in the road went under the tires.

She tried to open her eyes, found she couldn't, and tried again. As the effort exhausted her, she gave up. God, she was tired . . . like she had the flu. Ached all over, too, especially at her head and stomach. And she was nauseated. She tried to remember what had happened, how she'd gotten free, *if* she was free. But all she had was an image of the *lesser* who loved her coming through the door, covered in black blood. The rest was fog.

Patting her hand around, she found something covering her shoulders and pulled it closer. Leather. And it smelled . . . not at all like the cloying sweetness of a *lesser*. It was the scent of a male of her race. She took more breaths in through her nose. When she caught the baby-powder scent of the slayers, she was confused until she pressed her nose into the seat. Yes, in the upholstery. This was a *lesser*'s car. But then why was a male vampire's sweat on what she was wearing? And there was something else, another smell . . . a dark musk with an evergreen spice.

Bella started to tremble. She remembered the scent well, remembered it from the first time she had gone to the Brotherhood's training compound, remembered it from later, when she had been to their mansion.

Zsadist. Zsadist was in the car with her.

Her heart pounded. She struggled to open her eyes, but either her lids refused to obey or maybe they were already open and it was just too dark for her to see.

Am I rescued? she asked. *Did you come for me, Zsadist?*

Except no sound came out of her mouth, though she moved her lips. She formed the words again, forcing air through her voice box. A hoarse groan was released, nothing more.

Why weren't her eyes working?

She started to thrash around and then heard the sweetest sound that had ever reached her ears.

"I got you, Bella." Zsadist's voice. Low. Full of strength. "You're safe. You're out of there. And you're never going back."

He had come for her. He had come for her. . . .

She started to sob. The car seemed to slow, but then their speed redoubled.

Her relief was so great, she slid into blackness.

Zsadist kicked open the door to his room, busting the lock mechanism clean off. The crack of sound was loud, and Bella stirred in his arms, moaning. He froze as her head turned from side to side in the crook of his arm.

This was good, he thought. This was very good.

"Come on, Bella, come back to me. Wake up." But she didn't regain consciousness.

He went over to his pallet and laid her down where he slept. When he glanced up, Wrath and Phury were in his doorway, the two huge males blocking out most of the light from the hall.

"She needs to go to Havers's," Wrath said. "She needs to be treated."

"Havers can do what he has to here. She's not leaving this room."

Z ignored the long silence that followed, totally caught up in watching Bella breathe. Her chest was going up and down in a regular pump, but it seemed so shallow.

Phury's sigh was one he'd know anywhere. "Zsadist—"

"Forget it. He'll see her here. And no one is touching her without my permission or my presence." When he glared up at his brothers, Wrath and Phury seemed totally dumbfounded. "For chrissakes, you want me to say it in the Old Language in case you two forgot English? She goes *nowhere.*"

With a curse, Wrath flipped open his cell phone and spoke fast and hard.

When he closed the thing, he said, "Fritz is already in town, and he's going to pick the doctor up. They'll be here in twenty."

Z nodded and looked at Bella's eyelids. He wished he could be the one to take care of what had been done to them. He wanted her to be relieved now. *Oh, God . . .* How she must have suffered.

He became aware that Phury had come over, and he didn't like it as the brother knelt down. Z's instinct was to barricade Bella's body with his own, preventing his twin, Wrath, the doctor, *any* male from seeing her. He didn't understand the impulse, didn't know its origin, but it was so strong he nearly launched himself at Phury's neck.

And then his twin reached out his hand as if to touch her ankle. Z's lips peeled off his fangs, a growl launching out of his mouth.

Phury's head snapped up. "Why are you acting like this?"

She's mine, Z thought.

Except the instant the conviction came to him, he pushed it aside. What the fuck *was* he doing?

"She's hurt," he muttered. "Just don't mess with her, okay?"

Havers arrived fifteen minutes later. The tall, thin doctor had a black leather suitcase in his hand and looked like he was

ready to do his business. But as he came forward, Z sprang up
and intercepted the male into the wall. Havers's pale eyes
popped wide behind his tortoiseshell glasses, and his case
clattered to the floor.

Wrath cursed. "Jesus Christ—"

Z ignored the hands trying to pull him off and pegged the
doctor with a glare. "You treat her better than you would your
own blood. She suffers one unnecessary flinch and I will take
it out of your hide a hundred times over."

Havers's slender body trembled, his mouth working
silently.

Phury gave a good pull and got nowhere. "Z, go easy—"

"Stay out of this," he snapped. "We clear, Doctor?"

"Yes . . . yes, sire." When Z released him, Havers coughed
and pulled at his bow tie. Then frowned. "Sire . . . ? You
bleed. Your leg—"

"You don't worry about me. You worry about her. *Now.*"

The male nodded, fumbled with his suitcase, and went
over to the pallet. As he got down on his knees beside Bella,
Z willed lights on in the room.

Havers's harsh inhalation was probably as close to a curse
as the refined male could get. Under his breath he murmured
in the Old Language, "To do this to a female . . . merciful
Fade."

"Take the stitches out," Z demanded, looming over the
physician.

"First the exam. I have to see if there are more serious
injuries."

Havers opened up his case and pulled out a stethoscope, a
blood-pressure cuff, and a penlight. He checked her heart rate
and breathing, looked into her ears and nose, took her BP.
When he opened her mouth she winced a little, but then he
lifted her head and she began to struggle in earnest.

Just as Zsadist lunged at the doctor, Phury's heavy arm
clamped around Z's chest and jerked him back. "He's not
hurting her and you know it."

Z fought the hold, hating the sensation of Phury's body
against him. But when his twin didn't let up, he knew it was

for the best. He was on a hair trigger, and taking out the doctor would be a stupid move. Hell, he probably shouldn't be armed right now.

Phury was obviously thinking along similar lines. He removed Z's daggers from their chest holster and handed them to Wrath. The guns were taken as well.

Havers looked up and seemed greatly relieved that weapons were gone. "I . . . ah, I'm going to give her some light pain medication. Her respiration and pulse rate are strong enough so she'll handle it fine, and it will make the rest of the examination and what follows easier for her to tolerate. Okay?"

It wasn't until Z nodded that the doctor administered a shot. When the tension in Bella's body eased, the doctor took out a pair of scissors and went to the bottom of the bloodied nightgown she had on.

As he lifted up the hem, Z felt a red rage. "Stop!"

The doctor braced himself for a blow to the head, but all Z did was meet Phury's stare and then Wrath's. "Neither of you is to look at her naked. Close your eyes or turn around."

Both stared at him for a moment. Then Wrath offered his back and Phury lowered his lids, though he kept his hold on Z's chest strong.

Zsadist stared hard at the doctor. "If you're going to remove her clothing, you cover her with something."

"What shall I use?"

"A towel from the bathroom."

"I'll get it," Wrath said. After he handed one over, he resumed his post facing the door.

Havers spread the towel over Bella's body and then cut the nightgown along one side. He glanced up before lifting anything. "I'm going to need to see all of her. And I'm going to have to touch her belly."

"What for?"

"I have to palpate her internal organs to determine whether any are swollen from trauma or infection."

"Make it quick."

Havers pulled the towel aside—

Z swayed against his twin's hard body. "Oh . . . *nalla.*" His voice cracked. "Oh, sweet Jesus . . . *nalla.*"

Something was scratched into the skin on her stomach in what looked like three-inch block letters in English. As he was illiterate, he didn't know what it said, but he had a horrible feeling. . . .

"What does it read?" he hissed.

Havers cleared his throat. "It is a name. David. It says 'David.'"

Wrath growled. "*In her skin?* That animal—"

Z cut his king off. "I will kill that *lesser.* So help me God, I will chew on his bones."

Havers inspected the cuts, his hands light and careful. "You must see that no salt gets anywhere near these. Otherwise the scars will heal as is."

"No shit." As if he didn't have experience with how wounds became permanent.

Havers covered her up and went to her feet, inspecting them and then her calves. He pushed the nightgown out of the way as he went to her knees. Then he moved one of her legs out to the side, parting her thighs.

Z surged forward, dragging Phury with him. "What the fuck are you doing!"

Havers whipped back his hands, holding them up over his head. "I need to perform an internal exam. In the event she has been . . . violated."

With a quick move, Wrath stepped in front of Z and clamped his arms around Z's waist. Through the sunglasses, the king's stare burned. "Let him do it, Z. It's better for her if he does."

Zsadist couldn't watch. He dropped his head down into Wrath's neck, getting lost in the male's long black hair. The hard bodies of his brothers were sandwiching him, but he was too horrified to panic at the contact. He squeezed his eyes shut and breathed deeply, the scents of Phury and Wrath invading his nose.

He heard a rustling noise, as if the doctor were searching around in that suitcase of his. Then there were two snapping sounds, as though the male were pulling on gloves. A shifting of metal against metal. Some whispering noises. Then . . . silence. No, not really. Little noises. Then a couple of clicks.

Z reminded himself that all *lessers* were impotent. But he could just imagine how they made up for the deficiency.

He trembled for her until his teeth chattered.

Chapter Eight

John Matthew looked across the Range Rover's front seat. Tohr was preoccupied as they went deep into the rural part of Caldwell, and though John was scared to meet Wrath, the king, he was more worried about all this quiet. He couldn't understand what was wrong. Bella had been saved. She was safe now. So everyone should be happy, right? Except when Tohr had come home to pick John up, he'd wrapped his arms around Wellsie in the kitchen and stayed there a long time. His words, low and in the Old Language, had come out of what sounded like a choked throat.

John wanted to know the details of what had happened, but it was hard to pry in the car in the dark, what with him having to sign or write. And Tohr didn't look like he was into talking.

"Here we are," Tohr said.

With a quick swing to the right he shot them onto a cramped dirt road, and John realized he suddenly couldn't really see anything out the windows. There was an odd haze to the wintry forest around them, a buffering that made him vaguely nauseous.

From out of nowhere a huge gate materialized from the foggy landscape, and they skidded to a halt. There was another set of gates right beyond it, and as they entered the space in between, they were caged like a bull in a cattle chute. Tohr put down his window, entered some kind of code on an intercom pad, and they were free to go out the other side into a . . .

Jesus, what is this?

An underground tunnel. And as they headed down into the earth on a steady decent, several more gates appeared, the barricades getting more and more fortified until the last one. This was the biggest of them all, a shiny steel monster that had a HIGH VOLTAGE sign smack-dab in the middle. Tohr looked up into a security camera, and then there was a clicking noise. The gates slid apart.

Before they went forward, John tapped Tohr's forearm to get the man's attention. *Is this where the Brothers live?* he signed slowly.

"Sort of. I'm taking you through the training center first and then we'll go to the mansion." Tohr hit the gas. "When classes start you'll come here Monday through Friday. Bus will pick you up in front of our house at four o'clock. My brother Phury's on site, so he's covering the early classes." At John's look, Tohr explained, "The compound is all interconnected underground. I'll show you how to access the tunnel system that links the buildings together, but you keep it to yourself. Anyone who shows up uninvited somewhere is going to have a serious problem. Your classmates are not welcome, you feel me?"

John nodded as they pulled into the parking area he remembered from a night long ago. God, it felt like a hundred years had passed since he'd come here with Mary and Bella.

He and Tohr got out of the Range Rover. *Who will I be training with?*

"A dozen other males about your age. They all have some warrior blood in their veins, which is why we chose them. Training will last through your transitions and then quite a while afterward, until we think you're ready to go out in the field."

They walked up to a pair of metal doors that Tohr opened wide. On the other side was a corridor that seemed to go on forever. As they went along Tohr showed off a classroom, the gym, a weight room, then a locker room. The male stopped when he got to a door made of frosted glass.

"This is where I hang when I'm not home or in the field."

John walked in. The room was pretty empty and very un-remarkable. The desk was metal and covered with computer equipment, phones, and papers. File cabinets lined the back wall. There were only two places to sit, if you assumed flip-ping the wastepaper basket over was not an option. One chair was standard-issue office equipment, over in the corner. The other was behind the desk and hump-ugly: a ragged, avocado green leather monstrosity with dog-eared corners, a sagging seat, and a set of legs that gave new meaning to the word *sturdy.*

Tohr put his hand on the thing's high back. "Can you be-lieve Wellsie made me get rid of this?"

John nodded and signed, *Yes, I can.*

Tohr smiled and walked over to a floor-to-ceiling cabinet. When he opened the door and punched in a series of numbers on a keypad, the back of the thing released outward into a dim kind of passageway.

"Here we go."

John stepped inside even though he couldn't see much.

A metal tunnel. Wide enough to fit three people walking side by side, and so tall there was some space above even Tohr's head. Lights were set into ceiling every ten feet or so, but they didn't carry far through the darkness.

This is the coolest thing I've ever seen, John thought as they started walking.

The sound of Tohr's shitkickers rebounded off the smooth, steel walls, and so did his deep voice.

"Look, about meeting Wrath. I don't want you to worry. He's intense, but he's nothing to fear. And don't be freaked out by the sunglasses. He's nearly blind and hypersensitive to light, so he has to wear them. But even though he can't see, he's going to read you like a book anyway. He'll know your emotions clear as day."

A little later, a shallow staircase appeared to the left, lead-ing up to a door and another keypad. Tohr stopped and pointed down the tunnel, which continued forever, as far as John could tell.

"If you keep going straight here, you'll be at the gatehouse in another hundred and fifty yards."

Tohr went up the flight of stairs, hit the keypad, and threw open the door. Bright light flooded in, like water released from a dam.

John looked up, an odd feeling ringing in his chest. He had the weirdest sense he was dreaming.

"'S all good, son." Tohr smiled, his harsh face softening a little. "Nothing's going to hurt you up there. Trust me."

"Okay, it's done," Havers said.

Zsadist opened his eyes, seeing only Wrath's thick black hair. "Has she been . . . ?"

"She's just fine. No signs of forcible intercourse or trauma of any kind." There was a snapping sound, as if the doctor were removing his gloves.

Zsadist sagged and his brothers accepted his weight. When he finally lifted his head, he saw that Havers had removed the bloody nightgown, put Bella's towel back in place, and was pulling on a fresh pair of gloves. The male leaned over his case, took out a pair of needle-nose scissors and some tweezers, then looked up.

"I'll do her eyes now, all right?" When Z nodded, the doctor held up the instruments. "Be of care, sire. You startle me and I could blind her with these. Do you understand?"

"Yeah. Just don't hurt—"

"She won't feel a thing. I promise you."

This Z watched, and it took forever. He had some vague thought halfway through that he wasn't holding himself up anymore. Phury and Wrath were keeping him on his feet, his head lolling on the side of Wrath's massive shoulder as he stared down.

"Last one," Havers murmured. "Okay. The sutures are out."

All the males in the room took deep breaths, even the doctor, and then Havers went back to his supplies and picked up a tube. He smoothed some ointment onto Bella's lids; then he packed up his suitcase.

As the physician got to his feet, Zsadist broke away from his brothers and walked around a little bit. Wrath and Phury stretched their arms.

"Her injuries are painful, but not life-threatening at this point," Havers said. "They will heal by tomorrow or the day after, provided they are left alone. She is malnourished and she needs to feed. If she's staying in this room, you need to turn up the heat and move her to the bed. Food and drink should be brought in for when she comes around. And there's one other thing. On the internal exam, I found . . ." His eyes bounced between Wrath and Phury, then settled on Zsadist. "Something of a personal nature."

Zsadist went over to the doctor. "What?"

Havers drew him into the corner and spoke softly.

Z was stunned speechless when the male was finished. "You sure?"

"Yes."

"When?"

"I don't know. But fairly soon."

Z looked down at Bella. *Oh, Christ . . .*

"Now, I am assuming you have aspirin or Motrin in the house?"

Z had no clue; he never took pain meds. He glanced at Phury.

"Yes, we do," the brother said.

"Let her take them. And I'll give you something stronger as backup in case they don't work well enough."

Havers took out a small glass bottle that had a red rubber seal as a top and palmed two hypodermic syringes that were in sterile packs. He wrote on a little pad, then handed the paper and the supplies to Z.

"If it's daytime and she's in a great deal of pain when she wakes up, you may give her a shot of this according to my directions. It's the same morphine I just gave her, but you must mind the dosage information. Call me if you have questions or you want me to walk you through the injection procedure.

Otherwise, if the sun is down, I'll come and give her the shot myself." Havers glanced down at Z's leg. "Would you like for me to examine your wound?"

"Can I bathe her?"

"Yes, definitely."

"Now?"

"Yes." Havers frowned. "But, sire, your leg . . ."

Z walked into his bathroom, cranked the Jacuzzi's faucets, and stuck his hand under the rush. He waited until it was warm enough; then he went back for her.

By this time, the doctor had gone, but Mary, Rhage's female, was in the bedroom's doorway, wanting to see Bella. Phury and Wrath talked to her briefly and shook their heads. She left, looking stricken.

As the door shut, Z knelt down next to the pallet and started to pick Bella up.

"Hold it, Z." Wrath's voice was hard. "Her family should be caring for her."

Z stopped and thought of whoever had fed her fish. God . . . this was probably not right. Keeping her here, away from those who had proper cause to attend her in her pain. But the idea of letting her go out into the world was unbearable. He'd only just found her. . . .

"She'll go to them tomorrow," he said. "Tonight and today she stays here."

Wrath shook his head. "It's not—"

"You think she's ready to travel like this?" Z snapped. "Leave the female alone. Have Tohr call her family and tell them she will be given over to them at nightfall tomorrow. Right now she needs a bath and some sleep."

Wrath's lips tightened. There was a long silence. "Then she goes to another room, Z. She's not staying with you."

Zsadist rose to his feet and walked over to the king, getting all up in the male's grille. "You just try and move her."

"For chrissakes, Z," Phury barked. "Back off—"

Wrath leaned forward until their noses almost touched. "Careful, Z. You know damn well that threatening me won't just get you cracked in the jaw."

Yeah, they'd been through it over the summer. Legally Z could be executed under the old rules of conduct if he pushed this much further. The king's life was valued over all others'.

Not that Z gave a shit at the moment.

"You think I care about a death sentence? *Please.*" He narrowed his eyes. "But I'll tell you this. Whether you decide to go majesty all over my ass or not, it'll take you at least a day to condemn me with the Scribe Virgin. So Bella's still sleeping here tonight."

He walked back to her and picked her up as carefully as he could while making sure the towel stayed where it needed to be. Without looking at Wrath or his twin, he swept her into the bathroom and kicked the door shut behind him.

The tub was already halfway filled, so he kept a hold on her as he leaned down and checked the temperature. Perfect. He lowered her into the water and then stretched her arms over the sides so she was braced up.

The towel quickly dampened and fused with her body. He saw clearly the gentle swells of her breasts, the small rib cage, the flat expanse of her stomach. As the water rose, the hem of the towel floated loose and flirted with the tops of her thighs.

Z's heart kicked in his chest and he felt like a lecher, staring at her when she was hurt and out of it. Hoping to shield her from his eyes and wanting to give her the modesty she deserved, he went to the cabinet to find some bubble bath. There was nothing except bath salts, and he sure as hell wasn't using them.

He was about to turn back to her when he was struck by how big the mirror over the sink was. He didn't want her to see what she looked like, because the less she knew about what had been done, the better. He covered the glass with two large towels, tucking the thick terry cloth behind the frame.

When he returned to her, she'd slid down into the water, but at least the top of the towel was still sticking to her shoulders and basically staying in place. He took hold of her under one of her arms and hitched her up, then grabbed a washcloth. The instant he started washing the side of her neck, she thrashed around, the water splashing up onto him. Low, panicky noises came out of her mouth, and they didn't stop even after he'd put the little towel aside.

Talk to her, you idiot.

"Bella . . . Bella, it's all right. You're okay."

She fell still and frowned. Then her eyes opened slightly and she started to blink a lot. When she tried to wipe at her lids, he took her hands away from her face.

"No. That's medicine. Leave it there."

She froze. Cleared her throat until she could speak. "Where . . . where am I?"

Her voice, groggy and hoarse as it was, sounded beautiful to him.

"You're with . . ." *Me.* "You're with the Brotherhood. You're safe."

As her glassy, unfocused eyes moved around, he leaned up to a switch on the wall and dimmed the lights. Even though she was delirious and no doubt mostly blind from the ointment, he didn't want her to see him. The last thing she needed to worry about was what would happen if her scars didn't heal smoothly.

When she dropped her arms into the water and braced her feet against the tub's base, he cut the faucet off and sat back on his heels. He wasn't good at touching people, so it wasn't a big surprise that she couldn't stand his hands on her. But goddamn, he had no idea what to do to relieve her. She looked miserable—way past crying and into numb agony.

"You're safe . . ." he murmured, though he doubted she believed it. He wouldn't have if he'd been her.

"Is Zsadist here?"

He frowned, not knowing what to make of that. "Yeah, I'm right here."

"You are?"

"Right here. Right beside you." He reached out awkwardly and squeezed her hand. She squeezed back.

And then she seemed to slide into a delirium. She mumbled, making little sounds that might have been words, and jerked around. Z grabbed another towel, rolled it up, and put it under her head so she wouldn't bump it against the hard edge of the Jacuzzi.

He racked his brain for what he could do to help her, and because it was the only thing he could think of, he hummed a little. When that seemed to calm her, he began to sing softly, choosing an Old Language hymn to the Scribe Virgin, one about blue skies and white owls and green fields of grass.

Gradually Bella went lax and took a deep breath. Closing her eyes, she eased back against the towel pillow he'd made for her.

As his singing was the only comfort he could give her, he sang.

Phury stared down at the pallet where Bella had just lain, thinking that the torn nightgown she'd had on made him ill. Then his eyes shifted to the skull on the floor to the left. The female skull.

"I can't allow this," Wrath said as the sound of running water got cut off in the bathroom.

"Z's not going to hurt her," Phury muttered. "Look at the way he treats her. Christ, he's acting like a bonded male."

"What if his mood changes? You want Bella on that list of females he's killed?"

"He'll hit the ceiling if we take her away."

"Tough shit—"

The two of them froze. Then they both slowly looked toward the bathroom door. The sound coming from the other side was soft, rhythmic. As if someone were . . .

"What the hell?" Wrath murmured.

Phury couldn't believe it either. "He's singing to her."

Even muted, the purity and beauty of Zsadist's voice were striking. His tenor had always been like that. On the rare occasions he sang, the sounds that came out of his mouth were stunners, capable of making time grind to a halt and then slide into infinity.

"God . . . damn." Wrath pushed his sunglasses up on to his forehead and rubbed his eyes. "Watch him, Phury. Watch him well."

"Don't I always? Look, I have to go to Havers's myself tonight, but only long enough to get my prosthesis refitted. I'll have Rhage keep an eye on things until I get back."

"You do that. We're not going to lose that female on our watch, we clear? Jesus Christ . . . that twin of yours would drive anyone right off a cliff, you know that?" Wrath stalked out of the room.

Phury looked back down to the pallet and imagined Bella lying there next to Zsadist. This was all wrong. Z didn't know a fricking thing about warmth. And that poor female had spent the last six weeks in the cold ground.

It should be me in there with her. Washing her. Easing her. Caring for her.

Mine, he thought, glaring at the door the singing was coming out of.

Phury started for the bathroom, suddenly pissed off beyond belief. The territorial anger lit his chest up like a bonfire, teeing off a blaze of power that roared in his body. He clamped his hand on the doorknob—and heard that beautiful tenor changing tune.

Phury stood there, shaking. As his anger slid into a yearning that frightened him, he put his forehead on the jamb. *Oh, God . . . no.*

He squeezed his eyes shut, trying to find another explanation for his behavior. There wasn't one. And he and Zsadist were twins, after all.

So it would make sense that they would want the same female. That they would end up . . . bonding with the same female.

He cursed.

Holy shit, this was trouble—of the bury-your-dead variety. Two bonded males tied to the same female were a lethal combination to begin with. Make that two warriors and you had the potential for serious injury. Vampires were animals, after all. They walked and talked and were capable of higher reasoning, but fundamentally they were animals. So there were some instincts that even the smartest brain couldn't override.

Good thing he wasn't quite there yet. He was attracted to Bella and he wanted her, but he hadn't descended into the deep possessiveness that was the calling card of a bonded male. And he hadn't caught the bonding scent coming off of Z, so maybe there was hope.

They'd both have to get away from Bella, though. Warriors, probably because of their aggressive natures, bonded hard and quick. So hopefully she would leave soon and go back to her family, where she belonged.

Phury peeled his hand off the doorknob and backed out of the room. Like a zombie he walked downstairs and headed outside to the courtyard. He wanted the cold to slap some clear thinking into him. Except all it did was make his skin tight.

He was about to light a blunt of red smoke when he noticed that the Ford Taurus, the one Z had hot-wired and driven Bella home in, was parked in front of the mansion. It was still running, forgotten in all the drama.

Yeah, that was not the kind of lawn sculpture they needed. God only knew what kind of tracking device was in it.

Phury got into the sedan, threw the thing into gear, and headed out.

Chapter Nine

As John stepped free of the underground tunnel, he was momentarily blinded by brightness. And then his eyesight adjusted. *Oh, my God. It's beautiful.*

The vast lobby was rainbow vivid, so colorful he felt like his retinas couldn't take it all in. From the green and red marble columns to the multihued mosaic floor to the gold leafing everywhere to the—

Holy Michelangelo, look at that ceiling.

Three stories up, paintings of angels and clouds and warriors on great horses covered an expanse that seemed as big as a football field. And there was more. . . . All around the second floor there was a gold-leafed balcony that had panels inset with similar depictions. Then there was the grand staircase with its own ornate balustrade.

The proportions of the space were perfect. The colors luscious. The art sublime. And it wasn't Donald Trump rent-a-royalty. Even John, who didn't know anything about style, had this funny sense that what he was looking at was the real deal. The person who had built this mansion and decorated it knew his stuff and had the money to buy top-drawer everything: a true aristocrat.

"Sweet, isn't it? My brother D built this place in 1914." Tohr put his hands on his hips as he glanced around, then cleared his throat briskly. "Yeah, he had fabulous taste. The best of the best for him."

John measured Tohr's face carefully. He'd never heard that tone of voice come out of the man before. Such sadness . . .

Tohr smiled and urged John forward with a hand to the shoulder. "Don't look at me like that. I feel like an unwrapped sausage when you do."

They headed for the second floor, walking up dark red carpeting so lush it was like stepping on a mattress. When John got to the top, he looked over the balcony at the lobby's floor design. The mosaics coalesced into a spectacular depiction of a fruit tree in full bloom.

"Apples play a role in our rituals," Tohr said. "Or at least, they do when we observe them. Not a lot of that's been going on lately, but Wrath's convening the first winter solstice ceremony in a hundred or so years."

That's what Wellsie's been working on, right? John signed.

"Yeah. She's handling a lot of the logistics. The race is hungry to get back to the rituals, and it's about time."

When John didn't look away from the splendor, Tohr said, "Son? Wrath's waiting for us."

John nodded and followed, going across the landing to a set of double doors marked with some kind of seal. Tohr was just lifting his hand to knock when the brass handles turned and the interior was revealed. Except no one was on the other side. So how had the things opened?

John glanced in. The room was cornflower blue and reminded him of pictures from a history book. It was French, wasn't it? With all the curlicues and fancy furnishings—

John suddenly had trouble swallowing.

"My Lord," Tohr said, bowing and then walking forward.

John just stood there in the doorway. Behind a spectacular French desk that was way too pretty and way too little for him, there was a massive man with shoulders bigger than even Tohr's. Long black hair fell straight from a widow's peak, and that face . . . the hard composite of it spelled out do-not-fuck-with-me. God, the wraparound sunglasses made him look positively cruel.

"John?" Tohr said.

John went to Tohr's side and hid a little. Yeah, it was a pansy thing to do, but he'd never felt smaller or more dispensable in his life. Hell, next to the power of the guy in front of them, he was almost convinced he didn't actually exist.

The king shifted in his chair, leaning onto the desk.

"Come here, son." The voice was low and accented, the *r* stretching out quite a while before its word ended.

"Go on." Tohr gave him a nudge when he didn't move. "It's all right."

John stumbled over his feet, making it across the room with absolutely no finesse. He halted in front of the desk as if he were a rock that had rolled to a stop.

The king rose and kept rising until he seemed tall as an office building. Wrath had to be six-foot-seven or more, and the black clothes he wore, particularly the leathers, made him even larger.

"Come behind here."

John glanced back to make sure Tohr was still in the room.

"It's okay, son," the king said. "I'm not going to hurt you."

John moved around, his heart beating like a mouse's. As he tilted his head and looked up, the king's arm stretched out. The insides of it, from wrist to elbow, were covered with black tattoos. And the designs were like the ones John had seen in his dreams, the ones he'd put on the bracelet he wore. . . .

"I'm Wrath," the man said. There was a pause. "You want to shake my hand, son?"

Oh, right. John reached out, half expecting his bones to be crushed. Instead he just felt steady warmth as they made contact.

"That name on your bracelet," Wrath said. "It's Tehrror. Do you want to go by that or John?"

John panicked and glanced back at Tohr, because he didn't know what he wanted and didn't know how to communicate that to the king.

"Easy, son." Wrath laughed softly. "You can decide later."

The king's face suddenly snapped to the side, as if he'd

focused on something out in the hall. Just as abruptly a smile stretched his hard lips into an expression of total reverence.

"*Leelan,*" Wrath breathed.

"Sorry I'm late." The female voice was low and lovely. "Mary and I are so worried about Bella. We're trying to figure out how to help her."

"You two will find a way. Come meet John."

John turned to the door and looked at a woman—

White light suddenly took the place of his vision, just wiped out everything he saw. It was like being hit with a halogen beam. He blinked, blinked, blinked. . . . And then from out of the infinite nothing, he saw the woman again. She was dark-haired, with eyes that reminded him of someone he'd loved. . . . No, not reminded . . . hers were the eyes of his . . . What? Of his *what?*

John swayed. Heard voices coming at him from a distance.

On the inside of him, in his chest, down deep in the chambers of his beating heart, he felt a splintering, like he'd split in half. He was losing her . . . he was losing the dark-haired woman . . . he was . . .

He felt his mouth go wide, working as if he were trying to speak, but then spasms overtook him, jerking through his little body, flopping him off the soles of his feet, sending him tumbling to the ground.

Zsadist knew it was time to get Bella out of the tub, because she'd been in it for almost an hour and her skin was pruning up. Except then he glanced through the water at the towel he kept pulling into place over her body.

Shit . . . getting her out with that thing on was going to get messy.

With a wince, he reached over and pulled it off.

Looking away quickly, he slung the wet load to the floor and grabbed a dry one, which he put right next to the tub. Gritting his teeth, he leaned forward and pushed his arms into the water, going for her body. His eyes ended up right on the level of her breasts.

Oh, God . . . They were perfect. Creamy white with little

pink tips. And the water flirted with her nipples, teasing them with rippling kisses that made them glisten.

He squeezed his lids shut, pulled his arms out of the tub, and sat back on his heels. When he was ready to try again, he focused on the wall ahead and arched over . . . only to feel a quick shot of pain at his hips. He looked down, confused.

There was a swollen bulge in his pants. The *it* was so hard, a tent had popped out of the front of his warm-ups. Clearly the thing had gotten squeezed against the side of the tub when he'd leaned over, and that was what the stinger was about.

Cursing, he pushed the *it* around with the heel of his hand, hating the feel of the heavy weight, the way the hard length got tangled in his sweats, the fact that he had to deal with it at all. Except no matter how much he tried, he couldn't get the thing arranged right, at least not without putting his hand inside and working it around, which he was damn well not going to do. Eventually he gave up and left the erection caught at an angle, twisted and hurting.

Served the bastard right.

Zsadist took a deep breath, slid his arms into the water, and wrapped them under Bella's body. He lifted her out, shocked anew at how light she was; then he propped her against the marble wall using the outside of his hip and a hand on her collarbone. He picked up the towel he'd left on the Jacuzzi's edge, but before he put it around her, his eyes shifted to the letters on the skin of her stomach.

Something odd lurched in his chest, a heavy weight. . . . No, it was a descending sensation, as if he were falling down, though he was on a level. He was astonished. It had been so long since anything had broken through the anger or the numbness. He had a feeling he was . . . sad?

Whatever. She had goose bumps, was covered in them. So now was not the time to get all into himself.

He wrapped her up and carried her to the bed. Shoving the comforter aside, he laid her out flat, taking the damp towel off of her. As he covered her with the sheets and blankets, he caught sight of her belly again.

That weird tilting sensation came back, like his heart had taken a gondola ride into his gut. Or maybe his thighs.

He tucked her in and then went to the thermostat. Facing the dial, looking at numbers and writing he didn't understand, he had no idea what to turn it to. He moved the little pointer from all the way to the left to somewhere right of center, but he wasn't sure exactly what he'd done.

He glanced over to the bureau. The two syringes and the glass vial of morphine were sitting where Havers had left them. Z went over, picked up a needle, the drug, and the dosage instructions, then paused before leaving the room. Bella was so still in that bed, so small against all the pillows.

He imagined her in that pipe in the ground. Frightened. In pain. Cold. Then he imagined the *lesser* doing what he'd done to her, holding her down while she struggled and screamed.

This time Z knew what he felt.

Vengeance. Icy cold vengeance. So much of it the shit ran straight into infinity.

Chapter Ten

John woke up on the floor with Tohr by his side and Wrath staring down at him.

Where was the dark-haired woman? In a rush he tried to sit up, but heavy hands held him in place.

"Just chill for a little longer, my man," Tohr said.

John craned his neck around and there she was, looking anxious by the door. The moment he saw her, every neuron in his brain started to fire, and the white light came back. He began to shake, his body knocking against the floor.

"Shit, he's doing it again," Tohr muttered, bearing down to try and control the seizure.

As John felt himself getting sucked under, he threw a hand toward the dark-haired woman, trying to get to her, straining.

"What do you need, son?" Tohr's voice above him was fading in and out like a radio station with static. "We'll get it for you. . . ."

The woman . . .

"Go to him, *leelan*," Wrath said. "Take his hand."

The dark-haired woman came forward, and the instant their palms touched everything went black.

When he came to again, Tohr was talking. ". . . going to take him to see Havers anyway. Hey, son. You're back."

John sat up, head swimming. He put his hands to his face,

as if that would help him stay conscious, and looked to the doorway. Where was she? He had to . . . He didn't know what he had to do. But it was something. Something involving her . . .

He signed frantically.

"She's gone, son," Wrath said. "We're going to keep you two apart until we have an idea of what's doing."

John looked at Tohr and signed slowly. Tohr translated, "He says he needs to take care of her."

Wrath laughed softly. "I think I've got a handle on that job, son. That's my mate, my *shellan,* your queen."

For some reason John relaxed at that piece of news, and gradually he recalibrated back to normal. Fifteen minutes later he got to his feet.

Wrath pegged Tohr with a hard stare. "I want to talk strategy with you, so I need you here. Phury's going to the clinic tonight, though. Why doesn't he take the boy?"

Tohr hesitated and looked at John. "That okay with you, son? My brother's a good guy. All around."

John nodded. He'd already caused enough problems by checking out on the floor like he had a case of the vapors. After that stunt, he was *way* into being user-friendly.

God, what had it been about that woman? Now that she was gone, he couldn't remember what the big deal was. He couldn't even recall her face. It was like he had a snapshot case of amnesia.

"Let me take you down to my brother's room."

John put his hand on Tohr's arm. When he was finished signing, he looked at Wrath.

Tohr smiled. "John said it was an honor to meet you."

"Good to meet you, too, son." The king returned to the desk and sat down. "And Tohr? When you come back, have Vishous with you."

"No problem."

O kicked the side of U's Taurus so hard, his boot left a dent in the quarter panel.

The damn shit box was parked at the side of the road in the

sticks. On a random, nothing-special part of Route 14, twenty-five miles away from downtown.

It had taken him a good hour of sitting in front of U's computer to find the car, because the LoJack signal had been blocked for God only knew what reason. When the damn responder finally popped up on the screen, the Taurus had been moving swiftly. If O had had backup, he'd have made someone stay glued to the computer while he hit the truck and went after the sedan. But U was hunting downtown, and pulling him or anyone else off patrol would have caused a lot of attention.

And O already had trouble . . . trouble that was back again as his cell phone rang for the eight hundredth time. The thing had started going off about twenty minutes ago, and ever since then the calls had been nonstop. He took the Nokia out of his leather jacket. Caller ID showed the number as untraceable. Probably U, or worse, Mr. X.

Word must already be out that the center had been incinerated.

When the cell shut up, O dialed U's number. As soon as it was answered, O said, "You looking for me?"

"Christ, what happened out there? Mr. X said the place is gone!"

"I don't know what went down."

"But you were there, right? You said you were going there."

"You tell Mr. X that?"

"Yeah. And listen, you better watch yourself. The *Forelesser* is pissed off and looking for you."

O leaned against the cold body of the Taurus. *Holy hell.* He didn't have time for this. His wife was somewhere away from him, either breathing or being buried, and regardless of what state she was in, he needed to get her back. Then he had to go after that scarred Brother who'd stolen her and put that ugly bastard into the ground. Hard.

"O? You there?"

Goddamn it . . . Maybe he should have fixed it up so it looked like he'd died in the blast. He could have left the truck at the site and walked out through the woods. Yeah, but then what? He'd have no money, no vehicle, and no backup against the Brotherhood as he went after the one with the scar. He'd be an AWOL *lesser,* which meant that if anyone figured out his disappearing act, he'd be hunted down like a dog by the whole Society.

"O?"

"I honestly don't know what happened. When I got there, it was dust."

"Mr. X thinks you torched the place."

"Of course he does. The assumption's convenient for him, even though I had no motive. Look, I'll call you later."

He clipped the phone shut and shoved it into his jacket. Then he took the thing back out and turned it off.

As he rubbed his face, he couldn't feel anything at all, and it wasn't because of the cold.

Man, he was in deep shit. Mr. X was going to need to blame someone for that ash pile, and O was going to be it. If he wasn't put to death on the spot, the punishment lined up for him was going to be severe. God knew the last time he'd been reprimanded, he'd nearly died under the Omega. *Damn it . . .* What were his options?

When the solution came to him, his body shuddered. But the tactician in him rejoiced.

The first step was getting access to the Society's scrolls before Mr. X found him. This meant he needed an Internet connection. Which meant he was going back to U's.

John left Wrath's study and walked down the hall to the left, sticking close to Tohr. There were doors every thirty feet or so running opposite the balcony, as if the place were a hotel. How many people lived here?

Tohr stopped and knocked on one of them. When there was no answer he knocked again and said, "Phury, man, you got a sec?"

"You looking for me?" came a deep voice from behind them.

A man with a whole lot of nice-looking hair was coming

down the corridor. The stuff on his head was all kinds of different colors, falling down his back in waves. He smiled at John, then looked at Tohr.

"Hey, my brother," Tohr said. The two of them switched over to the Old Language as the guy opened the door.

John looked into the bedroom. There was a huge, antique canopied bed with pillows lined up on a carved headboard. Lots of fancy decorator stuff. Place smelled like a Starbucks.

The man with the hair switched to English and looked down with a smile. "John, I'm Phury. Guess we're both going to the doc's tonight."

Tohr put his hand on John's shoulder. "So I'll see you later, okay? You have my cell phone number. You just text-message me if you need something."

John nodded and watched Tohr stride off. Seeing those broad shoulders recede made him feel very alone.

At least until Phury said quietly, "Don't worry. He's never far, and I'll take good care of you."

John glanced up into warm yellow eyes. Wow . . . the things were the color of goldfinches. As he found himself relaxing, he connected the name. Phury . . . This was the guy who was going to be doing some of the teaching.

Good, John thought.

"Come on in. I just got back from a little errand."

As John breached the doorway, the smoky, coffee smell grew heavier.

"You ever been to Havers's before?"

John shook his head and spotted an armchair by a window. He went over and sat in the thing.

"Well, don't worry about it. We'll make sure you're treated right. So I guess they're going to try to get a bead on your bloodline?"

John nodded. Tohr had said that he was getting blood drawn and having a physical. Both of which were probably a good idea, given the stop, drop, and shiver he'd just pulled in Wrath's office.

He took out his pad and wrote, *Why are you going to the doctor's?*

Phury came over and looked at the scribbles. With an easy shift of his big body, he propped one huge shitkicker on the edge of the chair. John leaned away as the man pulled up his leathers a little.

Oh, my God . . . His lower leg was made up of a series of rods and bolts.

John reached out to feel the shiny metal, then looked up. He didn't realize he was touching his own throat until Phury smiled.

"Yeah, I know all about what it's like to be missing a part."

John glanced back at the artificial limb and cocked his head.

"How'd it happen?" When John nodded, Phury hesitated and then said, "I shot it off."

The door flew open and a hard male voice cut through the room. "I need to know—"

John shifted his eyes as the words died off. Then he cringed back in the chair.

The man in the doorway was scarred, his face distorted by a slash that ran right down the middle of it. But that wasn't what made John want to shrink out of sight. The black eyes in that ruined visage were like the shadows of a deserted house, full of things that probably would hurt you.

And to top it all off, the guy had fresh blood on his pant leg and left shitkicker.

That vicious gaze narrowed and hit John's face like a blast of cold air. "What are you looking at?"

Phury lowered his leg. "Z—"

"I asked you a question, *boy.*"

John fumbled with his pad. He wrote fast and flashed the page to the other man, but somehow that just made the situation worse.

That misshapen upper lip pulled up, revealing tremendous fangs. "Yeah, whatever, kid."

"Back off, Z," Phury cut in. "He has no voice. He can't talk." Phury tilted the pad his way. "He apologizes."

John resisted the urge to hide behind the chair as he got

raked over visually. But then the aggression radiating from the guy eased up.

"You can't talk at all?"

John shook his head.

"Well, I can't read. So we're SOL, you and me."

John worked his Bic quickly. As he showed the pad to Phury, the male with the black stare frowned. "What did the kid write?"

"He says that's okay. He's a good listener. You can do the talking."

Those soulless eyes shifted away. "Got nothing to say. Now what the hell do I set a thermostat at?"

"Ah, seventy degrees." Phury went across the room. "The dial should be here. See?"

"I didn't turn it up enough."

"And you've got to make sure this switch on the bottom of the unit is all the way over to the right. Otherwise, no matter what the dial is on, the heat won't kick in."

"Yeah . . . okay. And can you tell me what this says?"

Phury looked down at a square piece of paper. "It's the dosage information for the shot."

"No shit. So what do I do?"

"Is she uncomfortable?"

"Not right now, but I want you to fill this up for me and tell me what to do. I need one dose ready to go in case Havers can't get here fast enough."

Phury took the vial and unwrapped the needle. "Okay."

"Do it right." When Phury was finished with the syringe, he recapped it and the two spoke for a while in the Old Language. Then the scary guy asked, "How long will you be gone?"

"Maybe an hour."

"Do me a favor first, then. Lose that sedan I brought her back in."

"I already did."

The scarred man nodded and left, the door closing with a clap.

Phury put his hands on his hips and stared at the floor.

Then he went over to a mahogany box on a bureau and took out what looked like a blunt. Holding the hand-rolled between his thumb and forefinger, he lit it and breathed in deep, keeping the inhale down, closing his eyes. When he exhaled, the smoke smelled like roasting coffee beans and hot chocolate combined. Delicious.

As John's muscles relaxed, he wondered what the stuff was. Not marijuana, certainly. But it wasn't just a cigarette.

Who is he? John wrote, and showed the pad.

"Zsadist. My twin." Phury laughed a little when John's mouth went slack. "Yeah, I know, we don't look much alike. At least, not anymore. Listen, he's a little touchy, so you might want to give him some space."

No shit, John thought.

Phury slipped on a shoulder holster and popped a gun in on one side and a black-bladed dagger on the other. He went into a closet and came back wearing a black leather peacoat.

He put the joint or whatever it was out in a silver ashtray next to the bed. "All right, let's go."

Chapter Eleven

Zsadist was quiet as he stole back into his room. After he fixed the thermostat and put the medicine on the bureau, he went over to the bed and leaned against the wall, staying in the shadows. He became suspended in time as he loomed over Bella and measured the slight rise and fall of the covers that marked her breathing. He could feel the minutes dripping into hours, and yet he could not move even as his legs grew numb.

In the candlelight he watched her skin heal right in front of his eyes. It was miraculous, the bruises fading from her face, the swelling around her eyes draining away, the cuts disappearing. Thanks to the deep sleep she was in, her body was throwing off the damage, and as her beauty was revealed once again, he was so damned grateful. In the lofty circles she ran in, a female with imperfections of any kind would be shunned. Aristocrats were like that.

He pictured his twin's unmarred, handsome face and knew Phury should be the one taking care of her. Phury was perfect savior material, and it was obvious he was into her. Plus she would like to wake up to a male like that. Any female would.

So why the hell didn't he just pick her up and put her in Phury's bed? Right now.

But he couldn't move. And as he stared down at her while

she lay on pillows he'd never used, between sheets he'd never turned back for himself, he remembered the past . . .

Months had gone by since the slave first awoke in captivity. And in this time there was not anything that had not been done to him, in him, or on him, and there was a predictable rhythm to the abuse.

The Mistress was fascinated by his privates and felt the need to display them to other males she favored. She would bring these strangers into the cell, get out the salve, and show him off like a prized horse. He knew she did it to make the others insecure, for he could see the delight in her eyes as the males shook their heads in awe.

When the inevitable violations started up, the slave did his best to release himself from his skin and bones. It was so much more bearable when he could rise up into the air, rise higher and higher until he bounced along the ceiling, a cloud of himself. If he was lucky, he could transform entirely and just float along, watching them from above, playing witness to someone else's humiliation and pain and degradation. But it didn't always work. Sometimes he couldn't free himself, and was forced to endure.

The Mistress always had to use the salve on him, and of late he'd noticed something strange: Even when he was trapped in his body and everything being done to him was vivid, even as the sounds and the smells burrowed like rats into his brain, there was a curious displacement below his waist. Whatever he felt down there registered as an echo, as something removed from the rest of him. It was odd, but he was grateful. Any kind of numbing was good.

Whenever he was left alone, he worked at learning to control his huge, posttransition muscles and bones. This he succeeded at, and he'd attacked the guards a number of times, totally unrepentant about his acts of aggression. Verily, he no longer felt like he knew the males who watched over him and who found such disgust in their duty: Their faces were familiar to him in the manner of

*dream figures, naught but hazy leftovers from a wretched
life he should have enjoyed more.*

*Each time he'd struck out he'd been beaten for hours—
although only on the palms and the soles of his feet, because the Mistress liked him kept pleasing to the eye. As a
result of his offensives, he was now guarded by a revolv-
ing squad of warriors, all of whom wore chain mail if they
came inside his cell. Moreover, the bedding platform was
now fitted with restraints that could be sprung from outside, so that after he'd been used, the guards didn't have
to endanger their lives letting him go. And when the Mistress wanted to come calling, he was drugged into submission either through his food or by blow darts that
would be shot through a slot in the door.*

*The days passed slowly. He was focused on finding the
weakness in the guards and on removing himself as much
as he could from the depravity . . . when for all intents and
purposes he died. And died so hard that even when he was
out from under the Mistress, he would never truly live
again.*

*The slave was eating in his cell, trying to keep his
strength up for the next opening within the guards, when
he saw the sliding panel on the door shift open and a hollow tube protrude. He leaped up, though there was no
cover to be had, and felt the first sting in his neck. He
pulled out the dart as quickly as he could, but he was hit
with another and then another until his body grew heavy.*

He woke up on the bedding, shackled.

*The Mistress was sitting right next to him, her head
down, her hair shielding her face. As if she knew he had
found consciousness, her eyes shifted to his.*

"I am to be mated."

*Oh, sweet Virgin in the Fade . . . The words he'd
longed to hear. He would be free now, for she would need
no blood slave if she had a* hellren. *He could go back to
his duties in the kitchen. . . .*

The slave forced himself to address her with respect,

although to him she was no female of worth. "Mistress, will you let me go?"

There was only silence.

"Please let me go," he said raggedly. *Considering all he had been through, to throw his pride out for the possibility of being free was an easy sacrifice.* "I beg you, Mistress. Release me of this confinement."

When she looked at him, tears were in her eyes. "I find that I cannot. . . . I have to keep you. I must keep you."

He started to struggle, and the harder he fought the binds the more the look of love overtook her face.

"You are so magnificent," she said, *reaching down to touch him between his legs. Her face was wistful . . . nearly worshipful.* "Ne'er have I seen such a male as you. Would that you were not so far beneath me—I would show your face in my court as my consort."

He saw her arm moving slowly up and down and knew that she must be working that rope of flesh that interested her so. Mercifully, he could feel it not.

"Let me go. . . ."

"You never harden without the salve," she murmured in a sad voice. *"And you never find completion. Why is that?"*

She stroked him harder now until he felt a burning down where she was touching him. Frustration bled into her eyes, darkening them.

"Why? Why do you not want me?" When he stayed silent, she yanked at his male staff. *"I am beautiful."*

"Only to others," he said before he could catch the words.

Her breath stopped, as if he had choked her with his very hand. Then her eyes slid up his stomach and his chest to his face. They were still glossy with tears, but rage also filled them.

The Mistress rose from the bed and stared down at him. Then she slapped him so hard she must have hurt her palm. As he spit out blood, he wondered if one of his teeth wasn't leaving with it.

While her eyes bored into his, he thought for sure she was going to have him killed, and a calmness came over him. At least the suffering would be over then. Death . . . death would be glorious.

Abruptly she smiled at him, as if she knew his thoughts, as if she'd reached into him and taken them out of him, as if she'd stolen them just as she had laid larceny to his body.

"No, I shall not be sending you unto the Fade."

She leaned down and kissed one of his nipples, then sucked it into her mouth. Her hand drifted over his ribs, then onto his belly.

Her tongue flicked yet and still over his flesh. "You grow gaunt. You need to feed, do you not?"

She worked her way down his body, kissing and sucking. And then it happened quickly. The salve. Her getting up on top of him. That hideous merging of their bodies.

When he closed his eyes and turned his head, she slapped him once . . . twice . . . many more times. But he refused to look at her, and she was not strong enough to force his face around, even when she grabbed onto one of his ears.

As he denied her his eyes, her weeping grew as loud as the slap of her flesh against his hips. When it was over, she left in a swirl of silk, and not long thereafter the chains were released.

The slave eased himself up on one forearm and wiped his mouth. Looking down at his blood on his hand, he was surprised that it was still red. He felt so soiled, it wouldn't have been a shock to find it some kind of rusted brown.

He rolled off the bed, still groggy from the darts, and found the corner that he always went to. He sat with his back to the juncture of the walls and curled his legs up against his chest so his heels were tight to his male parts.

Sometime later he heard a struggle outside his cell, and

then the guards pushed a small female inside. She fell in a heap, but launched herself at the door as it closed.

"Why?" she yelled. "Why am I punished?"

The slave rose to his feet, not knowing what to do. He hadn't seen a female other than the Mistress since he'd woken up in captivity. This one was a maid of some sort. He remembered her from before. . . .

Blood hunger rose in him as he caught her scent. After all the Mistress had done to him, he couldn't see her as someone to drink from, but this diminutive female was different. He was suddenly dying of thirst, his body's needs coming out in a chorus of shouts and demands. He took lurching steps toward the maid, feeling nothing but instinct.

The female pounded on the door, but then seemed to realize she was not alone. When she turned around and saw who she was locked in with, she screamed.

The slave was nearly overcome by his drinking urge, but he forced himself away from her and scrambled back to where he had been. He crouched down, wrapping his arms around his trembling, naked body to keep it in place. Turning his face to the wall, he tried to breathe . . . and found himself on the verge of weeping over the animal he had been reduced to.

After a while the female stopped screaming, and after even longer she said, "'Tis truly you, is it not? The boy from the kitchen. The one who carried ale."

He nodded without looking at her.

"I had heard rumors you had been taken here, but I . . . I believed the others who said you'd died during your transition." There was a pause. "You are so large. Like a warrior. Why is that?"

He had no idea. He didn't even know what he looked like, as there wasn't a mirror in the cell.

The female cautiously approached him. When he looked up at her, she was eyeing his tattooed bands.

"Truly, what is done to you here?" she whispered.

"They say . . . terrible things are done to the male who dwells within this place."

When he said nothing, she sat beside him and softly touched his arm. He flinched at the contact and then realized he was soothed by it.

"I am here to feed you, am I not? That is why I was brought here." After a moment she peeled his hand free from his leg and put her wrist into his palm. "You must drink."

He wept then, wept from the generosity of her, from the kindness, from the feel of her gentle hand as it rubbed over his shoulder . . . the only touch he had welcomed in . . . forever.

Finally she pressed her wrist to his mouth. Though his fangs unsheathed and he craved her, he did naught but kiss her tender skin and refuse. How could he take from her what was regularly taken from him? She was offering, but she was forced into it, a prisoner of the Mistress just as he was.

The guards came in later. When they found her cradling him, they seemed shocked, but they were not rough with her. As she left she looked at the slave, concern on her face.

Moments later the darts came at him, so many through the door it was as if he were pelted with gravel. As he slid into oblivion, he thought vaguely that the frantic nature of the attack didn't bode well.

When he awoke, the Mistress was standing over him, furious. There was something in her hand, but he couldn't see what it was.

"Think you too good for the gifts I give you?"

The door opened and the young female's limp body was brought in. As the guards let go, she flopped onto the floor like so many rags. Dead.

The slave screamed in fury, the roar rebounding off the stone cell walls, magnifying to an earsplitting thunder. He strained against the steel bands until they cut him to

*the bone, until one of the posts cracked with a squeal . . .
and still he roared.*

*The guards backed away. Even the Mistress seemed un-
sure of the fury she'd released. But as always, it was not
long before she took control.*

"Leave us," she shouted to the guards.

*She waited until the slave wore himself out. Then she
leaned over him, only to grow pale.*

*"Your eyes," she whispered, staring down at him.
"Your eyes . . ."*

*She appeared to be momentarily frightened of him, but
then she cloaked herself in a regal forbearance.*

*"The females I present you with? You will drink from
them." She glanced over at the maid's lifeless body. "And
you'd best not let them comfort you, or I shall do that
again. You are mine and no one else's."*

"I will not drink," he shouted at her. "Ever!"

She stepped back. "Do not be ridiculous, slave."

*He bared his fangs and hissed. "Look upon me, Mis-
tress. Watch as I wither!" He screamed the last word at
her, his booming voice filling the room. As she went rigid
with fury, the door flew open and guards came in with
swords drawn.*

*"Leave us," she snarled at them, her face red, her body
shaking.*

*She lifted her hand up and a whip came with it. Slash-
ing her arm down, she brought the weapon across the
slave's chest. His flesh broke and bled, and he laughed
at her.*

*"Again," he hollered. "Do that again. I felt it not, you
are so weak!"*

*Some dam had burst within him, and the words would
not stop. . . . He railed against her as she whipped him
until the bedding platform flowed with what had been in
his veins. When finally she could lift her arm no more, she
was panting and blood-splattered and sweating. He was
focused, icy, calm in spite of the pain. Though he was the*

*one who had been beaten, she was the one who had bro-
ken first.*

*Her head fell downward as if in submission while she
dragged breath through her white lips.*

"Guard," she said hoarsely "Guard!"

*The door opened. The uniformed male who ran in
faltered when he saw what had been done, the soldier
blanching and teetering in his boots.*

*"Hold his head." The Mistress's voice was reedy as she
dropped the whip. "Hold his head, I say. Now."*

*The guard stumbled over, slipping on the slick floor.
Then the slave felt a meaty hand clap onto his forehead.*

*The Mistress leaned over the slave's body, still breath-
ing hard. "You are not . . . permitted . . . to die."*

*Her hand found his male flesh and then dipped down
underneath it to the twin weights below. She squeezed and
twisted, making his whole body spasm. As he cried out,
she bit her wrist, held it over his open mouth, and bled
into him.*

Z backed away from the bed. He didn't want to think of the
Mistress in Bella's presence . . . as if all that evil could escape
his mind and endanger her as she slept and healed.

He went over to his pallet and realized he was curiously
tired. Exhausted, actually.

As he stretched out on the floor, his leg throbbed like a
bitch.

God, he'd forgotten he'd been shot. He stripped out of his
shitkickers and pants and willed a candle to light beside him.
Cocking his leg around, he inspected the wound on his calf.
There was both an entrance and an exit hole, so he knew the
bullet had passed through. He'd live.

He extinguished the candle with his breath, draped his
pants over his hips, and lay back. Opening himself up to the
pain in his body, he became a basin for the agony, catching all
the nuances of his aches and stings—

He heard an odd noise, like a small cry. The sound was repeated, and then Bella began to struggle on the bed, the sheets rustling as if she were flailing around.

He shot up from the floor and went around to her, just as her head tilted toward him and her eyes opened.

She blinked, looked up at his face . . . and screamed.

Chapter Twelve

"You want something to eat, my man?" Phury said to John as they walked into the mansion. The kid looked worn-out, but then anyone would. Getting poked and prodded at was hard work. Phury was a little wiped himself.

As John shook his head and the vestibule's door clamped shut, Tohr came jogging down the staircase looking very much like a nervous father. And this was in spite of the fact that Phury had called in a report on the way home.

The visit to Havers's had been all good, for the most part. Seizure notwithstanding, John was healthy, and the results on his bloodline test would be available soon. With luck, they would get a bead on his ancestry, and that would help John find his kin. So there was no cause for worry.

Still, Tohr put his arm around the boy's shoulders and the kid sagged. Some kind of wordless, eyeball-to-eyeball communication took place, and the brother said, "I think I'll take you home."

John nodded and signed something. Tohr looked up. "He says he forgot to ask you how your leg is."

Phury brought up his knee and knocked on his calf. "Better, thanks. You take care, John, okay?"

He watched as the two of them disappeared through the door under the stairwell.

What a good kid, he thought. And thank God they'd found him before his transition—

A female scream ripped into the lobby, as if the sound were alive and had taken a nosedive off the balcony.

Phury's spine turned to ice. *Bella.*

He bolted up to the second floor and pounded down the hall of statues. When he threw open Zsadist's door, light spilled into the room and the scene was instantly carved into memory: Bella on the bed, cowering against the headboard, sheets clenched to her throat. Z crouched in front of her, hands up, naked from the waist down.

Phury lost it and launched himself at Zsadist, grabbing his twin by the throat and throwing him against the wall.

"What is wrong with you!" he yelled as he crashed Z into the plaster. *"You fucking animal!"*

Z didn't fight back as he was slammed again. And all he said was, "Take her away. Take her somewhere else."

Rhage and Wrath burst into the room. Both started talking, but Phury couldn't hear anything for the roar between his ears. He'd never hated Z before. Had cut his twin slack for all he'd endured. But going after Bella . . .

"You sick fuck," Phury hissed. He nailed that hard body to the wall once more. "You sick fuck . . . God, you *disgust* me."

Z merely stared back, his black eyes like asphalt, opaque and flat.

Suddenly Rhage's massive arms clamped around them, gathering them up into a bone-crushing bear hug. In a whisper, the brother said, "Bella doesn't need this right now, boys."

Phury dropped his hold and pushed himself free. Yanking his coat back into place, he snapped, "Get him out of here until we move her."

God, he was shaking so badly he was almost hyperventilating. And the anger wouldn't quit, even as Z left voluntarily, with Rhage tight on his heels.

Phury cleared his throat and glanced at Wrath. "My lord, will you give me leave to attend to her in private?"

"Yeah, I will." Wrath's voice was a nasty growl as he

headed for the door. "And we'll make sure Z doesn't come back for a while."

Phury looked over at Bella. She was trembling as she blinked and wiped at her eyes. When he approached her, she shrank back against the pillows.

"Bella, it's Phury."

Her body relaxed a little. "Phury?"

"Yeah, it's me."

"I can't see." Her voice quavered like hell. "I can't . . ."

"I know, it's just the medicine. Let me get something to clean it off."

He went into the bathroom and came back with a damp cloth, figuring she needed to get a look at her surroundings more than she had to have the ointment.

She flinched as he took her chin in his palm.

"Easy, Bella . . ." When he put the cloth up to her eyes, she struggled, then clawed at him. "No, no . . . put your hands down. I'll get it off."

"Phury?" she said hoarsely. "Is it really you?"

"Yes, it's me." He sat down on the edge of the bed. "You're at the Brotherhood's compound. You were brought here about seven hours ago. Your family's been notified that you're safe, and as soon as you want to, you can call them."

When she put her hand on his arm, he froze. With a tentative touch, she felt her way up to his shoulder to his neck, then touched his face and finally his hair. She smiled a little when she felt the thick waves and then she brought some of it to her nose. She breathed in deep and put her other hand on his leg.

"It truly is you. I remember the smell of your shampoo."

The closeness and the contact sizzled through Phury's clothes and skin, going straight into his blood. He felt like a total bastard to feel anything sexual, but he couldn't stop his body. Especially as she patted her way down his long hair until she was touching his pectorals.

His lips opened, his breath getting short. He wanted to drag her against his chest and hold her tight. Not for sex, though it was true his body wanted that from her. No, right now he just needed to feel her warmth and reassure himself that she was alive.

"Let me take care of your eyes," he said. *Jesus,* his voice was deep.

When she nodded, he carefully wiped at her lids. "How's that?"

She blinked. Smiled a little. Put her hand on his face.

"I can see you better now." But then she frowned. "How did I get out of there? I can't remember anything except . . . I let the other civilian go and David came back. And then there was a car ride. Or was that a dream? I dreamt that Zsadist saved me. Did he?"

Phury was not up to talking about his twin, even tangentially. He rose to his feet and put the washcloth on the nightstand. "Come on, let's get you to your room."

"Where am I now?" She looked around, and then her mouth parted. "This is Zsadist's room."

How the hell did she know that? "Let's go."

"Where is he? Where's Zsadist?" Urgency threaded through her voice. "I need to see him. I need—"

"I'm going to take you to your room—"

"No! I want to stay—"

She was so agitated now he decided to stop trying to talk to her. He pulled back the sheets so he could help her up—

Shit, she was naked. He yanked the covers back into place.

"Ah, sorry . . ." He pushed a hand into his hair. *Oh, God* . . . The graceful lines of her body were something he was never going to forget. "Let me . . . um, let me get you something to wear."

He went to Z's closet and was stunned by how empty it was. There wasn't even a robe to cover her with, and he'd be goddamned if he'd put her in one of his twin's fighting shirts. He took off his leather peacoat and walked over to her again.

"I'll turn my back while you put this on. We'll find you a robe—"

"Don't take me away from him." Her voice cracked from pleading. "Please. That must have been him standing over the bed. I didn't know it, I couldn't see. But it must have been him."

It sure as hell was. And the bastard had been naked as sin and ready to jump her. Considering all she'd been through, the near-miss was a total cringer. *Man . . .* Years ago Phury had caught Z having sex in a back alley with a whore. It hadn't been pretty, and the idea of Bella's being subjected to that made him ill.

"Put on the coat." Phury turned away. "You are not staying here." When he finally heard the bedding move, and the creak of leather, he took a deep breath. "Are you decent?"

"Yes, but I don't want to go."

He looked over his shoulder. She was dwarfed by the coat he wore all the time, her long mahogany hair falling around her shoulders, the ends curled as if they'd gotten wet and had dried without being brushed. He imagined her in a tub, with clean water rushing over her pale skin.

And then he saw Zsadist looming over her, watching her with those soulless black eyes, wanting to fuck her, probably only because she was scared. Yeah, her fear would be the turn-on for him. It was well-known that terror in a female cranked him up more than anything lovely or warm or worthy.

Get her out of here, Phury thought. *Right now.*

His voice became unsteady. "Can you walk?"

"I'm light-headed."

"I'll carry you." He approached her, on some level unable to believe he was going to put his arms around her body. But then it was happening. . . . He slid his hand around her waist and reached down, taking her behind her knees. Her weight barely registered, his muscles accepting her easily.

As he started for the door she eased into him, laying her head on his shoulder, taking some of his shirt into her hand.

Oh . . . Sweet Virgin. This felt so right.

Phury carried her down the hall to the other side of the house, to the room next to his.

John was on autopilot as he and Tohr left the training facility and walked across the parking area where they'd left the Range Rover. Their footsteps echoed up to the low concrete ceiling, bouncing through the empty space.

"I know you have to go back for the result," Tohr said as they got into the SUV. "I'll go with you that time, no matter what's happening."

Actually, John kind of wished he could take himself.

"What's the matter, son? Are you upset that I didn't take you tonight?"

John put his hand on Tohr's arm and shook his head vigorously.

"Okay, just wanted to make sure."

John looked away, wishing he'd never gone to the doctor's. Or that at least when he'd been there, he'd kept his mouth shut. *Holy hell.* He shouldn't have said a word about what had happened to him almost a year ago. Trouble was, after all the questions about his health, he'd been in answering mode. So when the doctor had asked about his sexual history, he'd alluded to the thing back in January. Question. Answer. Just like all the others . . . sort of.

For a moment it had been a relief. He'd never gone to a doctor or anything afterward, and in the back of his mind he'd always worried that he should have. At least by coming forward, he'd figured he could get a full checkup and really be done with the attack. Instead, the doctor had started in on him about therapy and the necessity of talking about the experience.

Like he wanted to relive it? He'd spent months burying the damn thing, so no way was he digging up that rotting corpse. It had taken too much effort to put it in the ground.

"Son? What's doing?"

Like hell he was going to see some therapist. Past trauma. *Screw that.*

John took out his pad and wrote, *Just tired.*

"You sure?"

He nodded and looked at Tohr so the man would think he wasn't lying. Meanwhile he was withering in his own skin. What the hell would Tohr think if he knew what had happened? Real men did not allow that to be done to them no matter what kind of weapon was at their throats.

John wrote, *Next time I want to go to Havers's alone, okay?*

Tohr frowned. "Ah . . . that's not really smart, son. You need a guard."

Then it needs to be someone else. Not you.

John couldn't look at Tohr when he flashed the paper. There was a long silence.

Tohr's voice became very low. "Okay. That's . . . ah, that's fine. Maybe Butch can take you."

John closed his eyes and exhaled. Whoever this Butch was would work for him.

Tohr started the car. "It's whatever you want, John."

John. Not *son.*

As they headed out, all he could think was, *Dear God, please don't let Tohr ever find out.*

Chapter Thirteen

As Bella hung up the phone, she had a passing thought that what was going on inside her chest was so explosive, she was going to shatter at any moment. There was just no way her brittle bones and her fragile skin could hold in the kind of emotion she was feeling.

In desperation she looked around the room, seeing the vague, blurry outlines of oil paintings and antique furniture and lamps made from Oriental vases and . . . Phury staring at her from a chaise longue.

She reminded herself that, like her mother, she was a lady. So she should at least pretend to have some self-control. She cleared her throat. "Thank you for staying while I made that call to my family."

"Of course."

"My mother was . . . greatly relieved to hear my voice."

"I can imagine."

Well, at least her mother had spoken words of relief. Her affect had been as smooth and calm as always. God . . . the female was ever the still-watered pond, unshaken by earthly events no matter how grim. And all because of her devotion to the Scribe Virgin. To *mahmen,* everything happened for a reason . . . yet nothing ever seemed particularly important.

"My mother . . . is greatly relieved. She . . ." Bella stopped.

She'd already said those words, hadn't she? "*Mahmen* was . . . she really was . . . she was relieved."

But it would have helped if she had at least choked up. Or shown anything but the beatific acceptance of the spiritually enlightened. For chrissakes, the female had buried her daughter and then been witness to a resurrection. You'd think that would call for some kind of emotional reaction. Instead it was as if they'd just spoken yesterday, and nothing of the past six weeks had occurred.

Bella glanced back down at the phone. Wrapped her arms around her stomach.

With no warning whatsoever, she cracked wide-open. The sobs came out of her like sneezes: fast, hard, shocking in their ferocity.

The bed dipped, and strong arms came around her. She fought the pull, thinking that a warrior wouldn't want to deal with such sloppy weakness.

"Forgive me. . . ."

"It's okay, Bella. Lean on me."

Oh, hell . . . She collapsed against Phury, wrapping her arms around his tight waist. His long, beautiful hair tickled her nose and smelled good and felt wonderful under her cheek. She burrowed into it, breathing deep.

When she finally calmed down she felt lighter, but not in a good way. The angry emotions had filled her out, given her contours and weight. Now, because her skin was nothing more than a sieve, she was leaching out, becoming air . . . becoming nothing.

She didn't want to disappear.

She inhaled and broke free of Phury's embrace. Blinking rapidly, she tried to focus her eyes, but the blurriness from the ointment persisted. God, what had that *lesser* done to her? She had a feeling it had been bad. . . .

She reached up to her eyelids. "What did he do to me?"

Phury just shook his head.

"Was it that ugly?"

"It's over. You're safe. That's all that matters."

None of it feels over to me, she thought.

But then Phury smiled, his yellow stare impossibly tender, a balm that soothed her. "Would it be easier if you were at home? Because if you want, we can find a way to get you there, even though the dawn's coming very soon."

Bella pictured her mother and couldn't imagine being in the same house with that female. Not right now. And even more to the point, there was Rehvenge. If her brother saw her with any kind of injury he'd go crazy, and the last thing she needed was him on the warpath against the *lessers*. She wanted the violence to stop. As far as she was concerned, David could go to hell right this minute; she just didn't want anyone she loved risking their lives to send him there.

"No, I don't want to go home. Not until I'm completely healed. And I'm so very tired. . . ." Her voice drifted off as she glanced at the pillows.

After a moment Phury got up. "I'm right next door if you need me."

"Would you like your coat back?"

"Oh, yeah . . . let me see if there's a robe in here." He disappeared into a closet and came back with black satin draped over his forearm. "Fritz stocks these guest rooms for males, so this is probably going to be too big."

She took the robe and he turned away. When she shrugged out of his heavy leather coat the air chilled her, so she quickly wrapped the satin around herself.

"Okay," she said, grateful for his discretion.

As he pivoted back to her, she put the leather into his hands.

"I'm always saying thank-you to you, aren't I?" she murmured.

He looked at her for a long time. Then in slow motion, he lifted his coat to his face and breathed in deeply.

"You're . . ." His voice trailed off. Then he dropped the leather to his side and an odd expression hit his face.

Actually, no, that wasn't an expression. It was a mask. He'd gone into hiding.

"Phury?"

"I'm glad you're with us. Try to get some sleep. And eat some of what I brought you, if you can."

The door shut behind him without a sound.

The drive back to Tohr's house was awkward, and John spent the time staring out the side window. Tohr's cell phone rang twice. Both conversations were in the Old Language, and the name Zsadist kept reappearing.

When they pulled into the driveway there was an unfamiliar car parked in it. A red Volkswagen Jetta. Yet Tohr didn't seem surprised as he eased past the thing and went into the garage.

He killed the Range Rover's engine and opened his door. "By the way, classes start the day after tomorrow."

John looked up from undoing his seat belt. *So soon?* he signed.

"We had the last trainee sign up tonight. We're good to go."

The two of them walked in silence through the garage. Tohr was in front, his big shoulders moving with the long steps he took. The man's head was down, as if he were looking for cracks in the concrete floor.

John stopped and whistled.

Tohr slowed, then halted. "Yeah?" he said quietly.

John took out his pad, scribbled something, and held it out.

Tohr's brows came down as he read. "There's nothing to be sorry for. Whatever makes you feel comfortable."

John reached out and squeezed the man's biceps. Tohr shook his head.

"It's all right. Come on, I don't want you to catch cold out here." The man glanced over when John didn't move. "Ah, hell . . . I'm just . . . I'm there for you. That's all."

John put his pen to the paper. *I don't doubt that for a moment. Ever.*

"Good. You shouldn't. Straight up, I feel like I'm your . . ." There was a pause as Tohr rubbed his thumb back and forth across his forehead. "Look, I don't want to crowd you. Let's go inside."

Before John could beg him to finish the sentence, Tohr

opened the door into the house. Wellsie's voice drifted out . . . and so did another woman's. John frowned as he came around the corner into the kitchen. And then stopped dead as a blond female looked over her shoulder.

Oh . . . wow.

Her hair was cut off at her jawline and her eyes were the color of new leaves. Those hip-hugger jeans she was wearing were so short-waisted . . . God, he could see her belly button and about an inch of flesh underneath. And her black turtleneck was . . . Well, he could tell exactly how perfect her body was, put it like that.

Wellsie grinned. "You guys got here just in time. John, this is my cousin Sarelle. Sarelle, this is John."

"Hi, John." The female smiled.

Fangs. Oh, yeah. Look at those fangs . . . Something traveled like a hot breeze over his skin, leaving him tingling from head to foot. Out of confusion, he opened his mouth. Then thought, *uh-huh, right.* As if anything was coming out of his useless piehole?

While flushing to all hell and gone, he lifted his hand in a wave.

"Sarelle's helping me with the winter festival," Wellsie said, "and she's going to stay for a bite to eat before dawn breaks. Why don't you two set the table?"

As Sarelle smiled again, that funny tingling thing got so strong, he felt as if he were levitating.

"John? You want to help set the table?" Wellsie prompted.

He nodded. And tried to remember where the knives and forks were.

O's headlights swung across the front of Mr. X's cabin. The *Fore-lesser*'s everyman minivan was parked right next to the door. O stopped his truck behind the Town & Country, blocking it in.

As he got out and the cold air shot into his lungs, he was aware that he was in the zone. In spite of what he was about to do, his emotions lay like smooth feathers over his chest, all arranged, nothing out of place. His body was just as unruffled, moving with its power checked, a gun ready to fire.

The scrolls had taken a long time to wade through, but he'd found what he needed. He knew what had to happen.

He opened the cabin's door without knocking.

Mr. X looked up from the kitchen table. His face was impassive, showing no frown, no sneer, no aggression of any kind. No surprise, either.

So they were both in the zone.

Without a word, the *Fore-lesser* rose, one hand going around to his back. O knew what was there, and he smiled as he unsheathed his own knife.

"So, Mr. O—"

"I'm ready for a promotion."

"Excuse me?"

O turned his blade on himself, putting the tip to his sternum. With a two-handed jabbing motion, he stabbed his own chest.

The last thing he saw before the great white inferno crisped the shit out of him was the shock on Mr. X's face. Shock that quickly shifted to terror as the man figured out where O was going. And what O was going to do when he got there.

Chapter Fourteen

Lying in bed, Bella listened to the quiet sounds around her: male voices down the hall, low-pitched, rhythmic . . . the wind outside pushing against the mansion, capricious, uneven . . . the creak of a floorboard, quick, high-pitched.

She forced herself to close her eyes.

A minute or so later she was up and pacing around, the Oriental on the floor soft under her bare feet. None of her elegant surroundings made sense, and she felt like she had to awkwardly transcribe what she was seeing. The normalcy, the safety she was steeping in seemed like another language, one she had forgotten how to speak or read. Or was this a dream?

In the corner of the room the grandfather clock chimed five A.M. How long had she been free, exactly? How long since the Brothers had come for her and taken her from the earth back into the air? Eight hours now? Maybe, except it felt like minutes. Or maybe it felt like years?

The fuzzy quality of time was like her blurry vision, insulating her, scaring her.

She pulled the silk robe around her more tightly. This was all wrong. She should be rejoicing. After God only knew how many weeks in that pipe in the ground with that *lesser* standing over her, she should be weeping with sweet relief.

Instead everything around her felt fake and insubstantial, as if she were in a life-size dollhouse filled with papier-mâché fakes.

She paused in front of a window and realized that only one thing felt real. And she wished she were with him.

Zsadist must have been the one who had come to the side of the bed as she'd first woken up. She'd been dreaming of being back in the hole, back with the *lesser*. When she'd opened her eyes, all she'd seen was a massive black shape standing over her, and for a moment she hadn't been able to separate reality from nightmare.

She was still having trouble with that.

God, she wanted to go to Zsadist now, wanted to return to his room. But in the middle of all the chaos after she'd screamed, he hadn't prevented her from leaving him, had he? Maybe he preferred her elsewhere.

Bella ordered her feet to start moving again and she made herself a little track: around the foot of the gigantic bed, over to the chaise, quick loop by the windows, then a big scenic swing past the highboy and the door to the hall and the old-fashioned writing desk. The home stretch took her by the fire-place and the bookshelves.

More pacing. More pacing. More pacing.

Eventually she went into the bathroom. She didn't stop in front of the mirror; didn't want to know what her face looked like. What she was after was some hot water. She wanted to take a hundred showers, a thousand baths. She wanted to strip off the first layer of her skin and shave off the hair that *lesser* had loved so much and clip her nails and clean her ears and scrub the soles of her feet.

She fired up the showerhead. When the spray was warm, she dropped the robe and stepped under the water. The second the rush hit her back, she covered herself out of instinct, one arm over her breasts, one hand shielding the apex of her thighs . . . until she realized she didn't have to hide. She was alone. She had privacy here.

She straightened and forced her hands to her sides, feeling like it had been forever since she'd been allowed to wash in private. The *lesser* had always been there, staring, or worse, helping.

Thank God, he'd never tried to have sex with her. Rape had been one of her greatest fears in the beginning. She'd been terrified, sure he was going to force her, but then she'd discovered he was impotent. No matter how hard he stared at her, his body had always remained flaccid.

With a shudder, she reached to the side for the bar of soap, lathered her hands, and ran them over her arms. She sudsed up her neck and then across her shoulders and worked her way down. . . .

Bella frowned and bent forward. There was something on her belly . . . faded scratches. Scratches that . . . *Oh, God.* That was a *D,* wasn't it? And the next . . . that was an *A.* Then a *V* and an *I* and another *D.*

Bella dropped the bar of soap and covered her stomach with her hands, falling back against the tile. His name was on her body. In her skin. Like a gruesome parody of her species' highest mating ritual. She truly was his wife. . . .

Stumbling from the shower, slipping on the marble floor, she grabbed a towel and wrapped herself up. Grabbed another and did the same. She would have gone for three, four . . . five, if she'd found more.

Shaky, nauseous, she went up to the mirror that was fogged over. Taking a deep breath, she rubbed her elbow across the condensation. And looked at herself.

John wiped his mouth and somehow managed to drop his napkin. Cursing to himself, he bent down to pick it up . . . and so did Sarelle, who got to the thing first. He mouthed the words *thank you* when she handed it to him.

"You're welcome," she said.

Boy, he loved her voice. And he loved the way she smelled like lavender body lotion. And he loved her long, thin hands.

But he'd hated dinner. Wellsie and Tohr had done all the talking for him, giving Sarelle a glossed-over version of his life. What little he'd written on his pad had seemed like stupid filler.

As his head came up to level, Wellsie was smiling at him. But then she cleared her throat, as if trying to play it cool.

"So, as I was saying, a couple of females from the aristocracy used to run the winter solstice ceremony back in the Old Country. Bella's mother was one of them, as a matter of fact. I want to check in with them. Make sure we don't forget anything."

John let the conversation amble along, not paying too much attention until Sarelle said, "Well, I guess I'd better get going. It's thirty-five minutes to dawn. My parents will have a conniption."

She pushed her chair out, and John stood up as everyone else did. While good-byes were said, he found himself fading into the background. At least until Sarelle looked right at him.

"Would you walk me out?" she asked.

His eyes shot to the front door. Walk her out? To her car?

In a sudden rush, some kind of raw male instinct flooded his chest, so powerful he shook a little. Abruptly his palm started to tickle, and he looked down at it, feeling as though there were something in it, that he was holding something . . . so he could protect her.

Sarelle cleared her throat. "Okay . . . um . . ."

John realized she was waiting for him and snapped out of his little trance. Stepping forward, he indicated with his hand the way to the front door.

As they went outside, she said, "So are you psyched to train?"

John nodded and found his eyes roaming the environs, searching the shadows. He felt himself tense up, and that right palm of his started to hum again. He wasn't sure exactly what he was looking for. He just knew he had to keep her safe at all costs.

Keys jingled as her hand came out of her pocket.

"I think my friend is going to be in your class. He was supposed to sign up tonight." She unlocked the car door. "Anyway, you know why I'm really here, don't you?"

He shook his head.

"I think they want you to feed from me. When your transition hits."

John coughed from shock, sure that his eyeballs had popped out of his skull and were rolling down the driveway.

"Sorry." She smiled. "Guess they didn't tell you."

Yeah, he would have remembered that conversation.

"I'm cool with it," she said. "Are you?"

Oh. My. God.

"John?" She cleared her throat. "Tell you what. Do you have something I can write on?"

Numbly, he shook his head. He'd left his pad in the house. *Idiot.*

"Give me your hand." When he reached out, she got a pen from somewhere and bent over his palm. The nub ran across his skin smoothly. "That's my e-mail address and my IM info. I'll be online in about an hour. Messie me, okay? We'll talk."

He looked at what she'd written. Just stared at it.

She shrugged a little. "I mean, you don't have to or anything. Just . . . you know. I thought we could get to know each other that way." She paused, as if waiting for a response. "Um . . . whatever. No pressure. I mean—"

He grabbed her hand, whipped the pen out of it, and flattened her palm.

I want to talk to you, he wrote.

Then he looked straight into her eyes and did the most amazing, ballsy thing.

He smiled at her.

Chapter Fifteen

As dawn came and shutters went down over the windows, Bella drew on the black robe and bolted out of the bedroom she'd been given. With quick eyes, she checked up and down the hallway. No witnesses. *Good.* Closing the door quietly, she glided over the Persian runner, making no sound at all. When she got to the head of the grand staircase she paused, trying to remember which way to go.

The corridor with the statues, she thought, remembering another trip down that long stretch so many, many weeks ago.

She walked fast and then ran, clutching the lapels of the robe and holding the slit on the bottom closed over her thighs. She passed statues and doors, until she got to the end and stopped in front of the last pair. She didn't bother to collect herself, because she was uncollectible. Loose, ungrounded, in danger of disintegration—there was no collecting anything. She knocked loudly.

Through the door came, "Fuck off. I've crashed."

She turned the knob and pushed. Light from the hall barged in, slicing a pie wedge out of the darkness. As the glow hit Zsadist, he sat up on a pallet of blankets in the far corner. He was naked, his muscles flexing into ridges under his skin, his nipple rings flashing silver. His face, with that scar, was a billboard for the rankly pissed-off male.

"I said, *fuck o*— Bella?" He covered himself with his hands. "Jesus Christ. What are you doing?"

Good question, she thought as her courage dimmed. "Can . . . can I stay here with you?"

He frowned. "What are you— No, you can't."

He grabbed something off the floor and held it in front of his hips as he stood up. With no apologies for her stare, she drank in the sight of him: the tattooed slave bands around his wrists and neck, the gauge in his left earlobe, his obsidian eyes, his skull-trimmed hair. His body was as starkly lean as she remembered, all striated muscles and hard-cut veins and evident bones. Raw power emanated from him like a scent.

"Bella, get out of here, okay? This is not the place for you."

She ignored the command in his eyes and his tone, because although her bravery was gone, desperation gave her the strength she needed.

Now her voice no longer faltered. "When I was so out of it in the car, you were behind the wheel, weren't you?" He didn't respond, but she didn't need him to. "Yes, you were. That was you. You spoke to me. You were the one who came for me, weren't you?"

He flushed. "The Brotherhood came for you."

"But you drove me away. And you brought me here first. To your room." She looked at the luxurious bed. The covers were thrown back, the pillow dented from where her head had lain. "Let me stay."

"Look, you need to be safe—"

"I am safe with you. You saved me. You won't let that *lesser* get me again."

"No one can touch you here. This place is wired like the goddamned Pentagon."

"Please—"

"No," he snapped. "Now get the hell out of here."

She started to shake. "I can't be alone. Please let me stay with you. I need to . . ." She needed him specifically, but didn't think he'd respond well to that. "I need to be with someone."

"Then Phury's more what you're looking for."

"No, he's not." She wanted the male in front of her. For all his brutality, she trusted him instinctually.

Zsadist ran his hand over his head. A number of times. Then his chest expanded.

"Don't make me go," she whispered.

When he cursed, she exhaled in relief, figuring that was as close to a yes as she was going to get.

"I have to put some pants on," he muttered.

Bella stepped inside and closed the door, lowering her eyes for only a moment. When she looked up again, he'd turned away and was pulling a pair of black nylon sweats up his thighs.

His back, with its streaks of scars, flexed as he bent over. Seeing the cruel pattern, she was struck with the need to know exactly what he'd been through. All of it. Each and every lash. She'd heard the rumors about him; she wanted his truth.

He'd survived what had been done to him. Maybe so could she.

He turned around. "Have you eaten?"

"Yes, Phury brought me food."

A flicker of expression passed over his face, but it was gone so fast she couldn't read it.

"Are you in pain?"

"Not particularly."

He walked over to the bed and plumped up the pillows. Then he stood to one side, looking down at the floor.

"Get in."

As she came forward she wanted to throw her arms around him, and he stiffened, as though he'd read her mind. God, she knew he didn't like to be touched, had learned that the hard way. But she wanted to get close anyway.

Please look at me, she thought.

She was just about to ask him to when she noticed he had something around his throat.

"My necklace," she breathed. "You're wearing my necklace."

She reached out to it, but he flinched away. With a quick

movement he took off the fragile gold chain with its little diamonds and dropped the thing in her hand.

"Here. Take it back."

She looked down. Diamonds by the Yard. By Tiffany. She'd worn it for years . . . her staple piece of jewelry. The thing had been so much a part of her, she'd always felt naked without it on. Now the fragile links seemed totally foreign to her.

It was warm, she thought, fingering a diamond. Warm from his skin.

"I want you to keep it," she blurted.

"No."

"But—"

"Enough with the talk. Get in or get out of here."

She put the necklace into the pocket of the robe and glanced at him. His eyes were locked on the floor, and as he breathed his nipple rings caught the light.

Look at me, she thought.

Except he didn't, so she got into the bed. When he leaned down she scootched over to make room for him, but all he did was pull the covers over her and then go back to the corner, to the pallet on the floor.

Bella stared at the ceiling for a few minutes. Then she grabbed a pillow, slid out of the bed, and went over to him.

"What are you doing?" His voice was high. Alarmed.

She dropped her pillow and lay down, easing onto the floor beside his big body. His scent was so much stronger now, smelling of evergreen and distilled male power. Seeking the heat of him, she inched closer until her forehead hit the back of his arm. He was so hard, like a stone wall, but he was warm, and her body relaxed. Next to him she was able to feel the weight of her own bones, the hard floor underneath her, the currents in the room as the heat came on. Through his presence, she connected to the world around her again.

More. Closer.

She pushed herself forward until she was flush against the side of him, from breast to heel.

He shifted away with a jerk, moving back until he hit the wall.

"I'm sorry," she whispered, pushing herself up to him again. "I need this from you. My body needs"—*you*—"something warm."

Abruptly he leaped to his feet.

Oh, no. He was going to kick her out—

"Come on," he said gruffly. "We're going to the bed. I can't stand the idea of you on the floor."

Whoever said you couldn't sell something twice had never met the Omega.

O rolled over onto his stomach and propped his body up on weak arms. The retching was easier like this. Gravity helped.

As he gagged, he remembered the first little deal he'd made with the father of all *lessers*. On the night of O's induction into the Lessening Society, he'd traded his soul, along with his blood and heart, to become an immortal, sanctioned, supported killer.

And now he'd done another trade. Mr. X was no more. O was now the *Fore-lesser.*

Unfortunately, O was also now the Omega's bitch.

He tried to lift his head. When he did the room spun, but he was too exhausted to bother getting more nauseated. Or maybe there was nothing left on the downside in that department.

The cabin. He was in Mr. X's cabin. And going by the light, it was past dawn. As he blinked in the weak glow, he looked down at himself. He was naked. Marked with bruises. And he hated the taste in his mouth.

Shower. He needed a shower.

O dragged himself off the floor using a chair and the edge of the table. As he stood, his legs made him think of lava lamps for some insane reason. Probably because both were liquid inside.

His left knee gave out and he collapsed into the seat. While he wrapped his arms around himself, he decided the wash-off could wait.

Man . . . the world was new again, wasn't it? And he'd learned so many things during the course of his promotion. Before his change in status, he hadn't known the *Fore-lesser* was much more than just the leader of the slayers. In fact, the Omega was trapped on the other side and needed a conduit to get temporal. The number one *lesser* was the beacon the Omega used to find his way during the crossover. All the *Fore-lesser* had to do was open up the channel and make like a lighthouse.

And there were serious benes to being the *lesser* in charge. Benes that made that body-freeze technique Mr. X had used look like child's play.

Mr. X . . . good old sensei. O laughed. However shitty he felt this morning, Mr. X felt worse. Guaranteed.

Things had gone so smoothly after that blade-in-the-chest routine. When O had landed at the Omega's feet, he'd made his case for a regime change. He'd pointed out that the Society's ranks were dropping in number, especially among Primes. The Brothers were getting stronger. The Blind King had ascended. Mr. X was not holding a strong front.

And all of that was true. But none of it was what cinched the deal.

No, the closing had happened on account of the Omega's whim for O.

In the Society's history, there had been some instances when the Omega had taken a personal interest, if you could call it that, in a specific *lesser*. It wasn't the boon you'd think. The Omega's affections were intense and short-lived, and the breakups were gruesome, according to the rumors. But O was willing to beg and pretend and lie to get what he needed, and the Omega had taken what was offered.

What a horrible way to kill a couple of hours. But so worth it.

He wondered idly what was happening to Mr. X right now. When O had been released the Omega had been about to call the other slayer home, and it must have happened already. The former *Fore-lesser*'s weapons were on the table, his cell phone and BlackBerry, too. And there was a scorched star-burst over there by the front door.

O glanced up at the digital clock across the room. Even though he felt like roadkill, it was time to motivate. He picked up Mr. X's phone, dialed, and held the thing to his ear.

"Yeah, sensei?" U answered.

"Been a change in leadership. I want you to be my second in command."

Silence. Then: "Holy shit. What happened to Mr. X?"

"He's eating his pink slip right now. So are you in?"

"Ah, yeah. Sure. I'm your boy."

"You're in charge of the check-ins from now on. No reason to do it in person. E-mail's fine. And I'm keeping the squads as is. Primes in pairs. Betas in groups of four. Get the announce-ment out about Mr. X. Then get your ass here to the cabin."

O hung up. He didn't give a shit about the Society. Couldn't care less about the stupid war with the vampires. He had two objectives: Get his woman back dead or alive. And kill the scarred Brother who'd taken her.

As he stood up, he happened to look down at his body, at his limp maleness. A horrible thought snaked through his mind.

Vampires, unlike *lessers,* were not impotent.

He pictured his beautiful, pure wife . . . saw her naked, her hair all over her pale shoulders, the elegant curves of her slen-der body catching the light. Gorgeous. Perfect, perfect, per-fect. Utterly feminine.

Something to be worshiped and possessed. But never fucked. A Madonna.

Except anything with a cock would want that. Vampire, human, *lesser.* Anything.

Violence threaded through him, and abruptly he hoped she was dead. Because if that ugly bastard had tried to have sex with her . . . man, O was going to castrate that brother with a spoon before killing him.

And God *help* her if she enjoyed it.

Chapter Sixteen

When Phury woke up, it was three fifteen in the afternoon. He'd slept like crap, still so pissed off at what had happened the night before that his adrenal glands were working overtime. Which was hardly conducive to shut-eye.

He reached for a blunt and lit it. As he drew the red smoke into his lungs and held on tight, he tried not to imagine going to Zsadist's room and waking the brother up with a jaw shot. But the fantasy was righteous appealing.

Goddamn it, he couldn't believe Z had tried to take Bella like that, and actually hated his twin for the depravity. Hated himself, too, for being stupidly surprised. For so long he'd been sure that something had survived Z's slavery . . . that some small flicker of a soul was left in the male. After last night? No more doubts about his twin's cruel nature. None.

And, shit, the real ass burner was knowing he'd let Bella down. He should never have left her in Z's bedroom. Couldn't stand that he'd sacrificed her safety for his need to believe.

Bella . . .

He thought about how she'd allowed him to hold her. In those fleeting moments he'd felt powerful, capable of protecting her against an army of *lessers*. For that short time, she'd transformed him into a true male, one who was needed and served a purpose.

What a revelation to be something other than a reactive half-wit chasing after a destructive, suicidal madman.

He'd desperately wanted to stay the night with her, and he'd left only because it was the right thing to do. She was exhausted, but more than that—and in spite of his vow of celibacy—he was untrustworthy. He'd wanted to succor her with his body. He'd wanted to worship her and make her whole with his skin and bones.

But he couldn't think like that.

Phury inhaled deeply on the blunt, his breath going in with a hiss. Keeping the smoke inside him, he felt the tension ease out of his shoulders. As the calm came over him, he eyed his stash. It was running low already, and as much as he hated going to see the Reverend, he needed more.

Yeah, considering how he was feeling toward Z, he was going to need a lot more. Red smoke was just a mild muscle relaxant, really, nothing like marijuana or any of the dangerous stuff. But he relied on the blunts to keep him level, like other folks used cocktails. If he didn't have to go to the Reverend to get the stuff, he'd say that it was a perfectly harmless pastime.

Perfectly harmless and the only ease he had in life.

When he was finished with the hand-rolled, he stabbed the little end in an ashtray and got out of bed. After he attached his prosthesis, he went into the bathroom to shower and shave; then he pulled on a pair of slacks and one of his silk shirts. He pushed his real foot and then the one he couldn't feel into a pair of Cole Haan loafers.

He checked himself in the mirror. Smoothed his hair down a little. Took a deep breath.

He went to the bedroom next to his and knocked softly. When there was no answer he tried again, and then opened the door. The bed was mussed, but empty, and she wasn't in the bathroom.

As he walked back out to the hall, alarm rang in his ears. Before he knew it he was in a jog, then a run. He raced past the head of the stairway and pounded down the statuary corridor. He didn't bother knocking on Z's door, just threw it open.

Phury stopped dead.

His first thought was that Zsadist was going to fall off the bed. The brother's body was on top of the comforter and right on the edge of the mattress, as far over as possible. *Jesus* . . . The position looked uncomfortable as hell. Z's arms were wrapped around his bare chest as if he were holding himself together, and his legs were bent and twisted to the side with the knees hanging in midair.

But his head was turned in the opposite direction. Toward Bella. And those distorted lips were parted ever so slightly instead of sneering. And his brows, usually drawn down in aggression, were loose, relaxed.

His expression was one of somnolent awe.

Bella's face was tilted up to the male beside her, her expression as peaceful as nightfall. And her body was cuddled up next to Z's, as close as all the sheets and blankets she was under would let her get. Hell, it was obvious that if she could have been wrapped around him, she would have been. And it was just as obvious that Z had tried to get away from her until he could go no farther.

Phury cursed softly. Whatever had been going on the night before, the situation had not been about Z pulling a nasty on her. No way. Not with what the pair of them looked like now.

He closed his eyes. Shut the door.

Like a total lunatic, he briefly considered going back in and fighting Zsadist for the right to lie next to her. He could see himself throwing the hand-to-hand around, having an old-fashioned *cohntehst* with his twin over who was allowed to have her.

But this was not the Old Country. And females had the right to choose who they sought out. Who they slept beside. Who they mated with.

And she had known where Phury stayed. He'd told her his room was right next door. If she had wanted to, she could have turned to him.

Z became aware of the oddest sensation as he came out of sleep: He was warm. Not overheated, just . . . warm. Had he forgotten to turn the heat off again after Bella had left? Must be it. Except he noticed something else. He wasn't on the pallet. And he had pants on, didn't he? He moved his legs around, trying to pin that one down, thinking that he always slept naked. As his warm-ups shifted, he realized the *it* was hard. Hard and heavy. *What the f—*

His eyes popped open. *Bella.* He was on the bed with Bella. He jerked away from her—

And fell off the mattress, landing on his ass.

Instantly she scrambled after him. "Zsadist?"

As she leaned over the side, the robe she was wearing fell open and his eyes latched onto the breast that was exposed. She was just as perfect as she'd been in the tub, her pale skin so smooth and her little nipple so pink. . . . God, he knew the other one was just the same, but for some reason he needed to see it anyway.

"Zsadist?" She stretched down farther, her hair slipping off her shoulder and pouring over the edge of the bed, a gorgeous fall of deep mahogany.

The *it* between his thighs strained. Pulsed with the beat of his heart.

He jacked his knees up and clamped his thighs together, not wanting her to see.

"Your robe," he said roughly. "Close it. Please."

She glanced down and then dragged the lapels together, blushing. *Oh, hell . . .* Now her cheeks were as pink as her nipple, he thought.

"Will you come back to bed?" she asked.

The very well buried, decent part of him pointed out that wasn't a good idea.

"Please?" she whispered, tucking her hair behind her ear.

He measured the arch of her body and the black satin that barred her skin from his stare and her wide, sapphire blue eyes and the slender column of her throat.

No . . . it *really* was not a good idea to get near her right now.

"Move over," he said.

As she shuffled back, he glanced down at the tent between

his legs. Christ, that goddamn thing in there was huge; he looked like he had another arm in his pants. And hiding a log like that would require scaffolding.

He eyed the bed. In a smooth movement he hopped between the sheets.

Which was an *achingly* bad idea. The moment he was underneath, she molded herself to his hard edges until she was another blanket. A soft, warm, breathing . . .

Z panicked. There was so much of her against him that he didn't know what to do. He wanted to shove her away. He wanted her even closer. He wanted . . . *Oh, man.* He wanted to mount her. He wanted to take her. He wanted to fuck her.

The instinct was so strong he saw himself doing the deed: rolling her onto her stomach, pulling her hips off the bed, rearing up behind her. He imagined pushing the *it* inside of her and pumping with his hips—

God, he was *loathsome.* To want to take that dirty thing and force it into her? He might as well shove a toilet brush in her mouth.

"You tremble . . ." she said. "Are you cold?"

She shifted even closer to him, and he felt her breast, soft and warm, on the back of his forearm. The *it* twitched wildly, popping against his pants.

Shit. He had a feeling that punch action meant he was dangerously aroused.

Yeah, ya think? Hell, the bastard was throbbing, and the balls under the thing ached, and he was having visions of rutting on her like a bull. Except a female's fear was the only thing that got it hard, and she wasn't scared. So what was he responding to?

"Zsadist?" she said softly.

"What?"

The four words she spoke next turned his chest into a cinder block and made his blood freeze up solid. But at least all that other crap went away.

When Phury's door opened without any warning, his hands froze on the T-shirt he was pulling over his head.

Zsadist stood between the jambs, naked to the waist, black eyes burning.

Phury cursed softly. "I'm glad you came. About last night . . . I owe you an apology."

"I don't want to hear it. Come with me."

"Z, I was wrong to—"

"Come. With. Me."

Phury yanked the shirt hem down and checked his watch. "I have to teach class in a half hour."

"This won't take long."

"Ah . . . well, okay."

As he followed Z down the hall, he figured they could get through the apology on the road.

"Look, Zsadist, I'm really sorry about last night." His twin's silence was not a surprise. "I jumped to the wrong conclusion. About you and Bella." Z walked even faster. "I should have known you wouldn't hurt her. I would offer you a *rythe*."

Zsadist stopped and glared over his shoulder. "What the hell for?"

"I offended you. Last night."

"No, you didn't."

Phury could only shake his head. "Zsadist—"

"I *am* sick. I *am* disgusting. I *can't* be trusted. Just because you've got half a brain and have figured that out doesn't mean you need to stroke my ass with this apology bullshit."

Phury's mouth dropped. "Jesus . . . Z. You're not—"

"Oh, for fuck's sake, will you get the lead out?"

Z marched down to his room and opened his door.

Bella sat up on the bed, gathering the lapels of the silk robe close to her neck. She seemed totally confused. And too beautiful for words.

Phury looked back and forth between her and Z. Then he focused on his twin. "What is this?"

Z's black eyes stuck to the floor. "Go to her."

"Excuse me?"

"She needs to feed."

Bella made a choked noise, like she'd swallowed a gasp. "No, wait, Zsadist, I want . . . you."

"You can't have me."

"But I want—"

"Tough. I'm out of here."

Phury felt himself get shoved into the room and then the door slammed shut. In the silence that followed, he wasn't sure whether he wanted to scream with triumph or . . . just plain scream.

He took a deep breath and glanced at the bed. Bella was curled up on herself, her knees to her chest.

Good God, he'd never let a female drink from him before. As a celibate, he hadn't wanted to risk it. With his sexual urges and his warrior blood, he'd always been afraid that if he let a female take his vein, he'd become overwhelmed and try to get inside her. And if it was Bella, he'd find it even harder to stay in neutral.

But she needed to drink. Besides, what good was a vow if it was easy to uphold? This could be his crucible, his chance to prove his discipline under the most extreme circumstances.

He cleared his throat. "I would offer myself to you."

As Bella's eyes lifted to his, his skin got too small for his skeleton. Which was what rejection did to a male. Just shriveled you right up.

He looked away and thought of Zsadist, who he could sense was right outside the room. "He may not be able to do this. You are aware of his . . . background, aren't you?"

"Is it too cruel of me to ask?" Her voice was full of strain, deepened by her conflict. "Is it?"

Probably, he thought.

"It would be better if you used someone else." *God, why can't you take me? Why can't you need me instead?* "I don't think it would be appropriate to ask Wrath or Rhage, as they are mated. Maybe I could get V—"

"No . . . I need Zsadist." Her hand shook as she brought it to her mouth. "I'm so sorry."

So was he. "Wait here."

When he stepped out into the hall, he found Z just beyond the door. The male's head was in his hands, his shoulders caved in.

"Is it over with so fast?" he asked, dropping his arms.

"No. It didn't happen."

Z frowned and looked over. "Why not? You gotta do it, man. You heard Havers—"

"She wants you."

"—so will you go in there and open a vein—"

"She'll only have you."

"She needs it, so just—"

Phury raised his voice. "I won't feed her!"

Z's mouth clamped shut and his black eyes narrowed. "Fuck you. You will do this for me."

"No, I won't." *Because she won't let me.*

Z surged forward, locking a vise grip on Phury's shoulder. "Then you will do this for her. Because it's the best thing for her and because you're feeling her and because you want to. Do this for *her.*"

Christ. He would kill to. He was dying to go back into Z's bedroom. Rip off his clothes. Fall onto the mattress. And have Bella crawl up his chest and sink her teeth into his neck and straddle him, taking him inside of herself both between her lips and between her thighs.

Z's nostrils flared. "God . . . I can smell how badly you want to do this. So go. Be with her, feed her."

Phury's voice cracked. "She won't have me, Z. She wants—"

"She doesn't know what she wants. She's coming out of hell."

"You are the one. For her, you are the one." As Zsadist's eyes slid to the closed door, Phury pushed, even though it killed him. "Listen to what I'm saying, my brother. She wants you. And you can do this for her."

"The hell I can."

"Z, do it."

That skull-trimmed head shook back and forth. "Come on, the shit in my veins is corroded. You know that."

"No, it isn't."

With a snarl, Z leaned back and held out his wrists, flashing the blood-slave bands tattooed at his pulse points. "You

want her biting through these? Can you stand the thought of
her mouth on them? Because I sure as hell can't."

"Zsadist?" Bella's voice drifted over. Without their notic-
ing, she'd gotten up and opened the door.

As Z's eyes squeezed shut, Phury whispered, "You are the
one she wants."

Z's reply was barely audible. "I'm contaminated. My
blood will kill her."

"No. It won't."

"Please . . . Zsadist," Bella said.

The sound of the humble, yearning request turned Phury's
ribs into a cage of ice, and he watched, frozen, numbed out,
as Z slowly turned to her.

Bella stepped back a little, keeping her eyes on him.

Minutes became days . . . decades . . . centuries. And then
Zsadist walked over and went inside. The door closed.

Phury was blind as he pivoted away and went down the
corridor.

Wasn't there someplace he needed to be?

Class. Yes, he was going to . . . to teach class now.

Chapter Seventeen

At ten after four, John climbed up into a shuttle bus lugging his duffel bag along with him.

"Hello, sire," the *doggen* behind the wheel said cheerfully. "Welcome."

John nodded and looked at the twelve guys who were seated in pairs and staring at him.

Whoa. Really not feeling the love here, fellas, he thought.

He took the empty seat behind the driver.

As the bus started to move, a partition came down so that the trainees were locked in the back together and none of them could see out the front. John shuffled around so he sat sideways. Keeping an eye on what was happening behind him seemed like a good idea.

The windows were all darkened, but the running lights on the floor and ceiling were bright enough so he could get a bead on his classmates. They were all like him, thin and small, though they had different hair colors, some blond, some dark. One was a redhead. Like John, they were all dressed in white martial-arts *jis*. And they all had the same duffel at their feet, a black nylon Nike bag big enough to fit a change of clothes and a lot of food. Each of them had a backpack, too, and he guessed they had the same stuff in it that he had in his: a notebook and some pens, a cell phone, a calculator. Tohr had sent out a list of required supplies.

John tucked his pack in close to his stomach and felt himself getting stared at. It helped to think about all the numbers he could text-message, so he repeated them in his head over and over again. Home. Wellsie's cell. Tohr's cell. The Brotherhood's number. Sarelle's . . .

Thinking of her made him smile. They'd spent hours online last night. Man, IM'ing, once he got the hang of it, was the perfect way to communicate with her. With them both typing words, he felt like they were equals. And if he'd liked her over dinner, he was really into her now.

"What's your name?"

John looked over a couple of seats. A guy with long blond hair and a diamond earring had spoken up.

At least they're using English, John thought.

As he unzipped the pack and took out a notebook, the guy said, "Hello? You deaf or something?"

John wrote his name and turned the pad around.

"John? What the hell kind of name is that? And why are you writing?"

Oh, man . . . This school thing was going to suck.

"What's your problem? Can't talk?"

John met the guy right in the eye. The laws of probability mandated that within every group, there was one alpha-male pain in the ass, and this towhead with the sparkler in his earlobe was clearly it.

John shook his head to answer the question.

"You can't speak? At all?" The guy raised his voice as if to make sure everyone heard. "What the hell are you doing training to be a soldier if you can't talk?"

You don't fight with words, do you? John wrote.

"Yeah, and all those muscles you're popping are *really* scary."

So are yours, he wanted to scribble.

"Why do you have a human name?" This question came from the redhead in the seat behind him.

John wrote, *Raised by them,* and then turned the pad around.

"Huh. Well, I'm Blaylock. John . . . wow, weird."

On impulse, John pulled up his sleeve and flashed the bracelet he'd made, the one with the characters he'd dreamed about on it.

Blaylock leaned over. Then his pale blue eyes shot up. "His real name's Tehrror."

Whispers. Lots of whispers.

John retracted his arm and eased back against the window again. He wished he'd kept his sleeve down. What the hell were they thinking now?

After a moment Blaylock pulled a polite one and introduced the others. They all had odd names. The blond's was Lash. And how fricking appropriate was that?

"Tehrror . . ." Blaylock murmured. "That's a very old name. That's a real warrior's name."

John frowned. And even though it would be better to get himself off these boys' high-def wide-screen, he wrote, *Isn't yours? And the rest of theirs?*

Blaylock shook his head. "We have some warrior blood in us, which is why we were chosen to come train, but none of us has a name like that. What line are you descended from? God . . . are you bred from the Brotherhood?"

John frowned. It had never dawned on him that he could be related to the Brothers.

"Guess he's too good to answer you," Lash said.

John let that one pass. He knew he was tripping all kinds of social wires, setting off land mines right and left, what with his names and the raised-by-humans thing and his inability to talk. He had a feeling this school day was going to be one hell of an endurance test, so he might as well save his energy.

The trip lasted about fifteen minutes, with the last five or so involving a lot of stopping and going, which meant they were going through the gate system into the training compound.

When the bus halted and the partition retracted, John shouldered his duffel and his backpack and got out first. The underground parking facility was just as it had been last night: still no cars, just another shuttle bus like the one they'd come in. He stood off to the side and watched the others mill about, a flock of white *jis*. Their nattering voices reminded him of the sound of pigeon wings clapping.

The center's doors swung open, and the group got good and transfixed.

But Phury could do that to a crowd. With his spectacular hair and his big body in black, he was enough to make anyone freeze.

"Hey, John," he said, lifting his hand. "What's doing?"

The guys turned and stared at him.

He smiled up at Phury. Then got busy trying to fade into the background.

Bella watched Zsadist pace around the bedroom. He reminded her of how she'd felt the night before when she'd sought him out: Caged. Miserable. Pushed too hard.

Why the hell was she forcing this?

As she opened her mouth to call the whole thing off, Zsadist stopped in front of the bathroom door.

"I need a minute," he said. Then shut himself away.

At a loss, she went over and sat on the bed, expecting him to be right back out. When the shower came on and stayed on, she fell into a churning introspection.

She tried to picture herself going back to her family's house and walking through those familiar rooms and sitting in chairs and opening doors and sleeping in her childhood bed. It felt all wrong, like she'd be a ghost in that place she knew so well.

And how would she deal with her mother and her brother? And the *glymera*?

In the aristocratic world she'd been disgraced before she'd been abducted. Now she would be shunned outright. Being handled by a *lesser* . . . trapped in the ground . . . The aristocracy didn't handle that kind of ugliness well, and they would blame her. Hell, that was probably why her mother had been so reserved.

God, Bella thought. What was the rest of her life going to be like now?

As dread choked her, the only thing that held her together was the thought of staying in this room and sleeping for days with Zsadist right next to her. He was the cold that made her condense into herself again. And the heat that stopped her from shivering.

He was the killer who made her safe.

More time . . . more time with him first. Then maybe she could face the outside world.

She frowned, realizing he'd been in the shower for quite a while.

Her eyes shifted to the pallet in the far corner. How did he sleep there night after night? The floor would be so hard on his back, and there was no pillow for his head. No covers to pull up against the chill, either.

She focused on the skull beside the folded blankets. The black leather strap between the teeth proclaimed it as one he had loved. Obviously he had been mated, though she hadn't heard that in the rumors about him. Had his *shellan* gone unto the Fade of natural causes or had she been taken from him? Was that why he was so angry?

Bella looked toward the bathroom. What was he doing in there?

She went over and knocked. When there was no answer, she opened the door slowly. A cold rush shot out and she jerked back.

Bracing herself, she leaned into the freezing air. "Zsadist?"

Through the glass door of the shower, she saw him sitting under an ice-cold spray of water. He was rocking back and forth, moaning, scrubbing his wrists with a washcloth.

"Zsadist!" She ran over and pushed the glass aside. Fumbling with the fixtures, she turned off the water. "What are you doing?"

He looked up at her with wild, crazy eyes as he kept rocking and scrubbing, rocking and scrubbing. The skin around the black-tattooed bands was brilliant red, completely raw.

"Zsadist?" She struggled to keep her tone gentle and steady. "What are you doing?"

"I . . . I can't get clean. I don't want you to get dirty, too." He lifted his wrist and blood oozed down his forearm. "See? Look at the dirt. It's all over me. Inside of me."

His voice alarmed her even more than what he'd done to himself, his words carrying the eerie, groundless logic of insanity.

Bella picked up a towel, stepped inside the stall, and fell into a crouch. Capturing his hands, she took the washcloth from him.

As she carefully dried off his ragged flesh, she said, "You are clean."

"Oh, no, I'm not. I'm really not." His voice started to rise, a terrible momentum growing. "I'm filthy. I am so very dirty. I am dirty, dirty. . . ." Now he babbled, the words running together, the volume lifting until hysteria pinged off the tiles and filled the bathroom. "Can you see the dirt? I see it *every-where.* It coats me. It seals me in. I can feel it on my skin—"

"Shh. Let me . . . just . . ."

Keeping an eye on him, as if he were going to . . . God, she didn't even know what . . . she grabbed blindly for another towel and dragged it into the shower. With a reach around his big shoulders, she draped him in it, but when she tried to pull him into her arms, he shrank back.

"Don't touch me," he rasped. "You'll get it on you."

She sank down to her knees in front of him, her silk robe catching the water, drinking it up. She didn't even notice the cold.

Jesus . . . He looked like someone who'd been in a ship-wreck: his eyes wide and demented, his soaked sweatpants clinging to the muscles of his legs, the skin of his chest covered in goose bumps. His lips were blue and his teeth chattered.

"I'm so sorry," she whispered. And she wanted to reassure him that there was no dirt on him, but knew that would just set him off again.

As water dripped from the showerhead onto the tile, the

rhythmic sound was loud as a snare drum between them. In between the beats, she found herself remembering the night
she'd followed him up to this room . . . the night when he'd
touched her aroused body. Ten minutes after he had she'd found
him curled over the toilet, throwing up because he'd put his
hand on her.

I'm filthy. I am so very dirty. I am dirty, dirty. . . .

Clarity came to her in the shifting way of a nightmare,
cleaving into consciousness with chilling illumination, showing her something ugly. It was obvious he'd been beaten as a
blood slave, and she'd assumed that was why he didn't like to
be touched. Except getting hit, however painful and frighten-
ing, didn't make you feel dirty.

But sexual abuse would do it.

His black eyes suddenly focused on her face. As if he'd felt
the conclusion that had found her.

Driven by sympathy, she leaned in toward him, but the
anger that bled into his face stopped her.

"Christ, female," he snapped. "Will you cover yourself?"

She glanced down. Her robe was open to her waist, the
swells of her breasts showing. She yanked the lapels together.

In the tight silence it was hard to meet his stare, so she focused on his shoulder . . . then followed the line of muscle to
his collarbone, to the base of his neck. Her eyes drifted up his
thick throat . . . to the vein that pumped just under his skin.

Hunger shot through her, making her fangs elongate. *Oh,
hell.* Like she needed bloodlust right now?

"Why do you want me?" he muttered, clearly sensing her
need. "You're better than this."

"You are—"

"I *know* what I am."

"You are not dirty."

"Damn it, Bella—"

"And I only want you. Look, I'm really sorry, and we don't
have to—"

"You know what? No more talking. I'm tired of the talking." He stretched his arm out on his knee, wrist up, and his

black eyes became devoid of any emotion, even anger. "It's your funeral, female. Do it if you want."

Time stopped as she stared at what he grudgingly offered. God help them both, but she was going to have him. With a quick move she arched over his vein and scored him cleanly. Though it must have hurt, he didn't jerk at all.

The instant his blood hit her tongue, she moaned in bliss. She'd fed from aristocrats before, but never from a male of the warrior class, and certainly never, ever a member of the Brotherhood. His taste was a delicious roar in her mouth, an invasion, an epic, screaming blast, and then she swallowed. The torrent of his power ripped through her, a forest fire in the marrow of her bones, an explosion that pumped into her heart in a glorious rush of strength.

She trembled so badly she almost lost contact with his wrist and had to grab onto his forearm to steady herself. She drank in great, greedy pulls, starved not just for the strength, but for him, for this male.

For her, he was . . . the one.

Chapter Eighteen

Zsadist fought to keep still as Bella fed. He didn't want to disturb her, but with every pull on his vein he was getting closer to losing it. The Mistress was the only one who'd ever fed from him, and the memories of those violations were as sharp as the fangs buried in his wrist now. Fear came to him, hard and vivid, no shadow of the past anymore, now a very present panic.

Holy shit . . . He was going totally light-headed here. About to black out like a stone-cold sissy.

In a desperate attempt to bring himself back to center, he focused on Bella's dark hair. There was a lock of it close to his free hand, and the strand gleamed in the shower's overhead light, so lovely, so thick, so different from the Mistress's blond.

God, Bella's hair looked really soft. . . . If he'd had the nerve, he would bury his hand—no, his whole face—in those mahogany waves. Could he handle that? he wondered. Being so close to a female? Or would he choke when even more fear hit him?

If it was Bella, he thought he might be able to do it.

Yeah . . . he'd really like his face there, in her hair. Maybe he would burrow through it and find his way to her neck and he would . . . press a kiss to her throat. Just real softly.

Yeah . . . and then he might move up and brush his lips against her cheek. Maybe she would let him do that. He wouldn't go near her mouth. He couldn't imagine she'd want to be that close to his scar and his upper lip was all fucked up anyway. Besides, he didn't know how to kiss. The Mistress and her minions had known enough to keep away from his fangs. And afterward he'd never wanted to get that tight with a female.

Bella paused and tilted her head, her sapphire blue eyes shifting up to his, checking to make sure he was okay.

The concern bit into his pride. Christ, to think he was so weak that he couldn't handle feeding a female . . . and what a cringer to realize she *knew* this while she was at his vein. Even worse, there had been that expression on her face a few moments ago, that dawning horror that meant she'd figured out what else he'd been used for as slave besides his blood.

He couldn't stand her sympathy, didn't want those worried looks, wasn't interested in being coddled and stroked. He opened his mouth, ready to take her head off, but somehow the anger got lost on the trip between his gut and his throat.

"It's okay," he said roughly. "Rock steady up here. Rock steady."

The relief in those eyes of hers was another slap in the ass.

As she started drinking again, he thought, *I hate this.*

Well . . . some of it he hated. Okay, the shit in his head he hated. But as the gentle pulls on his wrist continued, he realized he kind of liked them.

At least until he thought about what she was swallowing. Dirty blood . . . rusted blood . . . corroded, infected, nasty blood. Man, he just couldn't fathom why she'd turned down Phury. The male was perfect inside and out. Yet here she was on cold, hard tile, biting through a slave band with him. Why did she . . .

Zsadist shut his eyes. No doubt after all she'd been through, she figured she deserved no better than someone who was polluted. That *lesser* had probably torn the self-respect right out of her.

Man, as God was his witness, he was going to have that bastard's last breath squeezing out between his palms.

With a sigh, Bella released his wrist and eased back against the shower wall, her lids low, her body limp. The silk of the dressing down was wet and it clung to her legs, outlining her thighs, her hips . . . the juncture in their midst.

As the *it* in his pants thickened in a rush, he wanted to cut the thing off.

Her eyes lifted to his. He half expected her to go into seizures or something, and he tried not to think of all that ugliness she'd swallowed.

"You all right?" he asked.

"Thank you," she said huskily. "Thank you for letting me—"

"Yeah, you can stop that." God, he wished he'd protected her from himself. The Mistress's very essence pumped through him, the echoes of that female's cruelty trapped within the endless circuit of his arteries and veins, going around and around his body. And Bella had just taken some of that poison into her gut.

He should have fought harder against this.

"I'm going to carry you to the bed," he said.

When she didn't object, he picked her up, took her out of the shower, and paused by the sink to grab a towel for her.

"The mirror," she murmured. "You covered the mirror. Why?"

He didn't answer her as he headed for the bedroom, couldn't bear to talk about the horrible things she'd endured.

"Do I look so bad to you?" she whispered into his shoulder.

When he got to the bed, he set her on her feet. "The robe is wet. You should take it off. Use this to dry if you want."

She took the towel and started to loosen the tie at her waist. He quickly turned around, listening to a rush of cloth, some flapping, then the shifting of sheets.

As she settled in, some very base, ancient core of him demanded that he lay with her now. And not as in hold her. He wanted to be inside of her, moving . . . releasing. Somehow that seemed like the right thing to do, to give her not just the blood in his veins but the completion of the sexual act, too.

Which was *totally* fucked up.

He dragged a hand over his hair, wondering where the hell that bad idea had come from. Man, he had to get away from her—

Well, that was going to happen soon, wasn't it. She was leaving tonight. Leaving to go home.

His instincts went nuts, making him want to fight to make her stay in his bed. But screw that stupid, primeval core of him. He needed to go do his job. He needed to go out and find that one particular *lesser* and slaughter the fucker for her. That was what he had to do.

Z headed for the closet, pulled on a shirt, and armed up. As he grabbed for his chest holster, he considered asking her for a description of the slayer who'd taken her. Except he didn't want to traumatize her . . . No, he would get Tohr to ask, because the brother would handle that kind of thing well. When she was returned to her family tonight, he would have Tohr talk to her then.

"I'm heading out," Z said as he buckled the leather dagger holder across his ribs. "You want me to have Fritz bring you food before you go?"

When there was no answer, he looked around the doorjamb. She was on her side, watching him.

Another wave of heavy-handed instinct pounded through him.

He wanted to see her eat. After the sex, after he came inside of her, he wanted to have her eat food he'd brought her, and he wanted her to take the stuff from his hand. Hell, he wanted to go out and kill something for her, bring the meat back, cook it himself, and feed her until she was full. Then he wanted to lie beside her with a dagger in his hand, protecting her as she slept.

He ducked back into the closet. Man, he was going crazy. Straight-up *loco*.

"I'll have him bring you something," he said.

He checked the blades on his two black daggers, testing

them on the inside of his forearm, slicing into his skin. As the pain tingled into his brain, he stared at the puncture marks Bella had left on his wrist.

Shaking himself back into focus, he put his gun holster around his hips and ran through his twin SIG Sauers. Both nine-millimeters had full bullet loads, and there were another two clips of hollow tips on the belt. He slipped a throwing knife into a buckle at the small of his back and made sure he had some *hira shuriken* with him. Shitkickers were next. Light windbreaker to cover the portable arsenal was last.

When he came out, Bella was still looking up at him from the bed. Her eyes were so blue. Blue as sapphires. Blue as night. Blue as—

"Zsadist?"

He fought the urge to smack himself. "Yeah?"

"Am I ugly to you?" As he recoiled, she put her hands over her face. "Never mind."

While she hid from him, he thought of the very first moment he'd seen her, back when she'd surprised him in the gym so many weeks ago. She'd astounded him then, struck him dead-stupid in his boots, and she still had that effect on his brain. It was like he had an off switch that only she had the remote to.

He cleared his throat. "You are as you have always been to me."

He turned away, only to hear a sob. Then another. And another.

He looked over his shoulder. "Bella . . . holy hell . . ."

"I'm sorry," she said into her palms. "I'm s-sorry. Just go. I'm f-fine. . . . I'm sorry, I'm fine."

As he went over and sat on the edge of the bed, he wished he had the gift of words. "You've got nothing to be sorry for."

"I've invaded your room, your b-bed. Forced you to sleep next me. M-made you give me your vein. I'm so . . . sorry." She took a deep breath and collected herself, but even still her despair lingered, carrying the earthy scent of raindrops on a hot sidewalk. "I know I should leave here, I know you don't want me here, but I just need . . . I can't go to my farmhouse.

The *lesser* took me from there, so I can't stand the idea of going back. And I don't want to be with my family. They won't understand what's going on for me right now, and I don't have the energy to explain. I just need some time, I need some way to get what is in my head out of it, but I can't be alone. Even though I don't want to see anyone except . . ."

As she petered out, he said, "You stay here for as long as you want."

She started sobbing again. *Damn it.* That was the wrong thing to say.

"Bella . . . I . . ." What was he supposed to do?

Reach out to her, asshole. Take her hand, you piece of shit.

He couldn't do it. "You want me to move out? Give you some space?"

More crying, somewhere in the middle of which she mumbled, "I need you."

God, if he'd heard that right, he pitied her.

"Bella, stop crying. Stop crying and look at me." Eventually she took a deep breath and wiped her face. When he was sure he had her attention, he said, "You don't worry about anything. You're staying here as long as you want to. Are we clear?"

She just stared at him.

"Nod for me, so I know you heard that." When she did, he stood up. "And I'm the last thing you need. So you just drop that bullshit right now."

"But I—"

He headed for the door. "I'll be back before dawn. Fritz knows how to find me—er, all of us."

After leaving her, Z strode down the corridor of statues, hung a louie, and shot past Wrath's study and the grand staircase. Three doors down he knocked. No answer. He knocked again.

He headed downstairs and found what he was looking for in the kitchen.

Mary, Rhage's female, was peeling potatoes. A lot of potatoes. Like, an army load of them. Her gray eyes lifted and her paring knife stilled on an Idaho golden. She glanced around, as if figuring he must be looking for someone else. Or maybe she just hoped she wasn't alone with him.

"Could you put this off for a while?" Z said, nodding at the pile.

"Um, sure. Rhage can always eat something else. Besides, Fritz is having a conniption that I was going to cook, anyway. What . . . ah, what do you need?"

"Not me. Bella. She could use a friend right now."

Mary put the knife and the half-naked potato down. "I'm so anxious to see her."

"She's in my room." Z pivoted around, already thinking about which alleys to hit downtown.

"Zsadist?"

He stopped with his hand on the butler's door. "What."

"You're taking very good care of her."

He thought of the blood he'd let her swallow. And the urge he had to orgasm in her body.

"Not really," he said over his shoulder.

Sometimes you have to start at the beginning, O thought as he jogged through the forest.

About three hundred yards from where he'd parked the truck, the trees gave way to a flat meadow. He stopped while still hidden among the pines.

Across the white blanket of snow was the farmhouse where he had first found his wife, and in the fading light of day her home was all Norman Rockwell, Hallmark-card, Middle America perfect. The only thing that was missing was some smoke coming out of the redbrick chimney.

He took out his binocs and scanned the area, then focused on the house. All the tire tracks in the driveway and the footprints to the door made him worry that the place had changed hands and movers had come. But there was still furniture inside, furniture he recognized from when he'd been in there with her.

He dropped the binocs, letting them hang around his neck, and crouched down. He would wait for her here. If she was alive, either she would go to her house or whoever was taking care of her would come for some of her things. If she was dead, someone would start moving her shit out.

At least, he hoped something like that would happen. He had nothing else to go on, didn't know her name or her family's whereabouts. Couldn't guess where else she might be. His only other option was to go out and question civilians about her. As no other female had been abducted lately, surely she'd have been a topic of conversation within her race. Trouble was, that route could take weeks . . . months. And information from persuasive techniques wasn't always solid.

No, watching her house was more likely to get him results. He would sit and wait until someone tipped a hand and led him back to her. Maybe his job would get even easier and that scarred brother would be the one who showed.

That would be just about perfect.

O settled back on his heels, ignoring the cold wind.

God . . . he hoped she was alive.

Chapter Nineteen

John kept his head down and tried to pull it together.

The locker room was filled with steam and voices and the snapping of wet towels on bare butts. The trainees had ditched their sweaty *jis* and were showering before they took a food break and then hit the classroom part of the session.

It was all standard guy stuff, except John *so* did not want to get naked. Even though they were all his size, this was straight out of every high school nightmare he'd ridden out until he'd quit the system when he was sixteen. And right now he was just too flat-out exhausted to deal with the scene.

He figured it was about midnight by now, but he felt as though it were four A.M. . . . like, the day after tomorrow. Training had been grueling for him. None of the other guys was strong, but all of them could keep up with the stances Phury and then Tohr introduced. Hell, a few were even naturals. John was a mess. His feet were slow, his hands were always in the wrong place at the wrong time, and he had no physical coordination. Man, no matter how hard he tried, he couldn't find his balance. His body was like a shifting, lurching bag of water; if he moved in one direction, the whole thing flopped over on him.

"You'd better hurry," Blaylock said. "We've only got eight more minutes."

John eyed the shower's doorway. The jets were still on but there was no one in it as far as he could see. He stripped out of the *ji* and the jockstrap and walked quickly into the—

Shit. Lash was in the corner. Like he'd been waiting.

"Hey, big man," the guy drawled. "Really showed us a thing or two out—"

Lash stopped talking and just stared at John's chest.

"You little kiss-ass," he snapped. And then stormed out of the shower.

John looked down at the circular mark over his left pectoral, the one he'd been born with . . . the one that Tohr had told him members of the Brotherhood received on their initiations.

Terrific. Now he could add that birthmark to the growing list of stuff he didn't want to hear about from his classmates.

When he came out of the shower with a towel around his waist, all the guys, even Blaylock, were standing together. While they looked him over as a solid, silent unit, he wondered whether vampires had pack instincts, like wolves or dogs.

As they continued to stare at him, he thought, *Um, yeah. That would be a big affirmative.*

John ducked his head and went to his locker, desperate for the day to be over.

Around three A.M., Phury walked quickly down Tenth Street to ZeroSum. Butch was waiting outside the club's glass-and-chrome entrance, lounging casually in spite of the cold. In his full-length cashmere coat and with his Red Sox hat pulled down low, he looked good. Anonymous, but good.

"What's doing?" Butch asked as they clapped palms.

"Night was for crap on the *lesser* side. No one found any. Hey, man, thanks for company, I need it."

"No problem." Butch tugged his Sox cap down even more. Like the Brothers, he kept a low profile. As a homicide detective, he'd helped send a number of drug-trade folks to jail, so it was better for him not to be too conspicuous.

Inside the club, the techno music was annoying. So were

the flashing lights and all the humans. But Phury had his reasons for coming, and Butch was being polite. Sort of.

"This place is just too frickin' precious," the cop said, eyeing a guy dressed in a hot pink leisure suit with makeup to match. "Give me rednecks and home-grown beer any day of the week over this X-culture bullshit."

When they got to the VIP section, the satin rope was lowered immediately so they could pass.

Phury nodded to the bouncer, then looked at Butch. "I won't take long."

"You know where to find me."

As the cop went for their table, Phury walked to the back of the high-ticket area, stopping in front of the two Moors who guarded the Reverend's private door.

"I'll tell him you're here," the one on the left said.

A split second later Phury was let in. The office was a cave, dimly lit with a low ceiling, and the vampire behind the desk dominated the space, especially as he got to his feet.

The Reverend was a jacked-up six foot six, and the tight mohawk he wore his hair in suited him as well as his fancy-ass Italian threads did. His face was pitiless and intelligent, placing him rightfully in the dangerous business he was in. His eyes, though . . . his eyes didn't fit. They were curiously beautiful, the color of amethysts, a deep purple that glowed.

"Back so soon?" the male said, his voice low, deep, harder than usual.

Get the product, then get a move on, Phury thought.

He took out his roll and peeled off three large. He fanned out the thousand-dollar bills on top of the chrome desk. "Twice the usual. And I want it quartered."

The Reverend smiled coolly and swiveled his head to the left. "Rally, get the male what he needs. And pad those O-Zs." A minion came out of the darkness and scooted through a pocket door in the far corner of the room.

When they were alone, the Reverend came around the desk slowly, moving like he had oil in his veins, all sinuous power. As he circled, he closed in enough to have Phury slip his hand into his coat and find one of his guns.

"Sure we can't interest you in something more hard-core?" the Reverend said. "That red smoke is for low dosers."

"If I wanted something else, I'd ask for it."

The vampire stopped beside him. So very close.

Phury frowned. "There a problem?"

"You have beautiful hair, you know that? It's like a female's. All those different colors." The Reverend's voice was strangely hypnotic, his purple eyes purely cunning. "Speaking of females, I hear you don't take advantage of what's offered by my ladies here. That true?"

"Why do you care?"

"Just want to make sure your needs are served. Customer satisfaction is so damned important." The male moved even closer and nodded at Phury's arm, the one that disappeared into his coat. "Your hand's on a gun butt right now, isn't it? Afraid of me?"

"Just want to make sure I can take care of you."

"Oh, really?"

"Yeah. In case you need a little Glock-to-mouth resuscitation."

The Reverend grinned, his fangs flashing. "You know, I've heard this rumor . . . about a member of the Brotherhood who's celibate. Yeah, go figure, a warrior who abstains. And I've heard a few other things about this male. He's down to one leg. Has a scarred sociopath for a twin. You wouldn't by any chance know of such a Brother?"

Phury shook his head. "Nope."

"Huh. Funny, I've seen you hanging around with a guy who looks like he's wearing a Halloween mask. Actually, I've seen you with a couple of big males who kind of fit some descriptions I've heard. You don't suppose—"

"Do me a favor and get me my leaves. I'll be outside waiting." Phury turned away. He was in a bad mood to begin with: frustrated that he hadn't found a fight, bleeding inside over being shut down by Bella. Now was not the time for conflict. He was on his last fucking nerve.

"Are you celibate because you like males?"

Phury glared over his shoulder. "What is with you tonight?

You're always shifty, but right now you're also being a real asshole."

"You know, maybe you just need to get laid. I don't traffic in the males, but I'm sure we could find you one who'd be obliging."

For the second time in twenty-four hours, Phury snapped. He surged across the office, took the Reverend by his Gucci lapels, and nailed him into the wall.

Phury leaned on the guy's chest. "Why are you picking a fight with me?"

"You going to kiss me before the sex?" the Reverend murmured, still playing. "I mean, it's the least you can do, considering we only know each other professionally. Or aren't you into foreplay?"

"Fuck you."

"Now there's an original comeback. I would have expected something a little more interesting from you."

"Fine. How's this?"

Phury laid a hard one on the male's mouth, the kiss a punch between faces, not anything even remotely sexual. And he did it only to wipe the expression off the bastard's face. It worked. The Reverend stiffened and growled, and Phury knew he'd called the guy's bluff. But just to make sure the lesson was learned, he clipped the male's lower lip with a fang.

The instant blood hit his tongue, Phury yanked back, his mouth falling open. Through his shock, he breathed, "Well, what do you know, sin-eater."

At the sound of the word the Reverend cut all the bullshit, getting good and dead serious. In the silence he seemed to be considering his plausible denials.

Phury shook his head. "Don't even try. I can taste it."

Amethyst eyes narrowed. "The politically correct term is *symphath*."

Phury's hands tightened on the male out of reflex. *Holy shit.* A *symphath.* Here in Caldwell and living among the species. Trying to pass itself off as just another civilian.

Man, this was crucial information. The last thing Wrath needed was another civil war in the race.

"I should point something out," the Reverend said softly. "You turn me in and you're going to lose your supplier. Think about it. Where're you going to get what you need if I'm out of the picture?"

Phury stared into those purple eyes, still running through the implications. He was going to tell the Brothers as soon as he got home, and he was going to watch the Reverend closely. As for turning the guy in . . . The discrimination *symphaths* had faced throughout history had always struck him as unfair— provided they didn't start pulling shit out of their trick bags. And the Reverend had been running the club for at least five years with no problems linked to *symphath* behavior.

"We're going to strike a little deal," Phury said, glaring hard into that violet stare. "I keep quiet and you stay on the down-low. You also don't try to fuck with me again. I'm not going to roll over for you sucking on my emotions, which was what you were doing right now, wasn't it? You wanted me irate because you were hungry for the feeling."

The Reverend's mouth opened just as the door to the office swung wide. A female vampire barged in, only to stop dead as she saw what was undoubtedly a picture: two male bodies close together, the Reverend's lip bleeding, blood on Phury's mouth.

"Get the hell out of here," the Reverend snapped.

The female backed away so quickly she tripped and slammed her elbow into the doorjamb.

"So do we have a deal?" Phury bit out after she left.

"If you admit you're a Brother."

"I'm not."

The Reverend's eyes flashed. "Just so you know, I don't believe you."

Phury had the sudden notion that it was no accident the Brotherhood thing had come up tonight. He leaned into the male. Hard. "Wonder how you'd fare if your identity got out?"

"We"—the Reverend dragged in a breath—"have a deal."

Butch looked up as the woman he'd sent to check on Phury came back. Usually the buys were over and done with quickly, but it had been a good twenty minutes.

"My boy in there still?" Butch asked, noting absently that she was rubbing her elbow like it hurt.

"Oh, he's in there, all right." As she shot him a tight smile, he abruptly realized she was a vampire. That little grin thing was a move they all pulled when they were out among humans.

And she was kind of attractive, he supposed, what with the long blond hair and the black leather at her breasts and hips. As she slid into the booth next to him, he caught her scent and thought idly of sex for the first time in . . . well, since he'd met Marissa over the summer.

He took a long drink, finishing the Scotch in his glass. Then he glanced at the female's breasts. Yeah, sex was on his mind, but more as a physical reflex than anything else. The interest was nothing like it had been with Marissa. Then the need had been . . . consuming. Reverent. Important.

The female beside him shot him a look as if she knew the direction of his thoughts. "Your friend might be in there for a while."

"Yeah?"

"They were just starting to get down to it."

"The buy?"

"The sex."

Butch's head whipped up and he locked eyes with her. "Excuse me?"

"Oh, whoops . . ." She frowned. "Are you two together or something?"

"No, we're not together," he snapped. "What the hell are you talking about?"

"Yeah, I didn't really think you were like that. You dress well, but you don't give off that kind of vibe."

"And my buddy's not into men, either."

"You sure about that?"

He thought about the celibacy and started to wonder.

Whatever. He needed another drink; he did not need to get into Phury's biz. Lifting his arm, he waved to a waitress, who rushed over.

"Another double Scotch," he said. To be polite, he turned to the female next to him. "You want something?"

Her hand landed on his thigh. "As a matter of fact, I do. But she can't give it to me."

As the waitress left, Butch leaned back in the booth, stretching both arms out, opening himself. The female took the invite, leaning into him, moving that hand south. His body stirred, its first sign of life in months, and he had some passing thought that maybe he could get Marissa out of his head if he had some sex.

While the female stroked him through his pants, he watched her with clinical interest. He knew where this was headed. He'd end up doing her in one of the private bathrooms over there. Would take maybe ten minutes, if that. He'd get her off, do his business, then beat feet to get away from her.

God, he'd pulled that quickie routine hundreds of times over the course of his life. And it was really just masturbation disguised as sex. No big deal.

He thought of Marissa . . . and felt his tear ducts sting.

The female next to him moved so that her breasts were on his arm. "Let's go to the back, daddy."

He put his hand over hers at his crotch and she made some kind of purring noise in his ear. At least until he removed her palm.

"I'm sorry. I can't."

The female pulled away and looked at him as if he had to be playing her. Butch stared right back.

He wasn't prepared to say he was never going to have sex again. And he sure as shit didn't understand why Marissa had gotten to him as much as she had. All he knew was that his old pattern of balling random women wasn't doing it for him. Tonight.

Abruptly Phury's voice cut through the ambient noise of the club. "Hey, cop, you want to stay or go?"

Butch glanced up. There was a slight pause as he speculated about his friend.

The Brother's yellow eyes narrowed. "What's doing, cop?"

"I'm ready to go," Butch said, smoothing over the awkward moment.

As he got up, Phury gave the blond a hard look. A real keep-your-yap-shut special.

Wow, Butch thought as they headed for the door. So Phury really was gay.

Chapter Twenty

Bella woke up hours later to a soft scraping sound. She glanced over to a window and watched as its steel shutter came down. Dawn must be close.

Anxiety tingled in her chest, and she looked at the door. She wanted Zsadist to come through it, wanted to clap her eyes on him and reassure herself he was in one piece. Even though he'd seemed back to normal when he'd left, she'd put him through a lot.

She rolled over onto her back and thought about Mary showing up. How had Zsadist known she'd needed a friend? And God, the fact that he'd gone to Mary and—

The bedroom door opened wide without any warning.

Bella sat up in a rush, pulling the covers to her throat. But then Zsadist's shadow was a stunning relief.

"It's just me," he said gruffly. As he came inside, he was carrying a tray, and there was something on his shoulder. A duffel bag. "You mind if I hit the lights?"

"Hi . . ." *I'm so glad you're home safe.* "Not at all."

He called to life several candles, and she blinked in the sudden glow.

"I brought you some things from your house." He put the tray of food on the bedside table and opened up the bag. "I got you clothes and a parka. The bottle of shampoo that was in your shower. A brush. Shoes. Socks to keep your feet warm. Your diary, too—don't worry, I haven't read it or anything."

"I'd be surprised if you had. You're more trustworthy than that."

"No, I'm illiterate."

Her eyes flared.

"Anyway"—his voice was hard as his jawline—"I figured you'd want some of your own stuff."

As he put the duffel next to her on the bed, she just stared up at him until, overwhelmed, she reached out to take his hand. When he flinched back, she flushed and looked at what he'd brought her.

God . . . she was nervous about seeing her things. Especially the diary.

Except it turned out to be comforting to pull out her favorite red sweater, put the thing to her nose, and catch a whiff of the perfume she'd always worn. And . . . yes, the brush, *her* brush, the one she liked with the broad, square head and metal bristles. She grabbed her shampoo, popped the top, and inhaled. *Ahhhh* . . . Biolage. Nothing like the scent of what the *lesser* had made her use.

"Thank you." Her voice trembled as she took out her journal. "Thank you so much."

She stroked her diary's leather cover. She would not open it. Not now. But soon . . .

She glanced up at Zsadist. "Will you . . . will you take me back to my house?"

"Yeah. I can do that."

"I'm frightened to go there, but I probably should."

"You just tell me when."

Gathering her courage, suddenly interested in getting one of the big "firsts" out of the way, she said, "When light falls this evening. I want to go then."

"Okay, we will." He pointed at the tray. "Now eat."

Ignoring the food, she watched him go into the closet and disarm. He was careful with his weapons, checking them thoroughly, and she wondered where he had been . . . what he had done. Though his hands were clean, there was black blood on his forearms.

He had killed tonight.

She supposed she should feel some kind of triumph that a *lesser* had been taken down. But as Zsadist walked over to the bathroom with a pair of sweats draped over his arm, she was more interested in his well-being.

And also . . . his body. He moved like an animal in the best sense of the word, all latent power and sleek strides. The sex that had stirred in her the very first time she'd seen him rocked her again. She wanted him.

As the bathroom door shut and the shower started to run, she rubbed her eyes and decided she was out of her mind. The male pulled away at the threat of her hand on his arm. Did she actually think he'd want to lay with her?

Disgusted with herself, she looked over at the food. It was some kind of herbed chicken with roasted potatoes and squash. There was a glass of water and a glass of white wine, as well as two bright green Granny Smith apples and a piece of carrot cake. She picked up a fork and pushed the chicken around. She wanted to eat what was on the plate only because he'd been thoughtful enough to bring it to her.

When Zsadist came out of the bathroom with only the nylon sweats on, she froze and couldn't stop staring. His nipple rings caught the candlelight, and so did the hard muscles of his stomach and arms. Along with the star-shaped mark of the Brotherhood, his bare chest had a fresh, livid scratch across it and a bruise.

"Are you injured?"

He came over and measured the plate. "You haven't eaten much."

She didn't reply as her eyes got caught on the curving hip bones that rose above the low waistband of the sweats. God . . . just a little lower and she would be able to see everything.

Abruptly she remembered him scrubbing himself raw because he thought he was filthy. She swallowed, wondering what had been done to him, to his sex. Wanting him as she did seemed . . . inappropriate. Invasive. Not that it changed the way she felt.

"I'm not terribly hungry," she murmured.

He pushed the tray closer to her. "Eat anyway."

When she started in on the chicken again, he took the two apples and walked across the room. He bit into one and sank down to the floor, sitting cross-legged with his eyes lowered. One arm settled across his stomach as he chewed.

"Did you have dinner downstairs?" she asked.

He shook his head and took another hunk out of the apple, the crack ricocheting around the room.

"Is that all you'll have?" When he shrugged, she muttered, "And you're telling me to eat?"

"Yeah, I am. So why don't you get back to work there, female."

"You don't like chicken?"

"I don't like food." His eyes never wavered from the floor, but his voice got pushier. "Now eat."

"Why don't you like food?"

"Can't trust it," he said tightly. "Unless you make it yourself, or can see it whole, you don't know what's in it."

"Why do you think someone would tamper—"

"Have I mentioned how much I don't like talking?"

"Will you sleep beside me tonight?" She blurted out the request, figuring she'd better get her answer before he shut up completely.

His brows flickered. "You really want that?"

"Yes, I do."

"Then, yeah. I will."

As he polished off the two apples and she cleaned the plate, the silence wasn't exactly easy, but it didn't crackle, either. After she was finished with the carrot cake, she went into the bathroom and brushed her teeth. By the time she came back, he was working the last apple core with his fangs, picking off the little bits of flesh that were left.

She couldn't imagine how he fought on such a diet. Surely he must eat more.

And she felt like she should say something, but instead slid into bed and curled up, waiting for him. As minutes ticked by, and all he did was surgically trim that apple, she couldn't stand the tension.

Enough, she thought. She really should go somewhere else in the house. She was using him as a crutch, and that wasn't fair.

She reached out to throw the covers back just as he uncoiled from the floor. As he walked to the bed, she froze. He dropped the apple cores next to her plate, then picked up the napkin she had used to wipe her own mouth. After rubbing his hands with the thing, he took the tray and carried it out of the room, setting it right outside the door.

When he came back he went to the other side of the bed, and the mattress dipped down as he stretched out on top of the duvet. Crossing his arms over his chest and his feet at the ankles, he shut his eyes.

One by one the candles went out around the room. When there was just a single wick that burned, he said, "I'll leave that going so you can see."

She looked at him. "Zsadist?"

"Yeah?"

"When I was . . ." She cleared her throat. "When I was in that hole in the ground, I thought of you. I wanted you to come for me. I knew you could get me out."

His brows went down even though his lids were lowered. "I thought of you, too."

"You did?" His chin moved up and down, and still she said, "Really?"

"Yeah. Some days . . . you were all I could think of."

Bella felt her eyes stretch wide. She rolled toward him and propped her head up on one arm.

"Seriously?" When he didn't reply, she had to press. "Why?"

His big chest expanded and he blew out his breath. "Wanted to get you back. That's all."

Oh . . . so he'd just been doing his job.

Bella dropped her arm and turned away from him. "Well . . . thank you for coming for me."

In the silence she watched the candle burn on the night-stand. The tear-shaped flame undulated, so lovely, so grace-ful. . . .

Zsadist's voice was quiet. "I hated the idea that you were frightened and alone. That someone had hurt you. I couldn't . . . let it go."

Bella stopped breathing and glanced over her shoulder.

"I didn't sleep for those six weeks," he murmured. "All I could see when I shut my eyes was you, calling out for help."

God, even though his face was harsh, his voice was so soft and beautiful, like the candle flame.

His head swiveled toward her and his eyes opened. His black stare was full of emotion. "I didn't know how you could have survived that long. I was so sure you were dead. But then we found the place and I lifted you out of that hole. When I saw what he'd done to you . . ."

Bella slowly turned over, not wanting to startle him into a retreat. "I don't remember any of it."

"Good, that's good."

"Someday . . . I'm going to need to know. Will you tell me?"

He closed his eyes. "If you really have to have the details."

They were silent for a time, and then he shifted toward her, rolling onto his side. "I hate to ask you this, but what did he look like? Can you remember anything specific about him?"

Plenty, she thought. *Too much.*

"He, ah, he colored his hair brown."

"What?"

"I mean, I'm pretty sure he did. Every week or so he'd go into the bathroom and I could smell the chemicals. And he'd get rooty in between. A little line of white right at his scalp."

"But I thought paling out was good because it meant they'd been in the Society longer."

"I don't know. I think he had . . . or has . . . a position of power. From what I could hear from the hole, the other *lessers* were careful around him. And they called him 'O.' "

"Anything else?"

She shivered, going back into the nightmare. "He loved me."

A growl vibrated out of Zsadist, low and nasty. She liked the sound of it. It made her feel protected. Gave her the strength to keep talking.

"The *lesser,* he said he . . . loved me, and he did. He was obsessed with me." She released a breath slowly, trying to calm her fluttering heart. "In the beginning I was terrified of him, but after a while I used his feelings against him. I wanted to hurt him."

"Did you?"

"Sometimes, yes. I made him . . . cry."

Zsadist's expression took on the oddest cast. As if he were . . . envious. "What did that feel like?"

"I don't want to say."

"Because it was good?"

"I don't want you to think I'm cruel."

"Cruelty is different from retaliation."

In a warrior's world, she imagined that was true. "I'm not sure I agree."

His black eyes narrowed. "There are those who would *ahvenge* you. You know that, right?"

She thought about him going out into the night to hunt the *lesser* and couldn't bear the idea that he would get hurt. Then she pictured her brother, all angry and prideful, ready to tear into the slayer, too.

"No . . . I don't want you doing that. You or Rehvenge or anyone else."

A draft shot through the room, like a window had been thrown open. She looked around and realized the frigid wave had come out of Zsadist's body.

"Do you have a mate?" he asked abruptly.

"Why do you . . . Oh, no, Rehvenge is my brother. Not my mate."

Those big shoulders eased up. But then he frowned. "Have you ever?"

"Had a mate? For a little while I did. But things didn't work out."

"Why?"

"Because of my brother." She paused. "Actually, that's not true. But when the male couldn't stand up to Rehv, I lost a lot of respect for him. And then . . . then the guy let the details of our relationship out to the *glymera* and things got . . . complicated."

Actually, they got awful. The male's reputation had stayed intact, of course, whereas hers got shredded to pieces. Maybe that was why she was so attracted to Zsadist. He didn't care what anyone thought of him. There was no subterfuge, no courtly manners to hide his thoughts and instincts. He was honest, and that candor, even if it just served to reveal his anger, made it safe to trust him.

"Were you two . . ." His voice trailed off.

"Were we what?"

"Lovers?" In a harsh rush, Zsadist cursed. "Never mind, that's none of my—"

"Ah, yes, we were. Rehv found out, and that was when the problems started. You know how the aristocracy is. A female who lays with someone she's not mated to? You'd swear she was tainted for life. I mean, I've always wished I'd been born a civilian. But you can't opt out of your bloodline, can you?"

"Did you love the male?"

"I thought so. But . . . no." She thought of the skull next to Zsadist's pallet. "Have you ever been in love?"

The corner of his mouth lifted into a snarl. "What the fuck do you think?"

As she recoiled, he closed his eyes. "Sorry. I mean, no. That would be no."

So why did he keep that skull? Whose was it? She was about to ask when he cut the question off. "Your brother thinks he's going after that *lesser?*"

"Undoubtedly. Rehvenge is . . . Well, he's been head of my household since my father died when I was very young, and Rehv is very aggressive. Extremely so."

"Well, you tell him to sit tight. I'm going to *ahvenge* you."

Her eyes shot to Zsadist's. "No."

"Yes."

"But I don't want you to." She couldn't live with herself if he got killed in the process.

"And I can't stop myself." He squeezed his eyes shut. "Christ . . . I can't breathe for knowing that bastard is out there. He has to die."

Fear and gratitude and something altogether warm squeezed her chest. On impulse, she leaned in and kissed him on the lips.

He jerked back with a hiss, eyes wider than if she'd slapped him.

Oh, hell. Why had she done that? "I'm sorry. I'm sorry, I—"

"No, it's cool. We're cool." He rolled onto his back and lifted his hand to his mouth. His fingers rubbed back and forth across his lips, like he was wiping her off him.

When she sighed good and hard, he said, "What's the matter?"

"Am I so distasteful?"

He dropped his arm. "No."

What a lie. "Maybe I'll get you a washcloth, how about that?"

When she would have shot out of bed, his hand clamped on her arm. "That was my first kiss, okay? I just didn't expect it."

Bella stopped breathing. How was that possible?

"Oh, for chrissakes, don't look at me like that." He let go and went back to staring at the ceiling.

His first kiss . . . "Zsadist?"

"What."

"Will you let me do that again?"

There was a long, long pause. She inched over to him, pushing her body through the sheets and blankets.

"I won't touch you anywhere else. Just my lips. On yours."

Turn your head, she willed him. *Turn your head and look at me.*

And then he did.

She didn't wait for an engraved invitation or for him to change his mind. She pressed her lips to his lightly, then hovered over his mouth. When he stayed where he was, she dipped down again and this time stroked at him. His breath sucked in.

"Zsadist?"

"Yes," he whispered.

"Relax your mouth for me."

Careful not to crowd him, she propped herself up on her forearms and got in close again. His lips were shockingly soft except for where the upper one was scarred. To make sure he knew the imperfection didn't matter to her, she deliberately attended to that place, returning there again and again.

And then it happened: He kissed her back. It was just the slightest movement of his mouth, but she felt it all the way to her core. When he did it again, she praised him by moaning a little and letting him take the lead.

God, he was so tentative, feeling his way across her mouth with the most gentle of brushings. He kissed her sweetly and with care, tasting like apples and male spice. And the contact between them, though light and slow, was enough to have her aching.

When she sneaked her tongue out and licked him, he pulled away sharply. "I don't know what I'm doing here."

"Yes, you do." She leaned in to keep the connection. "You really do."

"But—"

She quieted him with her mouth, and it wasn't long before he was back in the game. This time when her tongue stroked over him he opened his lips, and his own met hers, slick and warm. A slow twirl started . . . and then he was in her mouth, pushing against her, seeking.

She felt the sex stir in him, the heat and urgency in his big body growing. She was hungry for him to reach out and drag her against him. When he didn't, she eased back and looked at him. His cheeks were flaming, his eyes glittering. He was hungry for her, but he made no move to get closer. And he wouldn't, either.

"I want to touch you," she said.

But as she brought her hand up, he stiffened and gripped her wrist hard. Fear hovered just below the surface of him;

she could sense it weaving through his body, making him tense. She waited for him to make up his mind, not about to push him on this.

His hold slowly loosened. "Just . . . go slow."

"I promise."

She started with his arm, running her fingertips up and down his smooth, hairless skin. His eyes tracked the movement with a suspicion she took no offense at, and his muscles twitched, flickering as she passed. She stroked him slowly, letting him get used to her touch, and when she was sure he was comfortable, she leaned down and put her lips on his biceps. His shoulder. His collarbone. The top of his pectoral.

She was heading for his pierced nipple.

When she was close to the silver ring with the little ball, she glanced up at him. His eyes were wide, so wide the whites showed all around his black irises.

"I want to kiss you here," she said. "All right?"

He nodded and licked his lips.

The moment her mouth made contact, his body jerked like someone had yanked all of his arms and legs at once. She didn't stop. She sucked the piercing in and twirled her tongue around it.

Zsadist moaned, the low sound a great rumble in his chest; then he inhaled with a hiss. His head pitched back into the pillow, but he kept it at an angle so he could keep watching her.

When she flicked the silver hoop, then tugged on it a little, he arched off the bed, one leg bending up, his heel digging into the mattress. She tickled his nipple again and then again until he balled the comforter in his fists.

"Oh . . . *fuck*, Bella . . ." He was breathing in a hard, raw rhythm, heat radiating out of him. "What are you doing to me?"

"Do you want me to stop?"

"Either that or do it harder."

"How about a little more?"

"Yeah . . . a little more."

She worked him with her mouth, playing with the ring, driving him until his hips started to swivel.

When she looked down his body, she lost her rhythm. His erection was massive as it pushed up against the thin nylon of his warm-ups, and she saw all of it: the blunt head with its graceful ridge, the thick shaft, the twin weights below.

Good Lord. He was . . . huge.

She went utterly wet between her thighs and shifted her gaze to meet his. His eyelids were still peeled back and his mouth open as awe and shock and hunger warred in his face.

She reached up and pushed her thumb between his lips. "Suck me."

He latched on with a great pull, watching her as she kept going. A frenzy was taking hold of him; she could sense it. The lust was building in him, turning him into a powder keg, and holy hell, she wanted him. She wanted him to explode all over her. Inside of her.

She released his nipple, pulled her thumb out of his mouth, and reared up to thrust her tongue between his lips. At the invasion he groaned wildly, his great body bucking against the hold he kept on the covers.

She wanted him to let go and touch her, but she couldn't wait. This first time, she would have to take control. She pushed the covers away, slid her upper body onto his chest, and threw her leg over his hips.

The instant her weight came on top of him, he went stiff and stopped kissing her back.

"Zsadist?"

He threw her off of him with so much force, she bounced on the mattress.

Zsadist bolted from the bed, panting and whacked-out, his body trapped between the past and the present, stretched thin between the two.

Part of him wanted more of what Bella was doing to him. Hell, he was dying to keep exploring his first taste of arousal. The sensations were incredible. A revelation. The only thing good he'd felt in . . . forever.

Dear Virgin in the Fade, no wonder males killed to protect their mates.

Except he couldn't bear having a female on top of him, even if it was Bella, and the wild panic pounding through him right now was dangerous. What if he lashed out at her? For God's sake, he'd already thrown her across the damn bed.

He glanced at her. She looked so achingly beautiful in the tangled sheets and scattered pillows. But he was terrified of her, and because of that, terrified *for* her. The touching and the kissing, however much he'd been into them in the beginning, were too much of a trigger for him. And he couldn't put himself in a position where he got this upset when he was around her.

"We're not going there again," he said. "That shit's not happening."

"You liked it." Her voice was soft but strong. "I could feel your blood race under my hands."

"No arguments."

"Your body's hard for me."

"Do you want to get hurt?" As she tightened her hold on a pillow, he pressed harder. "Because, straight up, sex and I only go one way, and it's nothing you want to be a part of."

"I liked the way you kissed me. I want to lay with you. Make love with you."

"Make love? *Make love?*" He spread his arms out. "Bella . . . all I've got to offer you is fucking. You won't like it, and frankly I won't like doing it to you. You're so much better than that."

"I felt your lips on mine. They were gentle—"

"Oh, *please*—"

"Shut up and let me finish!"

Z's mouth dropped open, sure as if she'd booted him in the ass. No one ever took that tone of voice with him. The anomaly alone would have gotten his attention, but the fact that it was her stunned him out.

Bella pushed her hair over her shoulder. "If you don't want to be with me, fine. Just say so. But don't hide behind wanting to protect me. You think I don't know the sex would be rough with you?"

"Is that why you want it?" he asked in a dead voice. "You think you only deserve to be hurt now, after the *lesser?*"

She frowned. "Not at all. But if that's the only way I can have you, then that's how I'll take you."

He ran his hand back and forth over his skull trim, hoping the friction might get his brain to work.

"I think you're confused." He looked down at the floor. "You have no idea what you're saying right now."

"You arrogant bastard," she snapped.

Z's head shot up. Well, that was slap in the ass number two. . . . "Excuse me?"

"Do us both a favor and don't try to think for me, okay? Because you're going to get it wrong every damn time." With that, she marched into the bathroom and slammed the door.

Zsadist blinked a couple of times. *What the hell just happened?*

He looked around the room as if the furniture or maybe the drapes could help him out. Then his acute hearing tuned in to a quiet sound. She was . . . crying.

With a curse he went over to the bathroom. He didn't knock, just turned the knob and went inside. She was standing next to the shower, arms crossed, tears pooling in her sapphire eyes.

Oh . . . God. What was a male supposed to do in this situation?

"I'm sorry," he muttered. "If I . . . uh, hurt your feelings or something."

She glared at him. "I'm not hurt. I'm pissed off and sexually frustrated."

His head snapped back on his spine. *Well . . . then. Okaaaaay.*

Man, he was going to need a neck brace after this conversation.

"I'll say it again, Zsadist. If you're not into laying with me, that's okay, but do not try to tell me I don't know what I want."

Z planted his palms on his hip bones and looked down at the marble tile. *Don't say a thing, asshole. Just keep your mouth—*

"It's not that," he blurted. As the words floated out into the air, he cursed himself. Talking was bad. Talking was a real piss-poor idea. . . .

"It's not what? You mean you want me?"

He thought of the *it* that was still trying to claw a way out of his pants. She had eyes. She could see the damn thing. "You know I do."

"So if I'm willing to take it . . . hard . . ." She paused, and he had a feeling she was blushing. "Then why can't we be together?"

His breath shortened until his lungs burned and his heart pounded. He felt as if he were looking over the edge of a ravine. Good Lord, he wasn't actually going to tell her? Was he?

His stomach rolled as the words came out. "She was always on top. The Mistress. When she . . . came to me, she was always on top. You, uh, you rolled over onto my chest and . . . yeah, that doesn't work for me."

He rubbed his face, as much to try to hide from her as to relieve the headache he suddenly had.

He heard breath being exhaled. Realized it was hers.

"Zsadist, I'm so sorry. I didn't know—"

"Yeah . . . fuck . . . maybe you can forget I said that." God, he needed to get away from her before that mouth of his got flapping again. "Look, I'm going to—"

"What did she do to you?" Bella's voice was thin as a hair.

He shot her a hard look. *Oh, not likely,* he thought.

She took a step toward him. "Zsadist, did she . . . have you against your will?"

He turned away. "I'm going to the gym. I'll see you later."

"Wait—"

"*Later,* Bella. I can't . . . do this."

On his way out, he grabbed his Nikes and his MP3 player.

A good, long run was just what he needed right now. A long . . . run. So what if it got him exactly nowhere. At least he could have the sweaty illusion he was getting away from himself.

Chapter Twenty-one

Phury looked across the mansion's pool table with disgust while Butch measured his shot. Something was off with the human, but as the cop sank three balls with one cue stroke, it sure as hell wasn't his game.

"Jesus, Butch. Four wins in a row. Remind me why I bother playing with you?"

"Because hope springs eternal." Butch tossed back the tail end of his Scotch. "You want another game?"

"Why not. My odds can't get worse."

"You rack while I get a refill."

As Phury collected the balls from the pockets, he realized what the problem was. Every time he turned away, Butch got to staring at him.

"You have something on your mind, cop?"

The male poured himself a couple of fingers of Lagavulin, then took a long drink from his glass. "Not particularly."

"Liar. You've been giving me the hairy eyeball since we got back from ZeroSum. Why don't you get real and spill it."

Butch's hazel eyes met his glare head-on. "You gay, my man?"

Phury dropped the eight ball and dimly heard it bouncing on the marble floor. "What? Why would you—"

"I heard you were getting close with the Reverend." As Phury cursed, Butch picked up the black ball and sent it rolling back over the green felt. "Look, I'm cool if you are. I honestly don't give a rat's ass who you're into. But I would like to know."

Oh, this is just great, Phury thought. Not only was he pining after the female who wanted his twin; now he was supposedly dating a frickin' *symphath.*

That female who'd walked in on him and the Reverend clearly had a big mouth and . . . *Christ.* Butch must have already told Vishous. The two were like an old mated couple, no secrets between them. And V would squeal to Rhage. And once Rhage knew, you might as well have popped the news flash on the Reuters wire.

"Phury?"

"No, I'm not gay."

"Don't feel like you need to hide it or anything."

"I wouldn't. I'm just not."

"You bi, then?"

"Butch, drop it. If any of the Brothers are down with the kinky shit, it's your roommate." At the cop's bug-eyed look, he muttered, "Come on, you have to know about V by now. You live with him."

"Obviously not— Oh, hey, Bella."

Phury wheeled around. Bella was standing on the threshold of the room, dressed in that black satin robe. He could not look away from her. The glow of health was back in her lovely face, the bruises gone, her beauty revealed. She was . . . astonishing.

"Hello," she said. "Phury, do you think I could talk with you for a moment? After you're finished?"

"Butch, you mind if we take a breather?"

"That's cool. See you later, Bella."

As the cop left, Phury put his pool cue away with unnecessary precision, sliding the slick, blond wood into the wall rack. "You look well. How do you feel?"

"Better. Much better."

Because she'd fed from Zsadist.

"So . . . what's going on?" he asked, trying not to imagine her at his twin's vein.

Without replying, she went over to the French doors, the robe trailing across the marble floor behind her like a shadow. As she walked, the ends of her hair brushed against the small of her back and moved with the sway of her hips. Hunger hit him hard, and he prayed she didn't catch the scent.

"Oh, Phury, look at the moon, it's almost full." Her hand went to the glass and lingered on the pane. "I wish I could . . ."

"You want to go outside now? I could get you a coat."

She smiled at him over her shoulder. "I have no shoes."

"I'll bring you those, too. Stay here."

In no time he came back with a pair of fur-lined boots and a Victorian cape that Fritz, homing pigeon that he was, had pulled out of some closet.

"You work fast," Bella said as he draped the bloodred velvet around her shoulders.

He knelt in front of her. "Let me get these on you."

She lifted one knee, and as he slid the boot on her foot, he tried not to notice how soft the skin of her ankle was. Or how much her scent tantalized him. Or how he could just part the robe out of the way and . . .

"Now the other one," he said hoarsely.

When he had her booted up he opened the door, and they walked out together, crunching through the snow that covered the terrace. At the lawn's edge she tugged the cape in tight around her and looked up. Her breath left her mouth in puffs of white, and the wind teased the red velvet around her body, as if stroking the cloth.

"Dawn is not far," she said.

"Coming soon."

He wondered what she wanted to talk about, but then her face grew serious and he knew why she'd come. Zsadist. Of course.

"I want to ask you about him," she murmured. "Your twin."

"What do you want to know?"

"How did he become a slave?"

Oh, God . . . He didn't want to talk about the past.

"Phury? Will you tell me? I would ask him, but . . ."

Ah, hell. There was no good reason not to answer her. "A nursemaid took him. She sneaked him out of the household when he was seven months old. We couldn't find them anywhere, and as far as I was able to find out, she died two years later. He was sold into slavery at that point by whoever found him."

"That must have been so hard on your whole family."

"The worst. A death with no body to bury."

"And when . . . when he was a blood slave . . ." She took a deep breath. "Do you know what happened to him?"

Phury rubbed the back of his neck. As he hesitated, she said, "I'm not talking about the scars or the forced feedings. I want to know about . . . what else might have been done to him."

"Look, Bella—"

"I need to know."

"Why?" Even though he knew the answer. She wanted to lay with Z, had probably already tried to. That was the *why* of it.

"I just have to know."

"You should ask him."

"He won't tell me, you know he won't." She put her hand on his forearm. "Please. Help me understand him."

Phury stayed quiet, telling himself it was becáuse he was respecting Z's privacy, and that was mostly true. Only the smallest part of him didn't want to help land Z in her bed.

Bella squeezed his arm. "He said he was tied down. And that he can't stand to have a female on top when—" She stopped. "What was done to him?"

Holy shit. Zsadist had *talked* about his captivity with her?

Phury cursed softly. "He was used for more than just his vein. But that's all I'm going to say."

"Oh, God." Her body sagged. "I just needed to hear it from someone. I needed to know for sure."

As a cold gust of wind came up, he took a deep breath and still felt suffocated. "You should go in before you get cold."

She nodded and started for the house. "Aren't you coming?"

"I'm going to have a smoke first. Go on now."

He didn't watch her head into the house, but heard the door click shut.

Putting his hands in his pockets he looked out over the rolling white lawn. Then he closed his eyes and saw the past.

As soon as Phury went through his transition, he searched to find his twin, canvassing the Old Country, seeking out households that were wealthy enough to have servants. Over time he heard a repeated rumor that there was a warrior-sized male being kept by a female high up within the glymera. *But he wasn't able to pin it down.*

Which made sense. Back then, in the early nineteenth century, the species was still relatively cohesive, and the old rules and social customs remained strong. If anyone had been found harboring a warrior as a blood slave, they would have faced death under the law. That was why he had to be discreet in his quest. If he'd demanded a congregation of the aristocracy and put out a call for his twin's return, or if he was caught trying to find Zsadist, he might as well put a dagger in the male's chest: Killing Zsadist and disposing of the body would be the captor's best and only defense.

By the late 1800s, he'd almost given up hope. His parents had both died of natural causes by then. Vampire society had fragmented in the Old Country, and the first of the migrations to America had begun. He was rootless, roaming Europe, chasing after whispers and innuendoes . . . when suddenly he found what he'd been looking for.

He was on English soil the night it happened. He'd gone to a gathering of his kind at a castle on the cliffs of Dover. Standing in a darkened corner of the ballroom, he overheard two males speaking of the hostess. They said she had an incredibly endowed blood slave and that she liked to be watched and sometimes even shared him.

Phury had courted the female starting that very night.

He wasn't worried that his face would give him away, even though he and Zsadist were identical twins. First of all, his clothes were those of a wealthy male, and no one would suspect someone of his station to be coming after a slave that had been rightfully purchased on the market as a small child. And second, he was always careful to keep disguised. He grew a short beard to dull his features, and he hid his eyes behind dark spectacles, which he explained away by claiming his vision was poor.

Her name had been Catronia. An aristocrat of wealth, she was mated to a half-breed merchant who conducted business in the human world. Evidently she was alone a lot, as her hellren traveled extensively, but the rumor was she'd had the blood slave before her mating.

Phury asked to be welcomed into her household, and as he was well-read and attentive, she permitted him to a room despite the fact that he was vague about his lineage. Courts were full of posers, and she was attracted to him, so she was obviously willing to overlook certain formalities. But she was cautious, too. Weeks passed, and though she spent a lot of time with him, she never took him to the slave she was said to possess.

Every chance he had he searched the grounds and the buildings, hoping to find his twin in a hidden cell of some kind. The problem was, there were eyes everywhere, and Catronia kept him busy. Whenever her hellren departed, which was often, she would come to Phury's quarters, and the more he evaded her hands, the more she wanted him.

Time . . . time was all it took. Time and her inability to resist showing off her prize, her toy, her slave. One evening right before dawn, she asked him to her bedroom for the first time. The secret entrance he had been searching for had been located in her antechamber, in the back of her wardrobe. Together they went down a vast, steep staircase.

Phury could still remember the thick oak door at the bottom swinging open, and the sight of the male chained naked, legs spread, on a tapestry-covered bedding platform.

Zsadist had been staring at the ceiling, his hair so long it fell onto the stone floor. He was clean shaven and oiled, as if he'd been prepared for her sport, and he smelled of expensive spices. The female went right to him and caressed him lovingly, those rapacious brown eyes of hers stamping ownership all over his body.

Phury's hand had gone for the dagger at his side before he'd known what he was doing. As if sensing the motion, Zsadist's head had slowly turned, and his dead black eyes had crossed the distance between them. There was no flash of recognition. Just seething hatred.

Shock and sorrow had rolled through Phury, but he'd kept focused, looking for the way out. There was another door across the cell, but that one had no knob or handle, just a little slot about five feet from the floor. He'd thought maybe he could break thr—

Catronia began to touch his brother intimately. She had some kind of salve on her hands, and as she stroked his twin's manhood, she was saying hateful things about what the size of him would be like. Phury bared his fangs at her and lifted the dagger.

The door across the way suddenly swung open. On the other side was an effete court male wearing an ermine-trimmed robe. He was frantic as he announced that Catronia's hellren *had returned unexpectedly and was searching for her. Rumors about her and Phury had evidently reached the male's ears.*

Phury crouched down, prepared to kill the female and her court-man. But the sound of pounding feet, many of them, echoed into the room.

The hellren *came pounding down the secret stairs, he and his private guard spilling into the room. The male had seemed flabbergasted, was clearly unaware that she had a blood slave. Catronia started speaking, but he slapped her so hard she ricocheted off the stone walls.*

Chaos exploded. The private guard went after Phury. The
hellren *went after Zsadist with a knife.*

*Killing the court's soldiers was a long and bloody process,
and by the time Phury could get free of the hand-to-hand,
there was no sign of Zsadist, just a bloody trail out of the cell.*

*Phury took off down the corridor, running through the un-
derground of the castle, following the red streaks. When he
emerged from the keep it was nearly dawn, so he knew he had
to find Zsadist with alacrity. As he paused to get his bearings,
he heard a rhythmic noise snapping through the air.*

A whipping.

*Over to the right, Zsadist had been strung up from a tree
on the cliff, and against the vast backdrop of the sea, he was
being whipped raw.*

*Phury attacked the three guards who were lashing his twin.
Though the males fought hard, he was in a wild fury. He
slaughtered them and then released Zsadist, only to see more
guards coming out of the bulkhead in a block of five.*

*With the sun about to rise, and the glow burning his skin,
Phury knew there was no time left. He slung Zsadist over his
shoulders, grabbed one of the pistols the guards had been
armed with, and shoved the weapon into his belt. Then he
eyed the cliff and the ocean below. Not the best route to freedom, but far better than trying to fight his way toward the castle. He started running, hoping to launch them far enough out
so that they fell into the ocean.*

*A throwing dagger caught him in the thigh, and he stum-
bled.*

*There was no catching his balance or stopping his mo-
mentum. He and Zsadist tumbled over the lip of the cliff and
skidded down the rock face until Phury's boot got caught in a
crevice. As his body was yanked to a halt, he scrambled to
hold on to Zsadist, knowing damn well that the male was out
cold and going to drown if he fell into the water unattended.*

*Zsadist's blood-slick skin slid out of Phury's grip, slipped
free—*

*He caught his twin's wrist at the last second and squeezed
hard. There was a massive jerk as the male's heavy body was*

*stopped, and pain ricocheted up Phury's leg. His vision faded.
Came back. Faded again. He could feel Zsadist's body dangling in midair, a perilous sway that challenged his hold un-
mercifully.*

*The guards peered over the edge and then measured the
gathering light, shielding their eyes. They laughed, sheathed
their weapons, and left him and Zsadist for dead.*

*As the sun gathered on the horizon, Phury's strength
quickly drained, and he knew he couldn't hold Zsadist for
long. The light was awful, burning, adding to the agony he already felt. And no matter how hard he pulled his leg, his ankle
remained trapped.*

*He fumbled for the pistol, pulling it free of his waistband.
With a deep breath, he aimed the muzzle at his leg.*

*He shot himself below the knee. Twice. The pain was as-
tounding, a fireball in his body, and he dropped the gun. Gritting his teeth, he'd planted his free foot into the cliff and
pushed with everything he had in him. He screamed as his leg
splintered and came apart.*

And then there was the yawning void of empty air.

*The ocean had been cold, but it had shocked him into con-
sciousness and sealed up his wound, keeping him from bleeding out. Dizzy, nauseous, desperate, he'd forced his head
above the choppy waves, his death grip on Zsadist the only
constant. Dragging his twin into his arms, keeping the male's
head above water, Phury swam to shore.*

*Blessedly, there was a cave entrance not far from where
they'd taken the plunge, and he used his last reserve of
strength to get the two of them toward the dark mouth. After
dragging himself and Zsadist from the water, he was all but
blind as he went as far into the cave as he could. A curve in
the natural architecture was what saved them, giving them the
darkness they needed.*

*In the back, away from the sun, he sheltered them behind
large rocks. Gathering Zsadist into his arms to conserve their
body heat, he stared ahead into the blackness, utterly lost.*

Phury rubbed his eyes. God, the image of Zsadist chained on that bedding platform . . .

Ever since the rescue he'd had a repeating nightmare, one that never failed to be a fresh horror each time his subconscious coughed it up. The dream was always the same: Him racing down those hidden stairs and throwing open the door. Zsadist tied down. Catronia in the corner, laughing. As soon as Phury was in the cell, Z would turn his head and his black, lifeless eyes would look up from out of an unscarred face. In a hard voice he would say, "Leave me here. I want to stay . . . here."

That was Phury's cue to wake up in a cold sweat.

"What's doing, my man?"

Butch's voice was jarring, but welcome. Phury scrubbed his face, then glanced over his shoulder. "Just enjoying the view."

"Lemme give you a tip. That's what you do on a tropical beach, not standing out in this kind of cold. Look, come eat with us, okay? Rhage wants pancakes, so Mary's backed a dump truck full of Bisquick into the kitchen. Fritz is about to levitate, he's so worried about not being able to help."

"Yeah. Good deal." As they headed inside, Phury said, "Can I ask you something?"

"Sure. What do you need?"

Phury paused by the pool table and picked up the eight ball. "When you worked in homicide, you saw a lot of fucked-up people, right? People who'd lost their husbands or their wives . . . sons or daughters." When Butch nodded, he said, "Did you ever find out what happened to them? I mean, the ones who were left behind. Do you know if they ever got over the shit?"

Butch rubbed his thumb over his eyebrow. "I don't know."

"Yeah, I guess you don't really follow up—"

"But I can tell you I never did."

"You mean the sight of those bodies you worked on stuck with you?"

The human shook his head. "You forgot sisters. Brothers and sisters."

"What?"

"People lose husbands, wives, sons, daughters . . . and sisters and brothers. I lost a sister when I was twelve. Two boys took her behind the baseball diamond at school and used her and beat her until they killed her. I never got over it."

"Jesus—" Phury stopped, realizing they were not alone.

Zsadist stood bare-chested in the doorway to the room. He was flushed with sweat from his head to his Nikes, like he'd run for miles down in the gym.

As Phury stared at his twin, he felt a familiar sinking sensation. It was always like that, as if Z were some kind of low-pressure zone.

Zsadist's voice was hard. "I want both of you to come with me at nightfall."

"Where to?" Butch asked.

"Bella wants to go to her house, and I'm not taking her there without backup. I need a car in case she wants to take some of her shit with her when she leaves, and I want someone to case the place before we land there. The bennie is that there's an escape tunnel out from the basement if things get rough. I checked through it last night when I went to pick up a few things for her."

"I'm good to go," Butch said.

Zsadist's eyes shifted across the room. "You, too, Phury?"

After a moment, Phury nodded. "Yeah. Me, too."

Chapter Twenty-two

That night, as the moon lifted higher in the sky, O eased up from the ground with a groan. He'd been waiting on the edge of the meadow since the sun went down four hours ago, hoping that someone would show at the farmhouse . . . only there was nothing. And there hadn't been for the past two days. Well, he thought he'd seen something before dawn this past morning, some kind of shadow moving around inside the place, but whatever it was, he'd caught it just once and then not again.

He wished like hell he could use all the Society's resources to go after his wife. If he sent out every *lesser* he had . . . Except he might as well take a gun to his head. Someone would blab to the Omega that focus had been diverted to one inconsequential female. And then there would be big problems.

He checked his watch and cursed. Speaking of the Omega . . .

O had a command performance with the master tonight and no choice but to keep the damn date. Staying viable as a slayer was the only way to get his woman back, and he wasn't going to risk getting poofed out of existence because he'd spaced a meeting.

He took out his phone and called in three Betas to watch the farmhouse. As the spot was a known place of congregation for vampires, at least he had an excuse to assign the detail.

Twenty minutes later the slayers came through the woods, the sound of their jogging boots muffled by the snow. The trio of big-boned men were just out of their initiations, so their hair was still dark and their skin ruddy from the cold. They were clearly thrilled to be used and ready to fight, but O told them they were to watch and monitor only. If anyone showed up, they weren't to attack until whoever it was tried to leave, and then any vampires were to be taken alive, male or female. No exceptions. The way O figured it, if he were his woman's family, he'd send feelers out first before letting her demateri- alize anywhere near the house. And if she was dead and her relatives were moving her things out, then he wanted her kin captured in working order so he could find her grave.

After making it clear the Betas' heads were on the line, O went through the forest to his truck, which was hidden in a stand of pines. As he came out onto Route 22, he saw that the *lessers* had parked the Explorer they'd come in right on the road less than half a mile from the turnoff to the farmhouse's lane.

He called the idiots and told them to use their fucking heads and get that car good and concealed. Then he drove to the cabin. As he went along, images of his woman flickered through his mind, dimming his eyes to the road in front of him. He saw her at her loveliest, in the shower with wet hair and skin. She was especially pure like that. . . .

But then the visions shifted. He saw her naked on her back, underneath that ugly-ass vampire who'd taken her away. The male was touching her . . . kissing her . . . pumping inside of her. . . . And she liked it. The bitch liked it. Her head was back and she was moaning and coming like a slut and wanting more.

O's hands curled around the steering wheel until his knuckles nearly popped out of his skin. He tried to calm him- self, but his anger was a pit bull on a paper chain.

He knew then with absolute clarity that if she wasn't dead already, he was going to kill her when he found her. All he had to do was picture her with the Brother who'd stolen her and his higher reasoning clicked off completely.

And didn't that put O in a bind. Living without her would be horrible, and though going out in a suicidal rush after she died had a lot of appeal, pulling a stunt like that would just land him with the Omega for eternity. *Lessers,* after all, went back to the master if they were extinguished.

But then a thought occurred to him. He imagined his woman many years from now, her skin paled out, her hair blonded, her eyes the color of clouds. A *lesser* just like him. The solution was so perfect, his foot slipped from the accelerator, and the truck coasted to a stop right in the middle of Route 22.

She would be his forever that way.

As midnight neared, Bella put on a pair of her old blue jeans and that thick red sweater she liked so much. Then she went into the bathroom, pulled the two towels down from the mirror, and looked at herself. Her reflection was of the female she had always seen staring back at her: Blue eyes. High cheeks. Biggish lips. Lots of dark brown hair.

She lifted the edge of the sweater and peeked at her stomach. The skin there was flawless, no longer bearing the *lesser*'s name. She smoothed her hand over where the letters had been.

"You ready?" Zsadist asked.

She glanced up into the mirror. He loomed behind her, dressed in black, weapons hanging off his body. His coal eyes were pegged on the skin she exposed.

"The scars have healed," she said. "In just forty-eight hours."

"Yeah. And I'm glad."

"I'm scared to go to my house."

"Phury and Butch are coming with us. You've got plenty of protection."

"I know. . . ." She lowered the sweater. "It's just . . . what if I can't bear to go inside?"

"Then we try again another night. However long it takes."
He held out her parka.

Shrugging into the thing, she said, "You have better things
to do than watch over me."

"Not right now I don't. Give me your hand."

Her fingers trembled as she reached out. She had some
vague thought that it was the first time he'd asked her to touch
him, and she hoped the contact would lead to an embrace.

But he wasn't interested in hugging. He put a small gun in
her hand without even brushing her skin.

She recoiled in distaste. "No, I—"

"Hold it like—"

"Wait a minute, I don't—"

"—this." He positioned the little butt against her palm.
"Here's the safety. On. Off. Got it? On . . . off. You need to be
in tight to kill with this, but it's loaded with two bullets that
will slow a *lesser* down long enough so you can get away. Just
point and pull the trigger twice. You don't need to cock it or
anything. And aim for the torso, it'll be a bigger target."

"I don't want this."

"And I don't want you to have it. But it's better than sending you in light."

She shook her head and closed her eyes. So ugly this business of life sometimes was.

"Bella? Bella, look at me." When she did, he said, "Keep
that in the outside pocket of your coat on the right side. You
want it in your business hand if you have to use it." She
opened her mouth and he talked right over her. "You're going
to stay with Butch and Phury. And as long as you're with
them, it is *extremely* unlikely you will need to use that."

"Where will you be?"

"Around." As he turned away, she noticed he had a knife
at the small of his back—in addition to the two daggers on his
chest, and the pair of guns on his hips. She wondered how
many other weapons he had on him that she couldn't see.

He stopped in the doorway, head hanging low. "I'm going
to make sure you don't have to take out that gun, Bella. I
promise you. But I can't have you unarmed."

She took a deep breath. And slipped the little piece of metal into her coat pocket.

Out in the hall Phury was waiting, leaning against the balcony. He was also dressed for fighting, with guns and those daggers all over him, a deadly calm radiating from his body. When she smiled at him, he nodded and drew on his black leather coat.

Zsadist's cell phone rang and he flipped it open. "You there, cop? What's doing?" When he hung up, he nodded. "Good to go."

The three of them walked down to the foyer and then out into the courtyard. In the cold air both males palmed guns, and then all of them dematerialized.

Bella took form on her front porch, facing the glossy red door with its brass knocker. She could feel Zsadist and Phury behind her, two huge male bodies full of tension. Footsteps sounded and she looked over her shoulder. Butch was coming up onto the porch. His gun was drawn, too.

The idea of taking her time and easing into her house struck her as dangerous and selfish. She unlocked the door with her mind, then walked in.

The place still smelled the same . . . a combination of the lemon floor wax she used on the wide pine boards and the rosemary candles she liked to burn.

When she heard the door shut and the security alarm get turned off, she glanced back. Butch and Phury were tight on her heels, but Zsadist was nowhere to be seen.

She knew he hadn't left them. But she wished he were inside with her.

She took a deep breath and looked around her living room. Without any lights on, she only saw familiar shadows and shapes, more the pattern of the furniture and the walls than anything else.

"Everything seems . . . God, exactly the same."

Although there was a blank spot over her writing desk. A mirror was gone, a mirror that she and her mother had picked out together in Manhattan about a decade ago. Rehvenge had always liked it. Had he taken the thing? She wasn't sure whether to be touched or offended.

When she reached out to turn a lamp on, Butch stopped her. "No lights. Sorry."

She nodded. Walking deeper into the farmhouse, seeing more of her things, she felt as though she were among friends of long acquaintance whom she hadn't seen in years. It was delightful and sad. A relief most of all. She'd been so sure she would get upset. . . .

She stopped when she got to the dining room. Beyond the wide archway at the far end was the kitchen. Dread coiled in her gut.

Steeling herself, she walked into the other space and halted. As she saw everything so neat and unbroken, she remembered the violence that had taken place.

"Someone's cleaned it up," she whispered.

"Zsadist." Butch stepped by her, gun up at chest level, eyes scanning around.

"He . . . did all this?" She motioned her hand in a sweep.

"The night after you were taken. He spent hours here. Downstairs is neat as a pin, too."

She tried to imagine Zsadist with a mop and bucket, getting rid of the bloodstains and the glass shards.

Why? she wondered.

Butch shrugged. "He said it was personal."

Had she spoken out loud? "Did he explain . . . why that was?"

As the human shook his head, she was aware of Phury pointedly taking interest in the outdoors.

"You want to go to your bedroom?" Butch asked.

When she nodded, Phury said, "I'm staying up here."

Down in the basement she found everything in order, arranged . . . clean. She opened her closet, went through her dresser drawers, wandered around her bathroom. Small things captivated her. A bottle of perfume. A magazine dated from before the abduction. A candle she could remember lighting next to the claw-foot tub.

Lingering, touching, sliding back into place in some

profound way, she wanted to spend hours . . . days. But she
could feel Butch's increasing strain.

"I think I've seen enough for tonight," she said, wishing
she could stay longer.

Butch went first as they headed back to the first floor.
When he came into the kitchen, he looked at Phury. "She's
ready to head out."

Phury flipped open his phone. There was a pause. "Z, time
to go. Start the car for the cop."

As Butch shut the cellar door, Bella went over to her fish
tank and peered in. She wondered if she would ever live at the
farmhouse again. And had a feeling she wouldn't.

"Do you want to take anything with you?" Butch asked.

"No, I think—"

A gunshot rang outside, the hollow popping noise muffled.

Butch grabbed her and hauled her back against his body.
"Stay quiet," he said in her ear.

"Out front," Phury hissed as he fell into a crouch. He
pointed his gun down the hall at the door they'd come in
through.

Another gunshot. And another. Getting closer. Coming
around the house.

"We're out the tunnel," Butch whispered as he muscled her
around and pushed her toward the basement door.

Phury tracked the sounds with his gun muzzle. "I got your
back."

Just as Butch's hand fell on the cellar door's knob, time com-
pressed into fractals of seconds, then collapsed into nonsense.

The French door behind them smashed open, the wood
frame splintering, the glass shattering.

Zsadist took the whole thing out with his back as he was
pushed through the thing by some tremendous force. As he
landed on the kitchen floor, his skull jacked back and hit the
tile so hard it sounded like another gun had gone off. Then,
with a horrible yell, the *lesser* that had thrown him through
the door leaped on his chest and the two of them slid across
the room, heading right for the cellar stairs.

Zsadist was rock-still under the slayer. Dazed? Dead?

Bella screamed as Butch yanked her out of the way. The only place to go was against the stove, and he shoved her in that direction, shielding her with his body. Only now they were trapped in the kitchen.

Phury and Butch both leveled guns at the tangle of arms and legs on the floor, but the slayer didn't care. The undead lifted his fist and punched Zsadist in the head.

"No!" she roared.

Except, strangely, the hit seemed to wake Zsadist up. Or maybe her voice had done the trick. His black eyes flipped open and an evil expression came over his face. With a quick thrust he clamped his hands under the *lesser*'s armpits and twisted so hard, the slayer's torso contorted into a vicious arch.

In a flash Zsadist was on top, straddling the *lesser.* He grabbed hold of the slayer's right arm and stretched it into a bone-cracking bad angle. Then he jammed his thumb under the undead's chin so far you couldn't see half the finger and bared long fangs that glistened white and deadly. He bit the *lesser* in the neck, right through the esophageal column.

The slayer hollered in pain, thrashing wildly between his legs. And that was only the beginning. Zsadist tore his prey apart. When the thing no longer moved, he paused while panting and pushed his fingers into the *lesser*'s dark hair, splitting a section wide, clearly looking for white roots.

But she could have told him it wasn't David. Assuming she could find her voice.

Zsadist cursed and caught his breath, but stayed crouched over his kill, looking for signs of life. As if he wanted to keep going.

And then he frowned and glanced up, clearly realizing the battle was over and there had been witnesses.

Oh . . . Jesus. His face was marked with the black blood of the *lesser,* and more of the stain covered his chest and hands.

His black eyes shifted to hers. They were bright. Shiny. Just like the blood he'd spilled to defend her. And he quickly looked away, as if he wanted to hide the satisfaction he'd gotten from the kill.

"The other two are finished," he said, still breathing hard. He pulled out the bottom of his shirt and wiped his face.

Phury headed for the hallway. "Where are they? Front lawn?"

"Try the Omega's front door. I stabbed them both." Zsadist looked at Butch. "Take her home. Now. She's too shocked out to dematerialize. And Phury, you go with them. I want a call the moment she puts a foot in the foyer, we clear?"

"What about you?" Butch said, even as he was moving her around the dead *lesser.*

Zsadist stood up and unsheathed a dagger. "I'll poof this one and wait for others to come. When these fuckers don't check in, there'll be more."

"We'll be back."

"I don't care what you do as long as you get her home. So quit talking and start driving."

Bella reached out to him, though she wasn't sure why. She was horrified by what he had done and by what he looked like now, all bruised and beaten, his own blood running down his clothes along with the slayers'.

Zsadist slashed a hand through the air, dismissing her. "Get her the hell out of here."

John leaped from the bus, so damned relieved to be home he almost fell all over himself. Man, if the first two days of training were anything to go by, the next couple years were going to be hell.

As he came in the front door, he whistled.

Wellsie's voice drifted out of her study. "Hi! How'd it go today?"

While he took off his coat, he blew two quick whistles, which was kind of an *okay, fine, all righty* type of thing.

"Good. Hey, Havers is coming in an hour."

John headed for her study and paused in the doorway. Sitting at her desk, Wellsie was surrounded by a collection of old books, most of which were laid open. The sight of all those splayed, bound pages reminded him of eager dogs on their backs, waiting for belly attention.

She smiled. "You look tired."

I'm going to crash for a while before Havers comes, he signed.

"You sure you're okay?"

Absolutely. He smiled to give the fib some juice. He hated lying to her, but he didn't want to go into his failures. In another sixteen hours he was going to have to have them out on display again. He needed a break, and no doubt they were exhausted, too, from having had so much airtime.

"I'll wake you up when the doctor gets here."

Thanks.

As he turned away, she said, "I hope you know that no matter what that test says, we'll deal with it."

He glanced at her. So she was worried about the results, too.

In a quick rush he went over and hugged her, then headed for his room. He didn't even put his laundry in the chute, just dropped his bags and lay on the bed. Man, the cumulative effects of eight hours of derision was enough to make him want to sleep for a week.

Except all he could think about was Havers's visit. God, what if it was all a mistake? What if he wasn't going to turn into something fantastic and powerful? What if his visions at night were nothing more than an overactive Dracula fixation?

What if he was mostly human?

It would kind of make sense. Even though the training was just beginning, it was clear he wasn't like the other pretransitions in the class. He flat-out sucked at anything physical and was weaker than the other guys. Maybe practice would help, although he doubted it.

John closed his eyes and hoped for a good dream. A dream that would place him in a big body, a dream that would have him strong and . . .

Tohr's voice woke him up. "Havers is here."

John yawned and stretched and tried to hide from the sympathy on Tohr's face. That was the other nightmare about training: He had to screw up in front of Tohr all the time.

"How you are you doing, son—I mean, John?"

John shook his head and signed, *I'm fine, but I would rather be* son *to you.*

Tohr smiled. "Good. That's how I want it, too. Now come on, let's rip this Band-Aid off about the tests, okay?"

John followed Tohr to the living room. Havers was sitting on the couch, looking like a professor with his tortoiseshell glasses and herringbone jacket and red bow tie.

"Hello, John," he said.

John lifted a hand and sat in the wing chair closest to Wellsie.

"So I have the results of your blood test." Havers took a piece of paper out of the inside of his sport coat. "It took me a little longer, because there was an anomaly I didn't expect."

John glanced at Tohr. Then Wellsie. *Jesus . . .* What if he was wholly human? What would they do to him? Would he have to leave—

"John, you are a full-bred warrior. There is only the barest trace of nonspecies blood in you at all."

Tohr laughed in a loud burst and clapped his hands together. "Hot damn! That's great!"

John started to grin and kept going until his lips totally disappeared into a smile.

"But there's something else." Havers pushed his glasses up higher on his nose. "You are of the line of Darius of Marklon. So close you could be his son. So close . . . you must be his son."

A stony silence overtook the room.

John looked back and forth between Tohr and Wellsie. The two were frozen solid. Was this good news? Bad news? Who was Darius? Going by their expressions, maybe the guy was a criminal or something. . . .

Tohr burst up from the sofa and took John into his arms, squeezing so hard the two became one. Gasping for air, feet dangling, John looked over at Wellsie. She had both hands over her mouth, and tears were rolling down her face.

Abruptly Tohr let go and stepped back. He coughed a little, eyes shimmering. "Well . . . what do you know."

The man cleared his throat a number of times. Rubbed his face. Looked a little woozy.

Who is Darius? John signed as he sat down again.

Tohr smiled slowly. "He was my best friend, my brother in the fighting, my . . . I can't wait to tell you all about him. And this means you have a sister."

Who?

"Beth, our queen. Wrath's *shellan—*"

"Yes, about her," Havers said, looking at John. "I don't understand the reaction you had to her. Your CAT scans are all fine, so too your EKG, your CBC. I believe you when you say she was what caused the seizures, though I have no idea why that would be. I'd like you to stay away from her for a while so we can see if it happens in another environment, okay?"

John nodded, though he wanted to see the woman again, especially if he was related to her. A sister. How cool . . .

"Now, about the other issue," Havers said pointedly.

Wellsie leaned forward and put her hand on John's knee. "Havers has something he wants to talk to you about."

John frowned. *What?* he signed slowly.

The doctor smiled, trying to be all reassuring. "I'd like you to see that therapist."

John went cold. In a panic, he searched Wellsie's face, then Tohr's, wondering how much the doctor might have told them about what had happened to him a year ago.

Why would I go? he signed. *I'm fine.*

Wellsie's reply was level. "It's just to help you make the transition to your new world."

"And your first appointment is tomorrow evening," Havers said, tipping his head down. He stared into John's face over the top of the horn-rims, and the message in his eyes was: *Either you go or I'll tell them the real reason why you have to.*

John was outmaneuvered, and that pissed him off. But he figured it was better to submit to compassionate blackmail than to have Tohr and Wellsie know anything about what had been done to him.

Okay. I'll do it.

"I'll take you," Tohr said quickly. Then he frowned. "I mean . . . we can find someone to take you—Butch will take you."

John's face burned. Yeah, he didn't want Tohr anywhere near the therapist gig. No way.

The front doorbell rang.

Wellsie grinned. "Oh, good. That's Sarelle. She's come over to work on the solstice festival. John, maybe you'd like to help us?"

Sarelle was here again? She hadn't mentioned that when they'd IM'd last night.

"John? Do you want to work with Sarelle?"

He nodded and tried to keep it cool, although his body had lit up like a neon sign. He was positively tingling. *Yeah. I can do that.*

He put his hands in his lap and looked down at them, trying to keep his smile to himself.

Chapter Twenty-three

Bella was damn well coming home. Tonight.

Rehvenge was not the kind of male who handled frustration well under the best of circumstances. So he was *beyond* through waiting to have his sister back where she needed to be. Goddamn it, he was not just her brother, he was her *ghardian,* and that meant he had rights.

As he yanked on his full-length sable coat, the fur swirled around his big body, then fell to rest at his ankles. The suit he was wearing was black and by Ermenegildo Zegna. The twin nine-millimeter handguns under his arms were by Heckler & Koch.

"Rehvenge, please don't do this."

He looked at his mother. Madalina was standing beneath the chandelier in the hall, the picture of aristocracy with her regal bearing and her diamonds and her satin gown. The only thing out of place was the worry on her face, and that wasn't because the tension clashed with her Harry Winston and haute couture. She never got upset. Ever.

He took a deep breath. He was more likely to calm her down if he didn't show his infamous temper, but more to the point, in his current frame of mind he was liable to shred her where she stood, and that wasn't fair.

"She will come home this way," he said.

His mother's graceful hand lifted to her throat, a sure sign she was caught between what she wanted and what she thought was right. "But it's so extreme."

"You want her sleeping in her own bed? You want her where she should be?" His voice started to punch through the air. "Or do you want her staying with the Brotherhood? Those are warriors, *mahmen*. Bloodthirsty, blood-hungry *warriors*. You think they would hesitate to take a female? And you know damn well by law the Blind King can lay with whatever female he chooses. You want her in that kind of environment? I don't."

As his *mahmen* stepped back, he realized he was yelling at her. He sucked in another deep breath.

"But, Rehvenge, I spoke with her. She doesn't want to come home yet. And they are males of honor. In the Old Country—"

"We don't even know who's in the Brotherhood anymore."

"They saved her."

"Then they can give her back to her family. For God's sake, she's a female of the aristocracy. You think the *glymera* will accept her after this? She's already had that one affair."

And what a mess that had been. The male had been totally unworthy of her, a crumbling idiot, and yet the bastard had managed to walk away from the split without talk. Bella, on the other hand, had been whispered about for months, and though she'd tried to pretend it hadn't bothered her, Rehv knew it had.

He hated the aristocracy they were stuck in, he really did.

He shook his head, pissed off at himself. "She should never have moved out of this house. I should never have allowed that."

And as soon as he got her back, she was *never* going to be allowed out again without his approval. He was going to have her anointed as a *sehcluded* female. Her blood was pure enough to justify it, and frankly she should have been one all along. Once that was done, the Brotherhood was legally required to render her back to Rehvenge's care, and thereafter she would not be able to leave the house without his permission. And there was more. Any male who wanted to see her would have to go through him as head of her household, and he was going to deny every single one of the sons of bitches. He'd failed to protect his sister once. He wasn't going to let that happen again.

Rehv checked his watch even though he knew he was late for his business. He would make the petition for *sehclusion* to the king from his office. It was odd to do something so ancient and traditional through e-mail, but that was the way of things now.

"Rehvenge . . ."

"What."

"You will drive her away."

"Not possible. Once I take care of this, she'll have nowhere else to go but here."

He reached for his cane and paused. His mother looked so miserable, he leaned down and kissed her cheek.

"You don't worry about a thing, *mahmen*. I'm going to fix it so she never gets hurt again. Why don't you ready the house for her? You could take her mourning cloth down."

Madalina shook her head. In a reverent voice she said, "Not until she walks over the threshold. It would offend the Scribe Virgin to assume her safe return."

He held back a curse. His mother's devotion to the Mother of the Race was legendary. Hell, she should have been a member of the Chosen with all her prayers and her rules and her flinching fear that one word askance would bring certain doom.

But whatever. It was her spiritual cage, not his.

"As you wish," he said, leaning on his cane and turning away.

He moved slowly through the house, relying on the different kinds of floorings to tell him which room he was in. There was marble in the hall, a swirling Persian carpet in the dining room, wide-planked hardwood in the kitchen. He used his sight to tell him that his feet were landing squarely and that it was safe for him to put his weight on them. He carried the cane in case he misjudged and lost balance.

As he went out into the garage, he held on to the door frame before putting one foot and then the other down the four steps. After sliding into his bulletproof Bentley, he hit the garage door opener and waited for a clear shot out.

Goddamn it. He wished like hell he knew who those Brothers were and where they lived. He'd go there, blast through the door, and drag Bella away from them.

When he could see the driveway behind him, he threw the sedan in reverse and nailed the gas so hard the tires squealed. Now that he was behind the wheel, he could move at the speed he wanted to. Fast. Nimble. Free of caution.

The long lawn was a blur as he gunned down the winding drive to the gates, which were set back from the street. He suffered a quick pause while the things opened; then he tore out onto Thorne Avenue and proceeded down one of the wealthiest streets in Caldwell.

To keep his family safe and never lacking for anything, he worked at despicable things. But he was good at what he did, and his mother and his sister deserved the kind of life they had. He would give them anything they wanted, fulfill any whim they had. Things had been too hard on them for too long. . . .

Yeah, the death of his father had been the first gift he'd given them, the first of many ways he'd improved their lives and kept them out of harm's way. And he wasn't stopping the trend now.

Rehv was going at a clip and heading for downtown when the base of his skull began to tingle. He tried to ignore the sensation, but in a matter of moments it condensed into a tight grip, as if a vise had been clamped around the top of his spine. He lifted his foot from the accelerator and waited for the feeling to pass.

Then it happened.

With a stab of pain his vision went to shades of red, like he'd pulled a transparent veil over his face: The headlights of oncoming cars were neon pink, the road a dull rust, the sky a claret like burgundy wine. He checked the clock on the dash, the numbers of which were now a ruby glow.

Shit. This was all wrong. This shouldn't be hap—

He blinked and rubbed his eyes. When he opened them again, his depth perception was gone.

Yeah, the hell this isn't happening. And he wasn't going to make it downtown.

He wrenched the wheel to the right and pulled over into a strip mall, the one where the Caldwell Martial Arts Academy had been before it burned down. He killed the Bentley's lights and drove behind the long, narrow buildings, parking flush with the bricks so that if he had to drive off fast, all he had to do was hit the gas.

Leaving the engine running, he shrugged out of the sable coat, stripped off his suit jacket, then rolled up his left sleeve. Through the red haze, he reached into his glove compartment and took out a hypodermic syringe and a length of rubber tubing. His hands were shaking so badly he dropped the needle and had to stretch down and pick it up off the floor.

He patted his jacket pockets until he found the glass vial of the neuromodulator dopamine. He put the thing on the dash.

It took two tries to open the hypodermic's sterile packet, and then he nearly broke the needle off getting it through the rubber top on the dopamine lid. When the syringe was loaded, he wrapped the rubber tubing around his biceps using one hand and his teeth; then he tried to find a vein. Because he was working in a flat visual field, everything was complicated.

He just couldn't see well enough. All he had in front of him was . . . red.

Red . . . red . . . red . . . The word shot around his mind, banging on the inside of his skull. Red was the color of panic. Red was the color of desperation. Red was the color of his self-hatred.

Red was not the color of his blood. Not right now, at any rate.

Snapping himself to attention, he fingered his forearm and looked for an internal launching pad for the drug, a super-highway that would bring the shit up to the receptors in his brain. Except his veins were collapsing.

He felt nothing as he pushed the needle in, which was reassuring. But then it came . . . a little sting at the injection site. The numbness he preserved himself in was about to end.

As he hunted around under his skin for a usable vein, he started to feel things in his body: The sensation of his weight in the car's leather seat. The heat blowing on his ankles. The fast air moving in and out of his mouth, drying his tongue.

Terror had him shoving the plunger down and releasing the rubber tourniquet. God only knew if he'd had the right place.

Heart pounding, he stared at the clock.

"Come on," he muttered, starting to rock in the driver's seat. "Come on . . . kick in."

Red was the color of his lies. He was trapped in a world of red. And one of these days the dopamine wasn't going to work. He'd be lost in the red forever.

The clock changed numbers. One minute passed.

"Oh, shit . . ." He rubbed his eyes as if that might bring back the depth in his vision and the normal spectrum of color.

His cell phone rang and he ignored it.

"Please . . ." He hated the pleading in his voice, but he couldn't pretend to be strong. "I don't want to lose me. . . ."

All at once his vision returned, the red draining from his visual field, the three-dimensional perspective returning. It was like the evil had been sucked out of him and his body numbed up, its sensations evaporating until all he knew were the thoughts in his head. With the drug, he became a moving, breathing, talking bag that blessedly had only four senses to worry about now that touch had been medicated to the back burner.

He collapsed against the seat. The stress around Bella's abduction and rescue had gotten to him. That was why the attack had hit him so hard and fast. And maybe he needed to adjust the dosage again. He'd go to Havers and check about that.

It was a while before he was able to put the car in drive. As he eased out from behind the strip mall and slipped into traffic, he told himself he was just one more sedan in a long line of cars. Anonymous. Just like everyone else.

The lie eased him somewhat . . . and increased his loneliness.

At a stoplight, he checked the message that had been left for him.

Bella's security alarm had been turned off for an hour or so and had just come back on. Someone had been in her house again.

Zsadist found the black Ford Explorer parked in the woods about three hundred yards away from the entrance to Bella's mile-long driveway. The only reason he'd run across the thing was because he'd been scouring the area, too restless to go home, too dangerous to be in the company of anyone else.

A set of footprints in the snow headed in the direction of the farmhouse.

He cupped his hands and looked in the car's windows. The security alarm was engaged.

Had to be those *lessers*' ride. He could smell the sweet scent of them all over it. But with only one set of tracks, maybe the driver had dropped his buddies off, then hidden it? Or maybe the SUV had had to be moved from somewhere else?

Whatever. The Society would be back for its property. And wouldn't it be sweet to know where the hell it ended up? But how could he trail the damn thing?

He put his hands on his hips . . . and happened to look down at his gun belt.

As he unclipped his cell phone, he thought fondly of Vishous, that tech-savvy son of a bitch.

Necessity, mother, invention.

He dematerialized under the SUV so he left a minimal amount of tracks in the snow. As his weight was absorbed by his back, he winced. Man, he was going to pay for that little trip through the French door. And for the knock on the head. But he'd survived worse.

He took out a penlight and looked around the under-carriage, trying to pick the right spot. He needed somewhere fairly large, and it couldn't be near the exhaust system, because even in this cold, that kind of heat could be a problem. Of course, he'd have much preferred to get into the Explorer and tuck the phone under a seat, but the SUV's alarm system was a complication. If it were tripped he might not be able to reengage it, so the *lessers* would know someone had been in the car.

As if the punched-out window wouldn't be a clue.

Goddamn it . . . He should have gone through those *lessers*' pockets before stabbing them into oblivion. One of those bastards had had the keys. Except he'd been so pissed off, he'd moved too fast.

Z cursed, thinking of the way Bella had looked at him after he'd chewed up that slayer in front of her. Her eyes had been wide in her pale face, her mouth loose with shock at what he'd done.

The thing was, the Brotherhood's business of protecting the race was a nasty one. It was messy and ugly and sometimes deranged. Always bloody. And on top of all that, she had seen the killing lust in him. Somehow, he was willing to bet that was what disturbed her the most.

Focus, dumb ass. Come on, get out of your head.

Z poked around some more, shifting under the Explorer. Finally he found what he was looking for: a little cave in the undercarriage. He shrugged out of his windbreaker, wrapped the phone up, and shoved the wad in the hole. He tested the jury-rig to make sure it was in there good and tight, then dematerialized out from under the SUV.

He knew the setup wasn't going to last long under there, but it was so much better than nothing. And now Vishous would be able to track the Explorer from home, because that little silver-bullet Nokia had a GPS chip in it.

Z flashed over to the edge of the meadow so he could see the back of the farmhouse. He'd done an okay patch job on the busted kitchen door. Fortunately the frame of the thing had still been intact, so he'd been able to close it and reengage the alarm sensors. Then he'd found a plastic tarp in the garage and covered up the monster hole.

Fixed, but not really.

Funny . . . he didn't think he'd be any more successful if

he tried to rehab Bella's opinion of him. But—*goddamn it*—he didn't want to be a savage to her.

In the distance, two headlights turned off Route 22 and shined down the long private lane. The car slowed as it came up to Bella's house, then pulled into her driveway.

Was that a Bentley? Z thought. Sure looked like it.

Man, an expensive car like that? Had to be a member of Bella's family. No doubt they'd been notified that the security alarm had been off for a while and then been turned back on about ten minutes ago.

Shit. Now was not a good time for someone to do a look-see walk-through. Given Z's luck, the *lessers* would pick right this moment to come back for their SUV—and decide to do a drive-by of the farmhouse for kicks and giggles.

Cursing under his breath, he waited for one of the Bentley's doors to open . . . except no one got out of the car and the engine stayed idling. This was good. As long as the alarm was activated, maybe they wouldn't think to go inside. Because the kitchen was a mess.

Z sniffed the cold air, but couldn't catch a scent. Instinct told him, though, that it was a male inside the sedan. Her brother? Most likely. He'd be the one who'd check out the scene.

That's right, buddy. Look at the front windows. See? Nothing's wrong. No one's in the house. Now do us both a favor and get the fuck out of here.

The sedan stayed put for what seemed like five hours. Then it backed out, did a K-turn in the street, and took off.

Z grabbed a deep breath of air. *Christ* . . . His nerves were too tight tonight.

Time passed. As he stood alone among the pines, he stared at Bella's house. And wondered if she'd be scared of him now.

The wind picked up, the cold getting rough with him and bleeding into his bones. With desperation, he embraced the pain that came with it.

Chapter Twenty-four

John stared across the desk in the study. Sarelle's head was down as she leafed through one of the ancient books, her short blond hair hanging in her face so that her chin was all he could see. The two of them had spent hours making a list of incantations for the solstice festival. Meanwhile, Wellsie was in the kitchen, ordering supplies for the ceremony.

As Sarelle turned another page, he thought she had really pretty hands.

"Okay," she said. "I think that's the last one."

Her eyes flashed up to his and it was like getting struck by lightning: a shock of heat and then a spacey disorientation. Plus he would have believed he glowed in the dark now, too.

She smiled and closed the book. Then there was a long silence. "So . . . um, I guess my friend Lash is in your training class."

Lash was her friend? *Oh, terrific.*

"Yeah . . . and he says you have the mark of the Brotherhood on your chest." When John didn't respond, she said, "Do you?"

John shrugged and scribbled on the edge of the list he'd made.

"Can I see it?"

He squeezed his eyes shut. Like he wanted her to get a load

of his scrawny chest? Or that birthmark that had proven to be
such a pain in the ass?

"I don't think you did it yourself, like they do," she said
quickly. "And, I mean, it's not like I want to inspect it or
something. I don't even know what one is supposed to look
like. I'm just curious."

She moved her chair closer to his and he caught a whiff of
the perfume she wore . . . or maybe it wasn't perfume. Maybe
it was just . . . her.

"Which side is it on?"

As if his hand belonged to her, he patted his left pectoral.

"Unbutton your shirt a little." She leaned over to the side,
her head angled so she could look at his chest. "John? Can I
please see it?"

He glanced at the doorway. Wellsie was still talking on the
phone in the kitchen, so she probably wasn't going to come
barging in or anything. But the study still seemed way public.

Oh . . . God. Was he really going to do this?

"John? I just want to . . . see."

Okay, he *was* going to do this.

He stood up and nodded at the doorway. Without a word
Sarelle followed right behind him, going all the way down the
hall, all the way into his bedroom.

After they stepped inside, he shut the door most of the way
and reached for the top button of his shirt. He willed his hands
to be steady by vowing to saw them off if they embarrassed
him. The threat seemed to work, because he unbuttoned the
shirt down to his stomach without much trouble. He stretched
the left side open and looked away.

When he felt a light touch on his skin, he jumped.

"Sorry, my hands are cold." Sarelle blew on her fingertips,
then went back to his chest.

Good God. Something was happening in his body, some
kind of wild shifting inside his skin. His breath grew short,
strangled. He opened his mouth so he could get more air in.

"That is *really* cool."

He was disappointed when she dropped her hand. But then
she smiled at him.

"So do you think you might want to go out sometime? You know, we could go to the laser-tag place. That could be cool. Or maybe the movies."

John nodded like the dummy he was.

"Good."

Their eyes met. She was so pretty, she made him dizzy.

"Do you want to kiss me?" she whispered.

John's eyes cracked open. Like a balloon had popped behind his head.

"Because I'd like you to." She licked her lips a little. "I really would."

Whoa . . . Chance of a lifetime, right here, right now, he thought.

Do not pass out. Passing out would be a total buzz kill.

John quickly called on every movie he'd ever seen . . . and got no help at all. As a horror fan, he was just swamped by visions of Godzilla stomping across Tokyo and of Jaws chewing on the ass end of the *Orca. Big help.*

He thought of the mechanics. *Head tilt. Lean forward. Make the contact.*

Sarelle glanced around, flushing. "If you don't want to, that's cool. I just thought . . ."

"John?" Wellsie's voice came from down the hall. And got closer as she kept talking. "Sarelle? Where are you guys?"

He winced. Before he lost his nerve, he grabbed Sarelle's hand, pulled her forward, and planted a good one right on her mouth, his lips tight against hers. No tongue, but there wasn't time, and he'd probably need to call 911 after something like that anyway. As it was, he was practically hyperventilating.

Then he pushed her back. And worried about how he'd done.

He risked a look. *Oh . . .* Her smile was radiant.

He thought his chest would explode with happiness.

He was just dropping his hand as Wellsie stuck her head in the door. "I need to go to—ah . . . I'm sorry. I didn't know that you two . . ."

John tried to marshal a nothing-special smile and then noticed that Wellsie's eyes were fixated on his chest. He looked down. His shirt was wide-open.

Scrambling to button the damn thing up just made the situation worse, but he couldn't help himself.

"I'd better go," Sarelle said easily. "My *mahmen* wanted me home early. John, I'll be on the computer later, okay? We'll figure out what movie to go see or whatever. Night, Wellsie."

As Sarelle walked down toward the living room, he couldn't resist glancing around Wellsie. He watched as Sarelle took her coat out of the hall closet, put it on, and got her keys from her pocket. Moments later the muted sound of the front door closing drifted down the hall.

There was a long silence. Then Wellsie laughed and pushed back some of her red hair.

"I, ah, I have no idea how to handle this," she said. "Except to say that I like her a lot and she has good taste in males."

John rubbed his face, aware that he was the color of a tomato.

I'm going to go for a walk, he signed.

"Well, Tohr just called. He was going to swing by the house and pick you up. Thought you might want to hang with him at the training center, since he's got some admin work to do. Anyway, it's your choice to stay or not. And I'm off to a *Princeps* Council meeting."

He nodded as Wellsie started to turn away.

"Ah, John?" She paused and looked over her shoulder. "Your shirt's . . . um, it's buttoned up kind of off-kilter."

He glanced down. And started to laugh. Even though he made no sound he just had to let his joy out, and Wellsie smiled, obviously happy for him. As he did the buttons up the right way, he had never loved the woman more.

Bella spent the hours after she returned to the mansion sitting up in Zsadist's bed with her diary in her lap. She didn't do anything with the journal at first, too caught up in what had happened at her house.

Jesus . . . She couldn't say she was surprised that Zsadist was every bit the menace she'd thought he was. And he'd saved her, hadn't he? If that *lesser* he'd killed had gotten its hands on her, she would have ended up back in a hole in the ground.

The trouble was, she couldn't decide whether what he'd done was evidence of his strength or his brutality.

As she decided it was probably both, she worried about whether he was okay. He'd been hurt and yet he was still out there, probably trying to find more slayers. *God* . . . What if he—

What if. What if . . . She was going to drive herself crazy if she kept this up.

Desperate for something else to focus on, she leafed through what she'd written in her journal over the past year. Zsadist's name had played a prominent role in the entries right before she'd been abducted. She'd been so obsessed by him, and couldn't say that had changed. Matter of fact, her feelings were so strong for him now, even after what he'd done tonight, that she wondered if she didn't . . .

Love him. *Oh* . . . *man.*

Suddenly she couldn't be alone, not with that realization shooting around her head. She brushed her teeth and her hair and made a go for the first floor, hoping she'd run into someone. Except halfway down the stairs, she heard voices from the dining room and came to a halt. The last meal of the night was in progress, but the idea of joining all the Brothers and Mary and Beth seemed overwhelming. Besides, wouldn't Zsadist be there? And how could she face him without giving herself away? No way that male was going to deal well with her loving him. No way.

Ah, hell. She was going to have to see him sooner or later. And hiding wasn't her thing.

But when she got to the bottom of the staircase and stepped off onto the foyer's mosaic floor, she realized she'd forgotten to put any shoes on. How could she go into the king and queen's dining room with bare feet?

She looked back up at the second floor and became utterly

exhausted. Too tired to go up and come down again, too embarrassed to go forward, she just listened to the sounds of the
meal: Male and female voices chatted and laughed. A wine
bottle was uncorked with a pop. Someone thanked Fritz for
bringing out more lamb.

She looked down at her naked feet, thinking she was such
a fool. A shattered fool. She was lost because of what the
lesser had done to her. And shaky because of what she'd seen
Zsadist do tonight. And so alone after realizing what she felt
for that male.

She was about to throw in the towel and go back upstairs
when something brushed against her leg. She jumped and
looked down, meeting the jade green eyes of a black cat. The
feline blinked, purred at her, and rubbed its head against the
skin of her ankle.

Bending at the waist, she stroked its fur with unsteady
hands. The animal was incomparably elegant, all lean lines
and graceful, sliding movements. And for no good reason, her
eyes got blurry. The more emotional she got, the closer she
and the cat became, until she was sitting on the last step of the
staircase and the animal had crawled into her lap.

"His name is Boo."

Bella gasped and looked up. Phury was standing in front of
her, a towering male no longer dressed in war clothes, but
now in cashmere and wool. He had a napkin in his hand, as if
he'd just gotten up from the table, and he smelled really good,
like he'd recently showered and shaved. Staring at him, she
became aware that all the talk and sounds of eating had bled
from the air, leaving a silence that told her everyone knew
she'd come downstairs and gotten stuck on the periphery.

Phury knelt down and pressed his linen napkin into her
hand. Which was how she realized there were tears running
down her cheeks.

"Won't you come join us?" he said softly.

She blotted her face while still holding on to the cat. "Any
chance I can take him in with me?"

"Absolutely. Boo is always welcome at our table. And so
are you."

"I don't have shoes on."

"We don't care." He held out his hand. "Come on, Bella. Come join us."

Zsadist walked into the foyer, so cold and stiff he shuffled along. He'd wanted to stay until the very dawn at the farmhouse, but his body hadn't fared well in the frigid air.

Even though he wasn't going to eat, he headed for the dining room, only to stop in the shadows. Bella was at the table, sitting next to Phury. There was a plate of food in front of her, but she was paying more attention to the cat in her lap. She was petting Boo, and didn't miss a stroke as she looked up at something Phury said. She smiled, and when her head dropped again, Phury's eyes stayed on her profile as if he were drinking her in.

Z walked quickly over to the stairs, not about to fall into that scene. He was almost free when Tohr emerged from the hidden door below the first landing. The brother looked grim, but then he never was a party.

"Hey, Z, hold up."

Zsadist cursed, and not under his breath. He had no interest in getting waylaid by some policy-and-procedure shit, and that was all Tohr talked about lately. The guy was cracking down on the Brotherhood, organizing shifts, trying to turn four loose cannons like V, Phury, Rhage, and Z into soldiers. No wonder he always looked like his head hurt.

"Zsadist, I said, *wait.*"

"Not now—"

"Yeah, *now.* Bella's brother sent a request to Wrath. Asking that she be assigned *sehculsion* status with him as her *whard.*"

Oh, shit. If that happened, Bella was as good as gone. Hell, she was as good as luggage. Not even the Brotherhood could keep her from her *whard.*

"Z? Did you hear what I said?"

Nod your head, asshole, he told himself.

He barely managed a chin dip. "But why are you telling me this?"

Tohr's mouth tightened. "You want to front like she's nothing to you? Fine. Just thought you'd want to know."

Tohr headed for the dining room.

Z gripped the banister and rubbed his chest, feeling like someone had replaced the oxygen in his lungs with tar. He looked up the stairs and wondered if Bella would come back to his room before she left. She would have to, because her diary was there. She could leave her clothes behind, but not that journal. Unless, of course, she'd moved out already.

God . . . How would he tell her good-bye?

Man, there was one conversation to bail on. He couldn't imagine what he'd say to her, especially after she'd seen him do his nasty magic all over that slayer.

Z went into the library, picked up one of the phones there, and dialed Vishous's cell number by its pattern on the buttons. He heard the ring through the receiver as well as from across the foyer. When V answered, he told the Brother about the Explorer and the cell phone and the undercarriage antics.

"I'm on it," V said. "But where are you? There's a funky echo on the phone."

"Call me if that car moves. I'll be in the gym." He hung up and headed for the underground tunnel.

He figured he could scrounge up some clothes down in the locker room and run himself into a state of utter depletion. When his thighs were screaming and his calves had turned to stone and his throat was sore from the gasping, the pain would clear his mind, cleanse him. . . . He craved the hurt more than he craved food.

When he got to the locker room, he went to the cubicle assigned to him and pulled out his Air Shox and a pair of running shorts. He preferred going shirtless anyway, especially if he was alone.

He'd disarmed and was about to strip down when he heard something moving around the lockers. Tracking the sound in silence, he stepped out into the path of—a half-pint stranger.

There was a metal bang as that little body slammed into one of the locker banks.

Shit. It was the kid. What was his name? John something.

And John-boy looked as if he was going to faint as he stared up with bugged-out, glassy eyes.

Z glared down from his full height. His mood was utterly vicious at the moment, black and cold as space, and yet somehow, ripping the kid a new asshole for doing nothing wrong wasn't appealing.

"Get out of here, kid."

John fumbled with something. A pad and pen. As he put the two together, Z shook his head.

"Yeah, I don't read, remember? Look, just go. Tohr's up at the house."

Z turned away and yanked off his shirt. When he heard a gasp, he looked over his shoulder. John's eyes were on his back.

"Christ, kid . . . get the fuck out of here."

As Z heard the patter of feet leaving, he ditched his pants, threw on the black soccer shorts, and sat on the bench. He picked his Nikes up by the laces and let them dangle between his knees. As he stared at the running shoes, he had some stupid thought about how many times he'd shoved his feet into them and punished his body on the very treadmill he was headed for. Then he thought about how many times he'd deliberately gotten himself hurt in fights with the *lessers*. And how many times he'd asked Phury to beat him.

No, not asked. Demanded. There had been times when he'd demanded that his twin hit him over and over again until his scarred face swelled up and the pounding ache in his bones was all he knew. In truth, he didn't like having Phury involved. He'd have preferred the pain to be private and would have done the damage himself if he'd been able to. But it was hard to coldcock yourself with any force.

Z slowly lowered the running shoes to the floor and leaned back against the locker, thinking about where his twin was. Up in the dining room. Next to Bella.

His eyes drifted to the phone that was mounted on the locker room wall. Maybe he should call up to the house.

A low whistle sounded right next to him. He flipped his eyes to the left and frowned.

The kid was there with a water bottle in his hand, and he came forward tentatively, his arm stretched way out in front of him, his head tilted away. Kind of like he was cozying up to a panther and hoped to leave the experience with his limbs still attached.

John placed the Poland Spring bottle about three feet from Z on the bench. Then he turned and ran away.

Z stared at the door the kid tore out of. As the thing eased shut, he thought about other doors in the compound. The front ones of the mansion, specifically.

God. Bella would be leaving soon, too. She might even be leaving now.

Right this very minute.

Chapter Twenty-five

"Apples? What the fuck do I care about apples?" O yelled into his cell phone. He was ready to crack heads, he was so pissed off, and U was nattering on about goddamn *fruit?* "I just told you we've got three dead Betas. *Three* of them."

"But tonight there were fifty bushels of apples bought from four different—"

O had to start pacing around the cabin. It was either that or so help him he was going to hunt down U just to burn off his edge.

As soon as O had returned from the Omega he'd gone to the farmhouse, only to find two scorch marks on the lawn as well as the busted-up back door. Looking through a window into the kitchen, he'd seen black blood all over the place and another burn mark on the tile.

Damn it to hell, he thought, picturing the scene again. He knew a Brother had done the work, because given the mess in the kitchen, the *lesser* who'd been finished off on that floor had been shredded before he'd been stabbed.

Had his wife been with the warrior at the time? Or had the visit been about her family trying to move her stuff out and a Brother had just been guarding them?

Goddamn those Betas. Those three lousy-ass, weak-balled, useless mother*fuckers* of his had gotten themselves killed, so he'd never have answers. And whether his wife had been there not, sure as hell if she were alive she wasn't going back there anytime soon, thanks to the fighting that had gone down.

U's bullshit came back into focus. ". . . the shortest day of the year, December twenty-first, is coming up next week. The winter solstice is—"

"I have an idea," O snapped. "Why don't you cut the calendar crap. I want you to go to that farmhouse and pick up that Explorer those Betas left behind in the woods. Then—"

"Listen to what I'm saying. Apples are used in the solstice ceremony to honor the Scribe Virgin."

Those two words, *Scribe* and *Virgin,* got O's attention. "How do you know this?"

"I've been around for two hundred years," U said dryly. "The festival hasn't been held for . . . Christ, I don't know, a century maybe. The apples are supposed to represent the anticipation of spring. Seeds, growth, that kind of renewal shit."

"What type of festival are we talking about?"

"In the past hundreds of them gathered, and I guess they did some chanting, some ritual stuff. I don't really know. Anyway, for years we've been monitoring certain buying patterns in the local marketplace during specific times of the year. Apples in December. Raw sugarcane in April. It's been more out of habit than anything else, because those vampires have been so damn quiet."

O leaned back against the cabin's door. "But now their king has ascended. So they're firing up the old ways."

"And you've got to love the ISBN system. Much more efficient than just asking around, which is what we used to have to do. As I said before, a huge load of Granny Smith apples has been purchased at various locales. Like they're spreading the orders around."

"So you're saying that in a week a bunch of vampires are going to get together in one place. Do a little song-and-dance thing. Pray to the Scribe Virgin."

"Yes."

"Do they eat the apples?"

"That's what my understanding is."

O rubbed the back of his neck. He'd been reticent about bringing up the whole turning-his-wife-into-a-*lesser* thing during his session with the Omega. He needed to find out if she was alive first, and then he had to work up some spin for the concept. Obviously, the potentially insurmountable problem was that she was a vampire, and the only counterpoint he could make on that was that she'd be the ultimate secret weapon. A female of their own species? The Brotherhood would never see that coming. . . .

Although, of course, that was just rationale for the Omega. His wife would never fight anyone but him.

Yeah, the proposal was going to be a hard sell, but one thing he had going for him was that the Omega was open to flattery. So wouldn't a big, splashy sacrifice in his honor do wonders to soften him up?

U was still talking. ". . . thinking was that I could check out the markets . . ."

As U droned on, O started thinking about poison. A whole lot of poison. A vat of the stuff.

Poisoned apples. How Snow White was that?

"O? You there?"

"Yeah."

"So I'm going to go to the markets and find out when—"

"Not right now you're not. Lemme tell you what you're going to do."

As Bella left Wrath's study she was shaking with rage, and neither the king nor Tohr tried to stop her or talk sense into her. Which proved they were highly intelligent males.

She pounded down the hall in her bare feet to Zsadist's room, and after she slammed the door shut, she went for the phone as if the thing were a weapon. She dialed her brother's cell.

Rehvenge picked up and snapped, "Who are you and how did you get this number?"

"Don't you dare do this to me."

There was a long silence. Then: "Bella . . . I— Hold on a second." A shuffling sound came through the phone; then he said in a cutting voice, "He'd better get over here right now. We clear? If I have to go after him, he's not going to like it." Rehvenge cleared his throat as he came back on. "Bella, where are you? Let me come pick you up. Or have one of the warriors take you to our house and I'll meet you there."

"You think I'm coming *anywhere* near you now?"

"It's better than the alternative," he said grimly.

"And what's that?"

"The Brothers forcibly returning you to me."

"Why are you doing—"

"Why am I doing this?" His voice sank into the deep, demanding bass she was so used to. "Do you have any idea what the last six weeks have been like for me? Knowing that you were in the hands of those goddamned things? Knowing that I put my sister . . . my mother's daughter . . . in that place?"

"It was not your fault—"

"You should have been home!"

As always, the sandblast of Rehv's fury shook her, and she was reminded that on some basic level her brother had always scared her a little.

But then she heard him take a deep breath. And another. Then a curious desperation crept into his words. "Christ, Bella . . . just come home. *Mahmen* and I, we need you here. We miss you. We . . . I need to see you to believe you're really okay."

Ah, yes . . . Now the other side of him, the one she actually loved. The protector. The provider. The tenderhearted, gruff male who had always given her everything she had ever needed.

The temptation to submit to him was strong. But then she pictured herself never being allowed out of the house again. Which was something he was damn well capable of doing to her.

"Will you rescind the *sehclusion* request?"

"We'll talk about it when you're sleeping in your own bed again."

Bella gripped the phone. "That means no, doesn't it?" There was a pause. "Hello? Rehvenge?"

"I just want you home."

"Yes or no, Rehv. Tell me now."

"Our mother can't live through something like this again."

"And you think I can?" she shot back. "Excuse me, but *mahmen* wasn't the one who ended up with a *lesser*'s name carved into her stomach!"

The instant the words left her mouth, she cursed. Yeah, that kind of happy little detail was *really* going to bring him around. *Way to negotiate.*

"Rehvenge—"

His voice went utterly cold. "I want you home."

"I've just been in captivity, I'm not volunteering for jail."

"And just what are you going to do about it?"

"Keep pushing me around and you'll find out."

She ended the call and slammed the cordless unit down on the bedside table. *Goddamn him!*

On a crazy impulse, she grabbed the receiver and spun around, ready to hurl it across the room.

"Zsadist!" She fumbled with the phone, catching it, holding it against her chest.

Standing silently next to the door, Zsadist was wearing running shorts and no shirt . . . and for some absurd reason she noticed that he didn't have shoes on either.

"Throw it if you want," he said.

"No. I . . . ah . . . no." She turned away and put the thing back on its little stand, taking two tries to get it in right.

Before she faced Zsadist again, she thought of him crouched over that *lesser,* beating it to death. . . . But then she remembered him bringing her things from her house . . . and taking her there . . . and letting her have his vein though he'd cracked wide-open at the invasion. As she pivoted around toward him, she was tangled in the net of him, caught between the kindness and the cruelty.

He broke the silence. "I don't want you running half-cocked into the night because of what your brother's up to. And don't tell me that isn't what you're thinking."

Damn, he was smart. "But you know what he wants to do to me."

"Yeah."

"And by law the Brotherhood will have to give me up, so I can't stay here. You think I like the only option I've got?"

Except where would she go?

"What's so bad about heading home?"

She glared at him. "Yeah, I really want to be treated like an incompetent, like a child, like . . . an object my brother *owns*. That works for me. Totally."

Zsadist ran a hand over his skull trim. The movement flexed his biceps so they squeezed up thick. "Makes sense to get families under one roof. It's a dangerous time for civilians."

Oh, man . . . The last thing she needed right now was him agreeing with her brother.

"Dangerous time for *lessers*, too," she muttered. "Going by what you did to that one tonight."

Zsadist's eyes narrowed. "If you want me to apologize for that, I won't."

"Of course you wouldn't," she snapped. "You don't apologize for anything."

He shook his head slowly. "You want to pick a fight with someone, you're talking to the wrong male, Bella. I won't go there with you."

"Why not? You excel at being pissed off."

The silence that followed made her want to scream at him. She was going after his anger, something he gave freely to all comers, and she couldn't figure out why the hell he was showing self-control when it came to her.

He cocked an eyebrow, as if he knew what she was thinking.

"Ah, hell," she breathed. "I'm just needling you, aren't I? Sorry."

He shrugged. "Rock and a hard place makes anyone crazy. Don't sweat it."

She sat down on the bed. The idea of running off alone was ludicrous, but she refused to live under Rehvenge's control.

"You got any suggestions?" she asked softly. When she raised her eyes, Zsadist was looking at the floor.

He was so self-contained leaning back against the wall like that. With his long, lean body, he looked like a flesh-colored crack in the plaster, a fissure that had opened up in the very structure of the room.

"Give me five minutes," he said. He walked out, still shirtless.

Bella let herself fall back on the mattress, thinking that five minutes wasn't going to help the situation. What she needed was a different brother waiting for her at home.

Dear, sweet Scribe Virgin ... Getting away from the *lessers* should have made things better. Instead, her life still seemed totally out of her control.

Granted, she could pick her own shampoo now, though.

She lifted her head. Through the bathroom door she saw the shower and imagined herself standing under a rush of hot water. That would be good. Relaxing. Refreshing. Plus she could cry out her frustration without embarrassment there.

She got up, went into the bath, and cranked on the water. The sound of the rush hitting the marble was soothing, and so was the warm spray as she got under it. She didn't end up crying. Just hung her head and let the water run down her body.

When she finally stepped out, she noticed that the door to the bedroom had been shut.

Zsadist was probably back.

Wrapping a towel around herself, she had no hope whatsoever that he'd found a solution.

Chapter Twenty-six

When the bathroom door opened, Z looked over and kept his curse to himself. Bella was rosy from head to foot, her hair knotted up high on her head. She smelled like that fancy French soap Fritz insisted on buying. And that towel wrapped around her body just made him think how easy it would be to get her totally naked.

One pull. That was all he'd need.

"Wrath's agreed to be temporarily unreachable," he said. "Which is only a delay of forty-eight hours or so. Talk to your brother. See if you can bring him around. Otherwise Wrath has to respond, and he can't really say no, given your blood-line."

Bella hitched the towel up a little higher. "Okay . . . thank you. Thank you for making the effort."

He nodded and eyed the door, thinking it was back to plan A: running himself into the ground. Either that or having Phury go at him.

Except instead of leaving, he put his hands on his hips. "I am sorry for something."

"What? Oh . . . Why?"

"I'm sorry that you had to see what I did to that slayer." He lifted his hand, then dropped it, resisting the urge to rub his head raw. "When I said I won't apologize for it, I meant I

never regret killing those bastards. But I didn't . . . I don't like
you having those images in your head. I'd take them from you
if I could. I'd take all of this from you . . . bear it all for you.
I'm so . . . fucking sorry this happened to you, Bella. Yeah,
I'm just sorry about the whole thing, including . . . me."

This was his good-bye to her, he realized. And he was running out of steam, so he hurried his last words.

"You're a female of worth." He hung his head. "And I
know that you'll find . . ."

A mate, he finished to himself. Yeah, a female like her
would most certainly find a mate. In fact, there was one in this
very house who not only wanted her, but was right for her.
Phury was just around the corner, as a matter of fact.

Z looked up, intending to beat feet out of the room—and
jerked back against the door.

Bella was right in front of him. As he caught her scent up
close, his heart went jackrabbit on him, doing some kind of
flutter thing that got him light-headed.

"Is it true you cleaned up my house?" she said.

Oh, man . . . The only answer he had to that was too
revealing.

"Is it?"

"Yeah, I did that."

"I'm going to hug you now."

Z stiffened, but before he could get himself out of the way,
her arms wrapped around his waist and her head came up
against his bare chest.

He stood in her embrace without moving, without breathing, without returning it . . . All he could do was feel her
body. She was a tall female, but he had a good six inches on
her. And even though he was thin for a warrior, he carried at
least seventy pounds more on his bones than she did. And still
she overwhelmed him.

God, she smelled good.

She made a little noise, like a sigh, and burrowed into his
body even more. Her breasts pressed against his torso, and as
he looked down, the curve of her nape was too damn tempt-

ing. Then there was the *it* problem. That godforsaken thing
was hardening, swelling, lengthening. Fast.

He put his hands up to her shoulders, hovering just above
her skin. "Yeah, ah, Bella . . . I've got to go."

"Why?" Closer. She came closer. Her hips moved against
his, and he gritted his teeth as their lower bodies made full
contact.

Shit, she had to be feeling that thing between his legs. How
could she miss it? The stiff was pushing into her belly, and it
wasn't like the flipping shorts could hide the bastard.

"Why do you have to go?" she whispered, her breath
brushing over his pecs.

"Because . . ."

When he let the word drift, she murmured, "You know, I
like these."

"Like what?"

She touched one of his nipple rings. "These."

He coughed a little. "I, ah . . . I did them myself."

"They're beautiful on you." She stepped back and dropped
the towel.

Z swayed. She was so damned beautiful, those breasts and
that flat stomach and those hips. . . . And that graceful little
slit between her legs that he saw with shattering clarity. The
few humans he'd been with had had hair there, but she was of
his kind, so she was utterly bare, achingly smooth.

"I really have to go," he said hoarsely.

"Don't run."

"I have to. If I stay . . ."

"Lay with me," she said, easing up against him once more.
She pulled the tie in her hair out, and dark waves spilled all
over both of them.

He closed his eyes and tilted his head back, trying not to
get buried by her scent. In a gritty voice, he said, "Do you just
want to get fucked, Bella? Because that's all I've got in me."

"You have so much more—"

"I do not."

"You've been kind to me. You've taken care of me. You've
washed me and held me—"

"You don't want me inside of you."

"You already are, Zsadist. Your blood is in me."

There was a long silence. "Do you know my reputation?"

She frowned. "That's not relevant—"

"What do people say about me, Bella? Come on, I want to hear it from you. So I know you get it." Her despair was palpable as he pushed her, but he had to snap her out of whatever daze she was in. "I know you must have heard about me. Gossip reaches even your social level. *What do they say?*"

"Some . . . some think you kill females for sport. But I don't believe—"

"Do you know how I got that rep?"

Bella covered her breasts and stepped back, shaking her head. He bent down and handed her the towel, then pointed to the skull in the corner.

"I murdered that female. Now tell me, do you want to be taken by a male who could do something like that? Who could hurt a female like that? You want that kind of bastard on top of you, pumping into your body?"

"It was her," Bella whispered. "You went back and killed your mistress, didn't you?"

Z shuddered. "For a while I thought it could make me whole."

"It didn't."

"No shit." He brushed by her and walked around, pressure building in him until he opened his mouth and the words just shot out. "A couple of years after I got out, I heard she . . . shit, I heard she had another male in that cell. I . . . I traveled for two days straight and snuck in close to dawn." Z shook his head. He didn't want to talk, he really didn't, but his mouth just kept moving. "Christ . . . he was so young, so *young*, just like I was when she got me. And I didn't have any intention of killing her, but she came down right as I was leaving with the slave. When I looked at her . . . I knew if I didn't strike, she was going to call for her guards. I also knew that eventually she would take another male and chain him down there and make him . . . Ah, fuck. Why the hell am I telling you this?"

"I love you."

Z squeezed his eyes shut. "Don't be a tragedy, Bella."

He left the room in a rush, but couldn't go more than fifteen feet down the hall.

She loved him. *She loved him?*

Bullshit. She *thought* she loved him. And as soon as she got back to the real world, she was going to realize that. Christ, she'd come out of a horrific situation and was living in a bubble here at the compound. None of this was her life, and she was spending too much time with him.

And yet . . . God, he wanted to be with her. Wanted to lie side by side and kiss her. Wanted to do even more than that. Wanted . . . to do it all to her, the kissing and the touching and the sucking and the licking. But where exactly did he think all that was going to lead to? Even if he could get past the idea of penetrating her for the sex, he didn't want to risk coming inside of her.

Not that he'd ever done that with any female. Hell, he'd never ejaculated under any circumstances. When he'd been a blood slave, it wasn't as if he'd ever been sexually excited. And afterward, when he was with those few whores he'd bought and fucked, he hadn't been after an orgasm. Those anonymous interludes were just experiments to see whether sex was as bad as it always had been for him.

As for masturbating, he couldn't stand touching the damn thing to take a piss, much less when it stood up for attention. And he'd never wanted to relieve himself, never been all that aroused, even when the *it* was hard.

Man, he was so whacked with the sex shit. Like there was a short in his brain.

Actually, he had a lot of them, didn't he?

He thought about all the holes in him, the blank places, the voids where others felt things. When it came down to it, he was really just a screen, more empty than solid, his emotions blowing through him, only the anger catching and holding.

Except that wasn't entirely true, was it? Bella made him feel things. When she had kissed him on the bed before, she had made him feel . . . hot and hungry. Very male. Sexual, for the first time in his life.

From out of a sharp desperation, some echo of what he'd been before the Mistress had had him started looking for air-time. He found himself wanting again that feeling he'd gotten from kissing Bella. And he wanted to crank her up, too. He wanted her gasping and breathless and starved.

It wasn't fair to her . . . but he was a son of a bitch, and he was greedy for what she'd given him before. And she would be leaving soon. He had this one day now.

Zsadist opened the door and went back inside.

Bella was lying in the bed and obviously surprised he was back. As she sat up, the sight of her brought back a lick of de-cency. How the hell could he be with her? God, she was so . . . beautiful, and he was nasty, a nasty bastard.

His momentum lost, he stalled in the middle of the room. *Prove you're not a bastard by bailing,* he thought. *But explain yourself first.*

"I want to be with you, Bella, and not to fuck you, either." As she started to say something, he silenced her by holding up his hand. "Please, just listen to me. I want to be with you, but I don't think I've got it in me to give you what you need. I'm not the right male for you, and this is definitely the wrong time."

He released his breath, thinking he was such an asshole. Here he was telling her no, playing the gentleman . . . while in his mind he was yanking back those sheets and replacing them with a blanket of his own skin.

The thing hanging from the front of his hips pounded like a jackhammer.

What would she taste like, he wondered, in that soft, sweet place between her legs?

"Come over here, Zsadist." She opened the covers, baring herself to him. "Stop thinking. Come to bed."

"I . . ." Words he'd never spoken to anyone hovered on his lips, a confession of sorts, a treacherous unveiling. He looked away and let them go for no good reason he could think of. "Bella, when I was a slave things were . . . ah, things were done to me. Sexual shit." He should stop. Right now. "There were males, Bella. Against my will, there were males."

He heard a little gasping sound.

This was good, he thought, even as he cringed. Maybe he could get her to save herself by revolting her. Because what female could stand being with a male who'd had that kind of thing done to him? Not the heroic ideal. Not by a long shot.

He cleared his throat and stared a hole right through the floor. "Look, I'm not . . . I don't want your pity. The reason I'm telling you this is not to sap you out. It's just . . . I'm scrambled. It's like my wires are all crossed when it comes to the whole . . . you know, the fucking thing. I want you, but it's not right. You shouldn't be with me. You're cleaner than that."

There was a long silence. *Ah, shit* . . . He had to look at her. The moment he did, she rose from the bed as if she'd been waiting for him to lift his eyes. She walked to him naked, nothing on her skin except the candlelight from the single wick that burned.

"Kiss me," she whispered in the dimness. "Just kiss me."

"God . . . what is wrong with you?" As she winced, he said, "I mean, why? Of all the males you could have, why me?"

"I want you." She put her hand on his chest. "It's a natural, normal response to the opposite sex, isn't it?"

"I'm not normal."

"I know. But you're not dirty or contaminated or unworthy." She took his shaking hands and placed them on her shoulders.

Her skin was so fine, the idea of marring it in any way froze him. So did the image of him pushing the *it* into her. Except he didn't have to involve the lower half of his body, did he? This could be all about her.

Oh, yeah, he thought. This could be for her.

He turned her around and drew her back against his body. With slow sweeps he ran his hands up and down the curves of her waist and hips. When she arched her spine and sighed, he could see the tips of her breasts over her shoulder. He wanted to touch her there . . . and realized he could. He moved his hands over her rib cage, feeling up the pattern of delicate bones until his palms enveloped her breasts. Her head kicked back farther and her mouth parted.

As she opened for him like that, he had a screaming instinct to get inside of her any way he could. On reflex, he licked his upper lip while he rolled one of her nipples between his thumb and forefinger. He imagined himself thrusting his tongue into her mouth, going in between her teeth and fangs, taking her in that way.

Like she knew what he was thinking, she tried to turn and face him, but it seemed too close somehow . . . too real that she was giving herself to him, that she was going to let someone like him do intimate, erotic things to her body. He stopped her by grabbing her hips and pulling her hard into his thighs. He ground his teeth at the feel of her ass against that stiff thing straining his shorts.

"Zsadist . . . let me kiss you." She tried to turn around again and he stopped her.

As she struggled in his hold, he kept her in place easily. "It'll be better for you this way. If you can't see me, it'll be better."

"No, it won't."

He put his head down on her shoulder. "If I could just get Phury for you . . . I used to look like him once. You could pretend it's me."

She yanked her body free of his hands. "But it wouldn't be. And it's you I want."

As she looked at him with feminine expectation, he realized they were headed for the bed right behind her. And they were going to get down to it. But, God . . . he had no idea how to make her feel good. He might as well have been a virgin for all the shit he knew about pleasuring a female.

With that happy little revelation, he thought about the other male she'd had, that aristocrat who undoubtedly knew so much more about sex than he did. From out of nowhere, he was struck by a totally irrational urge to hunt down her previous lover and bleed him out.

Oh . . . hell. He closed his eyes. *Oh . . . shit.*

"What?" she asked.

This kind of violent, territorial impulse was characteristic of a bonded male. The hallmark of one, actually.

Z lifted his arm, put his nose to his bicep, and breathed in deep. . . . The bonding scent was coming out of his skin. It was faint, probably only recognizable to him, but it was there.

Shit. Now what was he going to do?

Unfortunately, his instincts answered. As his body roared, he picked her up and headed for the bed.

Chapter Twenty-seven

Bella stared at Zsadist's face while he carried her across the room. His black eyes were narrowed into slits, a dark, erotic greed glittering in them. As he put her on the bed and looked down at her body, she had the distinct thought that he was going to eat her alive.

Except he just loomed over her.

"Arch your back for me," he demanded.

Okay . . . not what she expected.

"Arch your back, Bella."

Feeling oddly exposed, she did as he asked, craning her body off the mattress. As she moved on the bed, she glanced at the front of his shorts. His erection gave a mighty jerk, and the idea that it was going to be inside of her soon helped loosen her up.

He reached down and brushed one of her nipples with his knuckle. "I want this in my mouth."

A delicious greed of her own took root. "Then kiss—"

"Shh." His knuckle traveled in between her breasts and down her stomach. He stopped when he got to her belly button. Took his forefinger and ran a little circle around her navel. Then paused.

"Don't stop," she moaned.

He didn't. He went lower until he brushed across the top

of her cleft. She bit her lip and eyed his body, that huge, warrior frame with all that stark, hard muscle. *God . . .* She was really getting ready for him.

"Zsadist—"

"I'm going to want to go down on you. And I won't be able to stop myself." With his free hand he rubbed his lips, as if he were imagining the act. "You prepared to let me do that?"

"Yes . . ."

He fingered the distorted side of his mouth as he stroked her slit. "Wish I had something better-looking to offer you. Because you're going to be perfect down there. I know it."

She hated the shame that came through his pride. "I think you're—"

"You've got one last chance to tell me no, Bella. If you don't right now, I'm going to be all over you. No stopping, and I don't think I can be gentle about it."

She held her arms out to him. He nodded once, as if they'd made some kind of pact, and then went to the end of the bed.

"Spread your legs. I want to see you."

A nervous flush came over her.

He shook his head. "Too late, Bella. Now . . . it's too late. Show me."

Slowly she cocked one of her knees up and gradually revealed herself.

His face melted, the tension and the harshness bleeding out of him. "Oh . . . God . . ." he whispered. "You're . . . beautiful."

Leaning down onto his arms, he prowled up the bed to her body, his eyes fixated on her secret skin as if he'd never seen anything like it. When he got in range, wide hands smoothed their way up the insides of her thighs, opening them even farther.

But then he frowned and looked up at her. "Wait, I'm supposed to kiss you on the mouth first, aren't I? I mean, males start at the top and work their way down, don't they?"

What an odd question . . . like he'd never done this at all?

Before she could reply he began to move back, so she sat up and captured his face in her hands.

"You can do whatever you like to me."

His eyes flashed and he held his position for a split second. Then he lunged at her, taking her down onto the bed. His tongue shot into her mouth and his hands tangled in her hair, pulling on her, arching her, trapping her head. The hunger in him was ferocious, a warrior's thick-blooded need for sex. He was going to take her with all the strength he had, and she was going to be sore when he was through using her. Sore and utterly blissed out. She couldn't wait.

Suddenly, he stopped and pulled back from her mouth. He was breathing deeply and had a flush on his cheeks as he looked her in the eye.

And then he smiled at her.

She was so surprised she didn't know what to do. She'd never seen that expression on his face before, and the lift in his mouth did away with the distortion in his upper lip, showing off his gleaming teeth and fangs.

"I like this," he said. "You underneath me . . . You feel good. You're soft and warm. Do I weigh too much? Here, let me . . ."

As he propped himself up on his arms, his arousal pressed into her core and his grin faded quick as a gasp. It was as if he didn't like the sensation, but how could that be? He was aroused. She could feel his erection.

With a lithe move he repositioned himself so her legs were closed and his knees were on either side of them. She couldn't guess what had happened, but wherever he'd gone in his head was not a good place.

"You're perfect on top of me," she said to distract him. "Except for one thing."

"What?"

"You've stopped. And lose the shorts."

His weight came down on her immediately and his mouth went to the side of her neck. As he nipped at her skin, she pushed her head back into the pillow and bared the column of her throat. Gripping the back of his head, she urged him against her vein.

"Oh, yes . . ." she moaned, wanting him to feed.

He made a noise that was a no, but before the rejection could ripple through her, he was kissing his way down to her collarbone.

"I want to latch onto your breast," he said against her skin. "Do it."

"You need to know something first."

"What?"

He lifted his head. "The night you came here . . . when I bathed you? I did my best not to look at you. I really did. I covered you with a towel even though you were in the water."

"That was kind—"

"But when I took you out . . . I saw these." His hand captured one of her breasts. "I couldn't help it. I swear. I tried to allow you your modesty, but you were . . . I couldn't stop my eyes. Your nipple was tight from the chill of the air. So small and pink. Lovely."

He moved his thumb back and forth across her hard tip, scrambling her mind.

"It's all right," she mumbled.

"It wasn't. You were defenseless and I was wrong to look at you."

"No, you—"

He shifted, and his erection pressed into the top of her thighs. "This happened."

"What hap— Oh, you got aroused?"

His mouth tightened. "Yeah. I couldn't stop it."

She smiled a little. "But you didn't do anything, right?"

"No."

"So it's okay." She arched her back and watched as his eyes clung to her breasts. "Kiss me, Zsadist. Right where you're looking. Right now."

His lips parted, and his tongue led the way as he dipped down. His mouth was warm on her flesh, and so very tentative, kissing, then sucking her nipple inside. He tugged, then ran a languid circle around her, then drew her in again . . . and all the while his hands stroked her waist and her hips and her legs.

How ironic that he'd worried he wouldn't be gentle. Far

from brutal, he was positively reverent as he suckled, his lashes down against his cheek as he savored her, his face worshipful and rapt.

"Christ," he murmured, moving to her other breast. "I had no idea it would be like this."

"How . . . so?" *Oh, God* . . . His mouth . . .

"I could tongue you forever."

She grasped his head with her hands, pulling him closer. And it took some wriggling, but she managed to split her legs and get one out from under him so that he was almost lying in the cradle of her body. She was dying to feel his arousal, except he just hovered over her.

When he pulled back she protested, but then his hands went to the insides of her thighs and he moved down her body. As he spread her legs, the mattress began to quiver underneath her.

Zsadist's whole body shook as he looked at her. "You're so delicate . . . and you glisten."

The first stroke of his finger down her core nearly threw her over the edge. As she let out a hoarse sound, his eyes flashed to hers and he cursed. "Goddamn it, I don't know what I'm doing. I'm trying to be careful—"

She grabbed his hand before he could take it away. "More . . ."

He looked doubtful for a moment. Then he touched her again. "You're perfect. And God, you're soft. I've got to know . . ."

He leaned down, his shoulders bunching up hard. She felt a velvet brush.

His lips.

This time when she jacked up off the bed and said his name, he just pressed another kiss to her again, and then there was the wet stroke of his tongue. As he lifted his head and swallowed, the growl of ecstasy he made stopped her heart in her chest. Their eyes met.

"Oh . . . Jesus . . . you're delicious," he said, going back down with his mouth.

He stretched out on the bed, looping his arms under her

knees and overflowing the space between her thighs . . . a male who wasn't going anywhere for a long while. His breath was hot and needy, his mouth hungry and desperate. He explored her with an erotic compulsion, licking and probing with his tongue, sucking with his lips.

When her hips bucked, one of his arms moved across her stomach, holding her in place. She lurched again and he paused without lifting his head.

"Are you okay?" he asked, raspy voice muffled, words vibrating into her core.

"Please . . ." It was the only thing that came to mind.

He pulled back a little, and all she could do was look at his glossy lips and think of where they had been.

"Bella, I don't think I can stop. There's this . . . roar in my head telling me to keep my mouth on you. How can I make this . . . okay for you?"

"Make me . . . finish me," she said hoarsely.

He blinked as if she'd surprised him. "How do I make you come?"

"Just keep doing what you're doing. Only faster."

He was a quick study as he figured out what made her go wild, and he was ruthless once he discovered how to give her an orgasm. He drove her hard, watching her as she shattered apart once, twice . . . many times. It was as if he fed from her pleasure and was insatiable.

When he finally lifted his head, she was limp.

He looked at her gravely. "Thank you."

"God . . . I'm the one who should be saying that."

He shook his head. "You let an animal into the most beautiful part of you. I'm the one with the gratitude."

He pushed away from her body, that flush of arousal still in his cheeks. That erection still straining.

She held her arms out to him. "Where are you going? We're not done."

As he hesitated, she remembered. She rolled over onto her stomach and braced herself up on all fours, a shameless offer. When he didn't move, she looked back at him. He'd closed his eyes as if in pain, and that confused her.

"I know you only do it this way," she said softly. "That's what you told me. It's okay with me. Really." There was a long silence. "Zsadist, I want to finish this between us. I want to know you . . . like this."

He rubbed his face. She thought he was going to leave, but then he shifted around so he was behind her. His hands fell lightly on her hips and he urged her to one side, onto her back.

"But you only—"

"Not with you." His voice was rough. "Not like that with you."

She opened her legs, ready for him, but he just sat back on his heels.

His breath left on a shudder. "Let me get a condom."

"Why? I'm not fertile now, so you don't need one. And I want you to . . . finish."

His brows dropped low over his black eyes.

"Zsadist . . . this hasn't been enough for me. I want to be with you."

She was about to reach for him when he rose up onto his knees and brought his hands to the front of his running shorts. He fumbled with the drawstring and then pulled the elastic waistband out and down, revealing himself.

Bella swallowed hard.

His arousal was *enormous*. A perfectly beautiful, rock-solid aberration of nature.

Holy . . . Moses. Would he even fit?

His hands trembled as he hooked the shorts under the twin weights below his erection. Then he leaned over her body, positioning himself at her core.

When she put her hand out to stroke him, he jerked away. *"No!"* As she recoiled, he cursed. "I'm sorry. . . . Look, just let me take care of it."

He moved his hips forward and she felt the head of him, blunt and hot, against her. His hand came behind one of her knees and he stretched her leg up; then he pushed inside a little, then a little farther. As sweat bloomed over his entire body, a dark scent reached her nose. For a moment, she wondered if . . .

No, he couldn't be bonding with her. It wasn't in his nature.

"God . . . you're tight," he croaked. "Oh . . . *Bella,* I don't want to tear you up."

"Keep going. Just be slow."

Her body surged under the pressure and the stretching. Even as ready as she was he was an invasion, but she loved it, especially as his breath exploded out of his chest and he shuddered. When he was all the way in, his mouth fell open, his fangs elongating from the pleasure he felt.

She ran her hands up his shoulders, feeling the muscles and the warmth of him.

"This all right?" he asked through gritted teeth.

Bella pressed a kiss to the side of his neck and swiveled her hips. He hissed.

"Make love to me," she said.

He moaned and started to move like a great wave on top of her, that thick, hard part of him stroking the inside of her.

"Oh, shit . . ." He dropped his head into her neck. His rhythm intensified, his breath shooting out of him, rushing into her ear. "Bella . . . shit, I'm scared . . . but I can't . . . stop. . . ."

With a groan he propped himself up on his arms and let his hips swing freely, each thrust nailing against her, pushing her farther up on the bed. She grabbed for his wrists to hold her body in place under the onslaught. As he pounded, she could feel herself getting near the edge again, and the faster he went, the closer she got.

Her orgasm slammed into her core, then raced throughout her body, the force of it stretching her out so she was infinitely long and infinitely wide. The sensations lasted forever, the contractions of her inner muscles grabbing onto the part of him that penetrated her.

When she was back in her own skin again, she realized he was unmoving, completely frozen above her. Blinking away tears, she looked into his face. The hard angles of it were tense, and so was the rest of his body.

"Did I hurt you?" he asked tightly. "You cried out. Loudly."

She touched his face. "Not from pain."

"Thank God." His shoulders eased as he exhaled. "I couldn't bear to hurt you like this."

He kissed her softly. And then he withdrew and got off the bed, yanking up the shorts as he went into the bathroom and closed the door.

Bella frowned. Had he finished? He'd seemed fully erect as he'd withdrawn.

She slid out of bed and looked down. When there was nothing on the inside of her thighs, she drew on the robe and went after him, not even bothering to knock.

Zsadist's arms were propped on the sink, his head hanging low. He was breathing uneasily and looked fevered, his skin slick, his stance unnaturally stiff.

"What, *nalla*," he said in a hoarse whisper.

She stopped, unsure she'd heard him right. But she had. . . . *Beloved.* He'd called her *beloved.*

"Why didn't you . . ." She couldn't seem to get the rest of the words out. "Why did you stop before you . . ."

When he just shook his head, she went over to him and turned him around. Through the shorts she could see that his arousal was throbbing, painfully rigid. In fact, he looked as if his whole body ached.

"Let me ease you," she said, reaching for him.

He backed up against the marble wall between the shower and the sink. "No, don't . . . Bella—"

She gathered the robe in her hands and started to kneel down at his feet.

"No!" He dragged her up his body.

She met him right in the eye and went for his waistband. "Let me do this for you."

He grabbed her hands and squeezed her wrists until they hurt.

"I want to do this, Zsadist," she said with strength. "Let me take care of you."

There was a long silence, and she spent the time measuring the sorrow and the yearning and the fear in his eyes. A chill shot through her. She couldn't believe the leap of logic her mind was taking, but she had a really vivid impression that he'd never let himself orgasm before. Or was she just jumping to conclusions?

Whatever. It wasn't like she was about to ask him. He was teetering on the brink of bolting, and if she said or did the wrong thing, he was going to tear out of the room.

"Zsadist, I won't hurt you. And you can be in control. We'll stop if it doesn't feel right. You can trust me."

It was a long time before his grip loosened on her wrists. And then finally he let go and set her back from his body. Haltingly, he pulled down the shorts.

That arousal shot out into the space between them.

"Just hold on to it," he said with a cracked voice.

"You. I'll hold on to you."

When she wrapped her palms around him he let out a moan, and his head fell back. God, he was hard. Hard as iron, yet surrounded by skin soft as his lips.

"You're—"

"Shh," he cut in. "No . . . talking. I can't . . . No talking."

He began to move in her grip. Slowly at first, and then with increasing urgency. He took her face in his hands and kissed her, and then his body completely took over with a wild pumping. He was going crazy, shooting higher and higher, his chest and hips so beautiful as he moved in that ancient male surging motion. Faster . . . faster . . . jerking back and forth . . .

Except then he reached some kind of plateau. He was straining, the cords of his neck nearly breaking through his skin, his body covered with sweat. But he couldn't seem to let go.

He stopped, panting. "This isn't going to work."

"Just relax. Relax and let it happen—"

"No. I need . . ." He took one of her hands and placed it on the sac below his arousal. "Squeeze. Squeeze hard."

Bella's eyes flashed up to his face. "What? I don't want to hurt you—"

He wrapped his hand around hers like a vise and twisted their grips until he cried out. Then he held her other wrist, keeping her palm against his erection.

She struggled against him, fighting to stop the pain he was inflicting on himself, but he was pumping again. And the harder she tried to pull away, the more he crushed her hand to that most tender place on a male. Her eyes went wide and unblinking at the pain of the act, the agony he must be—

Zsadist shouted, his loud bark ricocheting around the marble until she was sure everyone in the mansion must have heard him. Then she felt the mighty jerks of his release, hot pulses dampening her hands and the front of her robe.

He sagged onto her shoulders, his massive body falling all over her. He was breathing like a freight train, his muscles quivering, his big body trembling with aftershocks. When he released his hand from hers, she had to peel her palm from his testicles.

Bella was cold to the bone as she bore the weight of him.

Something ugly had sprouted between them just now, some kind of sexual evil that blurred the distinction between pleasure and pain. And though it made her cruel, she wanted to get away from him. She wanted to run from the cringing awareness that she had hurt him because he'd made her and he had orgasmed because of it.

Except then his breath caught on a sob. Or at least seemed to.

She held her breath, listening. The soft sound came again, and she felt his shoulders quake.

Oh, my God. He was crying. . . .

She wrapped her arms around him, reminding herself that he hadn't asked to be tortured as he'd been. Nor had he volunteered for the aftereffects.

She tried to lift his head to kiss him, but he fought against her, drawing her close, hiding in her hair. She cradled him, holding him and soothing him as he struggled to mask the fact that he wept. Eventually he pulled back and scrubbed his face with his palms. He refused to meet her eyes as he reached over and turned the shower on.

With a quick yank he stripped the robe from her body, then wadded it up and threw it into the trash.

"Wait, I like that robe—"

"I'll buy you a new one."

He urged her under the water. When she fought him he picked her up easily, put her in the spray, and began to soap her hands with undisguised panic.

"Zsadist, stop it." She pulled away, but he caught her. "I'm not dirty—Zsadist, *stop*. I don't need to be cleaned because you—"

He closed his eyes. "Please . . . I have to do this. I can't leave you all . . . covered with that stuff."

"Zsadist," she snapped. "Look at me." When he did, she said, "This is not necessary."

"I don't know what else to do."

"Come back to bed with me." She shut off the water. "Hold me. Let me hold you. That's the only thing you need to do."

And frankly, she needed it, too. She was rattled to the core.

She put a towel around herself and pulled him into the bedroom. When they were under the covers together, she curled herself around him, but she was as stiff as he was. She'd thought proximity would help. It didn't.

After a long while his voice came through the darkness. "If I had known how it had to be, I never would have allowed that to happen."

She turned her face up to his. "Was that the first time you ever came?"

The silence wasn't a surprise. That he eventually answered her was.

"Yeah."

"You've never . . . pleasured yourself?" she whispered, even though she knew the answer. *God* . . . What those years as a blood slave must have been like. All that abuse . . . She wanted to weep for him but knew he would feel awkward about it.

He exhaled. "I don't like to touch it at all. Frankly, I hate the fact that it was inside of you. I want you to be in a tub right now, surrounded by bleach."

"I loved being with you. I'm glad we laid together." It was only what had come later that she'd had difficulty with. "But about what happened in the bathroom—"

"I don't want you to be a part of that. I don't want you doing that to me so I . . . do that all over you."

"I liked giving you an orgasm. It's just . . . I care for you too much to hurt you. Maybe we could try—"

He pulled away. "I'm sorry . . . I have to . . . I'm going to V's. I've got some work to do."

She grabbed his arm. "What if I told you I thought you were beautiful?"

"I'd say you were riding a pity wave and it would piss me off."

"I'm not feeling sorry for you. I wish you'd finished inside of me, and I think you're gorgeous when you're aroused. You're thick and long, and I was dying to touch you. I still am. And I want to take you in my mouth. How about that?"

He shrugged out of her hold and got to his feet. With quick, jabbing motions, he got dressed. "If you need to cast that sex in a different light so you can deal with it, that's fine. But you're lying to yourself right now. In no time at all you're going to wake up to the fact that you're still a female of worth. And then you're going to regret the shit out of laying with me."

"I will not."

"Wait for it."

He was out the door before she could find the proper words to throw back at him.

Bella crossed her arms over her chest and seethed with frustration. Then she kicked off the covers. Damn, but it was hot in this room. Or maybe she was so worked up, she'd screwed with her internal chemistry.

Unable to stay in bed, she dressed and went down the hall of statues. She didn't care where she ended up; she just had to get out and walk off some of this heat.

Chapter Twenty-eight

Zsadist stopped in the underground tunnel, halfway between the main house and Vishous and Butch's place.

When he looked behind himself there was nothing but a row of ceiling lights. In front of him there was more of the same, a strip of glowing patches that went on and on. The door he'd entered from and the door he would exit out of were both unseen to him.

Well, wasn't this a perfect fucking metaphor for life.

He settled against the steel wall of the tunnel, feeling trapped in spite of the fact that he was held by nothing and no one.

Oh, but that was bullshit. Bella was trapping him. Chaining him. Tying him up with her beautiful body and her kind heart and that misplaced chimera of love that glowed in her sapphire eyes. Trapped . . . He was so trapped.

With a sudden shift, his mind latched onto the night Phury finally got him away from the slavery.

When the Mistress had shown up with yet another male, the slave had been disinterested. After ten decades the eyes of other males no longer bothered him, and the rapes and the invasions had no new horrors to teach him. His exis-

tence was an even-keeled stretch of hell, the only real torture resting in the infinite nature of his captivity.

But then he'd sensed something odd. Something . . . different. He'd turned his head and looked at the stranger. His
first thought was that the male was huge and dressed with
expense, so he had to be a warrior. His next was that the
yellow eyes staring at him held a shocking misery. Verily,
the stranger standing in the doorway had paled until his
skin was waxy.

When the smell of the salve assaulted the slave's nose,
he went back to looking at the ceiling, uninterested in what
would happen next. Yet as his manhood was manipulated, a
wave of emotion surged in the room. He looked back to the
male who was standing just inside the cell. The slave
frowned. The warrior was reaching for a dagger and looking at the Mistress as if he were going to kill—

The other door burst open and one of the courtmen
spoke with panic. Suddenly the cell was filled with guards
and weapons and anger. The Mistress was grabbed roughly by
the male at the front of the group and slapped so hard she
hit the stone wall. Then the male went for the slave, unsheathing a knife. The slave screamed as he saw the blade
come at his face. A searing pain cut through his forehead
and nose and cheek; then blackness claimed him.

When the slave came to consciousness, he was hanging
by his neck, the weight of his arms and legs and torso choking the life right out of him. His mental reappearance was
as if his body knew his last breath was coming and had
awoken him on the off chance his brain could help. A sorry
attempt at rescue, he thought.

Dear Virgin, shouldn't he feel pain? And he wondered if
he had been splashed with water, for his skin was wet. Then
he realized something thick was dripping into his eyes. His
blood. He was covered in his own blood.

And what was all that noise around him? Swords? Fighting?

While choking he lifted his eyes, and for a split second
all manner of suffocation left him. The sea. He was looking

out at the vast sea. Joy soared for a moment . . . and then his vision swam from lack of air. His lids flickered and he sagged, though he was grateful that he'd seen the ocean once more before he died. He pondered vaguely whether the Fade would be anything like that vast horizon, an infinite expanse that was both unknowable and a home.

Just as he saw a shining white light before him, the pressure at his throat ceased and his body was handled roughly. There were shouts and jerky movements, then a jarring, bouncing ride that ended abruptly. Along the way, agony bloomed all over him, rushing into his bones, beating at him with dull, pounding fists.

Two shots from a gun. Grunts of pain that were not his own. And then a scream and a blast of wind on his back. Falling . . . he was in the air, falling . . .

Oh, God, the ocean. Panic spread through him. The salt—

He felt the hard cushion of the water for only a moment before the sensation of the sea hitting his raw skin overloaded his mind. He blacked out.

When he came to once more, his body was nothing more than a loose sack holding in aches. He realized dimly that he was freezing cold on one side, moderately warm on the other, and he moved to see if he could. As soon as he did, he felt the warmth against him shift in response. . . . He was in an embrace. A male was against the back of him.

The slave shoved the hard body away from his own and dragged himself through the dirt. His blurry vision showed him the way, pulling a boulder out of the blackness, giving him something to hide behind. When he was sheltered he breathed through the discomfort of his vitals, smelling the brine of the sea and the wretched decay of dead fish.

And as well a tinny scent. A sharp, tinny . . .

He peered around the edge of the rock. Though his eyes were weak, he was able to pick out the form of the male who had come into the cell with the Mistress. The warrior was sitting up against the wall now, his long hair hanging in

*strings down his thick shoulders. His fancy clothes were
torn, and his yellow stare aglow with sorrow.*

That was the other smell, the slave thought. That sad
emotion the male was feeling had a scent.

As the slave sniffed again he felt an odd pulling in his
face, and he lifted his fingertips up to his cheek. There was
a groove, a rigid line in his skin. . . . He followed it up to his
forehead. Then down to his lip. And remembered the knife
blade coming at him. Remembered screaming as it cut.

The slave started to shiver and wrapped his arms around
himself.

"We should warm each other," the warrior said. "Truly,
that is all I was doing. I have no . . . designs upon you. I
would but ease you if I could."

Except all the Mistress's males had wanted to be with
the slave. That was why she brought them. She liked to
watch, too. . . .

Yet then the slave remembered the warrior raising that
dagger, looking as if he were going to gut the Mistress like
a pig.

The slave opened his mouth and asked hoarsely, "Who
are you, sire?"

His mouth didn't work as it had before, and his words
were garbled. He tried again, but the warrior cut him off.

"I heard your inquiry." The tinny smell of sadness got
stronger until it overrode even the fishy stench. "I am Phury.
I am . . . your brother."

"Nay." The slave shook his head. "Verily, I have no family. Sire."

"No, I'm not . . ." The male cleared his throat. "I am not
sire to you. And you have always had a family. You were taken
from us. I have searched for you for a century."

"I fear you wrong."

The warrior shifted as if he were going to get up, and the
slave jerked back, dropping his eyes and covering his head
with his arms. He couldn't bear to be beaten again, even if
he deserved it for his insubordination.

Quickly, he said in his now messy way, "I mean not to offend, sire. I offer only my respect to your better station."

"Sweet Virgin above." A strangled noise came from across the cave. "I will not strike you. You are safe. . . . With me, you are safe. You are found, my brother."

The slave shook his head again, unable to hear any of it, because he suddenly realized what was going to happen at nightfall, what had to happen. He was the property of the Mistress, which meant he would have to be given back.

"I beg of you," he moaned, "do not return me unto her. Kill me now. . . . Do not render me returned to her."

"I shall kill us both before I allow you to tarry there once more."

The slave looked up. The warrior's yellow eyes were burning through the darkness.

The slave stared into the glow for a passing time. And then he remembered, long, long ago, when he'd first awoken from his transition in capture. The Mistress had told him she loved his eyes . . . his canary yellow eyes.

Among his species, there were very few with irises of bright gold.

The words and the actions of the warrior began to penetrate. Why ever would a stranger fight to get him free?

The warrior shifted, winced, and picked up one of his thighs.

The male's lower leg was gone.

The slave's eyes grew wide at the lost limb. How had the warrior saved them both in the water with that injury? He must have struggled simply to keep himself afloat. Why had he not just let the slave go?

Only a blood tie could engender that kind of selflessness.

"You are my brother?" the slave mumbled through his ruined lip. "Verily, I am blood to you?"

"Aye. I am your twin."

The slave started to shake. "Untruth."

"Truth."

A curious dread set upon the slave, chilling him. He curled up into himself in spite of the raw flesh that covered

*him from head to foot. It had never occurred to him that he
was other than a slave, that he might have had a chance to
live differently . . . live as a male, not as property.*

*The slave rocked back and forth in the dirt. When he
stopped, he looked once again at the warrior. What of his
family? Why had this happened? Who was he? And . . .*

*"Do you know if I had a name?" the slave whispered.
"Was I ever given a name?"*

*The warrior drew a ragged breath, as if every one of his
ribs were broken.*

*"Your name is Zsadist." The warrior's breathing short-
ened and shortened until he choked out his words. "You are
the son . . . of Ahgony, a great warrior. You are the beloved
of our . . . mother, Naseen."*

*The warrior let out a wretched sob and dropped his head
into his hands.*

While he wept, the slave watched.

Zsadist shook his head, remembering those silent hours
that had followed. Phury and he had spent most of the time
just staring at each other. They'd both been in rough shape,
but Phury was the stronger of them even with his missing
limb. He'd gathered driftwood and strands of seaweed and
cobbled the stuff together into a rickety, unreliable raft. When
the sun had gone down they had dragged themselves into the
ocean and had floated down the coastline to freedom.

Freedom.

Yeah, right. He wasn't free; never had been. Those lost
years had stayed with him, the anger over what he'd been
cheated of and what had been done to him more alive than he
was.

He heard Bella saying that she loved him. And he wanted
to scream at something.

Instead, he started for the Pit. He had nothing worthy of
her except his vengeance, so he was damn well going to get
back to work. He would see all the *lessers* crushed before
him, stacked in the snow like logs, a testament to the only
thing he could offer her.

And as for the one who had taken her, the one who had
hurt her, there was a special death waiting for him. Z had no
love to give anyone. But the hatred he had he would channel
for Bella until the last breath left his lungs.

Chapter Twenty-nine

Phury lit a blunt and eyed the sixteen cans of Aqua Net that were lined up on Butch and V's coffee table. "What's doing with the hair spray? You boys going drag on us?"

Butch held up the length of PVC pipe he was punching a hole in. "Potato launcher, my man. Big fun."

"Excuse me?"

"Didn't you ever go to summer camp?"

"Basket weaving and woodcarving are for humans. No offense, but we have better things to teach our youngs."

"Ha! You haven't lived until you've gone on a midnight panty raid. Anyway, you put the potato in this end, you fill up the bottom with spray—"

"And then you light it," V cut in from his bedroom. He came out in a robe, rubbing a towel on his wet hair. "Makes a great noise."

"Great noise," Butch echoed.

Phury looked at his brother. "V, you've done this before?"

"Yeah, last night. But the launcher jammed up."

Butch cursed. "Potato was too big. Damn Idaho bakers. We're leading with red skins tonight. It's going to be great. Of course, trajectory can be a bitch—"

"But it's really just like golf," V said, dropping the towel across a chair. He pulled a glove over his right hand, covering the sacred tattoos that marked the thing from palm to finger-tip and all across the back. "I mean, you gotta think of your arc in the air—"

Butch nodded up a storm. "Yeah, it's just like golf. Wind plays a big role—"

"Huge."

Phury smoked along as they finished each other's sentences for another couple minutes. After a while he felt compelled to mention, "The two of you are spending *way* too much time together, you feel me?"

V shook his head at the cop. "The brother has no appreciation for this kind of thing. Never has."

"Then we aim for his room."

"True that. And it faces the garden—"

"So we don't have to work around the cars in the courtyard. Excellent."

The door from the tunnel swung open, and all three of them turned around.

Zsadist was in the doorway . . . and Bella's scent was all over him. Along with the sultry spice of sex. As well as the faintest hint of the bonding mark.

Phury stiffened and took a deep drag. *Oh, God . . .* They'd been together.

Man, the urge to race up to the house and check that she was still breathing was nearly irresistible. So was the desire to rub his chest until the aching hole in it disappeared.

His twin had had the very thing Phury was yearning for.

"Has that SUV moved?" Z said to Vishous.

V went around to the computers and punched a few keys. "Nope."

"Show me."

As Zsadist walked over and bent down, V pointed at a screen. "There it is. If it hits the road, I can track the path."

"Do you know how to break into one of those Explorers without setting off the alarm?"

"*Please.* It's just a car. If it's still there at nightfall, I'll get you in like Flynn."

Z straightened. "I need a new phone."

Vishous opened a desk drawer, took one out, and double-checked it. "You're good to go. I'll text-message everyone your new number."

"Call me if that thing moves."

As Zsadist turned his back on them, Phury took another drag and held the breath in tight. The door to the tunnel shut solidly.

Without even realizing what he was doing, Phury stabbed out the hand-rolled and went after his twin.

In the tunnel, Z halted when he heard another set of footsteps. As the male pivoted around, the light overhead picked out the hollows under his cheekbones and the blunt cut of his jaw and the line of the scar.

"What?" he asked, his deep voice echoing. Then he frowned. "Let me guess. This is about Bella."

Phury stopped. "Maybe."

"Definitely." Z's eyes flicked downward and stayed on the tunnel's floor. "You can smell her on me, can't you."

In the long silence between them, Phury wished desperately that he had a blunt between his lips.

"I just need to know . . . is she all right after you . . . laid with her?"

Z crossed his arms over his chest. "Yeah. And don't worry, she's not going to want to do that again."

Oh, God. "Why?"

"I made her . . ." Z's distorted lip thinned. "Whatever."

"What? What did you do?"

"I made her hurt me." As Phury recoiled, Z laughed with a low, sad sound. "Yeah, you don't need to get all protective. She's not coming near me again."

"How . . . What happened?"

"Uh-huh, right. Let me count all the ways you and I aren't going there."

Suddenly, without any warning, Z focused on Phury's face. The force of the stare was a surprise, because the male rarely looked anyone in the eye. "Straight up, my brother, I know how you're feeling her and I . . . ah, I hope that when things cool out a little, maybe you can . . . be with her or something."

Was he insane? Phury thought. Was he fucking *insane?*

"How the hell would that work, Z? You've bonded with her."

Zsadist rubbed his skull trim. "Not really."

"Bullshit."

"It doesn't matter, how about that? Pretty damn soon she's going to snap out of this post-traumatic whatever she's got going on and she's going to want someone real."

Phury shook his head, knowing damn well that a bonded male didn't give up his feelings for his female. Not unless he died.

"Z, you're crazy. How can you say you want me to be with her? It'll kill you."

Zsadist's face changed and the expression was a shocker. *Such sorrow,* Phury thought. Of a depth that seemed impossible.

And then the male came forward. Phury braced himself for . . . God, he had no idea what was coming at him.

When Z's hand lifted, it was not in anger or with violence. And as Phury felt his twin's palm land lightly on his face, he couldn't remember the last time Z had touched him with any gentleness. Or touched him at all.

Zsadist's voice was low and quiet as his thumb went back and forth on an unmarred cheek.

"You are the male I might have been. You are the potential I had and lost. You are the honor and the strength and the kindness she needs. You'll take care of her. I *want* you to take care of her." Zsadist dropped his hand. "It will be a good mating for her. With you as her *hellren,* she can hold her head up high. She can be proud to be seen with you at her side. She'll be socially invincible. The *glymera* won't be able to touch her."

Temptation swirled and condensed and became instinct in Phury. But what about his twin?

"Oh, God . . . Z. How could you stomach the idea that I was with her?"

Instantly all the softness was gone. "Whether it's you or

someone else, the pain is the same. Besides, you think I'm not used to hurting?" Z's lips curled into a nasty little smile. "For me, it's home sweet home, my brother."

Phury thought of Bella and how she'd refused his vein. "But don't you think she gets a vote in all this?"

"She'll see the light. She's not stupid. Not by a long shot." Z turned away and started walking. Then he stopped. Without looking back he said, "There's another reason I want you to have her."

"Is this one going to make sense?"

"You should be happy." Phury stopped breathing while Zsadist murmured, "You live less than half a life. You always have. She would care for you, and that . . . that would be good. I would like that for you."

Before Phury could say something, Z cut him off. "Do you remember back in that cave . . . after you got me out? You know, that day we sat together waiting for the sun to go down?"

"Yes," he whispered, measuring his twin's back.

"That place smelled like hell, didn't it? Do you remember that? The fish?"

"I remember everything."

"You know, I can still picture you against the cave wall, your hair all matted, your clothes wet and stained with blood. You looked like shit." Z laughed in a short burst. "I looked worse, I'm sure. Anyway . . . you said you would ease me, if you could."

"I did."

There was a long silence. Then a cold blast came out of Z's body, and he looked over his shoulder. His black eyes were glacial, his face dark as hell's groundless shadows.

"I'm past being eased. Ever. But sure as shit there's hope for you. So you take that female you want so badly. Take her and talk some sense into her. I'd throw her out of my room if I could, but she just won't leave."

Z strode away, his shitkickers pounding into the ground.

*   *   *

Hours later Bella was walking around the mansion. She'd passed some of the night with Beth and Mary, and their friendship had been appreciated. But now all was quiet, because the Brothers and everyone else had gone to bed. It was only her and Boo roaming the halls as the day passed, the cat at her side as if he knew she needed company.

God, she was exhausted, so tired she could barely stand up, and she was achy, too. Trouble was, there was a restlessness that animated her body; her internal engine refused to go into idle.

As a flush went through her, like someone had put a hair dryer to every inch of her skin, she figured she must be getting sick, although she didn't know how. She'd been with the *lessers* for six weeks, and it wasn't as if she could pick up a virus from them. And none of the Brothers or their *shellans* were ill. Maybe it was just emotional.

Yeah, you think?

She went around a corner and paused, realizing she'd found her way back to the statue corridor. She wondered if Zsadist was in the room now.

And was disappointed when she opened the door and he wasn't.

That male was like an addiction, she realized. Not good for her, but not something she could let go of.

"Time for bed, Boo."

The cat gave her a meow, as if he were relinquishing his escort duties, and then trotted off down the hall, silent as falling snow and just as graceful.

Bella shut the door just as another hot flash tackled her. Yanking off her fleece she went over to open a window, but of course the shutters were down: It was two in the afternoon. Desperate to cool off, she headed for the shower and stood under the cold water for God only knew how long. She felt even worse when she got out, her skin prickly, her head heavy.

Wrapping a towel around herself, she went to the bed and rearranged the messy covers. Before she got in she eyed the phone and thought she should call her brother. They needed to meet face-to-face, and they needed to do it soon, because Wrath's grace period wasn't going to last for long. And as Rehv never slept, he would be up.

Except, as another rolling wave of heat went through her, she knew she could not deal with her brother now. She'd wait until nightfall, after she got some rest. When the sun went down she would call Rehvenge and meet him somewhere neutral and public. And she would persuade him to cut the crap.

She sat down on the mattress edge and felt an odd pressure between her legs.

The sex with Zsadist, she thought. It had been so long since she'd taken a male inside. And her only other lover hadn't been built like that. Hadn't moved like that.

Images of Zsadist poised over her, his face tight and dark, his body straining and hard, sent a reverberation through her that left her trembling. In a rush, a sharp sensation speared her core exactly as if he were penetrating her again, a combination of honey and acid flooding her veins.

She frowned, dropped the towel, and looked down at her body. Her breasts seemed much larger than normal, the tips a deeper pink. Remnants of Zsadist's mouth? *Absolutely.*

With a curse, she lay down and pulled a sheet over herself. More heat boiled in her body, and she rolled over onto her stomach. Scissored her legs apart. Tried to cool herself down. The aching just seemed to get sharper, though.

As the snow started falling in earnest and the afternoon light began to fade a little, O drove his truck south on Route 22. When he got to the right spot he pulled over and looked at U.

"The Explorer is a hundred yards straight back from here. Get it the hell out of those woods. Then start buying those supplies we need and nail down those delivery dates. I want those apples tracked and I want that arsenic ready."

"Fine." U unclipped the seat belt. "But, listen, you need to address the Society. It's customary for the *Fore-lesser*—"

"Whatever."

O looked out the windshield, watching the wipers flip the snowflakes around. Now that he had U all over this solstice festival bullshit, he was back to racking his brain for answers to his main problem: How the hell was he going to find his wife now?

"But the *Fore-lesser* always addresses the membership when he first takes over."

Christ, U's voice was beginning to really bug the shit out of him. And so was the guy's by-the-book mentality.

"O, you need to—"

"Shut the fuck up, man. I'm not interested in meetings."

"Okay." U drew the word out, his disapproval obvious. "So where do you want the squadrons?"

"Where do you think? Downtown."

"If they find civilians between fights with the Brothers, do you want the teams to go for captives or just kills? And are we going to build another persuasion center?"

"I don't care."

"But we need . . ." U's voice droned on.

How was he going to find her? Where would she—

"O."

O glared across the interior of the truck, ready to explode. *"What."*

U's mouth did the fish thing for a moment. Opening. Closing. "Nothing."

"That's right. No more anything from your ass. Now get the hell out of my truck and get busy doing something other than yak at me."

He hit the gas the second U's boots hit the gravel. But he didn't go far. He turned off onto the farmhouse's lane and did some recon of his wife's place.

No tracks in the fresh snow. No lights on. Deserted.

Goddamn those Betas.

O turned around and headed downtown. His eyes were

dry from lack of sleep, but he wasn't about to waste night hours on recharging. *Fuck that.*

Man . . . If he didn't get to kill something tonight, he was going to go mad.

Chapter Thirty

Zsadist spent the day in the training facility. He worked the punching bag bare-knuckled. Lifted. Ran. Lifted some more. Practiced with his daggers. When he got back to the main house it was almost four, and he was ready to go out hunting.

The moment he set foot into the foyer, he stopped. Something was off.

He looked around the lobby. Glanced up to the second floor. Listened for weird sounds. When he sniffed the air, all he could smell was the breakfast that was being served in the dining room, and he went there, convinced something was wrong, but unable to tie down what it was. He found the Brothers seated and oddly quiet, though Mary and Beth were eating and talking with ease. Bella was nowhere to be seen.

He had little interest in food, but he headed for the empty seat next to Vishous anyway. As he sat down his body felt tight, and he knew it was from the heavy exercise he'd pulled during the day.

"Has that Explorer moved?" he asked his brother.

"Not up until I came here to eat. I'll check it as soon as I get back, but don't worry. The computer will track whatever route it takes even if I'm not there. We'll be able to see the path."

"You sure?"

Vishous sent him a dry look. "Yeah. I am. Designed the program myself."

Z nodded, then put a hand under his chin and cracked his neck. Man, he was stiff.

A second later, Fritz came by with two shiny apples and a knife. After thanking the butler, Z went to work on one of the Granny Smiths. While peeling the thing, he rearranged his body in the chair. Shit . . . his legs felt funny, and so did his lower back. Maybe he'd pushed it too hard? He shifted in his seat again, then refocused on the apple, turning it around and around in his hand, keeping the blade tight to the white flesh. He was almost through when he realized he was crossing and uncrossing his legs under the table like a fricking Rockette.

He glanced at the other males. V was flipping the top of his lighter open and closed and tapping his foot. Rhage was massaging his shoulder. Now his upper arm. Now his right pectoral. Phury was pushing his coffee cup around in circles and chewing his lower lip and drumming his fingers. Wrath was rolling his head on his neck, left, right, back, forth, tense as a high-voltage line. Butch seemed twitchy, too.

None of them, not even Rhage, had eaten a thing.

But Mary and Beth were normal enough as they stood up to clear their plates. They started laughing and arguing with Fritz that they should help him bring out more coffee and fruit.

The females had just left the room when the first wave of energy pushed through the house. The invisible surge went straight to the thing between Zsadist's legs, hardening it instantly. He stiffened and saw that the Brothers and Butch had all frozen, too, as if each one were wondering whether what he'd felt was right.

A moment later a second wave hit. The *it* in Z's pants thickened up even more, quick as the curse that left his mouth.

"Holy shit," someone said with a groan.

"This can't be happening," another growled.

The butler's door swung open and Beth came in, a tray of cut fruit in her hands. "Mary's bringing in more coffee—"

Wrath stood up so fast, his chair fell back and landed on

the floor. He stalked over to Beth, whipped the tray out of her hands, and tossed it carelessly on the table. As cut strawberries and pieces of cantaloupe bounced off the silver and landed on the mahogany, Beth shot him a glare.

"Wrath, what the—"

He pulled her against his body, kissing her deep and hard, bending her back as if he were going to crawl up inside of her right in front of the Brotherhood. Without breaking their mouths apart, he picked her up by her waist and held her by the ass. Beth laughed softly and locked her legs around his hips. The king's face was buried in his *leelan*'s neck as he strode out of the room.

Another surge reverberated through the house, rocking the male bodies in the room. Zsadist gripped the edge of the table, and he wasn't the only one. Vishous's knuckles were white with how hard he was holding on to the thing.

Bella . . . it must be Bella. Had to be. Bella had gone into her needing.

Havers had warned him, Z thought. When the doctor had done the internal exam on her, he'd said she'd seemed close to her fertile time.

Holy hell. A female in her need. In a house with six males.

It was only a matter of time before the Brothers got raw from their sexual instincts. And the danger to everyone became very real.

When Mary walked through the butler's door, Rhage went after her like a tank, tearing the coffeepot out of her hand and pitching it on the sideboard so it skidded and sloshed. He pushed her up against the wall and covered her with his body, his head dropping down, his erotic purring so loud it made the crystal on the chandelier tinkle. Mary's shocked gasp was followed by a very feminine sigh.

Rhage had her up in his arms and out of the room in a flash.

Butch looked down at his lap and then up at the rest of them. "Listen, I don't mean to get nasty, but is everyone else . . . ah . . ."

"Yes," V said through tight lips.

"You want to tell me what the hell is happening here?"

"Bella's gone into her needing," V said, throwing down his napkin. "Christ. How long before nightfall?"

Phury checked his watch. "Almost two hours."

"We'll be a mess by then. Tell me you have some red smoke."

"Yeah, plenty."

"Butch, do yourself a favor and get off the property fast. The Pit is not going to be far enough away from her. I didn't think humans would respond, but since you are, you'd better go before you get sucked in."

Another assault hit them, and Z collapsed back against the chair, his hips surging involuntarily. He heard the groans of the others and realized they were in deep shit. No matter how civilized they pretended to be, males couldn't help but respond to a female in her fertile time, and their sexual urges would increase as the needing progressed and strengthened.

If it weren't daylight they could have saved themselves by getting away. But they were trapped in the compound, and by the time it was dark enough for them to get out, it would be too late. After prolonged exposure, males would instinctually resist leaving the female's vicinity. No matter what their brains told them, their bodies would fight the call to get away, and if they did depart from her, they would suffer withdrawal pangs that were worse than their cravings. Wrath and Rhage had outlets for their response, but the rest of the Brothers were in trouble. Their only hope was to numb themselves out.

And Bella . . . *Oh, God* . . . She was going to hurt more than all of them combined.

V rose from the table, steadying himself on the back of his chair. "Come on, Phury. We need to start smoking up. Now. Z, you're going to her, right?"

Zsadist shut his eyes.

"Z? Z, you're going to serve her—*right?*"

John looked up from the kitchen table as the phone rang. Sal and Regin, the family's *doggen*, were out getting groceries. He picked up the call.

"John, that you?" It was Tohr on the downstairs line.

John whistled and took another bite of his white rice and ginger sauce.

"Listen, school's canceled for today. I'm calling all the families now."

John lowered his fork and whistled an ascending note.

"There's a . . . complication at the compound. But we should be back on tomorrow or the night after. We'll see how things go. In light of this, we've moved up your appointment at Havers's. Butch is going to come get you right now, okay?"

John whistled twice, in little short puffs.

"Good . . . he's a human, but he's cool. I trust him." The doorbell rang. "That's probably him—yeah, that's Butch. I can see him on the video monitor. Listen, John . . . about this therapist business. If it creeps you out, you don't have to go back, okay? I won't let anyone make you."

John sighed into the phone and thought, *Thank you.*

Tohr laughed softly. "Yeah, I'm not much for the emotive crap either— Ouch! Wellsie, what the hell?"

There was a rapid conversation in the Old Language.

"Anyway," Tohr said into the phone. "You text-message me when it's done, okay?"

John whistled twice, hung up, and put his dish and fork into the washer.

Therapist . . . training . . . Neither one was something to look forward to, but all things being equal, he'd take whatever shrink he was going to see over Lash any day. Hell, at least the appointment with the doc wouldn't last more than sixty minutes. Lash he had to deal with for hours.

On the way out he picked up his jacket and his notebook. As he opened the door the big human on the front stoop smiled down at him.

"Hey, J-man. I'm Butch. Butch O'Neal. Your taxi."

Whoa. This Butch O'Neal was . . . well, the man was dressed like a *GQ* model, for one thing. Under a black cashmere coat he had on a fancy pin-striped suit, an awesome red tie, a bright white shirt. His dark hair was pushed off his forehead in a casual, finger-brushed way that totally rocked out.

And his shoes . . . *wow.* Gucci, really Gucci . . . black leather, red-and-green band, shiny gold stuff.

Funny, he wasn't handsome, not in a Mr. Perfect kind of way, at least. The guy had a nose that had clearly been busted once or three times, and his hazel eyes were too shrewd and too exhausted to be classified as attractive. But he was like a cocked gun: He had a steely intelligence and a dangerous power about him that you respected. Because the combination was a flat-out killer, literally.

"John? We cool here?"

John whistled and stuck out his hand. They shook and Butch smiled again.

"So you good to go?" the man asked a little more gently. Like he'd been told John had to go back to Havers's to "talk to someone."

God . . . Was everyone going to know?

While John shut the door, he imagined the guys in his training class finding out, and wanted to throw up.

He and Butch walked over to a black Escalade with darkened windows and some serious chrome on the wheels. Inside, the car was warm and smelled like leather and the awesome aftershave Butch was wearing.

They took off and Butch hit the stereo, Mystikal pumping through the car. As John looked out the window at the flurries and the peach light that was bleeding from the sky, he really wished he were going anywhere else. Well, except to class.

"So, John," Butch said, "I'm not going to front. I know why you're heading to the clinic, and I wanna tell you, I've had to go to the shrink, too."

When John looked over with surprise, the man nodded. "Yeah, when I was on the police force. I was a homicide detective for ten years, and in homicide you see some pretty *f* ed up stuff. There was always some deeply sincere guy with granny glasses and a steno pad bugging me to talk. I hated it."

John took a deep breath, oddly reassured that the guy hadn't liked the experience any more than he was going to.

"But the funny thing was . . ." Butch came to a stop sign and hit a directional signal. A second later he shot out into traffic. "The funny thing was . . . I think it helped. Not when I was sitting across from Dr. Earnest, the share-your-feelings superhero. Frankly, I wanted to bolt the entire time, my skin crawled so bad. It was just . . . afterward, I'd think about what we'd talked about. And, you know, he had some valid points. It kind of cooled me out, even though I'd thought I was fine. So it was all good."

John cocked his head to one side.

"What did I see?" Butch murmured. The man was silent for a long time. It wasn't until they pulled into another very ritzy neighborhood that he answered. "Nothing special, son. Nothing special."

Butch turned into a driveway, stopped at a pair of gates, and put down the window. After he hit an intercom button and said his name, they were allowed to pass.

When the Escalade was parked behind a stuccoed mansion the size of a high school, John opened his door. As he met Butch on the other side of the SUV, he realized the guy had taken out a handgun: The thing was in his grip and hanging by his thigh, barely noticeable.

John had seen this trick before. Phury had armed himself in a similar way when the two of them had gone to the clinic a couple of nights ago. Weren't the Brothers safe here?

John looked around. Everything seemed really normal, for a big-money estate.

Maybe the Brothers weren't safe anywhere.

Butch took John's arm and walked quickly to a solid-steel door, all the while scanning the ten-car garage behind the house, the oak trees on the periphery, the two other cars parked by what looked like a kitchen entrance. John jogged to keep up.

When they were at the back door Butch showed his face to a camera, and the steel panels in front of them made a clicking noise, then slid back. They went into a vestibule, the doors closed behind them, and then a freight elevator opened up. They took it down one level and stepped out.

Standing in front of them was a nurse John recognized

from before. As she smiled and welcomed them, Butch put the handgun away in a holster under his left arm.

The nurse swept her hand toward a hallway. "Petrilla is waiting."

Squeezing his notebook, John took a deep breath and followed the woman, feeling as if he were going to the gallows.

Z stopped in front of his bedroom door. He was just going to check on Bella and then he was going to make a beeline for Phury's room and get himself good and stoned. He hated any kind of drugged-out feeling, but anything was better than this raging urge to have sex.

He cracked the door and sagged against the jamb. The fragrance in the room was like a garden in full bloom, the loveliest thing that had ever shot up the inside of his nose.

The front of his pants pounded, the *it* screaming to get out.

"Bella?" he said into the darkness.

When he heard a moan, he went inside, closing the door behind him.

Oh, God. The perfume of her . . . He started to growl deep in the back of his throat, and his fingers cranked into claws. His feet took over, marching him to the bed, his instincts leaving his mind behind.

Bella was writhing on top of the mattress, tangled in the sheets. When she saw him she cried out, but then she settled down, as if she'd willed herself calm.

"I'm okay." She rolled over onto her stomach, her thighs rubbing together as she pulled the duvet over her body. "I'm . . . really . . . It's going to be—"

Another shock wave came out of her, so strong it pushed him back as she jackknifed into a ball.

"Go," she groaned. "Worse . . . when you're here. Oh . . . *God* . . ."

As she let out a ragged curse, Z stumbled back to the door even though his body roared for him to stay.

Getting himself out into the corridor was like hauling a mastiff off a target, and once he shut the door he raced for Phury's.

From all the way down the hall of statues he could smell what his twin and V were lighting up. And when he burst inside the bedroom, the blanket of smoke was already thick as fog.

Vishous and Phury were on the bed, thick blunts between their fingers, mouths tight, bodies straining.

"What the hell are you doing here?" V demanded.

"Give me some," he said, nodding at the mahogany box between them.

"Why have you left her?" V sucked in hard, the hand-rolled's orange tip glowing bright. "The needing hasn't passed."

"She said it was worse when I was there." Z leaned over his twin and grabbed a blunt. He had trouble lighting the thing because his hands were shaking so badly.

"How's that possible?"

"Do I look like I have any experience with this shit?"

"But it's supposed to get better if a male's with her." V scrubbed his face, then looked over in disbelief. "Wait a minute—you didn't lay with her, did you? Z . . . ? Z, answer the fucking question."

"No, I didn't," he snapped, aware that Phury was very, very quiet.

"How could you leave that poor female unserved in her condition?"

"She said she was okay."

"Yeah, well, it's just getting started. She's not going to be okay. The only way to relieve the pain is if a male finishes inside of her, you feel me? You *can't* leave her like that. It's cruel."

Z paced over to one of the windows. The shutters were still down for the day, and he thought of the sun, that great, bright jailer. God, he wished he could get out of the house. He felt like a trap was closing in on him, and the urge to run was almost as bad as the lust he was crippled with.

He thought of Phury, who was keeping his eyes down and not saying a word.

Now's your chance, Z thought. *Just send your twin down the hall to her. Send him in to service her in her need.*

Go on. Tell him to leave this room and go to yours and take off his clothes and cover her with his body.

Oh . . . God . . .

Vishous's voice cut through his self-torture, the tone gratingly reasonable. "Zsadist, it's wrong and you know it, true? You can't do this to her, she's—"

"How 'bout you back the fuck off, my brother."

There was a short silence. "Okay, I'll take care of her."

Z's head whipped around just as Vishous stabbed out his hand-rolled and got to his feet. As he hiked up his leathers, his arousal was obvious.

Zsadist launched himself across the room so fast, he didn't even feel his feet. He tackled Vishous down to the floor and clamped his hands around his brother's thick throat. As his fangs shot out of his upper jaw like knives, he bared them with a hiss.

"You go near her and I'll kill you."

There was a mad scramble behind him, no doubt Phury rushing to separate them, but V put the kibosh on any rescue attempt.

"Phury! No!" V dragged some air in. "Between me . . . and him."

Vishous's diamond eyes were sharp as he looked up, and though he was struggling for breath, his voice was as forceful as always.

"Relax, Zsadist . . . you dumb fuck. . . ." Deep breath. "I'm going nowhere. . . . Just needed to get your attention. Now loosen . . . your grip."

Z eased his hold, but didn't get off the brother.

Vishous inhaled with a big suck. A couple of times. "You feel your flow right now, Z? You feel that territorial urge? You've bonded with her."

Z wanted to deny it, but that was tough to do, considering the linebacker routine he'd just pulled. And the fact that he still had his hands around the male's throat.

V's voice dropped to a whisper. "Your path out of hell is

waiting for you. She's down that hall, man. Don't be a fool. Go to her. It'll take care of both of you."

Z swung his leg up and dismounted, letting himself roll onto the floor. To avoid thinking about paths out and females and sex, he wondered idly what had happened to the blunt he'd been smoking. Glancing over at the window, he found he'd had the decency to balance it on the sill before he'd launched at Vishous like a rocket.

Well, wasn't he a gentleman.

"She can heal you," V said.

"I'm not looking to be healed. Besides, I don't want to get her pregnant, you feel me? What a fucking mess that would be."

"Is it her first time?"

"I don't know."

"If it is, the chances are practically zero."

" 'Practically' isn't good enough. What else can ease her?"

Phury spoke up from the bed. "You've still got the morphine, right? You know, that syringe I prepared from what Havers left? So use it. I've heard that's what unmated females do."

V sat up, balancing his thick arms on his knees. As he pushed his hair back, the sprawling tattoo at his right temple flashed. "It won't completely take care of the problem, but sure as shit it's better than nothing."

Another shock wave of heat rippled through the air. The three of them groaned and were momentarily incapacitated, their bodies whacking out, straining, wanting to go where they were needed, where they could be used to ease a female's pain.

As soon as Z was able to, he got to his feet. As he left, Vishous was climbing back onto Phury's bed and lighting up again.

When Z was back at the other end of the house, he braced himself before he reentered his room. Opening the door he didn't dare look in her direction as he forced his body over to the bureau.

He found the syringes and picked up the one Phury had

filled. Taking a deep breath, he turned around, only to discover that the bed was empty.

"Bella?" He walked over. "Bella, where . . ."

He found her crumpled on the floor, a pillow between her legs, her body trembling.

She started to sob as he knelt beside her. "It hurts. . . ."

"Oh, God . . . I know, *nalla.*" He brushed her hair out of her eyes. "I'll take care of you."

"Please . . . it hurts so badly." She rolled over, her breasts tight and bright red at the tips. . . . Beautiful. Irresistible. "It hurts. It hurts so badly. Zsadist, it won't stop. It's getting worse. It h—"

In a massive surge, she undulated wildly, a blast of energy coming out of her body. The strength of the hormones she emitted blinded him, and he got so caught up in his body's beastly response that he didn't feel anything . . . even as she grabbed his forearm with enough force to bend his bones.

When the peak faded, he wondered if she'd broken his wrist. It wasn't that he cared about the pain; he would take any of that she needed to give him. But if she was hanging onto him that desperately, he could just imagine what she was going through in her insides.

With a wince, he realized she'd bit her lower lip hard enough to make it bleed. He wiped the blood off her mouth with his thumb. Then had to rub the stuff on his pant leg so he didn't lap it up and want more.

"Nalla . . ." He looked at the syringe in his hand.

Do it, he said to himself. *Drug her. Take the hurt away.*

"Bella, I need to know something."

"What?" she moaned.

"Is this your first time?"

She nodded her head. "I didn't know it would be this bad— Oh, *God . . .*"

Her body spasmed again, her legs crushing the pillow.

He glanced back at the syringe. Better than nothing was not good enough for her, but his releasing into her seemed like a sacrilege. Goddamn it, his ejaculations were the worse of the two piss-poor options she had, but biologically speaking, he could do more for her than the morphine.

Z reached up and put the needle on the bedside table. Then he stood and kicked off his boots while he peeled his shirt over his head. He unzipped his fly, springing that hideous, aching length, and stepped out of his leathers.

He needed pain to orgasm, but he wasn't worried about that. Hell, he could hurt himself enough to trigger a release. That was why he had fangs, right?

Bella was writhing in misery as he picked her up and laid her out on the bed. She was so magnificent against the pillows, her cheeks flushed, her lips parted, her skin glowing from the needing. But she was in such pain.

"Shhh . . . easy," he whispered as he got on top of the bed. On top of her.

As their naked skin brushed, she moaned and bit into her lip again. This time he bent down and licked the fresh blood off her mouth. The taste of it, the electric tingle on his tongue, thrilled him. Scared him. Reminded him that he'd been living off weak sustenance for over a century.

With a curse he shoved all his stupid fucking baggage out of the way and focused on Bella. Her legs were sawing underneath him, and he had to force them wide with his hands, then pin them with his thighs. When he touched her core with his hand, he was shocked. She was on fire, drenched, swollen. She cried out, and the orgasm that followed relieved her struggles a little, her arms and legs going still, her breathing getting less harsh.

Maybe this was going to be easier than he thought. Maybe Vishous was wrong about her needing a male inside. In which case, he could just go down on her over and over again. Man, he would *love* to do that for a day. The first time he had put his mouth to her hadn't lasted nearly long enough.

He eyed his clothes. Probably should have kept them on—

The force of energy that came out of her then was so great, he was actually pushed upright from her body, as if invisible hands had punched at his torso. She screamed in misery as he hovered in midair above her. When the surge passed he fell back on top of her. The orgasm had obviously made the situation worse, and now she was weeping so hard tears no longer fell from her eyes. All she had was a case of the dry heaves as she twisted and contorted beneath him.

"Lie still, *nalla*," he said frantically. "Let me put it in you."

But she was too far gone to hear him. He had to muscle her to keep her in place, pushing down on her collarbone with a forearm while he forced one of her legs up and to the side. He tried to position the *it* for penetration by moving his hips, but couldn't manage to get the angle right. Even trapped under his superior strength and weight, she still managed to flail around.

With a nasty curse Z reached between his legs and grabbed the thing he needed to use on her. He guided the bastard to her threshold and then thrust hard, joining them deep. They both yelled.

And then he dropped his head and held on for dear life, getting lost in the sensation of her tight, slick sex. His body took over, his hips moving like pistons, the punishing, grinding rhythm creating a mighty pressure in his balls and a burning in his lower belly.

Oh, God . . . A release was coming for him. Just as it had in the bathroom when she'd held on as he pumped. Only hotter. Wilder. Out of control.

"Oh, Jesus!" he hollered.

Their bodies were slapping together and he was mostly blind and he was sweating all over her and the bonding scent was a screaming roar in his nose. . . . And then she called his name and seized up under him. Her core grabbed onto him in spasms that milked him until— *Oh, shit, God, no—*

On reflex he tried to pull out, but the orgasm tackled him from behind, shooting up his spine and nailing him in the back of the head just as he felt the release bullet out of his body into hers. And the damn thing didn't stop. He came in great waves, pouring into her, filling her up. There was nothing he could do to stop the eruptions even though he knew what he was spilling into her.

When the last shudder left him, he lifted his head. Bella's

eyes were closed, her breathing even, the deep grooves in her face gone.

Her hands ran up his ribs and onto his shoulders, and she turned her face into his bicep with a sigh. The quiet in the room, in her body, was jarring. So was the fact that he'd ejaculated only because she'd made him feel . . . good.

Good? No, that didn't go far enough. She'd made him feel . . . alive. Awakened.

Z touched her hair, spreading the dark waves across a creamy pillow. There had been no pain for him, for his body. Just pleasure. A miracle . . .

Except then he became aware of the wetness where they were joined.

The implications of what he'd done in her made him twitchy, and he couldn't fight the compulsion to clean her up. He pulled out and quickly headed for the bathroom, where he grabbed a washcloth. When he returned to the bed, though, she'd started to undulate again, the need in her rising. He looked down at himself and watched the thing that hung from his groin grow hard and long in response.

"Zsadist . . ." she moaned. "It's . . . back."

He put the washcloth aside and mounted her again, but before he pushed into her he looked at her glassy eyes and had an attack of conscience. How whacked was it that he was greedy for more when the consequences were so ugly for her? Good God, he'd ejaculated into her, and the shit was all over her beautiful parts and the smooth skin of her thighs and—

"I can drug you," he said. "I can make you feel no pain and you won't have me inside you. I can help you without hurting you."

He stared down at her, waiting for her answer, caught between her biology and his reality.

Chapter Thirty-one

Butch was a wired-out mess as he peeled off his coat and took a seat in the doctor's waiting room.

Good thing night had just fallen and any vampire clientele had yet to show up. Some alone time was what he needed. At least until he pulled himself together.

Thing was, this happy little clinic was located in the basement of Havers's mansion. Which meant Butch was now, at this very moment, in the same house as the guy's sister. Yup . . . Marissa, the female vampire he wanted like no one else on the planet, was under the same roof he was.

Man, this obsession with her was a new and different nightmare. He'd never had a case of the sweats like this for a woman before, and he couldn't say he recommended it. Nothing but a pain in the ass. And the chest.

Back in September, when he'd come to see her and she'd shut him down without even doing a face-to-face, he'd sworn he'd never bother her again. And he hadn't. Technically. Those drive-bys he'd done since, those pathetic, sissy drive-bys where the Escalade somehow found itself going by this very house, those weren't really bothering her. Because she didn't know about them.

He was *so* pathetic. But as long as she had no idea how whipped he was, he could almost handle it. Which was why he was on edge tonight. He didn't want to be caught hanging out in the clinic in case she thought he was after her. After all, a man had to have his pride. At least, as far as the outside world could see.

He checked his watch. A whopping thirteen minutes had passed. He figured this session with the shrink was an hour, so his Patek Philippe's long hand had to take forty-seven more trips around before he could stuff the kid back in the car and bust on out of here.

"Would you like some coffee?" a female voice said.

He looked up. A nurse dressed in a white uniform was standing in front of him. She looked young, especially as she fiddled with one of her sleeves. She also seemed desperate to do something.

"Yeah, sure. Coffee'd be good."

She smiled broadly, her fangs showing. "How do you like it?"

"Black. Black's fine. Thanks."

The whisper of her soft-soled shoes faded while she went down the corridor.

Butch unbuttoned his double-breasted jacket and leaned forward, putting his elbows on his knees. The Valentino suit he'd put on before coming was one of his favorites. So was the Hermès tie around his neck. And the Gucci loafers on his feet.

If he got busted by Marissa, he'd figured he might as well look as good as he ever did.

"Do you want me to drug you?"

Bella focused on Zsadist's face as he loomed above her. His black eyes were mere slits, and he had that beautiful flush of arousal on his stark cheekbones. He was heavy on top of her, and as the needing rose again she thought of him releasing inside of her. She'd felt a wondrous, cooling ease as soon as he'd started to come, the first relief she'd had since the symptoms of the needing had started a couple of hours ago.

But the drive was back now.

"Would you like me to put you out, Bella?"

Maybe it would be better if he drugged her. This was going

to be a long night, and from what she understood, it would only get harder and more intense as the hours churned. Was it really fair of her to ask that he stay?

Something soft stroked her cheek. His thumb, brushing over her skin.

"I won't leave you," he said. "No matter how long, no matter how many times. I'll serve you and let you take my vein until it's over. I will not abandon you."

Staring up into his face, she knew without asking that this would be their only time together. The resolve was in his eyes. She could see it clearly.

One night and no other.

Abruptly he lifted his body from hers and reached for the bedside table. His tremendous erection stood out straight from his hips, and just as he came back with a syringe, she grasped his hard flesh.

He hissed and swayed before catching himself by throwing a hand down to the mattress.

"You," she whispered. "Not the drug. I want you."

He dropped the needle on the floor and kissed her, spreading her thighs with his knees. She guided him into her body and felt a glorious rush as he filled her. With a mighty swell her pleasure rose and then broke into two separate needs, one for his sex, one for his blood. Her fangs elongated as she eyed the thick vein at the side of his neck.

As if he sensed what she needed, he twisted his body around so he could stay inside of her while giving her access to his throat.

"Feed," he said hoarsely, his body moving into her and pulling back. "Take what you need."

She bit him without hesitation, piercing right through the slave band, going deep into his skin. As his taste hit her tongue, she heard a roar leave him. And then the strength and the power of him washed over her, through her.

O fell still over his captive, unsure he'd heard right.

The vampire he'd caught downtown and brought to the shed behind the cabin was strapped to the table, a butterfly mounted.

He'd captured the male only with plans to work out his frustration. He'd never imagined he'd learn anything useful.

"What was that?" O put his ear down closer to the civilian's mouth.

"She is called . . . Bella. The one . . . the female who was taken . . . her name . . . Bella."

O straightened, a heady, balmy bloom flowing across his skin. "Do you know if she's alive?"

"I thought she was dead." The civilian coughed weakly. "She's been gone so long."

"Where does her family live?" When there was no immediate answer, O did something guaranteed to open the male's mouth. After the scream faded, O said, "Where is her family?"

"I don't know. I . . . don't honestly know. Her family . . . I don't know. . . . I don't know. . . ."

Babble, babble, babble. The civilian slid into the diarrhea-of-the-mouth stage of interrogation, becoming all but useless.

O slapped the thing into silence. "Address. I want an address."

When there was no reply, he provided another source of encouragement. The male gasped under the fresh onslaught, and then blurted, "Twenty-seven Formann Lane."

O's heart started pumping, but he leaned over the vampire casually. "I'm going to go there right now. If you've told the truth I'll set you free. If you haven't I'll kill you slowly as soon as I get back. Now, do you want to change anything?"

The civilian's eyes darted away. Came back.

"Hello?" O said. "You hear me?"

To hurry the civilian up, he applied pressure to a sensitive area. The thing yelped like a dog.

"Tell me," O said softly. "And I'll let you go. This will all stop."

The male's face squeezed into itself, his mouth peeling up and revealing gritted teeth. A tear snaked down his bruised cheek. Though there was the temptation to add another shot of agony as inducement, O decided not to upset the battle between conscience and self-preservation.

"Twenty-seven Thorne."

"Avenue, right?"

"Yes."

O wiped off the tear. Then slit the civilian's throat wide-open.

"You are such a liar," he said as the vampire bled out.

O didn't hang around, just grabbed his jacket full of weapons and left. He was damn sure the addresses were nothing. That was the problem with persuasion. You really couldn't trust the information you got.

He'd check out whatever was there on both streets, but he was clearly being jerked around.

Waste of fucking time.

Chapter Thirty-two

Butch swirled the last inch of coffee around the bottom of the mug, thinking that the stuff was the color of Scotch. As he tossed the cold swill back, he wished it were some high-test Lagavulin.

He checked his watch. Six minutes till seven. God, he hoped the session was only an hour. If everything went smooth, he could drop John at Tohr and Wellsie's and be sitting on his couch with a shot glass at his elbow before *CSI* came on.

He winced. No wonder Marissa wouldn't see him. What a frickin' catch. High-functioning alcoholic living in a world that wasn't his own.

Yay. Let's beat feet for the altar.

As he pictured himself at home, he had a passing thought about V's warning to get away from the compound. Trouble was, being out at a bar or on the streets alone was not a good plan, not with the mood he was in. He was as raw as the weather.

A few minutes later, voices drifted down the corridor, and John came around the corner with an older woman. The poor kid looked like he'd been pulled through a ringer. His hair was standing up like weeds, as if he'd been shoving his hands into it, and his eyes were glued to the floor. That notebook was clutched to his chest as though the thing were a bullet-proof vest.

"So we'll see about the next appointment, John," the female said softly. "After you've thought about it."

John didn't respond, and Butch forgot about all his own whiny crap. Whatever had come out in that office was still out, and the boy needed a buddy. He put his arm around the kid tentatively, and when John leaned into him, all of Butch's protective instincts reared up and snarled. He didn't care that the therapist looked like Mary Poppins; he wanted to yell at her for upsetting the little guy.

"John?" she said. "You'll get back in touch with me about the next—"

"Yeah, we'll call you," Butch muttered. *Uh-huh, right.*

"I told him there was no rush. But I do think he should come again."

Butch glanced over at the woman, thoroughly annoyed. . . . only to have her eyes scare the shit out of him. They were so damned serious, so very grave. What the hell had gone down in that session?

Butch looked at the top of John's head. "Let's go, J-man."

John didn't move, so Butch gave him a little push, and led the way out of the clinic, his arm still on the kid's thin shoulders. When they got to the car John climbed into the seat, but didn't put his belt on. He just stared straight ahead.

Butch shut his door and locked the SUV up tight. Then he turned and stared at John.

"I'm not even going to ask what's doing. The only thing I need to know is where you want to go. You feel like heading home, I'll take you to Tohr and Wellsie's. You want to hang at the Pit with me, we'll go over to the compound. You just want to drive, I'll take you to Canada and back. I'm up for anything, so you just say the word. And if you don't want to decide now, I'll tool around town until you figure it out."

John's little chest expanded and then contracted. He flipped open the notebook and took out his pen. There was a pause, and then he wrote something and flipped the paper around to Butch.

1189 Seventh Street.

Butch frowned. That was a really shitty part of town.

He opened his mouth to ask why there of all places, but then shut his yap. The kid had clearly had enough questions thrown at him tonight. Besides, Butch was armed, and it was where John wanted to go. A promise was a promise.

"Okay, buddy. Seventh Street coming up."

But drive around for a while first, the kid wrote.

"No problem. We'll just chill."

Butch started the engine. Just as he put the Escalade into reverse, he saw a flash of something behind them. A car was pulling up to the back of the mansion, a very large, very expensive Bentley. He hit the brakes so it could pass and—

Forgot how to breathe.

Marissa came out of the house from a side door. Her hiplength blond hair blew in the wind, and she huddled into the black cape she was wearing. Moving quickly across the back parking lot, she dodged chunks of snow, leaping from asphalt spot to asphalt spot.

The security lights picked up the refined lines of her face and her gorgeous pale hair and her perfectly white skin. He remembered what it had felt like to kiss her, that one time he had, and his chest stung like his lungs were being crushed. Overcome, he wanted to rush out of the car, throw himself down in the slush, and beg like the dog he was.

Except she was heading for the Bentley. He watched as the door opened for her, as if the driver had leaned across and popped the handle. When the lights came on in the interior Butch couldn't see much, only enough to tell him that it was a man, or male, who was behind the wheel. Shoulders that big didn't come on female bodies.

Marissa gathered her cape with her hands and slid inside, shutting the door.

The light went off.

Dimly Butch heard some kind of shuffling next to him, and he glanced at John. The kid had shrunk back against the far window and was looking across the seats with fear in his eyes. That was when Butch realized he had palmed his gun and was growling.

Totally creeped out by the insane reaction, he took his foot off the Escalade's brake and stomped on the gas pedal.

"Don't worry, son. Nothing doing."

As he spun them around he looked in the rearview mirror at the Bentley. It was moving now, doing its own turn in the parking lot. With a grim curse Butch tore off down the driveway, his hands gripping the steering wheel so hard his knuckles stung.

Rehvenge frowned as Marissa got into his Bentley. God, he'd forgotten how beautiful she was. And she smelled just as good . . . the clean scent of the ocean filling his nose.

"Why won't you let me come to the front door?" he said, taking in her fair hair and her flawless skin. "You should have let me pick you up properly."

"You know how Havers is." The door shut with a solid sound. "He'll want us mated."

"That's ridiculous."

"And you're not the same way with your sister?"

"No comment."

As he waited for an Escalade to clear out of the parking lot, Marissa laid a hand on his sable sleeve. "I know I said this before, but I'm so sorry for everything that happened to Bella. How is she?"

How the hell would he know? "I'd rather not talk about her. No offense, but I'm just . . . Yeah, I don't want to go there."

"Rehv, tonight doesn't have to happen. I know you've been through a lot, and frankly I was surprised you would see me at all."

"Don't be ridiculous. I'm glad you called on me." He reached out and squeezed her hand. The bones under her skin were so delicate that he reminded himself he was going to have to be very gentle with her. She was not what he was used to.

As he drove them downtown, he could sense her nerves tightening. "It's going to be all right. I really am cool that you called."

"I'm rather embarrassed, actually. I just don't know what to do."

"We'll take it slow."

"I've only ever been with Wrath."

"I know. That's why I wanted to pick you up in the car. I thought you'd be too nervous to dematerialize."

"I am."

As they came up to a stoplight, he smiled at her. "I'm going to take good care of you."

Her pale blue eyes looked over at him. "You are a good male, Rehvenge."

He ignored that miscalculation and concentrated on the traffic.

Twenty minutes later they were stepping out of a high-tech elevator and into the vestibule of his penthouse apartment. His place took up half of the thirty-story building's top floor, overlooking the Hudson River and all of Caldwell. With the vast blocks of windows, he never used the place during the day. But it was perfect for the night.

He kept the lights low and waited as Marissa walked around and looked at things a decorator had bought for his lair. He didn't care about the stuff or the views or the fancy gadgets. He cared about the privacy from his family. Bella had never been here, and neither had their mother. In fact, neither knew he had the penthouse.

As if realizing she was wasting time, Marissa turned and faced him. Under the lights her beauty was absolutely stunning, and he was grateful for the extra hit of dopamine he'd pumped into his system about an hour ago. In *symphaths*, the drug had an opposite effect than when it was administered to humans or vampires. The chemical increased certain neurotransmitter activity and reception, ensuring that the *symphath* patient could feel no pleasure, no . . . nothing. With Rehv's sense of touch gone, his brain could better control the rest of his impulses.

Which was the only reason Marissa was safe to be alone with him, considering what they were going to do.

Rehv removed his coat, then walked over to her, relying on his cane more than usual because he could not take his eyes off her. Balancing the staff against his thighs, he slowly undid the bow that held her cape together. She stared down at his hands, trembling as he slid the folds of black wool from her shoulders. He smiled as he slung the weight over a chair. Her dress was the kind of thing his mother would wear and exactly what he wished his sister would put on more often: a pale blue satin gown that was fitted perfectly. It was Dior. It had to be.

"Come here, Marissa."

He drew her over to a leather sofa and pulled her down beside him. In the glow from the windows, her blond hair was like a shawl of silk, and he took some between his fingers. Her hunger was so strong, he could feel it clearly.

"You've waited for a long time, haven't you?"

She nodded and looked at her hands. They were knotted together in her lap, ivory against the light blue satin.

"How long?"

"Months," she whispered.

"Then you'll need a lot, won't you?" As she blushed, he pushed her. "Won't you, Marissa?"

"Yes," she breathed, obviously uncomfortable with her hunger.

Rehv smiled fiercely. It was good to be around a female of worth. Her modesty and her gentleness were damned appealing.

He took off his jacket and unknotted his tie. He'd been prepared to offer her his wrist, but now that she was in front of him, he wanted her at his neck. It had been forever since he'd allowed a female to feed from him, and he was surprised by how excited he was at the prospect.

He popped the buttons of his collar and undid the rest of them, all the way down his chest. With a surge of anticipation he yanked the shirt free and opened it wide.

Her eyes went round as she looked at his bare chest and his tattoos.

"I didn't know you were marked," she murmured, her voice shaking along with her body.

He eased himself back into the sofa, spreading his arms out, bringing one of his legs up. "Come here, Marissa. Take what you need."

She looked at his wrist, which was covered by a French cuff.

"No," he said. "This is the way I want you to do it. At my throat. It's the only thing I ask."

As she hesitated, he knew the rumors about her were true. She was indeed untouched by any male. And the purity of her was . . . something to be taken.

He squeezed his eyes shut as the darkness in him shifted and breathed, a beast locked in a cage of medication. Christ, maybe this wasn't a good idea.

But then she was moving on him slowly, crawling up his body, her smell so like the ocean's. He cracked his eyelids to see her face and knew he was helpless to stop the feeding. And he was not going to miss this; he had to let a few sensations come to him. Slipping loose his discipline, he opened the channel to his sense of touch, and it received with greed even with the drug, all kinds of heady information surging through the dopamine fog.

The satin of her gown was soft against his skin, and he felt the warmth of her body mingling with his own heat. Her slight weight was braced on his shoulder and . . . yes, her knee was between his thighs.

Her mouth parted and her fangs unsheathed.

For a split second the evil in him howled, and he called on his mind in a panic. Thank the Virgin, the damn thing came to the rescue, the rational side of him rushing forward, chaining his instincts, quieting the very sexual need to dominate her.

She wobbled as she leaned down toward his throat, unsteady as she held herself above him.

"Lie on me," he said in a guttural voice. "Lay yourself . . . upon me."

With a wince she let the lower half of her body sink into the cradle of his hips. Clearly she was worried about bumping up against an erection, and when she encountered nothing of the sort she glanced between their bodies, as if thinking she'd hit the wrong place.

"You don't have to worry about that," he murmured, running his hands up her slender arms. "Not from me." Her relief was so palpable he was offended. "Would laying with me be such a chore?"

"Oh, no, Rehvenge. No." She glanced down at the thick muscles of his chest. "You are . . . quite lovely. It's just . . . there is another. For me, there is another."

"You still love Wrath."

She shook her head. "No, but I cannot think of the one I want. Not . . . now."

Rehv tilted her chin up. "What kind of idiot wouldn't feed you when you needed it?"

"Please. No more talk like that." Abruptly, her eyes fixated on his neck and dilated.

"Such hunger," he growled, thrilled to be used. "Go ahead. And don't worry about being gentle. Take me. The harder the better."

Marissa bared her fangs and bit him. The two sharp penetrations shot through the drug haze, and the sweet pain speared into his body. As he moaned, he thought that he'd never been grateful for his impotence before, but he was now. If his cock had worked at all, sure as hell he'd have pushed that gown out of the way, parted her legs, and had her nice and deep as she fed.

Almost immediately she pulled back and licked at her lips.

"I'm going to taste different from Wrath," he said, counting on the fact that because she'd fed from only one male, she wouldn't know exactly why his blood hit her tongue in an odd way. Actually, her inexperience had been the only reason he'd been able to help her. Any other female who'd been around a little would know too much. "Go on, take some more. You'll get used to it."

Her head dropped again and he felt the tingling sting of another bite.

He wrapped his heavy arms around her fragile back and hugged her close as he shut his eyes. It had been so long since he'd held anyone, and though he couldn't afford to let in much of the experience, he found it sublime.

As she sucked at his vein, he had the absurd impulse to cry.

*   *   *

O eased up on the truck's accelerator and glided past another high stone wall.

Damn, the houses were huge on Thorne Avenue. Well, not that you could see the mansions from the street. He just assumed that with hedges and ramparts like these, there weren't a lot of split-levels and Cape Cods going on.

When this particular barricade split to allow for a driveway, he hit the brakes. To the left there was a little brass plaque that read, 27 THORNE AVENUE. He leaned forward, stretching for a look beyond, but with the drive and the wall disappearing into the darkness, he couldn't tell what was on the other side.

On a what-the-hell whim, he turned in and proceeded down the lane. A good hundred yards from the street there was a towering set of black gates, and he stopped, noting the cameras mounted on the top of them and the intercom system and the air of keep-out.

Well . . . this was interesting. The other address had been for shit, just an average house in an average neighborhood with humans in the living room watching TV. But whatever was behind a setup like this was big business.

Now he was curious.

Although infiltrating these barriers would require a coordinated strategy and some careful execution. And the last thing he needed was the inconvenience of tangling with the police just because he'd broken into some highflier's McMansion.

But why would that vampire have pulled this address out of his ass to save himself?

Then O saw something weird: a black ribbon tied to the gate. No, two of them, one on each side, waving in the wind.

Like they were for mourning?

Fixated by his own dread, he got out of the truck and crunched over the ice, heading for the ribbon on the right. It was mounted seven feet off the ground, so he had to stretch up his arm to finger it.

"Are you dead, wife?" he whispered. He dropped his hand and looked through the gates into the black night beyond.

He went back to the truck and reversed down the driveway.

He needed to get past that wall. Had to find someplace to dump the F-150.

Five minutes later he was cursing. *Damn it.* There was nowhere to park on Thorne that wasn't totally conspicuous. The street was nothing but walls, with barely any shoulder. *Fucking rich people.*

O hit the gas and looked left. Right. Maybe he could leave the truck down at the bottom of the hill and jog up from the main drag. It was a half mile at an incline, but he could cover the distance quickly enough. The streetlights he'd have to pass under were a bitch, of course, but it wasn't like anyone living on this road could see out from their ivory towers.

His cell phone went off and he answered it with a nasty, "What."

U's voice, which he was beginning to hate, was tense. "We've got a problem. Two *lessers* were arrested by the police."

O squeezed his eyes shut. "What the hell did they do?"

"They were taking down a civilian vampire and an unmarked patrol car went by. Two policemen engaged the slayers and more cops showed up. The *lessers* were taken into custody, and I got the call just now from one of them."

"So bail them out," O snapped. "Why are you calling me?"

There was a pause. Then U's tone had the stench of *well, duh* all over it. "Because *you* need to know this. Listen, they were packing plenty of concealed weapons, none of which they had permits for, all of which had come off the black market, with no serial numbers on the barrels. No way they're going to get bail in the morning. No public defender is that good. You need to get them out."

O scanned left and right and then turned around in a driveway the size of a football field. Yeah, there was definitely noplace to park around here. He had to go down to where Thorne Avenue dumped out on Bellman Road and leave the truck in that little village.

"O?"

"I have things I have to do."

U coughed as if he were choking back a boatload of pissed-off. "No offense, but I can't imagine anything's as important as this. What if those slayers get into a fight in general holding? You want black blood flowing so that some EMT type figures out they're not human? You have to contact the Omega and get him to call those two home."

"You do it." O accelerated even though he was headed down the hill now.

"What?"

"Reach out and touch the Omega." He came to a rolling stop at the bottom of Thorne and picked left. There were all kinds of cutie-pie, homey-ass shops on the street, and he parked in front of one called Kitty's Attic.

"O . . . That kind of request needs to come from the *Fore-lesser.* You know that."

O paused before turning off the ignition.

Terrific. Just what he wanted. More quality time with the bastard master. *Goddamn it.* He couldn't live with not knowing the fate of his woman any longer. There wasn't time for this Society bullshit.

"O?"

He put his head down on the steering wheel. Banged it a couple of times.

On the other hand, if that contact with the humans down at the police station exploded in his face, the Omega was going to come looking for him. And then where would he be?

"Fine. I'll go see him now." He cursed as he put the truck in gear. Before he pulled out he looked up Thorne Avenue again.

"And O, I have a concern about the membership. You need to meet with the slayers. Things are slipping."

"You're handling the check-ins."

"They want to see you. They're questioning your leadership."

"U, you know what they say about messengers, right?"

"Excuse me?"

"Too much bad news will get you shot." He turned off the phone and flipped it shut. Then hit the gas.

Chapter Thirty-three

As Phury sat on his bed, he was so strung out from the need to have sex, he could barely pour himself another shot of vodka. The bottle shook, the glass shook. Hell, the whole mattress was shaking.

He looked at Vishous, who was leaning back against the headboard beside him. The brother was just as twitchy and miserable as he nodded his head to 50 Cent's *The Massacre*.

Five hours into Bella's fertile time and they were both a mess, their bodies mostly instinct, their minds mostly fog. The compulsion to stay at the mansion couldn't be overridden, the needing pulling them in tight, paralyzing them. Thank God for the red smoke and the Grey Goose. The numbing out helped a lot.

Though not with everything. Phury tried not to think about what was going on in Z's room. Because when the brother hadn't come back, it was obvious that his body was being used, not the morphine.

Dear God . . . the two of them. Together. Over and over again . . .

"How you doing?" V asked.

"'Bout the same as you, my man." He took a deep drink from his glass, his body swimming, lost, drowning in the erotic sensations trapped under his skin. He eyed the bathroom.

He was about to get up and head for a little privacy again when Vishous said, "I think I'm in trouble."

Phury had to laugh. "This won't last forever."

"No, I mean . . . I think there's something wrong. With me."

Phury narrowed his eyes. His brother's face looked strained, but otherwise it was the same as always. Handsome lines, goatee around the mouth, swirling tattoos at the right temple. Those diamond eyes were sharp, undimmed even by the Grey Goose, the blunts, the needing. Their superblack centers shined with a vast, incomprehensible intelligence, a genius so powerful it was unnerving.

"Like what kind of trouble, V?"

"I, ah . . ." Vishous cleared his throat. "Only Butch knows this. You don't tell anyone else, true?"

"Yeah. No problem."

V stroked his goatee. "My visions have dried up."

"You mean you can't see—"

"What's coming. Yeah. I'm getting nothing anymore. The last thing I received was about three days ago, right before Z went after Bella. I saw them together. In that Ford Taurus. Coming here. After that, there's been . . . nothing."

"You ever have something like this happen before?"

"No, and I'm not getting anyone's thoughts anymore, either. It's like the whole thing dried up on me."

Abruptly the brother's tension seemed to have nothing to do with the needing. He seemed rigid from . . . fear. *Holy shit.* Vishous was scared. And the anomaly was downright jarring. Of all the brothers, V was the one who never was afraid. It was like he'd been born without fear receptors in his brain.

"Maybe it's just temporary," Phury said. "Or you think maybe Havers could help?"

"This isn't about physiology." V finished the vodka in his glass and held out his hand. "Don't hog the Goose, my brother."

Phury passed him the bottle. "Maybe you could talk to . . ."

But who? Where could V, who knew everything, go for answers?

Vishous shook his head. "I don't want . . . I don't want to talk about this, actually. Forget I said anything." As he poured, his face closed up tight, a house battened down. "I'm sure it will come back. I mean, yeah. It will."

He put the bottle on the table next to him and held up his gloved hand. "After all, this godforsaken thing still glows like a lamp. And until I lose this whacked-out night-light of mine, I figure I'm still normal. Well . . . normal for me."

They fell silent for a while, Phury looking into his glass, V staring into his, the rap in the background beating, thumping, switching to G-Unit.

Phury cleared his throat. "Can I ask you about them?"

"About who?"

"Bella. Bella and Zsadist."

V cursed. "I'm not a crystal ball, you know. And I hate telling fortunes."

"Yeah, I'm sorry. Forget it."

There was a long pause. Then Vishous muttered, "I don't know what's going to happen to them. I don't know because I just can't . . . see anymore."

As Butch got out of the Escalade, he looked up at the grungy apartment building and wondered again why in the hell John had wanted to come here. Seventh Street was nasty and dangerous.

"This it?"

When the boy nodded, Butch activated the security alarm on the SUV. He wasn't particularly worried about the thing being stripped while they were gone. Folks around here would be convinced one of their dealers was inside. Or someone even more picky about their shit who'd be packing heat.

John walked up to the tenement's door and pushed. The thing opened with a squeal. No locks. Big surprise. As Butch followed, he put his hand inside his suit coat so he could get at his gun if he needed to.

John went left down a long corridor. The place smelled like old cigarette smoke and moldy decay and was almost as cold as the great outdoors. The in-house residents were like rats: unseen, only heard, on the other side of thin walls.

Down at the end the boy pushed open a fire door.

A staircase jogged up to the right. The steps had been worn down to the particleboard, and there was the sound of dripping water from somewhere a couple of flights up.

John put his hand on a banister that was screwed loosely into the wall, and he went up slowly until he got to the landing between the second and third floors. Up above, the fluorescent light that was sunk into the ceiling was in its death-rattle stage, the tubes flickering as if desperately trying to keep up a useful life.

John stared at the cracked linoleum on the floor, then looked up at the window. Starburst patterns covered the thing as if it had been pummeled with bottles. The only reason the grimy glass hadn't broken was because it was embedded with chicken wire.

From the floor above there was a splatter of curses, a kind of verbal shotgun that was undoubtedly the beginning of a fight. Butch was about to suggest that they get out of Dodge when John turned away of his own accord and started jogging down the stairs.

They were back in the Escalade and heading out of the bad part of town less than a minute and a half later.

Butch came to a stop at a traffic light. "Where to?"

John wrote and then flashed the pad.

"Home it is," Butch murmured, still having no idea why the kid had wanted to visit that stairwell.

John said a passing hello to Wellsie when he came into the house and then took off for his room. He was grateful that she seemed to understand he needed some space. After he shut his door he dropped his notebook on the bed, shrugged out of his coat, and immediately headed for the shower. While the water was heating up, he stripped out of his clothes. Once he was under the spray, he stopped shaking.

When he came back out, he put on a T-shirt and a pair of sweatpants, then eyed his laptop on the desk. He sat down in front of it, thinking that maybe he should write something. The therapist had suggested it.

God . . . Talking to her about what had happened to him

had been almost as bad as living through the experience the first time. And he hadn't meant to be as candid as he'd been. It was just . . . about twenty minutes into the session, he'd cracked and his hand had started scribbling and he hadn't been able to stop once the story had begun.

He closed his eyes and tried to remember what the man who'd cornered him had looked like. Only a vague picture came to mind, but he remembered the knife clearly. It had been a five-inch, double-sided switchblade with a point on it sharp as a scream.

He ran his forefinger over the mouse square on the laptop and the Windows XP screen saver blinked off. His e-mail account had a fresh message in it. From Sarelle. He read the thing three times before trying to reply.

In the end, he sent her back: *Hey, Sarelle, tomorrow night's not going to work for me. I'm really sorry. I'll get back with you sometime. TTYL, John.*

He really . . . didn't want to see her again. Not for a while, at any rate. He didn't want to see any females except for Wellsie and Mary and Beth and Bella. There was going to be nothing even remotely sexual in his life until he came to terms with what had been done to him almost a year ago.

He moved out of Hotmail and opened a fresh document in Microsoft Word.

He rested his fingers on the keyboard for only a moment. And then they started to fly.

Chapter Thirty-four

Z sadist dragged his head over to the side and looked at the clock. Ten in the morning. Ten . . . ten o'clock. How many hours? Sixteen . . .

He closed his eyes, so exhausted he could barely breathe. He was flat on his back, legs splayed out, arms lying wherever. He'd been in that position since he'd rolled off Bella maybe an hour ago.

He felt like it had been a year since he'd come back into the room the night before. His neck and wrists burned from the number of times she'd fed from him, and the thing between his legs was sore. The air around them was saturated with the bonding scent, and the sheets were wet with a combination of his blood and the other thing she had needed from him.

He wouldn't have traded a moment of it.

As he closed his eyes, he wondered if he could sleep now. He was starved for food and blood, so hungry not even his penchant for keeping himself on edge could override the needs. But he couldn't move.

When he felt a hand brush over his lower belly, he peeled his lids apart to look at Bella. The hormones were rising in her again, and the response she called from him answered, the *it* growing hard once more.

Zsadist struggled to roll over so he could go where he needed to be, but he was too weak. Bella shifted against him and he tried to lift himself again, but his head weighed a thousand pounds.

Reaching out, he grabbed her arm and pulled her on top of him. As her thighs parted over his hips, she looked at him in shock and began to scramble off.

"'S okay," he croaked. He cleared his throat, but it didn't help with all the gravel. "I know it's you."

Her lips came down on his and he kissed her back even though he couldn't lift his arms to hold her to him. God, how he loved kissing her. He loved feeling her mouth against his, loved having her right up close all in his face, loved her breath in his lungs, loved . . . her? Was that what had happened in the night? Had he fallen?

The bonding scent that was all over the both of them gave him his answer. And the realization should have shocked him, but he was too tired to bother to fight it.

Bella eased up and slid the *it* inside of her. As beat as he was, he groaned in ecstasy. The feel of her was something he couldn't get enough of, and he knew it wasn't because of her needing.

She rode him, planting her hands on his pecs and finding a rhythm with her hips because he couldn't thrust anymore with his. He felt himself gearing up for another explosion, especially as he watched her breasts sway with her movements.

"You are so beautiful," he said in his hoarse voice.

She paused to bend down and kiss him again, her dark hair falling around him, a gentle shelter. When she straightened, he marveled at the sight of her. She was glowing with health and vitality from everything he had given her, a resplendent female who he . . .

Loved. Yes, loved.

That was the thought that shot through his brain as he came inside of her again.

Bella collapsed on top of him, exhaled in a shudder, and suddenly the needing was over. The roaring female energy just drifted out of the room, a storm that had passed. Sighing in relief, she shifted off of him, separating her gorgeous sex from his thing. As the *it* flopped lifeless on his belly, he felt the cold of the room on that flesh, so unappealing compared to her warmth.

"Are you okay?" he asked.

"Yes . . ." she whispered, settling on her side, already easing into sleep. "Yes, Zsadist . . . yes."

She was going to need food, he thought. He needed to go get her food.

Gathering his will, he took a deep breath, and another and another . . . and finally forced his upper body off the bed. His head swam wildly, the furniture and the floor and the walls spinning, trading places, until he wasn't sure whether he was on the ceiling or not.

The vertigo got worse as he shifted his legs off the mattress, and when he stood his balance deserted him completely. He fell into the wall, slamming into the thing, and had to hold himself up by clinging to some drapes.

When he was ready, he pushed free and leaned down to her. Lifting her up in his arms was a struggle, but his need to care for her was stronger than the exhaustion. He took her to his pallet and laid her down, then covered her with the comforter they'd long ago shoved to the floor. He was turning away when she took his arm.

"You have to feed," she said, trying to draw him close. "Come to my throat."

God, he was tempted.

"I'll be back," he said, stumbling to his feet. He lurched over to the closet and drew on a pair of boxers. Then he stripped the bed of the sheets and mattress pad and left.

Phury opened his eyes and realized he couldn't breathe.

Which made sense, he supposed. His face was mashed into a wad of blankets. He moved his mouth and nose free of the jam-up and tried to get his eyes to focus. The first thing he saw, about six inches from his head, was an ashtray full of dead blunts. On the floor.

What the hell? Oh . . . He was hanging off the foot of the mattress.

When he heard a groan, he shoved himself up, turned his head around—and came face-to-face with one of Vishous's feet. Beyond the size-fourteen was Butch's thigh.

Phury had to laugh, and that brought the cop's groggy gaze up out of a pillow. The human looked over himself and then Phury. He blinked a couple of times, like he was hoping to wake up for real.

"Oh, man," he said with more gravel than voice. Then he glanced at Vishous, who was passed out next to him. "Oh . . . *man,* this is too weird."

"Get over yourself, cop. You're not that attractive."

"Fair enough." He scrubbed his face. "But that doesn't mean I'm all into waking up with two men."

"V told you not to come back."

"True. That was my bad call."

Talk about a long night. Eventually, when even the feel of clothing against their skin had gotten to be too much, they'd lost any pretense of modesty. It had just been a matter of enduring the need: lighting up red smoke after red smoke, hitting the Scotch or the vodka, slipping into the bathroom alone to relieve themselves privately.

"So is it over?" Butch asked. "Tell me it's over."

Phury shuffled off the bed. "Yeah. I think so."

He picked up a sheet and pitched it at Butch, who covered himself and Vishous. V didn't even twitch. He was sleeping like the dead on his stomach, his eyes squeezed shut, a soft snore coming out of his mouth.

The cop cursed and rearranged his body, propping a pillow up against the headboard and leaning back. He rubbed his hair until it stood straight off his head and yawned so wide Phury heard the guy's jaw crack.

"Damn, vampire, I never thought I'd say this, but I have absolutely no interest in sex. Thank God."

Phury pulled on a pair of nylon warm-ups. "You want food? I'm going to make a kitchen trip."

Butch's eyes blissed out. "You're actually going to bring it up here? As in, I don't have to move?"

"You're going to owe me, but yeah, I'm willing to deliver."

"You are a god."

Phury put on a T-shirt. "What do you want?"

"Whatever's in the kitchen. Hell, make yourself really useful and drag that refrigerator on up here. I'm starved."

Phury went downstairs to the kitchen and was about to start foraging when he heard sounds coming from the laundry room. He went over and pushed the door open.

Zsadist was cramming sheets into the washer.

And dear Virgin in the Fade, he looked like hell. His stomach was a shrunken hole; his hips stood out from his skin like tent posts; his rib cage looked like a plow field. He must have lost ten, fifteen pounds overnight. And—*holy hell*—his neck and wrists were chewed raw. But . . . he smelled of beautiful dark spices, and there was a peace about him, so deep and unlikely Phury wondered if his senses were playing tricks on him.

"My brother?" he said.

Z didn't look up. "Do you know how to work this thing?"

"Ah, yeah. You put some of that stuff in the box in and you move that dial around— Here, let me help."

Z finished stuffing the belly of the washer and then stepped back, his eyes still locked on the floor. When the machine was filling up with water, Z muttered a thank-you and headed into the kitchen.

Phury followed, his heart in his throat. He wanted to ask if everything was okay, and not just with Bella.

He was trying to choose his words carefully when Z took a roasted turkey out of the refrigerator, tore the leg off, and bit into it. He chewed desperately, cleaning the meat from the bone as fast as he could, and the moment he was done he ripped the other drumstick free and did the same thing.

Jesus . . . The brother never took meat. Then again, he'd never been through a night like last night before. None of them had.

* * *

Z could feel Phury's eyes on him, and would have stopped eating if he could have. He hated people looking at him, especially when he was chewing on something, but he just couldn't get the food in fast enough.

He kept shoving stuff in his face as he took out a knife and a plate and started slicing off thin shavings of the turkey breast. He was careful to take only the very best parts of the meat for Bella. The odd bits, the corners, the stuff close to the core, that he ate himself, as it was not as good.

What else would she need? He wanted her to eat calorically dense things. And drink—he should bring her something to drink. He went back to the refrigerator and began making a pile of leftovers for review. He would choose carefully, taking to her only what was worthy of her tongue.

"Zsadist?"

God, he'd forgotten that Phury was still kicking around.

"Yeah," he said as he cracked a Tupperware bowl.

The mashed potatoes inside looked okay, though he really would have preferred bringing her some that he'd made. Not that he knew how to do that. Christ, he couldn't read, couldn't work a damn washing machine, couldn't cook.

He had to let her go so she could find a male who had half a brain.

"I don't mean to pry," Phury said.

"Yeah, you do." He took a loaf of Fritz's homemade sourdough bread out of the cupboard and squeezed the thing with his fingers. It was soft, but he sniffed at it anyway. Good, it was fresh enough for her.

"Is she okay? Are . . . you?"

"We're fine."

"What was it like?" Phury coughed a little. "I mean, I want to know not because it was Bella. It's just . . . I've heard a lot of rumors and I don't know what to believe."

Z took some mashed potatoes and put them on the plate with the turkey; then he spooned on wild rice and covered the lot with a good dose of gravy. He threw the heavy load into the microwave, glad this was one machine he knew how to work.

As he watched the food go around, he thought about his twin's question and remembered the feel of Bella getting up on his hips. That joining, of the dozens they'd had during the night, was the one that stuck out the most. She had been so lovely on top of him, especially as she'd kissed him. . . .

Throughout the needing, but mostly during that particular union, she'd chipped away at the past's hold on him, marking him with something good. He would treasure the warmth she'd given him for the rest of his days.

The microwave dinged and he realized Phury was still waiting for an answer.

Z put the food on a tray and grabbed some silverware so he could feed her properly.

As he turned and headed out of the room, he murmured, "She is more beautiful than I have words for." He lifted his eyes to Phury's. "And last night I was blessed beyond measure to serve her."

For some reason, the brother recoiled in shock and reached out. "Zsadist, your—"

"I have to bring my *nalla* her food. I'll see you later."

"Wait! Zsadist! Your—"

Z just shook his head and kept on going.

Chapter Thirty-five

"Why didn't you show me this as soon as I got home?" Rehvenge asked his *doggen*. As the servant flushed with shame and horror, he reached out to the poor male. "It's okay. Never mind."

"Master, I came to you when I realized you had returned for the day. But you were sleeping for once. I wasn't sure what the image was, and I didn't want to disturb you. You never rest."

Yeah, the feeding with Marissa had put him out like a light. First time he'd closed his eyes and lost consciousness in . . . God, whenever. But this was trouble.

Rehv sat down in front of the computer screen and re-played the digital file. It was the same as the first time he'd seen it: A man with dark hair and black clothes parking in front of the gates. Getting out of a truck. Coming forward to touch the mourning ribbons that had been tied on the iron bars.

Rehv increased the zoom until he saw the man's face clearly. Unremarkable, neither handsome nor ugly. But the body that went with it was big. And that jacket looked as if it was either padded or covering some weapons.

Rehv froze the image and did a copy on the date/time read-ing in the lower right-hand corner. He switched screens, call-

ing up the files from the other camera that monitored the front
gate, the heat-sensing one. With a quick paste action, he got
the recording from that piece of equipment at exactly the
same moment in time.

And what do you know. Body temperature of that "man"
was in the fifties. A *lesser.*

Rehv switched screens again and got in real tight on the
slayer's face while the killer looked at those ribbons. Sadness,
fear . . . anger. None of which were anonymous emotions; all
of which were tied to something personal. Something lost.

So this was the bastard who took Bella. And he was coming back for her.

Rehv wasn't surprised the *lesser* had found the house.
Bella's capture had been news within the species, and the
family's address had never been hidden from the race . . . in
fact, with *mahmen*'s spiritual advising, the Thorne Avenue
mansion was well-known. All it would take would be the capture of one civilian who knew where they lived.

The real question was, Why hadn't the slayer come
through the gates?

God. What time was it? Four in the afternoon. *Shit.*

"That is a *lesser*," Rehv said, punching his cane into the
floor and rising quickly. "So we evacuate the house right now.
You will find Lahni immediately and tell her the mistress
must be dressed. Then you will take them both through the
tunnel and drive them to the safe house in the van."

The *doggen* blanched. "Master, I had no idea that it was
a—"

Rehv put a hand on the male's shoulder to quell the wheel-
spin panic. "You did well with what you knew. But move
quickly now. Go get Lahni."

Rehv walked as quickly as he could to his mother's bedroom.

"*Mahmen?*" he said as he opened her door. "*Mahmen,*
wake up."

His mother sat up in her bed of silken sheets, her white hair
coiled in a cap for the day. "But it's . . . it is the afternoon still.
Why—"

"Lahni is coming to help you dress."

"Dear Virgin, Rehvenge. Why?"

"You are leaving this house."

"What—"

"Now, *mahmen*. I'll explain later." He kissed both her cheeks as her maid came in. "Ah, good. Lahni, you will dress your mistress fast."

"Yes, master," the *doggen* said with a bow.

"Rehvenge! What is—"

"Hurry. Leave with the *doggen*. I'll call you."

As his mother cried out his name, he went down to his private quarters and shut the doors so he wouldn't hear her. He picked up the phone and dialed the Brotherhood's number despising what he had to do. But Bella's safety had to come first. After he left a message that made his throat sting, he went to his walk-in closet.

Right now the mansion was sealed up tight for the daylight hours, so there was no way a *lesser* could get in. The shutters covering the windows and doors were bullet- and fireproof and the house was made of stone walls that were two feet thick. To top it off, there were enough cameras and security alarms so he'd know if anyone so much as sneezed on his property. But he wanted his *mahmen* out anyway.

Plus, as soon as darkness fell, he was going to open up the iron gates and roll out the welcome mat. He wanted that *lesser* inside.

Rehv stripped out of his mink robe and put on a pair of black pants and a thick turtleneck sweater. He wouldn't get out the weapons until his mother was gone. If she wasn't totally hysterical already, seeing him covered with metal was going to throw her right over the edge.

Before he went back to check on the progress of the evac, he glanced at the locked cabinet in his closet. It was getting time for his afternoon dopamine dose. *How perfect.*

Smiling, he left his room without injecting himself, ready to bring all his senses out to play.

*   *   *

As the shutters lifted for the night, Zsadist lay on his side next to Bella, watching her sleep. She was on her back, tight in the crook of his arm, her head at his chest level. No sheets or blankets covered her naked body, because she was still radiating heat from the remnants of the needing.

When he'd returned after his trip to the kitchen, she'd eaten from his hand and then snoozed as he'd made up the bed with fresh linens. They'd lain together in the pitch-dark ever since.

He moved his hand from her upper thigh to the underside of her breast and brushed at her nipple with his forefinger. He'd been like this for hours, petting her, humming to her. Though he was so tired his lids were at half-mast, the calm between them was better than any rest he could have gotten if he'd shut his eyes.

As she stirred against him her hip brushed his, and he was surprised as the urge to take her rose. By now he figured he'd be done with that for a while.

He leaned back and looked down his body. Through the slit in the front of his boxers, the head of that thing he'd used on her had escaped, and as the shaft lengthened, the blunt tip pushed out farther and farther.

Feeling as if he were breaking some kind of law, he took the finger that had been running circles around Bella's nipple and poked at the erection. It was stiff, so it moved right back into place.

He closed his eyes and, with a wince, captured the arousal in his palm. When he stroked it he was surprised at how the soft skin slid over the hard core. And the sensations were weird. Not unpleasant, really. Actually, they kind of reminded him of being inside of Bella, only not that good. Not by a long shot.

God, he was such a sissy. Afraid of his own . . . dick. Cock? Penis? What the hell should he call it? What did normal males call themselves? Okay, George wasn't an option. But somehow referring to it as . . . *it,* just didn't seem right anymore.

Now that they'd shaken hands, so to speak.

He let go of the thing and slid his palm under the waist-band of the boxers. He was queased out and nervous, but fig-ured he had to finish the Lewis-and-Clark routine. He didn't know when he'd have the heart to do this again.

He shuffled the . . . *dick,* yeah, he'd start with just calling it *dick* . . . around so it was inside, but out of the way, and then touched the balls underneath. He felt a shock ride up the erec-tion's shaft, and the tip tingled.

That felt kind of nice.

He frowned as he explored for the first time what the good Virgin had given him. Funny that all of it had been attached to him, hanging off of him, for so long and yet he'd never done what young, post-transition males no doubt spent whole days doing.

As he brushed over the balls again, they got tighter and the dick got even harder. Sensations boiled in his lower body, and images of Bella popped into his mind, images of the two of them having sex, of him stretching her legs up and going deep into her. He recalled with bone-aching clarity what she felt like beneath him, what that channel of hers did to him, how tight she was. . . .

The whole thing started to snowball, the pictures in his mind, the rolling currents of energy spreading out from where his hand was. His breath grew short. His mouth parted. His body did some kind of surge thing, his hips jerking forward. On impulse, he rolled over on to his back and shoved the box-ers down.

And then he realized what he was doing. Was he jerking off? Next to Bella? God, he was a *nasty* bastard.

Disgusted with himself, he released his hand and started yanking the boxers back up—

"Don't stop," Bella said softly.

A frigid blast shot down Z's spine. *Busted.*

His eyes went to hers as the blood hit his face.

But she just smiled at him and stroked his arm. "You're so beautiful. The way you arched just now. Finish it, Zsadist. I know that's what you want to do, and you have nothing to be embarrassed by. You're beautiful when you touch yourself."

She kissed his bicep, her eyes going to the tent of his boxers. "Finish it," she whispered. "Let me see you finish."

Feeling like an anxious fool, but curiously unable to stop himself, he sat up and got naked.

Bella made a little noise of approval as he lay down again. Taking strength from her, he slowly slid his hand down his stomach, feeling the ridges of his muscles and the smooth, hairless skin that covered them. He didn't really expect to be able to continue—

Holy shit. The thing was so hard, he could feel his heartbeat drumming through it.

He stared into Bella's deep blue eyes as he moved his palm up and down. Starbursts of pleasure began to shoot off and flow through his body. God . . . having her watch worked for him, even though it shouldn't have. When he'd been watched before—

No, the past was not welcome here. If he lingered on what had happened a century ago, he was going to lose this moment with Bella.

With a shove and a slam he locked away the memories of what had been done to him in front of an audience. *Bella's eyes . . . see them. Be in them. Drown in them.*

Her gaze was so lovely, shining up at him with warmth, holding him as if he were in her arms. He looked at her lips. Her breasts. Her stomach . . . The gathering need in his blood took a geometric leap, exploding so that every inch of him felt an erotic tension.

Bella's eyes drifted down. As she watched him work it, she took her bottom lip between her teeth. Her fangs were two little white daggers, and he wanted them in his skin again. He wanted her sucking on him.

"Bella . . ." he groaned. Fuck, he was *really* into this.

He cocked one of his legs up, moaning in the back of his throat as he moved his hand faster and then concentrated the motion at the tip. A second later he lost it. He cried out as his head punched back into the pillow and his spine curved up to the ceiling. Warm jets hit his chest and belly, and the rhythmic releases went on for a time as he finished himself off. He stopped when the head was too sensitive to touch anymore.

He was breathing hard and dizzy as hell as he leaned to the side and kissed her. When he pulled back, her eyes showed how clearly she read him. She knew that she'd helped him through this first time. Yet somehow she wasn't looking at him with pity. She didn't seem to care that he was a lame-ass who up until now hadn't been able to bear touching himself.

He opened his mouth. "I l—"

A knock cut off the declaration he had no business making.

"Do *not* open that door," he barked, wiping himself off with the boxers. He kissed Bella and pulled a sheet over her before going across the room.

He braced his shoulder against the door, as if whoever was on the other side might crash into the room. It was a stupid impulse, but there was no way anyone was going to see Bella in her postneeding glow. That was for him only.

"What," he said.

Phury's voice was muffled. "The Explorer you shoved your phone into moved last night. Went to the supermarkets where Wellsie's been buying the apples for the solstice festival. We've canceled the orders, but we've got to reconnoiter. The Brotherhood's meeting in Wrath's study in ten minutes."

Z closed his eyes and leaned his forehead on the wood. Real life was back.

"Zsadist? Did you hear me?"

He glanced at Bella, thinking their time together was over. And going by the way she gathered the sheets to her chin as if she were cold, she knew it too.

God . . . this hurts, he thought. He actually felt it . . . hurt.

"I'll be right there," he said.

Dropping his eyes from Bella, he turned and headed for the shower.

Chapter Thirty-six

While night fell, O was enraged as he stalked around the cabin and gathered up the ammo he needed. He'd gotten back only a half hour ago, and the last day had been for shit. First he'd gone to the Omega and received one fuck of a tongue-lashing. Literally. The master had been ripping pissed about the two *lessers* who had been arrested, as if it were all O's fault that those incompetents had gotten cuffed and stuffed.

After the Omega was through with his first wave of sharing, the bastard master had pulled the slayers out of the human world, retracting his hold on them as if they were dogs on a leash. Interestingly, it wasn't that easy for him. Calling members of the Society home was not a flick-of-the-wrist kind of thing, and the weakness was something to remember.

Not that the frailty had lasted. Man, O had no doubt those two *lessers* were ruing the day they had traded their souls. The Omega had started in on them immediately, and the scene was right out of a Clive Barker movie. And the thing was, the slayers were undead, so the punishment could go on and on until the Omega got bored.

He'd looked very focused as O had taken off.

The return to the temporal world had been a total buzz kill. In O's absence, an insurgency of Betas had taken root. A squadron of them, all four, had gotten bored and decided to attack some other *lessers*, a kind of hunt-and-kill game that resulted in a number of Society casualties. U's increasingly frantic voice mails, left over the course of six hours, were the kind of updates that made a man want to scream.

Goddamn it. U was a total failure as a second in command. He hadn't been able to control the Beta battles, and a human had been slaughtered during the violence. O didn't give a shit about the dead guy, but what he'd worried about was the body. The last thing they needed was the cops getting involved. Again.

So O had gone to the scene and gotten his hands dirty getting rid of the frickin' corpse; then he'd pissed away a couple of hours identifying the rogue Betas and paying each of them a visit. He'd wanted to kill them, but if there were any more vacancies in the Society's ranks, he was going to have another problem with the master.

By the time he'd finished beating the crap out of that quartet of idiots, which had been only a half an hour ago, he was in a total rage. And that was when U had called with the happy news that all the apple orders that had been put in for the solstice festival had been canceled. And why were all those buys offed? Because somehow the vampires had figured out they were being tracked.

Yeah, U was righteous on the stealth job. *Right.*

So the mass-murder tribute to the Omega had gone out the window. So O had nothing to butter the master up. So if his wife was alive, it was going to be harder to make her a *lesser.*

O had lost it at that point. Had screamed at U on the phone. Let loose all kinds of obscenities. And U had taken the on-air whipping like a pussy, getting quiet, hunkering down. The silence had driven O insane, but then he'd always hated it when people didn't fight back.

Christ. He'd thought U was stable, but in reality the bastard was weak, and O was sick of it. He knew he needed to put a knife in U's chest, and he was going to, but he'd had it with the distractions.

Fuck the Society and U and the Betas and the Omega. He had work to do that mattered.

O grabbed the truck's keys and left the cabin. He was going directly to 27 Thorne Avenue and he was going to get inside of that mansion. Maybe it was desperation talking, but he was certain the answer he was looking for was behind those iron gates.

Finally, he was going to find out the where and why of his wife.

O was almost at the F-150 when his neck started to hum, no doubt from all that screaming at U. He ignored the sensation and got behind the wheel. As he headed out, he pulled at the collar of his shirt, then coughed a couple of times, trying to loosen things up. *Shit.* This felt weird.

Half a mile later he was gasping for breath. Grabbing his throat, choking, he wrenched the steering wheel to the right and stomped on the brakes. Punching open the door, he stumbled out. The cold air brought him a second or two of relief and then he was back to the suffocation.

O went down on his knees. As he fell face-first in the snow, his vision flickered on and off like a broken lamp. And then went out.

As Zsadist walked down the hall to Wrath's study, his mind was sharp though his body was slow. When he stepped into the room the brothers were all there, and the group fell silent. Ignoring the bunch of them, he kept his eyes on the floor and went over to the corner he usually propped himself up in. He heard someone clear a throat to get the ball rolling. Probably Wrath.

Tohrment spoke. "Bella's brother called. He's tabled the *sehclusion* request and asked that she stay here for a couple of days."

Z jacked his head up. "Why?"

"He didn't give a reason—" Tohr's eyes narrowed on Z's face. "Oh . . . my God."

The others in the room glanced over, and there were a

couple of low gasps. Then the Brotherhood and Butch just stared at him.

"What the fuck are you looking at?"

Phury pointed to the antique mirror hanging on the wall next to the double doors. "See for yourself."

Zsadist marched across the room, ready to give them all hell. Bella was what mattered—

His mouth went lax at his reflection. With a shaky hand he reached out to the eyes in the old-fashioned leaded glass. His irises were no longer black. They were yellow. Just like his twin's.

"Phury?" he said softly. "Phury . . . what's happened to me?"

As the male came up behind him, the brother's face appeared right beside Z's. And then Wrath's dark reflection showed up in the mirror, all long hair and sunglasses. Then Rhage's star-fallen beauty. And Vishous's Sox cap. And Tohrment's brush cut. And Butch's busted nose.

One by one they reached out and touched him, their big hands landing gently on his shoulders.

"Welcome back, my brother," Phury whispered.

Zsadist stared at the males who were behind him. And had the oddest thought that if he were to let himself go limp and fall backward . . . they would catch him.

Shortly after Zsadist left, Bella walked out of his bedroom and went in search of him. She'd been about to call her brother and arrange for a meeting when she realized she had to take care of her lover before she got wrapped up in her family drama again.

Finally Zsadist needed something from her. And badly, too. He'd been nearly drained after his time with her, and she knew exactly how starved he was, knew just how desperate he was to feed. With so much of his blood in her veins, she could sense his hunger vividly, and she also knew, too, precisely where he was in the house. All she had to do was reach out her senses and she could feel him, find him.

Bella followed his pulse down the corridor of statues,

around the corner, and toward the open double doors at the head of the stairs. Angry male voices boiled out of the study, and Zsadist's was one of them.

"The hell you're going out tonight," someone shouted.

Zsadist's tone was downright evil. "Don't try to order me around, Tohr. It just pisses me off and wastes your time."

"Look at yourself—you're a fucking skeleton! Unless you feed, you're staying in."

Bella came into the room just as Zsadist said, "Try to keep me here and see where it lands you, *brother.*"

With all of the Brotherhood looking on, the two males were nose-to-nose, eyes locked, fangs bared.

Jesus, she thought. Such aggression.

But . . . Tohrment was right. She hadn't been able to see in the darkness of the bedroom, but here in the light Zsadist looked half-dead. The bones of his skull were pushing through his skin; his T-shirt was hanging from his body; his pants were sagging. His black eyes were intense as always, but the rest of him was in rough shape.

Tohrment shook his head. "Be reasonable—"

"I would see Bella *ahvenged.* That is *totally* reasonable."

"No, it isn't," she said. Her interjection brought all the heads her way.

As Zsadist looked at her, his irises changed color, flashing from the angry black she was used to into a glowing, incandescent yellow.

"Your eyes," she whispered. "What's happened to your—"

Wrath cut in. "Bella, your brother has asked that you stay here a little longer."

Her surprise was so great, she looked away from Zsadist. "What, my lord?"

"He doesn't want me to rule on your *sehclusion* right now, and he wants you to remain here."

"Why?"

"No idea. Maybe you could ask him."

God, as if things aren't confusing enough. She glanced back at Zsadist, but he was focused on a window across the room.

"You are, of course, welcome to stay," Wrath said.

As Zsadist stiffened, she wondered how true that was.

"I don't want to be *ahvenged*," she said loudly. When Zsadist's head whipped around, she spoke directly to him. "I'm grateful for everything you've done for me. But I don't want anyone hurt trying to get at the *lesser* who kept me. Especially not you."

His brows cranked down on his eyes. "That is not your call."

"The hell it's not." As she pictured him going to fight, terror overrode everything. "God, Zsadist . . . I don't want to be responsible for your going out and getting yourself killed."

"That *lesser*'s going to end up pine-boxing it, not me."

"You can't be serious! Dear Virgin, look at you. You can't possibly fight. You're so weak."

There was a collective hiss in the room, and Zsadist's eyes went black.

Oh . . . shit. Bella put her hand over her mouth. Weak. She'd called him weak. In front of the whole Brotherhood.

There was no greater insult. To merely insinuate that a male couldn't handle himself with strength was unforgivable in the warrior class, no matter the basis. But to come flat out and say so, in front of witnesses, was a complete social castration, an irrevocable condemnation of his worth as a male.

Bella rushed over. "I'm sorry, I didn't mean—"

Zsadist lifted his arms out of her reach. "Get away from me."

She put her hand back to her mouth as he stepped around her like she was a grenade. He headed out the door and his footsteps receded down the hall. When she was able, she met the disapproving eyes of his brothers.

"I will apologize to him immediately. And hear this now, I do not doubt his courage or his strength. I worry over him because . . ."

Say it to them, she thought. Surely they would understand.

"I love him."

Abruptly the tension in the room eased. Well, most of it. Phury turned away and went to the fire, leaning up against the mantel. His head dipped down as if he wanted to be in the flames.

"I'm glad you feel that way," Wrath said. "He needs it. Now go find him and apologize."

On her way out of the study, Tohrment stepped in front of her and gave her a level look. "Try to feed him while you're at it, okay?"

"I'm praying he'll let me."

Chapter Thirty-seven

Rehvenge prowled around his house, going from room to room with a restless, punching stride. His visual field was red, his senses alive, his cane left behind hours ago. No longer cold as he always was, he'd ditched the turtleneck, hanging his weapons on his bare skin. He felt all of his body, reveled in all the power of his muscles and bones. And there were other things, too. Things he hadn't experienced in . . .

God, it had been a decade since he'd let himself get this far gone, and because this was engineered, a deliberate recession into the madness, he felt in control—which was probably a dangerous fallacy, but he didn't give a shit. He was . . . liberated. And he wanted to fight his enemy with a desperation that was downright sexual.

So he was also frustrated as hell.

He looked out one of the library's windows. He'd left the front gate wide-open, trying to encourage visitors. Nothing. *Nada.* Zilch.

The grandfather clock chimed twelve times.

He'd been so sure the *lesser* would show, but no one had come through the gate, up the drive, to the house. And according to the periphery's security cameras, the cars that had passed by on the street were only those indigenous to the neighborhood: multiple Mercedes, a Maybach, several Lexus SUVs, four BMWs.

Goddamn it. He wanted that slayer, badly enough to scream, and the urge to fight, to *ahvenge* his family, to protect his turf, made sense. His bloodline reached back into the warrior elite on his mother's side, and aggression ran thick in him; it always had. Add to his core nature the anger about his sister and the fact that he'd had to rush his *mahmen* out of her home in broad fucking daylight, and he was a powder keg.

He thought of the Brotherhood. He would have been a good candidate for them, if they'd been recruiting before his transition. . . . Except who the hell knew what they did anymore? They'd gone underground as the vampire civilization had crumbled, becoming this hidden enclave, protecting themselves more than the race they were sworn to defend.

Hell, he couldn't help thinking that if they'd been more focused on their job and less on themselves, they could have prevented Bella's abduction. Or found her right away.

Fresh anger stirring, he continued to walk through the house in a random pattern, looking out of windows and doors, checking monitors. Eventually he decided the aimless waiting was bullshit. He was just going to lose his mind wandering around here all night, and he had business to take care of downtown. If he set the alarms and they were triggered, he could dematerialize in the blink of an eye.

When he got up to his room, he went to his closet and paused in front of the locked cabinet in the back. Going to work unmedicated was not an option, even if it meant he had to use a gun instead of hand-to-hand on the *lesser* if the bastard showed up.

Rehv took out a vial of dopamine as well as his syringe and tourniquet. As he prepared the needle and wrapped the rubber tube around his upper arm, he stared at the clear fluid he was about to pump into his vein. Havers had mentioned that at this kind of high dose, paranoia was a side effect in some vampires. And Rehv had been doubling up the prescribed load for . . . Jesus, ever since Bella had been abducted. So maybe he was losing it.

But then he thought about the body temperature of that thing that had stopped in front of the gates. Fifty degrees wasn't alive. Not for humans.

He injected himself and waited until his vision came back and his body went away. Then he dressed warmly, grabbed his cane, and headed out.

Zsadist stalked into ZeroSum, totally aware of Phury's silent worry looming behind him like a damp fog. Good thing he found his twin easy to ignore, or all that despair would have sucked him down.

Weak. You're so weak.

Yeah, well, he was going to take care of that.

"Give me twenty minutes," he told Phury. "Then meet me outside in the alley."

He didn't waste any time. He picked a working human whore who had her hair up in a chignon, gave her two hundred dollars, then practically pushed her out of the club. She didn't seem to care about his face or his size or the way he moved her around. Her eyes were not tracking at all, she was so high.

When they were out in the alley, she laughed too loudly.

"How do you want it?" she said, doing a little dance in her skyscraper heels. She stumbled, then put her hands up over her head and stretched in the cold. "You look like you take it rough. Which is fine with me."

He spun her to face the bricks and held her in place by the back of her neck. As she giggled and pretended to struggle, he restrained her and thought of the countless human females he'd sucked over the years. How clean did he get their memories? Did they wake up from nightmares of him when their subconscious stirred?

User, he thought. He was a user. Just like the Mistress.

The only difference was, he had no choice.

Or did he? He could have used Bella tonight; she'd wanted him to. But if he fed off her, it was only going to be harder for both of them to let go. And that was where they were headed.

She didn't want to be *ahvenged.* He could not rest while that *lesser* took up space on the earth. . . .

More than that, though, he couldn't bear to watch Bella destroy herself by trying to love a male she shouldn't. He had to get her to walk away from him. He wanted her to be happy and safe, he wanted a thousand years of her waking up with a peaceful smile on her face. He wanted her well mated, with a male she could take pride in.

In spite of the bonding he had for her, he wanted her to know joy more than he wanted her with him.

The prostitute wiggled. "We going to do this or what, daddy? 'Cause I'm getting kind of excited."

Z bared his fangs and reared back, prepared to strike.

"Zsadist—*no!*"

Bella's voice brought his head around. She was standing in the middle of the alley, about fifteen feet away. Her eyes were horrified, her mouth open.

"No," she said hoarsely. "Don't . . . do it."

His first impulse was to get her the hell back to the house and then yell at her for leaving. His second was that he had his chance to sever ties between them. It would be a surgical maneuver, involving a lot of pain, but she would heal from the amputation. Even if he wouldn't.

The whore looked over, then laughed, a high, happy trill. "Is she going to watch? 'Cause that'll cost you fifty bucks extra."

Bella put her hand up to her throat as Zsadist held the human between his body and the brick wall of a building. The pain in her chest was so great she couldn't breathe. To see him so close to another female . . . a human, a prostitute at that . . . and for the purpose of feeding? After all they had shared last night?

"Please," she said. "Use me. Take me. *Don't* do this."

He spun the female around so the two of them were facing front; then he clamped an arm across the woman's chest. The prostitute laughed and undulated against him, rubbing her body into his, her hips moving in a sinuous twist.

Bella put her hands out into the frigid air. "I love you. I didn't mean to insult you in front of the Brothers. *Please* don't do this to get back at me."

Zsadist's eyes locked on hers. Misery shone in them, an utter desolation, but he bared his fangs . . . then sank them into the woman's neck. Bella cried out as he swallowed; the human female laughed again with a lilting, wild sound.

Bella staggered back. And still his eyes didn't move from hers, even as he repositioned his bite and drank harder. Unable to watch for a moment longer, she dematerialized to the only place she could think of.

Her family's house.

Chapter Thirty-eight

"The Reverend wants to see you."

Phury looked up from the glass of seltzer he'd ordered. One of ZeroSum's bouncer mountains was looming over him, the Moor oozing a quiet threat.

"Any particular reason?"

"You're a valued customer."

"So he should leave me alone."

"Is that a no?"

Phury cocked an eyebrow. "Yeah, that's a *no*."

The Moor disappeared and came back with reinforcements: Two guys as big as he was. "The Reverend wants to see you."

"Yeah, you told me."

"Now."

The only reason Phury slid out of the booth was because the trio seemed ready to carry him off, and he didn't need the kind of attention that would come when he smacked them around.

The moment he walked into the Reverend's office, he knew the male was in a dangerous frame of mind. Not that that was a news flash.

"Leave us," the vampire murmured from behind his desk. As the room emptied out, he sat back in his chair, violet eyes shrewd. Instinct had Phury easing one hand behind his back, close to the dagger he carried on his belt.

"So I've been thinking about our last meeting," the Reverend said, making a temple out of his long fingers. The light over him picked out his high cheekbones and his hard jaw and his heavy shoulders. His mohawk had been trimmed, the black stripe no more than two inches off his skull. "Yeah . . . I've been thinking about the fact that you know my little secret. I'm feeling exposed."

Phury stayed silent, wondering where in the hell this was going.

The Reverend pushed back his chair and crossed his legs, ankle on his knee. His expensive suit fell open, revealing his broad chest. "You can imagine how I feel. How it keeps me up."

"Try some Ambien. That'll knock you out."

"Or I could light up a lot of red smoke. Just like you, right?" The male ran a hand over his mohawk, lips lifting into a sly grin. "Yeah, I really don't feel safe."

What a lie that was. The guy kept himself surrounded by Moors who were as smart as they were lethal. And he was definitely someone who could handle himself. Besides, *symphaths* had advantages in conflict that no one else did.

The Reverend stopped smiling. "I was thinking maybe you could cop to your secret. Then we'd be even."

"Don't have one."

"Bullshit . . . *Brother*." The Reverend's mouth pulled up at the corners again, but his eyes were a cold purple. "Because you *are* a member of the Brotherhood. You and those big males you come in here with. The one with the goatee who drinks my vodka. The guy with the fucked-up face who sucks my whores. Don't know what to say about that human you hang with, but whatever."

Phury stared hard across the desk. "You've just violated every social custom our species has. But then, why should I expect good behavior out of a drug dealer?"

"And users always lie. So the question was pointless anyway, wasn't it?"

"Tread carefully, my man," Phury said in a low voice.

"Or you'll what? You saying you're a Brother, so I'd better shape up before you hurt me?"

"Health should never be taken for granted."

"Why won't you admit it? Or are you Brothers afraid that the race you fail will rebel? Are you hiding from all of us because of the shitty job you've been doing lately?"

Phury turned away. "Don't know what you're talking to me for."

"About the red smoke." The Reverend's voice was bladed like a knife. "I've just run out of it."

A flicker of unease tightened Phury's chest. He looked over his shoulder. "There are other dealers."

"Have fun finding them."

Phury put his hand on the doorknob. When it refused to turn, he glanced back across the room. The Reverend was watching him, still as a cat. And trapping him in the office with his will.

Phury tightened his grip and pulled, tearing the piece of brass right off. As the door lolled open, he tossed the knob onto the Reverend's desk.

"Guess you're going to have to fix this."

He took two steps before a hand grabbed onto his arm. The Reverend's face was hard as stone, and so was his grip. With the blink of a violet eye, something flared between them, some kind of exchange . . . a current. . . .

From out of nowhere, Phury felt an overwhelming tide of guilt, like someone had popped the lid off all his deepest concerns and his fears for the future of the race. He had to respond to it, couldn't bear the pressure.

Riding the wave, he found himself saying in a rush, "We live and die for our kind. The species is our first and only concern. We fight every night and count the jars of the *lessers* we kill. Stealth is the way we protect the civilians. The less they know about us, the safer they are. That is why we disappeared."

As soon as the words left him, he cursed.

Goddamn it, you could never trust a symphath, he thought. Or the feelings you had while you were around them.

"Let go of me, sin-eater," he gritted. "And stay the fuck out of my head."

The hard grip dissolved and the Reverend bowed a little, a measure of respect that was a shocker. "Well, what do you know, warrior. A shipment of red smoke just came in."

The male brushed by and walked slowly into the crowd, his mohawk, his thick shoulders, his aura getting lost in the people whose addictions he fed.

Bella took form in front of her family's home. The exterior lights were off, which was strange, but she was crying, so it wasn't like she would have seen much anyway. She let herself in, turned off the security alarm, and stood in the foyer.

How could Zsadist do that to her? For all it hurt, he might as well have had sex in front of her. God, she'd always known he could be cruel, but that went too far, even for him. . . .

Except it wasn't about retaliation for the social slight, was it? No, that was too petty. She suspected he'd bitten that human for a declarative break. Because he wanted to send a message, a totally incontrovertible message that Bella wasn't welcome in his life.

Well, it worked.

Deflated, defeated, she glanced around her family's front hall. Everything was the same. The blue silk wallpaper, the black marble floor, the sparkling chandelier overhead. It was like stepping back in time. She'd grown up in this house, the last young her mother would ever bear, the cosseted sister of a brother who loved her, the daughter of a father she'd never known. . . .

Wait a minute. It was quiet. Way too quiet.

"*Mahmen*? Lahni?" Silence. She wiped her tears away. "Lahni?"

Where were the *doggen*? And her mother? She knew Rehv would be out doing whatever he did during the nights, so she didn't expect to see him. But the others were always home.

Bella walked over to the curving staircase and called out, "*Mahmen*?"

She went upstairs and jogged down to her mother's bed-

room. The sheets on the bed were thrown back, all a mess . . .
something the *doggen* would never have allowed normally.
With a feeling of dread she went down the hall to Rehvenge's
room. His bed was also disheveled, the Frette sheets and the
heaps and heaps of fur comforters he always used thrown to
one side. The disorder was unheard-of.

The house was not safe. That was why Rehv had insisted
she stay with the Brotherhood.

Bella rushed out into the hall and ran down the stairs. She
needed to be outdoors to dematerialize, because the walls of
the mansion were all inlaid with steel.

She tore out of the front door . . . and didn't know where
she could go. Not even she knew the address of her brother's
safe house, and that was where he would have taken *mahmen*
and the *doggen*. And she wasn't about to waste time calling
him, not in the house.

There was no choice. She was heartbroken, she was angry,
she was exhausted, and the idea of going back to the Brotherhood's compound made all of that worse. But she wasn't
about to be stupid. She closed her eyes and disappeared back
to the Brothers' mansion.

Zsadist finished quickly with the whore, then focused on
Bella. Because his blood was in her, he could sense her materializing somewhere to the south and east. He triangulated her
destination to the area of Bellman Road and Thorne Avenue:
a very ritzy neighborhood. Obviously she had gone to her
family's house.

His instincts fired up, because that call from her brother
had been too weird. Chances were, something was going
down over there. Why else would the male want her staying
with the Brotherhood after he'd been about to slap a *sehclusion* on her?

Just as Z was going to go get her, he sensed her traveling
again. This time she landed outside the Brotherhood's mansion. And she stayed there.

Thank God. He didn't have to worry about her safety for
the time being.

Abruptly, the club's side door opened, and Phury came out looking decidedly stark. "You feed?"

"Yeah."

"So you should go home and wait for the strength to kick in."

"Already has." *Sort of.*

"Z—"

Phury stopped talking, and both of them whipped their heads around toward Trade Street. At the alley's throat, three white-haired men dressed in black were walking past in I-formation. The *lessers* were staring straight ahead as if they'd found a target and were closing in.

Without a word spoken, Z and Phury took off at a silent jog, moving lightly across the fresh-packed snow. When they got to Trade Street it turned out the *lessers* hadn't found a victim but were meeting up with another pack of their kind—two of which had brown hair.

Z put his palm on one of his dagger handles and trained his eyes on the pair with the dark heads. Dear Virgin in the Fade, let one of them be what he was looking for.

"Hold up, Z," Phury hissed while taking out his cell. "You stay put and I'll get reinforcements."

"How 'bout you call"—he unsheathed the dagger—"while I kill."

Z took off, keeping the knife by his thigh, because this was a high-exposure area with humans around.

The *lessers* spotted him immediately, and they fell into attack posture, their knees bending, their arms coming up. To corral the bastards, he jogged in a fat circle around them, and they flowed with him, turning, coalescing into a triangle that faced him. When he backed into the shadows, they followed as a unit.

After darkness had swallowed them all, Zsadist lifted his black dagger high, bared his fangs, and attacked. He prayed like hell that when the violent song and dance was over one of the two dark-haired *lessers* had white roots at his scalp.

Chapter Thirty-nine

Dawn was just arriving as U walked up to the cabin and opened the door. He slowed as he stepped inside, wanting to savor the moment. The headquarters were his. He had become the *Fore-lesser.* O was no more.

U couldn't believe he'd gone and done it. He couldn't believe he'd had the balls to petition the Omega for a change of leadership. And he really couldn't believe that the master had agreed with him and called O home.

It wasn't in U's nature to lead, but he couldn't see that he had a choice. After everything that had happened yesterday with the rogue Betas and the arrests and the insurgencies, total anarchy among the slayers was coming fast and hard. Meanwhile, O was doing jack shit at the top. He'd even seemed annoyed that he had to do his job.

U had been put back against a wall. He'd been in the Society for almost two centuries, and he was damned if he was going to see the thing devolve into a loose confederation of sloppy, disorganized contract killers who occasionally went after vampires. For God's sake, they were already forgetting who their target was supposed to be, and it had been three fucking days since O had let things slide.

No, the Society had to be run with a focused, heavy hand in the temporal realm. So O had to be replaced.

U sat down at the rough table and fired up the laptop. First thing on deck was to call a general assembly and make a show of strength. That was the one thing O had done right. The other *lessers* had feared him.

U called up a list of Betas to find one to sacrifice as an example, but before he got far, he was IM'd with a nasty news flash. Last night a bloody fight had taken place downtown. Two members of the Brotherhood against seven slayers. Fortunately, it looked as if both the Brothers had been hurt. But only one of the *lessers* had survived, so more Society members were lost.

Man, recruiting was going to be paramount. But how the hell was he going to find the time? He had to gather the reins first.

U rubbed his eyes, thinking of the work in front of him.

Welcome to the job of Fore-lesser, he thought as he began to dial his cell.

Bella glared up at Rhage, not caring that the male had a hundred and fifty pounds and eight inches on her.

Unfortunately, the Brother didn't seem to mind that she was pissed off. And he didn't budge from the bedroom door he was blocking.

"But I want to see him."

"Now's not the best time, Bella."

"How seriously is he hurt?"

"This is Brotherhood business," Rhage said gently. "Leave it alone. We'll let you know what happens."

"Oh, sure you will. Just like you all told me he was injured. For God's sake, I had to find out from *Fritz.*"

At that moment, the bedroom door swung open.

Zsadist was as grim as she'd ever seen him, and he was marked up badly. One of his eyes was swollen shut, his lip was split, and his arm was in a sling. Little random cuts were all over his neck and skull, like he'd bounced on pebbles or something.

As she winced, he glanced at her. His eyes flashed from

black to yellow, but then he just looked at Rhage and spoke quickly.

"Phury's finally resting." He nodded in Bella's direction. "If she's come to sit by him, let her. He'll be eased by her presence."

Zsadist turned away. As he walked down the hall, he limped, his left leg dragging behind as if his thigh wasn't working right.

With a curse Bella went after him, even though she had no idea why she bothered. He would accept nothing from her, not her blood or her love . . . certainly not her sympathy. He didn't want a damn thing from her.

Well, except for her to go away.

Before she caught up with him, Zsadist stopped abruptly and glanced back at her. "If Phury needs to feed, will you let him take your vein?"

She froze. Not only did he drink from another, but he found it easy to share her with his twin. Work of a moment, nothing special. Christ, was she so disposable? Had nothing they'd shared meant something to him?

"Will you let him?" Zsadist's newly yellow eyes narrowed on her face. "Bella?"

"Yes," she said in a low voice. "I'll take care of him."

"Thank you."

"I think I despise you right now."

"It's about time."

She pivoted on her heel, ready to go striding back to Phury's room, when Zsadist said softly, "Have you bled yet?"

Oh, terrific, another cringer. He wanted to know if he'd gotten her pregnant. Would no doubt be relieved when he heard the good news he hadn't.

She glared at him over her shoulder. "I've been cramping. You have nothing to worry about."

He nodded.

Before he could get away, she bit out, "Tell me something. If I were with young, would you mate me?"

"I would provide for you and your babe until another male did."

"My babe . . . as if it wouldn't be half yours?" When he

said nothing, she had to push. "Would you not even acknowledge it?"

His only response was to cross his arms over his chest.

She shook her head. "Holy hell . . . you really are cold to the bone, aren't you."

He stared at her for a long time. "I've never asked you for anything, have I?"

"Oh, no. You've never done that." She let out a hard laugh. "God forbid you open yourself up for that."

"Take care of Phury. He needs it. So do you."

"Don't you *dare* tell me what I need."

She didn't wait for a response. She marched down the hall to Phury's doorway, shoved Rhage out of the way, and shut herself in with Zsadist's twin. She was so pissed off that it took her a second to realize she was in the dark and that the room smelled like red smoke, a lovely, chocolaty scent.

"Who's there?" Phury said hoarsely from the bed.

She cleared her throat. "Bella."

A ragged sigh rose into the air. "Hi."

"Hi. How are you feeling?"

"Downright perky, thanks for asking."

She smiled a little until she came up to him. With her night vision, she saw that he was lying on top of the covers with only a pair of boxers on. He had a gauze pad around his belly and was covered with bruises. And—*oh, God*—his leg . . .

"Don't worry," he said dryly. "I haven't had that foot-and-shin combo for over a century. And I really am okay. Just some aesthetic damage."

"Then why are you wearing that bandage like a sash?"

"It makes my ass look smaller."

She laughed. She'd expected him to be half-dead, and he did look like he'd been in a hell of a fight. But he wasn't on death's door.

"What happened to you?" she asked.

"I got hit in the side."

"With what?"

"A knife."

Now, that made her sway. Maybe he only seemed okay.

"I'm fine, Bella. Honestly. In another six hours I'm going to be ready to go back out." There was a short silence. "What's doing? Are you all right?"

"Just wanted to see how you are."

"Well . . . I'm fine."

"And, ah . . . do you need to feed?"

He stiffened, then abruptly reached for the comforter, pulling it over his hips. She wondered why he was acting like he had something to hide. . . . *Oh, right. Whoa.*

For the first time she assessed him as a male. He really was beautiful, with all that gorgeous, lush hair and a face that was classically handsome. His body was spectacular, layered with the kind of heavy muscle his twin lacked. But no matter how good he looked, he wasn't the male for her.

It was a pity, she thought. For both of them. God, how she hated hurting him.

"Do you?" she said. "Need to feed?"

"Are you offering?"

She swallowed. "Yes. I am. So would you . . . May I give you my vein?"

A dark fragrance permeated the room, so strong it eclipsed the red-smoke aroma: The smell was the thick, rich scent of a male's hunger. Phury's hunger for her.

Bella closed her eyes and prayed that if he accepted, she could get through it without crying.

As the sun went down later in the day, Rehvenge stared at the funeral drapes hanging off his sister's portrait. When his cell phone rang he looked at the caller ID and flipped it open.

"Hello, Bella," he said softly.

"How did you know—"

"It was you? Untraceable number. Very untraceable, if this phone can't locate the source." At least she was still safe at the Brotherhood's compound, he thought. Wherever that was. "I'm glad you called."

"I went home last night."

Rehv's hand crushed the phone. "Last night? What the hell! I didn't want you going—"

Sobs came through the phone, great, wretched sobs. The misery stole his words, his anger, his breath.

"Bella? What's wrong? Bella? *Bella!*" *Oh, Jesus . . . "Did one of those Brothers hurt you?"*

"No." She took a deep breath. "And don't yell at me. I can't bear it. I'm through with you and the yelling. No more."

He dragged air into his lungs, clamping down on his temper. "What happened?"

"When can I come home?"

"Talk to me."

Silence stretched out between them. Clearly his sister didn't trust him anymore. *Shit . . .* Could he blame her?

"Bella, please. I'm sorry. . . . Just talk to me." When there was no response, he said, "Have I . . ." He cleared his throat. "Have I so damaged things between us?"

"When can I come home?"

"Bella—"

"Answer the question, brother mine."

"I don't know."

"Then I want to go to the safe house."

"You can't. I told you long ago, if there's trouble, I don't want you and *mahmen* in the same place. Now, why do you want to leave there? Only a day ago you didn't want to be anywhere else."

There was a long pause. "I went through my needing."

Rehv felt the air leak out of his lungs and get trapped in his chest cavity. He closed his eyes. "Were you with one of them?"

"Yes."

Sitting down was a damn good idea right about now, but there was no chair close enough. He leaned on his cane and lowered himself to his knees on the Aubusson carpet. Right in front of her portrait. "Are you . . . well?"

"Yes."

"And he's claimed you."

"No."

"Excuse me?"

"He doesn't want me."

Rehv bared his fangs. "Are you pregnant?"

"No."

Thank God. "Who was it?"

"I wouldn't tell you that to save my life, Rehv. Now, I'd like to leave here."

Christ . . . Her in her needing in a compound full of males . . . full of thick-blooded warriors. And the Blind King—*shit.* "Bella, tell me it was only one who serviced you. Tell me it was only one and that he didn't hurt you."

"Why? Because you're afraid of having a slut for a sister? Afraid of the *glymera* shunning me again?"

"Fuck the *glymera*. It's because I love you . . . and I can't bear the thought of you being used by the Brotherhood when you were so vulnerable."

A pause followed. As he waited, his throat burned so badly, he felt as though he'd swallowed a box of thumbtacks.

"There was only one, and I love him," she said. "You might as well know that he gave me a choice between him and being drugged unconscious. I picked him. But I will never tell you his name. Frankly, I don't want to ever speak of him again. Now, when can I come home?"

Okay. This was good. At least he could get her away from there.

"Just let me find a place that's secure. Call me in thirty minutes."

"Wait, Rehvenge, I want you to rescind the *sehclusion* request. If you do that, I will voluntarily submit to a security detail whenever I go out, if that makes you feel safer. Is that a fair trade?"

He put his hand over his eyes.

"Rehvenge? You say you love me. Prove it. Rescind that request, and I promise we'll work together. . . . Rehvenge?"

He dropped his arm and looked up at the painting of her. So beautiful, so pure. He would keep her that way always if he could, but she wasn't a child any longer. And she was proving far more resilient and strong than he could have imagined. To have lived through what she did, to have survived . . .

"All right . . . I'll take it back."

"And I will call you in a half hour."

Chapter Forty

Night fell and the light bled from the cabin. U hadn't moved from the computer all day. Between e-mails and his cell phone, he'd tracked down the twenty-eight slayers remaining in Caldwell and scheduled a general-assembly meeting for midnight. At that time he was going to reorder them into squadrons and assign a five-man task force on recruiting.

Following tonight's meeting, he was putting only two Beta squadrons downtown. Civilian vampires weren't showing up at the bars the way they used to, because too many of their kind had been pinched from that vicinity for persuasion. It was time to shift focus elsewhere.

After some thought, he'd decided to send the rest of his men out into the residential areas. Vampires were active at night. In their homes. It was really a question of finding them among the humans—

"You are such a little shit."

U burst up from his chair.

O stood naked in the doorway to the cabin. His chest was covered in claw marks, as if something had held on to him hard, and his face was swollen, his hair a mess. He looked well used and pissed off.

And as he shut the two of them in with a crack, U was unable to move: None of his large muscles fell into the defensive crouch he was screaming for, and this told him all he needed to know about who was *Fore-lesser* now. Only the top slayer had this kind of physical control over his subordinates.

"You forgot two important things." O casually withdrew a knife from a holster that hung on the wall. "One, the Omega is very fickle. And two, he has a personal taste for me. It really didn't take me long to work my way back into the fold."

As that knife came toward him, U struggled, tried to run, wanted to scream.

"So say good night, U. And give the Omega a big fat 'hello' when you see him. He's expecting you."

Six o'clock. Almost time to go.

Bella looked around the guest room she was in and figured she'd packed up everything she'd brought with her. She hadn't had much to begin with, and anyway, she'd moved it all from Zsadist's room the night before. Most of it had already been in an L.L. Bean bag.

Fritz would be coming for her things any minute, and he would drive the stuff to Havers and Marissa's. Thank God the brother-and-sister pair were willing to grant Rehvenge a favor and take her in. Their mansion, and the clinic, were a real stronghold. Even Rehv was satisfied she'd be safe.

Then at six thirty she was going to dematerialize over there, and Rehv would meet her.

Compulsively she went into the bathroom and checked behind the shower curtain again to make sure she had her shampoo. Yup, nothing there. And there was nothing of her left in the bedroom. Or in the house at all, for that matter. When she left, no one would know she'd ever been at the mansion. No one would . . .

Oh, Christ. Shut up with that, she thought.

There was a knock on the door. She walked over and pulled the thing open. "Hi, Fritz, my bag is on the—"

Zsadist was standing in the hall, dressed for fighting. Leathers. Guns. Blades.

She jumped back. "What are you doing here?"

He came into the room, saying nothing. But Jesus, he looked ready to pounce on something.

"I don't need an armed guard," Bella said, trying to keep cool. "I mean, if that's what this is all about. I'm going to dematerialize there, and the clinic is perfectly safe."

Zsadist didn't speak a word. Just stared at her, all power and male strength.

"Did you come to loom at me?" she snapped. "Or is there a point to this?"

When he shut the door behind him, her heart started to pound. Especially as she heard the lock turn.

She backed up until she was against the bed. "What do you want, Zsadist?"

He came forward as if he was stalking her, his yellow eyes fixated. His body was all coiled tension, and suddenly it didn't take a genius to figure out what kind of release he was looking for.

"Do *not* tell me you came here to mate."

"All right, I won't." His voice was nothing but a deep, purring growl.

She put her hand out. Yeah, like that was going to make a difference. He could take her if he wanted to whether she said yes or not. Only . . . like an idiot she wouldn't turn him away. Even after all the crap he'd pulled, she still wanted him. *Goddamn it.*

"I'm not having sex with you."

"I'm not here for me," he said, coming up to her.

Oh, God. His scent . . . his body . . . so close. She was *such* a fool.

"Get away from me. I don't want you anymore."

"Yes, you do. I can smell it." He reached out and touched her neck, running his forefinger down her jugular. "And I can feel it pounding in this vein."

"I will hate you if you do this."

"You hate me already."

If only that were true . . . "Zsadist, there is no way I will lay with you."

He bent down so that his mouth was at her ear. "I'm not asking you for that."

"So what do you want?" She shoved against his shoulders. Got nowhere. "Damn you, why are you doing this?"

"Because I just came from my twin's room."

"Excuse me?"

"You didn't let him drink from you." Zsadist's mouth brushed against her neck. Then he pulled back and stared down at her. "You will never accept him, will you? You will never be with Phury, no matter how right he is for you socially, personally."

"Zsadist, for chrissakes, just leave me alone—"

"You will not have my twin. So you're never coming back here, are you?"

She exhaled in a rush. "No, I'm not."

"And that's why I had to come."

Rage boiled in her, rising to meet the desire for his sex. "I don't get it. You have taken *every* opportunity to push me away. Remember that little episode in the alley last night? You drank from her to get me to walk, didn't you? It wasn't about that comment I made."

"Bella—"

"And then you wanted me to be with your *brother*. Look, I know you don't love me, but you're well aware of how I feel about you. Do you have any conception what it's like to have the male you love tell you to *feed* someone else?"

He dropped his hand. Stepped away.

"You're right." He rubbed his face. "I shouldn't be here, but I couldn't let you go without . . . In the back of my mind I always figured you'd be back. You know, to be with Phury. I always thought that I would see you again, even if it was from a distance."

So help her, God, she was sick of this. "Why the *hell* would you care if you saw me?"

He just shook his head and turned for the door. Which made her nearly violent.

"Answer me! Why do you care if I don't ever come back?"

He had his hand on the knob as she screamed at him, *"Why do you care?"*

"I don't!"

She launched herself across the room, intending to hit him, claw him, make him hurt, she was so frustrated. But he wheeled around, and instead of slapping him she grabbed his head and dragged his mouth to hers. His arms snapped around her, holding her hard enough so she couldn't breathe. As his tongue shot into her mouth, he picked her up and headed for the bed.

Desperate, angry sex was a bad idea. A very bad idea.

They were tangled on the mattress in a split second. He had her jeans off and was about to bite through her panties when a knock sounded on the door.

Fritz's voice came through the panels, pleasant and respectful. "Madam, if your bags are ready—"

"Not now, Fritz," Zsadist said in a guttural voice. He bared his fangs, shredded the silk between her thighs, and licked up the center of her. *"Fuck . . ."*

His tongue went down again and he lapped at her, moaning. She bit her lip to keep from crying out and held on to his head, gyrating her hips.

"Oh, master, I beg your pardon. I thought you were at the training center—"

"Later, Fritz."

"But of course. How long would you—"

The rest of the *doggen*'s words were cut off as Zsadist's erotic growl told Fritz everything he needed to know. And probably a little more.

"Oh . . . my goodness. Forgive me, master. I will not return for her things until I, ah . . . see you."

Zsadist's tongue swirled around as his hands clamped on her thighs. He drove her hard, all the time whispering hot, starved things against her secret flesh. She pushed herself against his mouth, arching up. He was so raw, so voracious . . . she shattered apart. He teased the orgasm out for the longest time, keeping it going as if he were desperate not to have it fade.

The stillness afterward chilled her as much as his mouth's

release of her core. He rose up from between her legs, his hand wiping across his lips. As he looked down at her, he licked his palm, catching every last bit of what he'd removed from his face.

"You're going to stop now, aren't you," she said roughly.

"I told you. I didn't come here for sex. I only wanted this. I only wanted to have you against my mouth one last time."

"You selfish bastard." And how ironic was it to be calling him that for *not* fucking her. *God* . . . This was just awful.

As she reached for her jeans, he made a low sound in the back of his throat. "You think I wouldn't kill to be inside of you this very second?"

"Go to hell, Zsadist. Go there right—"

He moved fast as a lightning strike, taking her down hard to the bed, tackling her with his weight.

"I am in hell," he hissed, pushing his hips into her. He swiveled them against her core, that massive erection pushing into the soft place he'd just had with his mouth. With a curse, he pulled back, unzipped his leathers . . . and thrust into her, stretching her so wide it almost hurt. She cried out at the invasion, but tilted her hips up so he could go in even farther.

Zsadist grabbed her knees and stretched her legs up, balling her under him; then he pounded against her, his warrior body sparing her nothing. She held on to his neck, drawing blood, lost in the grinding rhythm. This was how she'd always thought it would be with him. Hard, heavy, wild . . . raw. As she orgasmed again, he came with a roar, crashing into her. Hot jets filled her, then spilled out onto her thighs as he kept pumping.

When he finally collapsed onto her, he released her legs and breathed against her neck.

"Oh, God . . . I didn't mean for that to happen," he said finally.

"I am very sure about that." She pushed him aside and sat up, more tired than she'd been in her whole life. "I have to meet my brother soon. I want you to leave."

He cursed, an aching, hollow sound. Then he handed over her pants, though he didn't let them go. He looked at her for a long while, and like a fool she waited for him to tell her what she wanted to hear: *I'm sorry I hurt you, I love you, don't go.*

After a moment he dropped his hand and stood up, arranging himself, zipping up his pants. He went to the door, moving with that lethal grace he'd always walked with. As he looked over his shoulder, she realized they'd made love while he'd been fully armed. Fully dressed, too.

Oh, but that had only been sex, hadn't it.

His voice was low. "I'm sorry—"

"Do *not* say that to me right now."

"Then . . . thank you, Bella . . . for . . . everything. Yeah, really. I . . . thank you."

And just like that he was gone.

John stayed behind in the gym as the rest of the class filed out to hit the locker room. It was seven at night, but he could have sworn it was three in the morning. What a day. Training had started at noon, because the Brotherhood wanted to go out early, and there had been hours of classwork on tactics and computer technology taught by two Brothers named Vishous and Rhage. Then Tohr had arrived right at sundown and the ass-kicking had started. The three-hour workout had been brutal. Running laps. Jujitsu. More hand-to-hand weapons training, including an introduction to nunchakus, or nunchucks.

Those two wooden sticks connected by a chain were a nightmare for John, exposing all his weaknesses, especially his god-awful hand-to-eye coordination. But he wasn't about to give up. As the other guys left to go shower, he went back to the equipment room and picked up one of the sets. He figured he'd practice until the bus came and then shower at home.

He started spinning the nunchucks slowly at his side, the whirling sound oddly relaxing. Gradually increasing the velocity, he set them flying at a clip and then switched them to his left. Took them back. Again and again, until the sweat was once more coming out on his skin. Again and again and—

And he clonked the shit out of himself. Right on the head.

The blow made him weak in the knees, and after fighting

the sag for a moment, he let himself sink down. Bracing himself with his arm, he put a hand to his left temple. Stars. Definitely seeing stars.

In the midst of all his blinking, soft laughter drifted up from behind him. The satisfaction of the sound told him who it was, but he had to look anyway. Glancing under his arm, he saw Lash standing about five feet away. The guy's pale hair was wet, his street clothes sleek, his smile cool.

"You are such a loser."

John refocused on the mat, not really caring that Lash had caught him nailing himself in the brain. The guy had already seen that in class, so there was no new humiliation here.

God . . . If he could only get his eyes to clear. He shook his head, stretched his neck . . . and saw another pair of nunchucks on the mat. Had Lash thrown them at him?

"No one likes you, John. Why don't you just leave? Oh, wait. That would mean you couldn't chase after the Brothers. Then what would you do all day?"

The guy's laughter cut off abruptly as a deep voice snarled, "You don't move, blondie, except to breathe."

A huge hand appeared in John's face and he looked up. Zsadist was standing over him, dressed in full war gear.

John grabbed hold of what was in front of him out of reflex and was pulled up easily from the floor.

Zsadist's black eyes were narrow, shimmering with anger. "The bus is ready, so get your shit. I'll meet you outside of the locker room."

John hustled across the mats, thinking that when a male like Zsadist told you to do something, you did it fast. When he got to the door, though, he had to glance back.

Zsadist had Lash around the neck and had lifted the guy off the mat so his feet dangled. The warrior's voice was graveyard cold. "I saw you put him on the ground, and I'd kill you right now for it, except I'm not interested in dealing with your parents. So listen good, boy. You *ever* do something like that again, I'm going to thumb out your eyes and feed them to you. We clear?"

In response, Lash's mouth worked like a one-way valve.

Air went in. Nothing came out. And then he pissed in his pants.

"I'll take that as a yes." Zsadist dropped him.

John didn't stick around. He ran to the locker room, grabbed his duffel, and was out in the hall a moment later.

Zsadist was waiting for him. "Come on."

John followed the Brother out into the parking lot to the van, all along wondering how he could thank the male. But then Zsadist paused by the bus and all but shoved him inside. Then he boarded the thing himself.

Every one of the trainees cringed back into their seats. Especially when Zsadist unsheathed one of his daggers.

"We sit here," he said to John, pointing the weapon's black blade to the first bench seat.

Yeah, okay. Right. Here is good.

John squeezed up against the window as Zsadist took an apple out of his pocket and lowered himself down.

"We're waiting for one more," Zsadist told the driver. "And John and I will be your last stop."

The *doggen* bowed low behind the wheel. "Of course, sire. As you wish."

Lash slowly came into the van, the red streak around his throat a stain on his pale skin. When he saw Zsadist, he stumbled.

"You're wasting our time, boy," Zsadist said while sliding the knife under the apple's skin. "Sit your ass down."

Lash did as he was told.

As the van took off, no one said a thing. Especially as the partition closed and they were all locked in the back together.

Zsadist peeled the Granny Smith in one long strip, the skin inching down until it reached the floor of the van. When he was finished, he draped the green ribbon over his knee, then cleaved off a slice of white flesh and held it out to John on the blade. John took the piece with his fingers and ate it while Zsadist cut a hunk for himself and carried it to his mouth on the knife. They alternated until the apple was nothing but a skinny core.

Zsadist took the skin and what was left and threw them in the little trash bag by the partition. Then he wiped the blade on his leathers and started to flip it into the air and catch it. He kept this up the whole ride to town. When they got to the first dropoff, there was a long hesitation after the partition opened. And then two of the guys shuffled by quickly.

Zsadist's black eyes followed them, and he stared hard, as if he were memorizing their faces. And all the time with the blade, up and down, the black metal flashing, the big palm catching it in the same place on the handle after every toss— even when he was looking at the guys.

This happened at each stop. Until John and he were alone.

As the partition closed, Zsadist slid the dagger into his chest holster. Then he moved to the seat across the aisle and leaned back against the window, shutting his eyes.

John knew better than to think the male was asleep, because his breathing didn't change and he didn't relax at all. He just didn't want to interact.

John took out his pad and pen. He wrote neatly, folded the paper, and held it in his hand. He had to say thank-you. Even if Zsadist couldn't read, he had to say something.

When the van stopped and the partition opened, John left the paper on Zsadist's seat, not even trying to give it to the warrior. And he made sure he didn't look up as he hit the steps and headed across the road. He did stop on the front lawn to watch the van leave, though, snow falling on his head and shoulders and duffel.

As the bus disappeared into the gathering storm, Zsadist was revealed standing across the street. The Brother flashed the note, holding it up in the air between his first and middle fingers. Then he nodded once, put it in his back pocket, and dematerialized.

John kept staring at the spot where Zsadist had been. Thick bundles of flakes filled up the footprints the male's shitkickers had left.

With a rumble the garage door opened behind him, and the Range Rover reversed its way over. Wellsie put the window down. Her red hair was coiled up high on her head, and she was wearing a black ski parka. The heater inside the car was going full blast, a dull roar almost as loud as the engine.

"Hi, John." She reached out her hand and he laid his palm on hers. "Listen, was that Zsadist I just saw?"

John nodded.

"What was he doing here?"

John dropped his duffel and signed, *He rode home on the bus with me.*

Wellsie frowned. "I'd like you to stay away from him, okay? He's . . . not right in a lot of ways. Do you know what I mean?"

Actually, John wasn't so sure about that. Yeah, the guy was enough to make you think fondly of the bogeyman sometimes, but clearly he wasn't all bad.

"Anyway, I'm off to pick up Sarelle. We've run into a snag with the festival and lost all our apples. She and I are going to make the rounds of some spiritual folks, see what we can do about this so close to the date. Do you want to come?"

John shook his head. *I don't want to get behind in Tactics.*

"Okay." Wellsie smiled at him. "I left you some rice and ginger sauce in the fridge."

Thank you! I'm starved.

"I figured you would be. See you soon."

He waved at her while she backed down the rest of the driveway and took off. As he headed for the house, he noticed absently how the chains Tohr had put on the Rover made sharp gouges in the fresh snow.

Chapter Forty-one

"Stop here." O opened the Explorer's door before the SUV even came to a halt at the base of Thorne Avenue. He angled a quick look up the hill, then shot the Beta behind the wheel a real wake-your-ass-up stare.

"I want you to circle this neighborhood until I call you. Then I want you to come to number twenty-seven. Don't head into the driveway, keep going. There's a corner in the stone wall about fifty yards later. That's where I want you." As the Beta nodded, O snapped, "You fuck this up and I'll put you under the Omega's feet."

He didn't wait for the slayer to throw out some kind of bullshit, have-confidence-in-me babble. He hit the pavement and ran up the road's gradual incline. As he jogged he was a mobile arsenal, his body weighed down by the weapons and explosives he'd hung on himself as if he were a paramilitary Christmas tree.

He went past number twenty-seven's twin pillars and eyed the driveway that disappeared between them. Fifty yards later he was at the juncture of the stucco wall where he'd told the fool Beta to pick him up. He took three running strides and leaped into the air, all Michael Jordan and shit as he went for the top lip of the ten-foot wall.

He closed the distance with no problem, but then his hands

made contact. The blast of electricity that shot through his body was a real hair curler. If he'd been human still he'd have been toasted, and even as a slayer, the jolt was enough to leave him breathless as he pulled himself up and then plunged down the other side.

Security lights flared, and he took shelter behind a maple tree, taking out his muzzled gun. If attack dogs came at him he was ready to pop them, and he waited for the barking. There was none. And there was no rush of lights going on in the mansion or the pounding feet of security guards either.

While he waited a minute longer, he assessed the place. Back of the house was grand, all red bricks and white trim and sprawling terraces with second-floor porches. Garden was a pip, too. *God . . .* The annual upkeep on a monster spread like this was probably more than average folks made in a decade.

Time to close in. He moved across the lawn toward the house in a crouch, running in a cramped shuffle with his gun up in front. When he got in tight with the bricks, he was elated. The window he was next to was fitted with tracks that ran down its long sides, and on the top of the thing there was a discreetly disguised boxy transom.

Steel retractable shutters. And there was a set on every window and door, it looked like.

In the Northeast, where you didn't have to worry about tropical storms and hurricanes, there was only one kind of homeowner who threw those puppies over every slice of glass: the kind who needed to be protected from the sun.

Vampires lived here.

The shutters were up because it was night, and O looked inside the house. It was dark, which wasn't encouraging, but he was going in anyway.

The question was how to do the breaking and entering. It went without saying that the place was alarmed up the ass and wired for sound. And he was willing to bet that anyone who ran electric current around the top of their fence wasn't going to ADT it. This was going to be some sophisticated technology.

He decided his best move was cutting the power, so he

went hunting for the main electrical line into the mansion. He found the utilities spinal cord around the back of the six-car garage, nestled in an enclave of HVAC shit that included three air-conditioning units, an exhaust blower, and a backup generator. The main power line's thick, metal-encased vein came up through the earth and split, plugging into a series of four meters that were whizzing along.

He put a short-fused load of C4 plastic explosive right at the trunk and then rigged another setup like that at the nerve center of the generator. Stepping behind the garage, he triggered both remotely. Two pops broke out, and the flare of light and the smoke faded quickly.

He waited to see if anyone came running. No one did. On impulse he peered into a couple of the garage bays. Two were empty; the others had very nice cars in them, so nice he couldn't even tell what kind one of them was.

With the juice cut off, he jogged around and cased the front of the house, skirting behind the boxwood hedge that ran down the facade. A set of French doors was perfect for entry. He put his gloved fist through one pane, shattering the glass, and then sprang the lock. As soon as he stepped inside, he started to reclose the door. It was critical that the contacts for the security alarm were in their proper place if an alternative generator kicked in— *Holy . . . Moses.*

Those were lithium-powered electrodes on the doors . . . which meant the contacts didn't run on a current. And— *shit*—he was standing right in the middle of a laser beam. *Jesus.* This was very high-tech . . . as in Museum of Fine Arts, the White House, the pope's bedroom high-tech.

The only reason he'd gotten into the house at all was because someone had wanted him to.

He listened. Total silence. A trap?

O stayed frozen, barely breathing, for a little longer and then made sure his gun was good to go before he silently walked through a bunch of rooms that were right out of some glossy magazine. As he went he wanted to slash the paintings on the walls and yank down the chandeliers and break the spindly legs of the fancy tables and chairs. He wanted to burn the drapes. He wanted to shit on the floors. He wanted to ruin it because it was beautiful, and because if his woman had ever lived here, it meant she was *way* better than he was.

He rounded a corner into some kind of living room and stopped dead.

Up on the wall, in an ornate gilded frame, was a portrait of his wife . . . and the thing was draped with black silk. Below the painting, on a marble-topped table, there was a gold chalice turned upside down and a square of white cloth with three rows of ten little stones. Twenty-nine were rubies. The last one, in the lower left-hand corner, was black.

The ritual was different from the Christian shit he'd lived with as a human, but this was a memorial to his wife.

O's intestines turned into snakes, seething and hissing in his lower belly. He thought about throwing up.

His woman was dead.

"Don't look at me like that," Phury muttered as he limped around his room. His side hurt like a bitch, and he was trying to get ready to go out, and Butch's mother-hen impression wasn't helping.

The cop shook his head. "You need to go to the doctor, big guy."

The fact that the human had a point burned Phury's ass even more. "No, I don't."

"If you were going to spend the day on the couch, maybe. But fighting? Come on, man. If Tohr knew you were going out like this he'd have your head on a stick."

True. "I'll be fine. Just have to warm up."

"Yeah, stretching's really going to help that hole in your liver. Matter of fact, maybe I can get you some Ben-Gay and we'll just massage the shit out of it. Good plan."

Phury glared across the room. Butch cocked an eyebrow.

"You're pissing me off, cop."

"You don't say. Hey, how about this . . . you can yell at me while I drive you to Havers's."

"I don't need an escort."

"But if I take you, I'll know you went." Butch dragged out

the Escalade's keys from his pocket and dangled them in the air. "Besides, I'm a good taxi. Just ask John."

"I don't want to go."

"Well . . . in the words of Vishous, want in one hand, shit in the other—see what you get the most of."

Rehvenge parked the Bentley in front of Havers and Marissa's and walked carefully up to the grand door. He lifted the heavy lion's-head knocker and let it fall, the sound reverberating. Immediately he was welcomed by a *doggen* and led into a parlor.

Marissa stood up from a silk couch, and he bowed to her while telling the butler he would keep his coat. When they were alone Marissa rushed over, her hands held out, her long, pale yellow gown trailing after her like mist. He captured both her palms and kissed them.

"Rehv . . . I'm so glad you called us. We want to help."

"I appreciate your taking Bella in."

"She's welcome to stay for however long she needs. Although I wish you would tell us what's wrong."

"Just dangerous times."

"True." She frowned and looked around his shoulder. "Is she not with you?"

"Meeting me here. It shouldn't be long." He checked his watch. "Yeah . . . I'm early."

He pulled Marissa over to the couch, and as they sat down the folds of his sable coat fell across her feet. She reached out and stroked the fur, smiling a little. They were silent for a time.

He was anxious to see Bella, he realized. Actually, he was . . . nervous.

"How are you feeling?" he asked, wanting to focus on something else.

"Oh, you mean, after . . ." Marissa blushed. "Fine. Very well. I . . . thank you."

He really liked her way. So soft and gentle. So shy and self-effacing, though she was one of the rare beauties of his species, and everyone knew it. Man, how Wrath had held himself back from her was anyone's guess.

"Will you come to me again?" Rehv said in a low voice. "Will you let me feed you again?"

"Yes," she replied, lowering her eyes. "If you will allow me."

"I can't wait," he growled. As her eyes flipped up to his, he forced himself to smile even though he didn't really feel like it. He wanted to do other things with his mouth at the moment, none of which would have put her at ease. Thank God for the dopamine, he thought. "Don't worry, *tahlly*. Just the drinking, I know."

She assessed him then nodded. "And if you . . . if you need to feed . . ."

Rehv lowered his chin and stared at her from underneath his lids, erotic images flashing through his mind. She pulled back, clearly alarmed by his expression, and he wasn't surprised. No way she could handle the kind of sick shit he was into.

Rehv lifted his head back to level. "That's a generous offer, *tahlly*. But we'll keep this one-sided."

As relief showed on her face his cell phone started to ring, and he took the thing out to check caller ID. His heart kicked up. It was the security monitoring people for his house. "Excuse me just a moment."

After he heard the report that an intruder had breached the wall, engaged a number of motion detectors in the backyard, and knocked out the power, Rehv told his people to turn all the interior alarms off. He wanted whoever was there to stay.

As soon as he saw Bella, he was heading straight for home.

"Something wrong?" Marissa asked while he clipped the phone shut.

"Oh, no. Not at all." *Quite the contrary.*

When the front door knocker sounded, Rehvenge stiffened.

A *doggen* passed in front of the parlor's doorway to go answer it.

"Would you like me to leave you two alone?" Marissa said.

The mansion's big door opened and closed. Soft voices were traded, one that of the *doggen,* the other . . . Bella's.

Rehv pushed into his cane and slowly rose to his feet as Bella appeared in the doorway. She was wearing blue jeans and a black parka, and her long hair was shiny on her shoulders. She looked . . . alive . . . healthy. But age showed in her face, new lines of stress and worry bracketing her mouth.

He expected her to race into his arms, but she just stared at him . . . insulated, unreachable. Or maybe she was just so numb after all she'd been through, she had no reactions left to show the world.

Rehvenge's eyes watered as he plugged his cane into the floor and went to her, rushing, though he couldn't feel the fine rug beneath his shoes. He caught the shock on her face as he pulled her against him.

Sweet Virgin. He wished he could feel the embrace he was giving her. Then it dawned on him that he didn't know if she was hugging him back. He didn't want to force her. He made himself let go.

As he dropped his arms, she clung to him, not moving away, but staying close. He embraced her again.

"Oh . . . God, Rehvenge . . ." She shuddered.

"I love you, sister mine," he said weakly, unashamed in the moment for being less of a male than he should be.

Chapter Forty-two

O walked right out the brick mansion's front door and he left the thing wide-open behind him. As he wandered down the driveway, snow swirled in the cold wind.

The sight of that portrait was an echo in his brain that wouldn't let up, wouldn't fade. He had killed his woman. Beaten her so badly she'd died. God . . . he should have taken her to a doctor. Or maybe if that scarred Brother hadn't stolen her, maybe she would have lived. . . . Maybe she'd died because she'd transported.

So had O killed her? Or would she have lived if she'd been allowed to stay with him? What if— *Oh, fuck it.* The search for the sequence of truth was bullshit. She was dead and he had nothing to bury because that bastard Brother had taken her from him. Period.

Abruptly, he caught the lights of a car up ahead. As he got a little closer, he saw that a black SUV had stopped before the gates.

That goddamned Beta. What the hell was he doing? O hadn't called the slayer for a pickup, and that was the wrong place— Wait, the car was a Range Rover, not an Explorer.

O jogged through the snow, staying in the shadows. He was a couple of yards away from the gate when the Rover's window came down.

He heard a female voice say, "With everything that's been going on about Bella, I don't know if her mother will be receiving. But we can at least give it a try."

O stepped up to the gates and took out his gun, hiding behind one of the pillars. He saw a flash of red hair as the female behind the wheel leaned out and rang the intercom. Beside her there was another female in the passenger seat, a short-haired blond. That one said something and the redhead smiled a little, revealing fangs.

As she pressed the intercom again, O spoke loudly. "Nobody's home."

The redhead looked up, and he leveled his Smith & Wesson at her.

"Sarelle, *run!*" she screamed.

O pulled the trigger.

John was deep in tactics, and ready to put his head through a plate-glass window from the brain strain, when someone knocked on his door. He whistled without looking up from the textbook.

"Hey, son," Tohr said. "How's the studying?"

John stretched his arms over his head, then signed, *Better than the physical training.*

"You don't worry about that. It'll come."

Maybe.

"No, really. I was the same way before my transition. All over the place. Trust me, it gets better."

John smiled. *So, you're home early.*

"Actually, I was going to go to the center and get some admin work done there. You wanna hang? You could study in my office."

John nodded and grabbed a fleece, then packed up his books. A change of scenery would be good. He was sleepy, and he still had another twenty-two pages to go through: Getting away from his bed was a great idea.

They were heading down the hall when Tohr suddenly swayed and banged into the wall. His hand went to his heart and he seemed to struggle for breath.

John grabbed for him, alarmed by the Brother's coloring. He'd gone positively gray.

"I'm cool. . . ." Tohr rubbed his sternum. Winced. Took a couple of deep draws through his mouth. "No, I'm . . . I just got a pain or something. Probably the stuff I ate from Taco Hell on the way home. I'm okay."

Except the man was pasty and sickly as they stepped into the garage and went over to the Volvo.

"I made Wellsie take the Range Rover tonight," Tohr said as they got in her car. "I put the chains on it for her. I hate her driving in the snow." He seemed to be talking for the sake of talking, the words fast, pressurized. "She thinks I'm overprotective."

Are you sure we should be going out? John signed. *You look sick.*

Tohr hesitated before starting the station wagon, all the while rubbing his chest under his leather jacket. "Oh, yeah, no. I'll be fine. It's no big deal."

Butch watched Havers go to work on Phury, the doctor's hands steady and sure as they removed the bandage.

Phury was clearly not charmed about his role as patient. Sitting on top of the examination table, his shirt off, his huge body dominating the little room, he had a glower on him like an ogre. Right out of the Brothers Grimm.

"This hasn't healed as it should," Havers pronounced. "You said you were hurt last night, correct? So this should all be scar tissue. Instead it's barely closed."

Butch shot Phury a big old I-told-you-so stare.

The Brother mouthed back, *Bite me,* then muttered, "It's okay."

"No, sire, it's not. When was the last time you fed?"

"I don't know. A while." Phury craned around and looked at the wound. He frowned, as though he were surprised by how bad it looked.

"You need to feed." The doctor ripped open a gauze pack and covered the slice. After he taped the thick white square in place, he said, "And you should do it tonight."

Havers snapped off his gloves, stuffed them in a biohazard container, and made a note in his chart. He hesitated by the door. "Is there someone you could go to now?"

Phury shook his head while he put on his shirt. "I'll deal with it. Thanks, Doc."

When they were alone, Butch said, "Where'm I taking you, big man?"

"Downtown. Time to hunt."

"Yeah, right. You heard the man with the stethoscope. Or do you think he was playing you?"

Phury slid off the exam table, his shitkickers landing with a boom. He turned away, going for his dagger holster.

"Look, cop, it takes time for me to get someone lined up," he said. "Because I'm not . . . because of the way I am, I only like to go to certain females, and I have to talk with them first. You know, see if they're willing to let me take their vein. Celibacy is complicated."

"Then you make the calls now. You're in no shape to fight, and you know it."

"So use me."

Butch and Phury both wheeled toward the doorway. Bella was standing in it.

"I didn't mean to eavesdrop," she said. "The door was open and I was walking by. My, ah . . . brother just left."

Butch glanced at Phury. The male was still as a photograph.

"What's changed?" Phury asked in a voice that had gone hoarse.

"Nothing. I still want to help you. So I'm giving you another opportunity to accept."

"You couldn't have gone through it twelve hours ago."

"Yes, I could have. You were the one who said no."

"You would have wept through the whole thing."

Whoa. This was way personal.

Butch eased over to the door. "I'll go wait out—"

"Stay, cop," Phury said. "If you don't mind."

Butch cursed and looked around. There was a chair right next to the exit. He lowered his butt into it and tried to make like an inanimate object.

"Did Zsadist—"

Bella cut Phury's question off. "This is about you. Not him."

There was a long silence. And then the air was permeated by something like dark spices, the scent emanating from Phury's body.

As if the fragrance were an answer of some kind, Bella came into the room, shut the door, and started to roll up her sleeve.

Butch glanced at Phury and saw that the guy was trembling, his eyes glowing like the sun, his body . . . Well, he was obviously getting aroused, put it like that.

Okay, time to go . . .

"Cop, I need you to stay while we do this." Phury's voice was more like a growl.

Butch groaned, even though he knew damn well why the Brother wouldn't want to be alone with that female right now. He was throwing off erotic heat like a stallion.

"Butch?"

"Yeah, I'll stay." Even though he wasn't going to watch. No way. For some reason that seemed like being on the fifty-yard line while Phury had sex.

With a curse, Butch leaned onto his knees, put his hand up to his forehead, and looked down at his Ferragamos.

There was the scratchy sound, as if the tissue paper on the exam table was shifting because someone was getting up on the thing. Then a whisper of cloth.

Silence.

Shit. He had to look.

Butch took a peek and then couldn't have peeled his eyes away to save his life. Bella was up on the table, her legs dangling over the side, her exposed inner wrist on her thigh. Phury was staring at her with hunger and an awful, cursed love on his face as he eased down onto his knees before her. With hands that shook, he took hold of her palm and her upper forearm and bared his fangs. The damn things were huge now, long enough to keep him from closing his mouth all the way.

With a hiss, he lowered his head to Bella's arm. She

twitched all over as he struck, though her dull eyes just stared straight ahead at the wall. Then Phury jerked, released, and looked up at her.

That was quick.

"Why did you stop?" Bella asked.

"Because you're—"

Phury glanced over at Butch. Who flushed and looked down at his loafers again.

The Brother whispered, "Have you bled yet?"

Butch winced. *Oh, yeah.* This was way awkward.

"Bella, do you think you're pregnant?"

Holy shit—this was awkward.

"Would you like me to leave?" Butch asked, hoping they would kick him out.

When they both said no, he went back to watching his shoes.

"I'm not," Bella said. "I'm really not . . . you know. I mean, I'm . . . cramping, okay? Next thing is bleeding and then it's all over."

"Havers needs to check you out."

"Do you want to drink or not?"

More silence. Then another hiss. Followed by a low moan.

Butch glanced over. Phury was crowding Bella's wrist, her slender arm buried in a cage of his body as he took greedy pulls. Bella was looking down at him. After a moment she took her hand and put it on his multicolored hair. Her touch was tender. Her eyes shimmered with tears.

Butch got up from the chair and slipped out the door, leaving them to their business. The sad intimacy of what was passing between them needed to be private.

Outside the room, he eased against the wall, somehow still caught up in the drama though he wasn't watching it anymore.

"Hello, Butch."

He snapped his head around. Marissa was standing at the other end of the hall.

Good Lord.

As she walked over to him he could smell her, that clean ocean scent drilling into his nose, into his brain, into his blood. Her hair was up and she was wearing a yellow gown with an empire waist.

Jesus . . . Most blondes would have looked half dead in the color. She was radiant.

He cleared his throat. "Hey, Marissa. What's doing?"

"You look well."

"Thanks." She looked fantastic, but he kept his mouth shut about that.

Man, it's just like getting stabbed, he thought. *Yeah* . . . Seeing this female and getting nailed with six inches of steel in the breastbone were just different faces of the same nasty coin.

Shit. All he could picture was her getting into that Bentley with that male.

"How have you been?" she asked.

How had he been? He'd been a mooning idiot for the past five months.

"Good. Real good."

"Butch, I—"

He smiled at her and straightened. "Listen, can you do me a favor? I'm going to go wait in the car. Will you let Phury know when he surfaces? Thanks." He smoothed his tie down and buttoned his suit jacket, then pulled his overcoat together. "Take care, Marissa."

He made a beeline for the elevator.

"Butch, wait."

God help him, his feet stopped.

"How . . . have you been?" she said.

He considered turning around, but refused to let himself get sucked in. "Like I said, Jim Dandy, thanks for asking. Take care of yourself, Marissa."

Shit. He'd just said that, hadn't he?

"I want to . . ." She stopped. "Would you call on me? Sometime?"

That had him pivoting around. *Oh, sweet Mary, mother of God* . . . She was so beautiful. Grace Kelly beautiful. And with her Victorian speech and her genteel manner, she made him feel like a total loser, all babbles and shuffles in spite of his expensive clothes.

"Butch? Maybe you could . . . call on me."

"Why would I do that?"

She flushed and seemed to wilt. "I had hoped . . ."

"Hoped what?"

"That perhaps . . ."

"What?"

"You might call on me. If you had some time. Perhaps you could come . . . calling."

Christ. He'd already done that and she'd refused to see him. No way he was volunteering for another crash course in ego bashing. This woman, female . . . whatever . . . was totally capable of whipping his ass, and he didn't need more of that kind of rash, thank you very much. Besides, Mr. Bentley was showing up at her back door.

At that thought, an evil, very male part of him wondered if she was still the untouched virgin she'd been when he'd met her over the summer. Probably not. Even if she was still shy, now that she was away from Wrath she must have taken a lover. Hell, Butch knew firsthand the kind of kiss she could lay on a man; there had been only that one time, but she'd had him tearing the arm off a chair, he got so cranked. So, yeah . . . she'd definitely found a man. Maybe a couple. And she'd show them a hell of a ride.

As she opened her perfect, pink, godforsaken rosebud of a mouth again, he cut her off. "No, I'm not going to call on you. But I do mean what I said. I hope you . . . take care of yourself."

Okay, that was three times with the little phrase. He needed to hit the road before he sported a fourth.

Butch strode over to the elevator. By some miracle the thing opened the moment he punched the *up* button. He stepped inside and kept his eyes from her.

As the doors closed, he thought she might have said his name one last time. But knowing him, he was just imagining it. Because he really wished she—

Oh, shut up, O'Neal. Just shut up and drop it.

When he strode out of the clinic, he was walking so fast, he was practically running.

Chapter Forty-three

Zsadist tracked the lone pale-haired *lesser* into the maze of downtown alleys. The slayer was moving quickly in the falling snow, alert, scanning, looking for prey among the straggling bar riders who were out in the cold in their club clothes.

Behind him Z was light over the ground, running on the balls of his feet, keeping close but not too close. Dawn was coming fast and hard, and even though he was skimming the edge of night right now, he wanted this kill. All he needed was to get the slayer away from prying, human eyes. . . .

The right moment came as the *lesser* slowed and considered the intersection between Eighth and Trade Street. It was just a pause, a short internal debate on whether to go left or right.

Zsadist struck fast, materializing right behind the slayer, wrapping an arm around the bastard's neck, and pulling him into the darkness. The *lesser* fought back, and the struggle sounded like flags flapping in the wind as two male bodies thrashed and jackets and pants whipped around in the cold air. The *lesser* was on the ground within moments, and Z looked into its eyes as he lifted his dagger. He plunged the black blade into a thick chest. The pop and flare faded quickly.

As Z stood up, there was no satisfaction at all. He was on

a violent kind of autopilot. Ready, willing, and able to kill, but moving in a dream state.

Bella was all that was on his mind. Actually, it went deeper than that. The absence of her was a tangible weight hanging from his body: He missed her with a crippling kind of desperation.

Ah, yes. So the rumors were true. A bonded male without his female might as well be dead. He'd heard that piece of bullshit before and never believed it. Now he was living the hard-core truth.

His cell phone rang and he answered the thing, because that was what you did when it went off. He had no real interest in who was on the other end.

"Z, my man," Vishous said. "Got a really weird message in the general voice mail. Some guy wanting to speak with you."

"He asked for me by name?"

"Actually, he was a little hard to follow because he was so wired, but he mentioned your scar."

Bella's brother? Z wondered. Although now that she was back out in the world, what would that male have to bitch about?

Well . . . other than the fact that his sister had been serviced in her need and there was no mating ceremony on the calendar. Yeah, that was something a brother would get pissed over.

"What's the callback number?"

Vishous recited the pattern of digits. "And he left the name Ormond."

Guess Bella's big, bad older bro wasn't it. "Ormond? That's a human name."

"Couldn't tell you. So you might want to take this careful."

Z hung up, dialed slowly, and waited, hoping he'd managed to hit the right numbers.

When the call was answered, there was no hello on the other end of the line. Just a low male voice that said, "Out of my network and untraceable. So it must be you, Brother."

"And you are?"

"I want to meet you in person."

"Sorry, I'm not into dating."

"Yeah, I can imagine with that face of yours you don't have much luck there. But I don't want you for sex."

"I'm so relieved. Now who the fuck are you?"

"My first name is David. Ring any bells?"

Fury clouded Z's vision until all he saw were the marks on Bella's stomach. He squeezed the phone until he heard the thing squeak, but he was through with the hotheaded stuff.

Forcing his voice into a drawl, he said, "'Fraid not, Davy. But refresh my memory."

"You took what is mine."

"I steal your wallet? I would have remembered that."

"My woman!" the *lesser* screamed.

Every marking instinct in Z's body fired off at once, and there was no holding back the growl that came out of his mouth. He whipped the phone away from his face until the sound faded.

". . . too close to dawn."

"What was that?" Z said with a nasty edge. "Bad connection."

"You think this is a fucking joke?" the *lesser* spat.

"Easy, there, wouldn't want you to throw an embolism."

The slayer panted with fury, but then got himself under control. "I want to meet you at nightfall. We've got a lot of ground to cover, you and I, and I don't want to be rushed by dawn. Besides, I've been busy the last few hours and I need a break. I took out one of your females, a nice-looking redhead. Popped her a good one. Buh-bye."

Now Z's growl got into the phone. The slayer laughed. "You Brothers are so protective, aren't you. Well, how about this. I got myself another one. Another female. I persuaded her to give me that number I dialed to find you. She was really forthcoming. Cute little blonde, too."

Z's hand went to one of his dagger handles. "Where do you want to meet?"

There was a pause. "First the terms. Naturally I want you to come alone, and here's how we're going to make sure that happens." Z heard a female moan in the background. "Any of my associates catch your Brothers around and this one gets sliced up. All it will take is a phone call. And they will do it slowly."

Zsadist shut his eyes. He'd so had it with death and suffering and pain. His own and others'. That poor female . . . "Where?"

"Six-o'clock showing of *The Rocky Horror Picture Show* in Lucas Square. You sit in the back. I'll find you."

The phone went dead, only to ring again immediately.

Now V's voice was strangled. "We have a situation. Bella's brother found Wellsie shot in his driveway. Get back home, Z. Right now."

John watched from across the desk as Tohr hung up the phone. The man's hands were shaking so badly the receiver rattled in its cradle.

"She probably forgot to turn that cell on. Lemme try the house again." Tohr picked up. Dialed quickly. Flubbed the numbers so he had to start over. And all the while he was rubbing at the center of his chest, his shirt in disarray.

As Tohr stared into space, frozen as their home phone rang, John heard footfalls coming down the hallway to the office. A horrible feeling went through him like a fever's bloom. He glanced at the door, then shifted his eyes to Tohr again.

Tohr obviously heard the heavy pounding, too. In slow motion he let the receiver fall to the desk, the sound of the ringing over the open line loud in the room. His eyes fixated on the door, his hands gripping the arms of his chair.

As the knob turned, voice mail kicked in and the sound of Wellsie's voice came out of the receiver. "Hi, this is Wellsie and Tohr. We can't get to the phone right now. . . ."

Every one of the Brothers was out in the hall. And Wrath was in front of the grim, silent group.

There was a clatter and John looked back at Tohr. The man had jacked up onto his feet and knocked his chair over. He was trembling from head to foot, sweating through his shirt in great patches under his arms.

"My brother," Wrath said. There was a helpless tone to his

voice, one totally at odds with his fierce face. And that powerlessness was terrifying.

Tohr moaned and grabbed at his sternum, rubbing in fast, desperate circles. "You . . . can't be here. Not all of you." He put one hand out as if to push them all away and then he backed up. Except there was nowhere to go. He banged against a file cabinet. "Wrath, don't . . . my lord, please, don't . . . oh, God. Don't say it. Don't tell me. . . ."

"I'm so sorry. . . ."

Tohr started to rock back and forth, arms going around his middle as if he were going to throw up. His short breaths went in so fast he began to hiccup, and he didn't seem to exhale at all.

John burst into tears.

He didn't mean to. But reality was dawning and the horror was too hard to bear. He dropped his head in his hands, and all he could think about was Wellsie backing out of the driveway like it was just another day.

When a big hand pulled him up out of the chair and he was held against a chest, he thought it was one of the Brothers. But it was Tohr. Tohr was holding him hard, clinging.

The male started to murmur like a crazy man, his words fast and incomprehensible until they finally coalesced into some kind of meaning. "Why wasn't I called? Why didn't Havers call me? He should have called me. . . . Oh, God, the baby took her. . . . I knew we shouldn't have gotten her pregnant. . . ."

Abruptly everything changed in the room, as if someone had turned up the lights or maybe the heat. John felt the shift in the air first, and then Tohr's words dried up as he obviously sensed it, too.

Tohr's arms loosened. "Wrath? It was . . . the baby, right?"

"Get the boy out of here."

John shook his head and held on to Tohr's waist with a death grip.

"How did she die, Wrath?" Tohrment's voice went flat and his hands fell from John. "You tell me now. Right fucking now."

"Get the kid out of here," Wrath barked at Phury.

John fought as Phury grabbed him around the waist and picked him up off the floor. At the same time Vishous and Rhage positioned themselves on either side of Tohr. The door closed.

Outside of the office, Phury put John down and held him in place. There was a moment or two of silence . . . and then a raw scream shattered the air as sure as if the oxygen were a solid.

The burst of energy that followed was so strong it shattered the glass door. Shards splintered and sprayed out while Phury sheltered John from the shrapnel.

One by one down both lengths of the hall, the fluorescent ceiling lights exploded, flashing bright and leaving streamers of sparks to bleed down from the fixtures. Energy vibrated up through the concrete floor, leaving cracks that ran into the cinder-block walls.

Through the busted door John saw a whirlwind in the office, and the Brothers were backing away from it, arms in front of their faces. Pieces of furniture whipped around a black hole in the center of the room, one that was vaguely shaped like Tohr's head and body.

There was another unearthly howl and then the inky void disappeared, the furniture came crashing down, the trembling in the floor stopped. Papers fluttered to a gentle rest over the chaos like snow over a traffic accident.

Tohrment was gone.

John pushed himself out of Phury's arms and ran into the office. As the Brothers looked on, his mouth opened and he screamed without making a sound:

Father . . . father . . . father!

Chapter Forty-four

Some days lasted forever, Phury thought much later. And when the sun went down, there was still no end to them.

As the shutters lifted for the evening, he took a seat on a spindly sofa and looked across Wrath's study at Zsadist. The other Brothers were just as speechless as he was.

Z had just dropped another bomb in what was already a blitz zone of blowups. First there had been Tohr, Wellsie, and that young female. Now this.

"Jesus, Z . . ." Wrath rubbed his eyes and shook his head. "You didn't think to mention this before now?"

"We've had other shit to deal with. Besides, I'm meeting with the slayer by myself no matter what you say. It's really not up for discussion."

"Z, man . . . I can't let you do that."

Phury braced for his twin's reaction. As did the others in the room. They were all exhausted, but knowing Z, he'd have enough juice left over to hit the fan.

The brother just shrugged. "The *lesser* wants me, and I want to take care of him. For Bella. For Tohr. Besides, what about the female hostage? I can't not go, and backup's not an option."

"My brother, you'd be walking into your coffin."

"So I'll do a hell of a lot of damage before they take me out."

Wrath crossed his arms over his chest. "No, Z, I can't let you go."

"They'll kill that female."

"There's another way to handle this. We just need to figure out what it is."

There was a heartbeat of a pause. Then Z said, "I want everyone out of this room so I can talk to Wrath. Except you, Phury. You stay."

Butch, Vishous, and Rhage looked around at one another, then focused on the king. When he nodded once, they left.

Z shut the door behind them and stayed with his back to the thing. "You can't stop me. I am *ahvenging* my *shellan*. I am *ahvenging* the *shellan* of my brother. You have no standing to prevent me. This is my right as a warrior."

Wrath cursed. "You never mated her."

"I don't need a ceremony to know she's my *shellan*."

"Z—"

"And what about Tohr? Are you saying he's not my brother? Because you were there the night I was brought into the Black Dagger Brotherhood. You know Tohrment is flesh of my flesh now. I own the right to *ahvenge* him as well."

Wrath leaned back in his chair, his weight making the thing creak in protest. "Christ, Zsadist, I'm not saying you can't go. I just don't want you to go alone."

Phury looked back and forth between the two of them. He'd never seen Zsadist so calm. The brother was focused to the point of stone, nothing but clearsighted eyes and deadly purpose. If it weren't so eerie, it would have been remarkable.

"I didn't make up the rules of this scenario," Z said.

"You'll die if you go by yourself."

"Well . . . I'm kind of ready to get off the ride."

Phury felt his skin get tight all over.

"Excuse me?" Wrath hissed.

Z stepped away from the door and walked through the dainty French room. He stopped in front of the fire, and the flames ricocheted off his ruined face. "I'm ready to end things."

"What the hell are you—"

"I want to go out like this, and I want to take that *lesser* with me when I do. Real blaze-of-glory shit. Up in flames with mine enemy."

Wrath's mouth went lax. "Are you asking me to sanction your suicide?"

Z's head went back and forth. "No, because short of chaining me, you aren't going to keep me from showing up at that movie theater tonight. What I'm asking you to do is make sure no one else gets hurt. I want you to command the others, especially him"—Z looked pointedly at Phury—"to stay away."

Wrath took off his sunglasses and rubbed his eyes again. When he looked up, his pale green irises glowed, the disks like floodlights in his face. "There's been too much death in the Brotherhood. Don't do this."

"Have to. Going to. So order the others to stay away."

There was a long, tense silence. Then Wrath gave the only answer he had. "So be it."

With the wheels set in motion for Z's death, Phury leaned forward and put his elbows on his knees. He thought of the taste of Bella's blood, and that very special spice his tongue had detected.

"I'm sorry."

As he felt Wrath and Z look over at him, he realized he'd spoken out loud. He got to his feet. "I'm sorry, will you both excuse me?"

Zsadist frowned. "Wait. I need something from you."

Phury stared at his twin's face, tracing the scar that intersected it, absorbing the nuances in a way he never had before. "Name it."

"Promise me you will not leave the Brotherhood after I'm gone." Z pointed to Wrath. "And do it over his ring."

"Why?"

"Just do it."

Phury frowned. "Why?"

"I don't want you to be alone."

Phury stared long and hard at Z, thinking about the patterns of both their lives. Man, the two of them really had been cursed, although the *why* of it was a total unknown. Maybe it was just bad luck, although he'd like to think there was a reason.

Logic . . . logic was better than a capricious fate that screwed you hard.

"I drank from her," he said abruptly. "Bella. I drank from her last night when I went to Havers's. Still feel like having someone watch over me?"

Zsadist closed his eyes. Like a cold draft, a wave of despair came out of him and passed through the room. "I'm glad you did. Now are you going to give me your word?"

"Come on, Z—"

"All I want is your vow. Nothing else."

"Sure. Whatever."

Christ, fine.

Phury walked over to Wrath, got down on bended knee, and hovered over the king's ring. In the Old Language, he said, "So long as I breathe, I shall remain within the Brotherhood. I humbly offer this vow, that it may be acceptable to thine ears, my lord."

"It is acceptable," Wrath replied. "Tender your lips to mine ring and seal the words upon your honor."

Phury kissed the king's black diamond and rose again. "Now, if the drama's over, I'm out of here."

Except when he got to the door, he stopped and looked back into Wrath's face. "Have I ever told you how honored I've been to serve you?"

Wrath recoiled a little. "Ah, no, but—"

"It really has been an honor." As the king's eyes narrowed, Phury smiled a little. "Don't know why that suddenly struck me. Probably the view of you from your feet just now."

Phury left and was glad when he ran into Vishous and Butch outside the study.

"Hey, boys." He touched them briefly on the shoulders. "The two of you are quite a pair, you know that? Our resident genius and a human pool shark. Who'd've thought?" As the two of them looked at him oddly, he asked, "Rhage go to his room?"

When they nodded, he went over and knocked on Holly-wood's door. Rhage answered and Phury smiled, putting his hand up to that thick neck. "Hey, my brother."

He must have paused for a little too long, because Rhage's eyes got shrewd. "What's doing, Phury?"

"Nothing." He dropped his hand. "Just a drive-by. You take care of that female of yours, you feel me? Lucky, lucky . . . you are a very lucky male. Later."

Phury went to his room, wishing that Tohr were around . . . wishing that they knew where the brother was. As he mourned for the male he armed himself, then checked the hall. He could hear the Brotherhood talking in Wrath's study.

To avoid them he dematerialized to the corridor of statues and went into the room next to Zsadist's. After shutting the door, he headed for the bath and flipped on the light. He stared at his reflection in the mirror.

Unsheathing one of his daggers, he grabbed a thick hunk of his hair and took the blade to it, cutting through the waves. He did this over and over again, letting the reds and the blonds and the browns fall to the floor in chunks that covered his shitkickers. When the stuff was about an inch long all the way around, he grabbed a can of shaving cream from the vanity, lathered up his skull, and took a razor out from under the sink.

When he was bald he wiped the residue off his scalp and brushed off his shirt. His neck itched from some of the hairs that had fallen into his collar, and his head felt too light. He rubbed his hand over his scalp, leaned into the mirror, and looked at himself.

Then he took the dagger and put it point-first to his fore-head.

With a hand that shook, he drew the knife down the center of his face, ending with an S-curve at his upper lip. Blood welled and dripped down. He wiped it off with a clean white towel.

Zsadist armed himself with care. When he was ready he stepped out of his closet. The bedroom was dark, and he walked through it out of habit more than sight, heading for the pool of light spilling out of the bathroom. He went to the sink, turned it on, and bent down over the rushing water, cupping the cold torrent in his hands. He splashed his face and rubbed his eyes. Drank a little from what he held between his palms.

When he went to dry off, he sensed that Phury had come into the bedroom and was moving around, though he couldn't see the male.

"Phury . . . I was going to come find you before I left."

With a towel under his chin, Z looked at his reflection in the mirror, seeing his new yellow eyes. He thought of the arc of his life and knew most of it was for shit. But there had been two things that hadn't been. One female. And one male.

"I love you," he said in a rough voice, realizing it was the first time he'd ever said the words to his twin. "Just wanted to get that out."

Phury stepped in behind him.

Z recoiled in horror at his twin's reflection. No hair. Scar down his face. Eyes flat and lifeless.

"Oh, sweet Virgin," Z breathed. "What the *fuck* did you do to yourself . . . ?"

"I love you, too, my brother." Phury raised his arm. In his hand was a hypodermic syringe, one of the two that had been left for Bella. "And you need to live."

Zsadist spun around just as his twin's arm swung down. The needle caught Z in the neck and he felt the rush of morphine go right into his jugular. Screaming, he grabbed onto Phury's shoulders. As the drug kicked in, he sagged and felt himself get eased onto the floor.

Phury knelt beside him and stroked his face. "I've only ever had you to live for. If you die I have nothing. I'm utterly lost. And you are needed here."

Zsadist tried to reach out, but couldn't lift his arms as Phury stood up.

"God, Z, I keep thinking this tragedy of ours is going to be over. But it just keeps going, doesn't it?"

Zsadist blacked out to the sound of his twin's boots heading from the room.

Chapter Forty-five

John lay on the bed, curled on his side, staring into the dark. The room he'd been given in the Brotherhoods' mansion was luxurious and anonymous and made him feel no better or worse.

From somewhere in the corner, he heard a clock chime once, twice, three times. . . . He kept counting the low, rhythmic tones until he got up to six. Rolling over onto his back, he considered the fact that in another six hours it would be the start of a new day. Midnight. No longer Tuesday, but Wednesday.

He thought of the days and weeks and months and years of his life, time that he owned because he'd experienced it and therefore could lay claim to its passage.

How arbitrary, this distinction of time. How like humans—and vampires—to have to cut the infinite down to something they could believe they controlled.

What a crock. You didn't control anything in your life. And neither did anyone else in theirs.

God, if only there was a way to do that. Or at least be able to do some things over. How wonderful would it be if he could just hit a rewind button and then edit the hell out of the past day? That way he wouldn't have to feel as he did now.

He groaned and turned onto his stomach. This pain was . . . unparalleled, a revelation of the worst kind.

His despair was like an illness, affecting his whole body, making him shiver though he was not cold, tossing his stomach though it was empty, causing aches to bloom in his joints and his chest. He'd never considered emotional devastation to be an affliction, but it was one, and he knew he was going to be ill from it for quite some time.

God . . . He should have gone with Wellsie, instead of staying home to work on tactics. If he'd been in that car, maybe he could have saved her . . . Or maybe he'd just be dead too?

Well, that would be better than this existence. Even if there was nothing in the afterlife, even if you just blacked out and that was it, surely that would be better than this.

Wellsie . . . gone, gone. Her body, it was ashes. From what John had overheard, Vishous had laid his right hand upon her at the scene and then taken what was left behind. A formal Fade ceremony, whatever that was, would be performed, except no one could do that without Tohr.

And Tohr was gone, too. Disappeared. Perhaps dead? It had been so close to dawn when he'd taken off. . . . In fact, maybe that had been the point. Maybe he'd just run out into the light so he could be with Wellsie's spirit.

Gone, gone . . . everything seemed gone.

Sarelle . . . lost to the *lessers* now, too. Lost before he had really known her. Zsadist was going to try to get her back, but who knew what would happen?

John pictured Wellsie's face and her red hair and her little pregnant bump. He saw Tohr's brush cut and his navy blue eyes and his broad shoulders in black leather. He imagined Sarelle poring over those old texts, her blond cap of hair hanging forward, her long, pretty hands working the pages.

The temptation to start with the tears again rose, and John sat up quickly, forcing the urge to level off. He was through with the crying. He would not weep again for any of them. Tears were utterly useless, a weakness not worthy of their memories.

Strength would be his offering to them. Power his eulogy. Vengeance the prayer at their graves.

John got off the bed, used the bathroom, then dressed, slipping his feet into the Nikes Wellsie had bought for him. Within moments he was downstairs, going through the secret door that led into the underground tunnel. He walked quickly down the steel labyrinth, eyes straight ahead, arms swinging in a soldier's precise rhythm.

When he stepped through the back of the closet and out into Tohr's office, he saw that the mess had been cleaned up: The desk was back where it had been before, and the ugly-ass green chair was tucked in behind it. The papers and the pens and the files and everything were tidied up. Even the computer and the phone were where they should be, though both had been broken into pieces the night before. They must be new ones. . . .

Order had been restored, and the three-dimensional lie worked for him.

He went to the gym and flipped on the cage lights in the ceiling. There were no classes today because of everything that had happened, and he wondered with Tohr gone whether the training would stop altogether.

John jogged across the mats to the equipment room, his sneakers smacking against the tough blue skins. From the knife cabinet he took out two daggers and then snagged a chest holster small enough to fit him. Once the weapons were strapped on, he went to the center of the gym.

Just as Tohr had taught him, he began by lowering his head.

And then he palmed the daggers and started to work them, clothing himself in anger against his enemy, picturing all the *lessers* he was going to kill.

Phury walked into the theater and took a seat in the back. The place was crowded, chatty, filled with young twosomes and legions of frat boys. He heard hushed voices and some that were loud. Listened to laughter and candy getting unwrapped, and slurping and munching.

When the movie came up the houselights dimmed, and everyone started yelling out lines.

He knew when the *lesser* approached. Could smell the sweetness in the air, even through the popcorn and the girlie perfumes emanating from the dating pairs.

A cell phone appeared in front of his face. "Take it. Put it up to your ear."

Phury did and heard harsh breaths on the line.

The crowd in the theater yelled, "Damn it, Janet, let's go screw!"

The *lesser*'s voice came from right behind his head. "Tell her you're going to come with me without a problem. Promise her that she'll live because you're going to do what you're told. And do it in English so I can understand you."

Phury spoke into the phone, the exact string of words he used unknown to him. All he tracked was the fact that the female started sobbing.

The *lesser* yanked the phone back. "Now put these on."

Steel handcuffs dropped in his lap. He cuffed himself and waited.

"You see that exit to the right? That's where we're headed. You're going first and there's a truck waiting just outside. You're getting in the passenger-side door. The whole time I'm right behind you with the phone to my mouth. You fuck with me, or I see any of your Brothers, and I'm going to have her slaughtered. Oh, and FYI, there's a knife at her throat so there's no time delay. We clear?"

Phury nodded.

"Now stand up and get moving."

Phury rose to his feet and headed for the door. As he walked along he realized he'd had some thought of coming out of this alive. He was vicious good with weapons, and he'd packed a few in hidden places. But this *lesser* was smart, hog-tying him, trapping him with the life of that civilian female.

As Phury kicked open the theater's side door, he knew without a doubt that he was kissing his ass good-bye tonight.

Zsadist came to by force of will, reaching out through the drug haze and grabbing onto consciousness. With a groan he dragged himself across the bath's marble floor and onto the rug in the bedroom. Clawing his way across the carpet, pushing with his feet, he barely had the strength to will the door open when he got to it.

As soon as he was in the hall of statues, he tried to yell. At first it was only hoarse whispers, but then he got a holler out. And another. And another.

The pounding, running footsteps made him dizzy with relief.

Wrath and Rhage knelt by him and rolled him over. He cut through their questions, unable to follow all the words. "Phury . . . gone . . . Phury . . . gone . . ."

When his stomach heaved, he lurched back onto his side and threw up. The voiding helped, making him feel a little more clearheaded after it stopped.

"Have to find him . . ."

Wrath and Rhage were still firing questions, talking fast, and Z thought they were probably the cause of all the buzzing in his ears. Either that or his head was about to explode.

As he pushed his face off the carpet his vision spun, and he thanked God that dose of morphine had been calibrated for Bella's weight. Because he was a mess.

His gut spasmed and he vomited again, losing it all over the rug. *Shit . . .* He never had been able to handle opiates.

More feet pounding down the hall. More voices. Someone wiping his mouth with a wet cloth. Fritz. When Z's throat started working up another round of gags, a wastepaper basket was shoved in his face.

"Thank you," he said as he threw up again.

With every heave, his mind was coming back online, his body, too. He stuffed two fingers down his throat to keep himself going. The faster he got that drug out of his system, the sooner he could go after Phury.

That heroic motherfucker . . . God. He was going to kill his twin for this, he really was. Phury was the one who was supposed to live.

But where the hell had he been taken? And how to find him? The movie theater was the starting place, but they wouldn't have stayed there long.

Zsadist started to do the dry-heave thing, because there was nothing left in his stomach. It was in the middle of the retching that the only solution came to him, and when it did, his stomach rolled from something other than the drug. The way to his twin violated every instinct he had.

More pounding down the hall. Vishous's voice. A civilian emergency. A family of six trapped in their house, surrounded by *lessers*.

Z lifted his head. Then his torso. Then he was up on his feet. His will, ever the only saving grace he had, came to the rescue again. It threw off more of the drug, focused him, cleared him out better than the vomiting.

"I'll get Phury," he told his brothers. "You go take care of business."

There was a brief pause. Then Wrath said, "So be it."

Chapter Forty-six

Bella sat in a Louis XIV chair, her legs crossed at the ankles, her hands in her lap. A blaze crackled in a marble fireplace to the left, and there was a cup of Earl Grey tea at her elbow. Marissa was across the way on a delicate sofa, drawing a strand of yellow silk up through an embroidery mesh. There was no sound to the movement.

Bella thought she was going to scream—

She leaped up, energized by instinct. Zsadist . . . Zsadist was close by.

"What is it?" Marissa said.

Pounding on the front door lit off like a drum, and a moment later Zsadist came into the parlor. He was dressed for his business, guns on his hips, daggers strapped on his chest. The *doggen* right on his heels looked scared stiff of him.

"Leave us," Marissa was told. "And take your servant with you."

As the female hesitated, Bella cleared her throat. "It's okay. It's . . . Go."

Marissa inclined her head. "I won't be far."

Bella held herself in place as they were left alone.

"I need you," Zsadist said.

She narrowed her eyes. God, those words she had wanted to hear. How cruel that they came so late. "For what."

"Phury took your vein."

"Yes."

"I need you to find him."

"Is he missing?"

"Your blood is in his veins. I need you—"

"To find him. I heard that. Tell me why." The brief pause that followed chilled her.

"The *lesser* has him. David has him."

Her breath left her lungs. Her heart stopped. "How . . . ?"

"I don't have time to explain." Zsadist came forward, looking as if he was going to take her hands, but then he stopped. "Please. You're the only one who can get me to him, because your blood is in him."

"Of course . . . of course I'll find him for you."

It was the chain of blood ties, she thought. She could locate Phury anywhere because he'd fed from her. And after she'd been at Zsadist's throat, he would be able to track her for the same reason.

He put his face right into hers. "I want you to get within fifty yards of him, no closer, we clear? And then you're dematerializing right back here."

She looked him in the eye. "I won't let you down."

"I wish there were another way to find him."

Oh, that hurt. "No doubt you do."

She left the parlor and got her coat, then stood in the foyer. She closed her eyes and reached out into the air, piercing first the walls of the entryway she was in, then the outer structure of Havers's house. Her mind cast out over the shrubs and the lawn and cut through other trees and houses. . . . Through cars and trucks and buildings and across parks and rivers and streams. Out farther still to the farmland and the mountains . . .

When she found Phury's energy source, a screaming pain assaulted her, as if that were what he felt. As she swayed, Zsadist gripped her arm.

She pushed him away. "I've got him. Oh, God . . . he's—"

Zsadist grabbed her arm again and squeezed. "Fifty yards. No closer. Are we clear?"

"Yes. Now let me go."

She went out the front door, dematerialized, and took form about twenty yards away from a small cabin in the woods.

She felt Zsadist take shape at her elbow. "Go," he hissed. "Get out of here."

"But—"

"If you want to help, leave so I don't have to worry about you. *Go.*"

Bella took one last look into his face and dematerialized.

Zsadist sidled up to the log cabin, grateful for the cold air that helped him throw off a little more of the morphine. As he flattened himself against a rough-hewn wall, he unsheathed a dagger and peered into one of the windows. There was nothing inside, just some rustic, shitty furniture and a computer setup.

Panic washed through him, a cold rain in his blood.

And then he heard the sound . . . a thump. Then another.

There was a smaller outbuilding with no windows about twenty-five yards back. He jogged over and listened for only a split second. Then he traded his knife for a Beretta and kicked down the door.

The sight before him was out of his own past: A male chained to a table, pounded raw. A demented psychopath standing over the victim.

Phury lifted his battered face, blood glistening on his swollen lips and beat-to-hell nose. The *lesser* with the brass knuckles whirled around and seemed momentarily confused.

Zsadist aimed his gun at the fucker, but the slayer was right in front of Phury: The slightest miscalculation and the bullet was going to drill into his twin. Z dropped the muzzle, squeezed the trigger, and nailed the *lesser* in the leg, shattering his knee. The bastard screamed and dropped to the floor.

Z went for him. Except just as he got a hold on the undead, another popping sound went off.

The blaze of pain shot through Z's shoulder. He knew he'd been plugged a good one, but he couldn't think about that right now. He focused on getting control over the *lesser*'s gun, which was the same thing the SOB was trying to do to Z's Sig. They struggled on the floor, each trying to get a grip on the other in spite of the blood that was oiling them up. Punches were thrown and hands grabbed and legs thrashed. Both guns were lost in the grappling.

About four minutes into the fight Z's strength started to flag with alarming speed. Then he was on the bottom, the *lesser* sitting on his chest. Z gave a push, willing his body to throw the weight on it off, but though his mind gave the command, for once his limbs refused to obey. He glanced at his shoulder. He was bleeding out, no doubt because that slug had hit an artery. And that shot of morphine didn't help.

In the lull of the fighting, the *lesser* was panting and wincing, like his leg was killing him. "Who . . . the fuck . . . are you?"

"The one . . . you want," Z shot back, breathing just as hard. *Shit . . .* He had to work to keep his vision from phasing out. "I'm the one . . . who took her . . . from you."

"How . . . do . . . I know that?"

"I watched the scars . . . on her stomach heal. Until your mark . . . on her disappeared."

The *lesser* froze.

Now would have been an excellent time to get the upper hand, except Z was too spent.

"She's dead," the slayer whispered.

"No."

"Her portrait—"

"She lives. Breathes. And you will . . . never find her again."

The slayer's mouth opened and a primal scream of fury came out like a blast.

In the midst of the noise Z calmed down. Suddenly breathing was easy. Or maybe he'd just stopped altogether. He watched as the slayer moved in slo-mo, unsheathing one of Z's black daggers and lifting the thing overhead with both hands.

Zsadist tracked his thoughts carefully because he wanted to know what his last one was going to be. He thought of

Phury and wanted to weep, because no doubt his twin wouldn't last long. *God.* He'd always failed that male, hadn't he . . . ?

And then he thought of Bella. Tears came to his eyes as images of her flickered through his mind . . . so vivid, so clear . . . until from over the *lesser*'s shoulder, a vision of her appeared. She was so real, it was as if she were actually standing in the doorway.

"I love you," he whispered as his own blade came down toward his chest.

"David," her voice commanded.

The *lesser*'s whole body jerked around, the dagger's trajectory getting transferred so it landed in the floorboards next to Z's upper arm.

"David, come here."

The *lesser* lurched to his feet as Bella held her arm out.

"You were dead," the *lesser* said, voice cracking.

"No."

"I went to your house. . . . I saw the portrait. Oh, God . . ." The *lesser* started to cry as he limped closer and closer to her, black blood trailing after him. "I thought I'd killed you."

"You didn't. Come here."

Z tried desperately to work his mouth, gripped by an awful suspicion that this was no vision. He started to yell, but it came out as a moan. And then the *lesser* was in Bella's arms and weeping openly.

Z watched as her hand came around and went up onto the slayer's back. In it was the little handgun, the one he'd given her before they'd gone to her house.

Oh, Sweet Virgin . . . No!

Bella was in a state of weird calm as she brought the gun higher and higher. Moving slowly, she kept murmuring words that soothed until the barrel was on a level with David's skull. She leaned back, and as he lifted his head to meet her eyes, he brought his ear right to the muzzle.

"I love you," he said.

She pulled the trigger.

The explosion kicked her hand out and spun her arm away, throwing her off balance. As the sound faded she heard a thud and looked down. The *lesser* was on his side, still blinking. She'd expected his head to blow up or something, but there was just a neat little hole at his temple.

Nausea hit her hard, but she ignored it, stepping over the body and going to Zsadist.

Oh, God. There was blood everywhere.

"Bella . . ." His hands lifted off the ground and his mouth worked slowly.

She cut him off by reaching for his chest holster and taking the remaining dagger from him. "I need to do it in his sternum, right?"

Ah, hell. Her voice was as bad as her body. Wobbly. Weak. "Run . . . get . . . out of—"

"In the heart, right? Or he's not dead. Zsadist, answer me!"

When he nodded, she went over to the *lesser* and pushed him onto his back with her foot. His eyes were staring up at her, and she knew she was going to be seeing them in her nightmares for years to come. Grabbing the knife with both hands, she put it up over her head, and plunged it down. The resistance the blade met sickened her to the point of gagging, but the popping sound and the flash of light were a closure of sorts.

She let herself fall back and hit the floor, but two breaths were all she could spare. She went to Zsadist, tearing off her coat and fleece. She wrapped the pullover around his shoulder, then stripped off her belt, looped it around the thick wad, and cinched it up tight to keep it in place.

The whole time Zsadist struggled against her, urging her to run, to leave them.

"Shut up," she told him, and bit into her own wrist. "Drink this or die, your choice. But make up your mind quick, because I need to check on Phury and then I've got to get the two of you out of here."

She held her arm out to him, right over his mouth. Her blood welled and dripped onto his closed lips.

"You bastard," she whispered. "Do you hate me so much—"

He lifted his head and latched onto her vein, his cold mouth telling her all she needed to know about how close to death he was. He drank slowly at first and then with increasing greed. Little sounds came out of him, sounds at odds with his big warrior body. He sounded as if he were mewing, a starved cat at a font of milk.

When he let his head fall back, his eyes closed with satiation. Her blood seeped into him; she watched him breathe through his open mouth. But there was no time to stare. She raced across the shed to Phury. He was unconscious, chained to the table, bloody as hell. But his chest was going up and down.

Damn it. Those steel chains had Master locks dangling from them. She was going to have to cut him free with something. She went over to the left, to a horrific selection of tools—

And that was when she saw the body in the corner. A young female with short blond hair.

Tears welled and flowed as she checked to make sure the girl was dead. When it was obvious she had passed unto the Fade, Bella swiped her own eyes clear and forced herself to focus. She needed to get the living out of here; they were her first priority. Afterward . . . one of the Brothers could come back and . . .

Oh . . . God . . . oh . . . God . . . oh . . . God.

Shuddering, close to hysterical, she picked up a Sawzall, fired the thing up, and made quick work of Phury's restraints. When he didn't come around after all the shrill noise, she got terrified again.

She looked at Zsadist, who had fought to get his upper body off the floor.

"I'm going to go get that truck by the cabin," she said. "You stay here and conserve your strength. I need you to help me move Phury. He's out cold. And the girl . . ." Her voice choked up. "We'll have to leave her. . . ."

Bella ran across the snow to the cabin, desperately hoping

to find the truck's keys, trying hard not to think what she would do if she didn't.

Merciful Virgin, they were on a hook by the door. She grabbed them, raced for the F-150, started the damn thing, and gunned it around to the shed. A quick skidding turn and she backed it bed-first to the doorway.

She was just getting out of the driver's side when she saw Zsadist weaving like a drunk between the jambs. Phury was in his arms, and Zsadist wasn't going to last long holding up all that weight. She popped the lip on the bed and the two fell in, all tangled limbs and blood. She shoved at their bodies with her feet, then jumped up and pulled them farther back by their belts.

When they were in far enough, she threw one leg over the gunwale of the truck and hopped to the ground. She slammed the lip shut and met Zsadist's eyes.

"Bella." His voice was a mere whisper, just a movement of his lips backed up by a sigh of sadness. "I don't want this for you. All this . . . ugliness."

She turned away from him. A moment later she hit the gas.

The one-lane road that led away from the cabin was her only option, and she prayed she didn't meet anyone on the way. When she came out onto Route 22, she said a prayer of thanks to the Scribe Virgin and headed for Havers's at a dead run.

Tilting the rearview mirror, she looked into the truck bed. It must have been freezing back there, but she didn't dare slow down.

Maybe the cold would slow the blood loss for both of them.

Oh . . . God.

Phury was aware of an icy wind blowing over his bare skin and across his bald head. He moaned and curled up into himself. God, he was cold. Was this what you had to go through to make it into the Fade? Then thank the Virgin it only happened once.

Something moved against him. Arms . . . there were arms

coming around him, arms that took him in close to a kind of warmth. Shivering, he gave himself up to whoever it was who held him so gently.

What was that noise? Close to his ear . . . a sound other than the roaring wind.

Singing. Someone was singing to him.

Phury smiled a little. How perfect. The angels that were taking him unto the Fade truly did have beautiful voices.

He thought of Zsadist and compared the lovely melody he heard now with the ones he had listened to in real life.

Yes, Zsadist had had a voice like an angel, as it turned out. He truly had.

Chapter Forty-seven

When Zsadist came awake, his first instinct was to sit up. *Bad fucking idea.* His shoulder let out a holler and nailed him with a shot of pain so intense, he blacked out again.

Round two.

This time when he woke up at least he remembered what not to do. He turned his head slowly instead of trying to get vertical. Where the hell was he? The place seemed halfway between a guest bedroom and a hospital setup—Havers. He was at Havers's clinic.

And someone was sitting in the shadows across the unfamiliar room.

"Bella?" he croaked.

"Sorry." Butch leaned forward, into the light. "Just me."

"Where is she?" Man, he was hoarse. "Is she all right?"

"She's fine."

"Where . . . where is she?"

"She's . . . ah, she's leaving town, Z. Actually I think she's already gone."

Zsadist closed his eyes. Considered briefly the merits of passing out again.

He couldn't blame her for getting away, though. Christ, the situations she'd been put in. Not the least of which was killing that *lesser.* It was better that she get far away from Caldwell.

Although he ached all over from the loss.

He cleared his throat. "Phury? Is he—"

"Right next door. Bunged up, but okay. The two of you have been out to lunch for a couple of days."

"Tohr?"

"No one has any idea where he is. It's like he vanished." The cop blew out his breath. "John's supposed to be staying at the mansion, but we can't get him out of the training center. He's been sleeping in Tohr's office. Any other updates you want?" As Z shook his head, the cop got to his feet. "I'll leave you alone now. I just assumed you'd feel better knowing where things stood."

"Thanks . . . Butch."

The cop's eyes flared at the sound of his name, making Z realize he'd never used it with the guy before.

"Sure," the human said. "No problem."

As the door eased shut, Zsadist sat up. While his head spun he yanked the monitors off his chest and his forefinger. Alarms started to go off, and he silenced them by pushing over the stand of machinery that was next to the bed. The tangle of monitors unplugged itself on the way to the floor and shut up.

He yanked the catheter out with a grimace and looked at the IV going into his forearm. He was about to rip it from his vein, but then figured chilling on that move might be smart. God only knew what was pumping into him. Maybe he needed it.

He stood up and his body felt like a beanbag, all loose inside his skin. The IV pole made a good walker, though, so he hit the hallway. As he started for the room beside his, nurses came running from all directions. He shrugged them off and pushed open the first door he got to.

Phury was lying on the king-size bed, lines plugged into him as if he were a switchboard.

The male's head turned. "Z . . . what are you doing up?"

"Giving the medical staff a workout." He shut the door and weaved into the room, heading for the bed. "They're pretty damn fast, actually."

"You shouldn't be—"

"Shut up and move over."

Phury looked startled as hell, but he pushed himself to the far side as Z heaved his exhausted body up onto the mattress. When he lay back against the pillows, the two of them let out identical sighs.

Z rubbed his eyes. "You're ugly without all that hair, you know."

"That mean you're going to grow some?"

"Nah. My beauty-queen days are over."

Phury chuckled. Then there was a long silence.

In the quiet, Zsadist kept picturing what it had been like to go into that *lesser's* shed and see Phury strapped to that table, his hair gone, his face beat to shit. Having to witness his twin's pain had been . . . an agony.

Z cleared his throat. "I shouldn't have used you like I did."

The bed wiggled as if Phury had jerked his head around. "What?"

"When I wanted to . . . hurt. I shouldn't have made you beat me."

There was no reply, and Z turned for a look, watching as Phury covered his eyes with his hands.

"That was cruel of me," Z said into the dim, tense air between them.

"I hated doing that to you."

"I know, and I knew it when I made you hit me until I bled. That I fed off your misery was the cruelest part. I'm never going to ask you to do that again."

Phury's bare chest rose and fell. "I'd rather it be me than anyone else. So when you need it, you let me know. I'll do it."

"Christ, Phury—"

"What? It's the only way you'll let me take care of you. The only way you'll let me touch you."

Now Z was the one covering stinging eyes with a forearm. He had to cough a couple of times before speaking. "Look, no more saving me, my brother, okay? That's over now. Finished. It's time for you to let go."

There was no reply. So Z glanced over again—just as a tear slid down Phury's cheek.

"Ah . . . fuck," Z muttered.

"Yeah. Pretty much." Another tear rolled out of Phury's eye. "God . . . damn. I'm leaking."

"Okay, brace yourself."

Phury scrubbed his face with his palms. "Why?"

"Because . . . I think I'm going to try to hug you."

Phury's hands dropped and he looked over with an absurd expression.

Feeling like an utter ass, Z pushed himself over to his twin. "Lift up your head, damn it." Phury craned his neck. Z slid his arm underneath. The two of them froze in the unnatural positions. "You know, this was a hell of a lot easier when you were out cold in the back of that truck."

"That was you?"

"You think it was Santa Claus or some shit?"

Z's hackles were rising all over the place. *God* . . . He was really exposed here. What the hell was he doing?

"I thought you were an angel," Phury said softly as he laid his head back onto Z's arm. "When you sang to me, I thought you were seeing me safely unto the Fade."

"I'm no angel." He reached up and smoothed his hand over Phury's cheek, sweeping the wetness away. Then he closed the male's eyelids with his fingertips.

"I'm tired," Phury murmured. "So . . . tired."

Z stared at his twin's face for what felt like the very first time. The bruises were already healing, the swelling going down, the jagged cut he'd given himself fading. What was revealed were lines of exhaustion and strain, not much of an improvement.

"You've been tired for centuries, Phury. It's time to let go of me."

"Don't think I can."

Zsadist inhaled deeply. "That night I was taken from the family . . . No, don't look at me. It's too . . . close. I can't breathe when you do. . . . Christ, just close your eyes, okay?" Z coughed some more, little chuffing sounds that were the only reason he could speak through his tight throat. "That night, it wasn't your fault you didn't get snatched. And you can't make up for the fact that you were lucky and I wasn't. I want you to stop looking after me."

Phury's breath shuddered out of him. "Do you . . . do you have any idea what it felt like to see you in that cell, naked and chained and . . . to know what that female had done to you for so long?"

"Phury—"

"I know it all, Z. I know everything that happened to you. I heard about it from males who . . . had been there. Before I knew it was you that they spoke of, I heard the stories."

Zsadist swallowed, though he'd gone queasy. "I had always hoped that you didn't know. Had prayed that you—"

"So you've got to understand why I die for you every day. Your pain is mine."

"No, it isn't. Swear to me you will stop this."

"I can't."

Z closed his eyes. As they lay together, he wanted to beg for forgiveness for all the shitty things he'd done since Phury had gotten him free . . . and he wanted to yell at his twin for being such a damn hero. But mostly he wanted to give all those wasted years back to Phury. The male deserved so much more than he had gotten out of life.

"Well, you're giving me no alternative, then."

Phury's head jerked off Z's arm. "If you kill yourself—"

"I guess I'd better take a stab at not giving you as much to worry about."

Z felt Phury's whole body go limp. "Oh . . . Jesus."

"Don't know how it'll work out, though. My instincts . . . they've been honed for anger, you know. I'm probably always going to be a quick trigger."

"Oh, Jesus . . ."

"But you know, maybe I could work on that. Or something. Fuck, I don't know. Probably not."

"Oh . . . Jesus. I'll help you. Any way I can."

Z shook his head. "No. I don't want help. I need to do this myself."

They were quiet for a time.

"My arm's falling asleep," Z said.

Phury lifted his head and Zsadist took the limb back, but he didn't move away.

Right before Bella left, she went to the room Zsadist had been given. She'd been delaying her departure for days, telling herself it wasn't because she was waiting for him to come around. Which was a lie.

The door was slightly ajar, so she knocked on the jamb. She wondered what he would say when she just walked right in. Probably nothing.

"Come in," a female said.

Bella stepped into the room. The bed was empty, and a splintered tree of monitoring equipment was lying on its side as if it were dead. A nurse was picking pieces of it off the floor and putting them into a trash can. Clearly Zsadist was up and around.

The nurse smiled. "Are you looking for him? He's next door with his brother."

"Thank you."

Bella went one room farther down and knocked quietly. When there was no response, she went inside.

The two of them were lying back-to-back, so tightly against each other it was as if their spines were fused. Their arms and legs were curled up in identical positions, their chins tucked into their chests. She imagined them in their mother's womb like that, resting together, innocent of all the horrors that waited for them on the outside.

Odd to think her blood was in both of them. It was her only legacy to the pair, the only thing she was leaving behind.

Without warning Zsadist's eyes flipped open. The yellow-gold glow was such a surprise, she jumped.

"Bella . . ." He reached for her. "Bella—"

She took a step back. "I came to say good-bye."

As he dropped his hand, she had to look away.

"Where are you going?" he asked. "Somewhere safe?"

"Yes." She was heading down the coast, to Charleston in

South Carolina, to extended family who were more than happy to take her in. "It's going to be a new start for me. A new life."

"Good. This is good."

She closed her eyes. Just once . . . just once she would have liked to hear some regret in his voice while she was leaving. Then again, as this was their last good-bye, at least she wouldn't have to be disappointed anymore.

"You were so brave," he said. "I owe you my life. His, too. You are so . . . brave."

The hell she was. She was about to break down completely. "I hope you and Phury heal up fast. Yeah, I hope . . ."

There was a long silence. Then she took one last look at Zsadist's face. She knew then that even if she mated somewhere down the line, no male would ever take his place.

And as unromantic as it sounded, that just plain sucked. Sure, she was supposed to triumph over loss and all that. But she loved him and she wasn't going to end up with him, and all she wanted to do was get in a bed somewhere, turn the lights off, and just lie there. For, like, a century.

"I need you to know something," she said. "You told me that someday I would wake up and regret being with you. Well, I do. But not because of what the *glymera* would say." She crossed her arms over her chest. "After having been burned by high society once, I'm no longer afraid of the aristocracy, and I would have been proud . . . to stand at your side. But yes, I am sorry I was with you."

Because leaving him was a shattering blow. Worse than everything she'd gone through with the *lesser.*

All things considered, it would have been better not to know what she was missing.

Without another word she turned and left the room.

As dawn creeped over the landscape, Butch walked into the Pit, took off his coat, and sat down on the leather sofa. SportsCenter was on mute. Kanye West's *Late Registration* was on surround sound.

V appeared in the kitchen's doorway, clearly just in from a

night of fighting: He was shirtless and sporting a shiner, still
in his leathers and shitkickers.

"How you doing?" Butch asked, eyeing another black-
and-blue that was popping up on his roommate's shoulder.

"No better than you. You look beat, cop."

"For real." He let his head fall back. Watching over Z had
seemed like the thing to do while the other Brothers had been
out doing their job. But he was exhausted, even though all
he'd done was park it in a chair for three days straight.

"I've got something to perk you up. Here."

Butch shook his head as a wineglass appeared in front of
his face. "You know I don't drink red."

"Try it."

"Nah, I need a shower and then something with a little
more bite in it." Butch planted his hands into his knees and
started to get up.

Vishous stepped in the way. "You need this. Trust me."

Butch let his ass sink back down as he took the glass. He
sniffed at the wine. Drank some. "Not bad. Little thick, but
not bad. Is this a merlot?"

"Not really."

He tilted his head back and swallowed seriously. The wine
was strong, burning its way to his stomach, making him a little light-headed. Which made him wonder when the last time
he'd eaten had been.

As he sucked back the last inch, he frowned. Vishous was
watching him far too closely.

"V? Something wrong?" He put the glass on a table and
cocked an eyebrow.

"No . . . no, everything's cool. Everything's going to be
cool now."

Butch thought about his roommate's troubles of late. "Hey,
I meant to ask about your visions. They still gone?"

"Well, I had one about ten minutes ago. So maybe they're
back."

"That'd be good. I don't like to see you all freaked out."

"You're all right, cop. You know that?" Vishous smiled
and pushed a hand through his hair. As his arm dropped,

Butch caught sight of the Brother's wrist. On the inside of it
there was a fresh red cut. Like, one that had been made minutes ago.

Butch looked at the wineglass. A horrible suspicion carried
his eyes to his roommate's drinking point again.

"Jesus . . . Christ. V, what . . . what did you do?" He shot
to his feet just as the first spasm overtook his stomach. "Oh,
God . . . *Vishous.*"

He ran for his toilet to throw up, but he didn't make it that
far. As soon as he flew into his room V tackled him from behind, taking him down onto the bed. When he started to gag,
Vishous flipped him over onto his back and pushed the heel
of his hand up against Butch's chin, keeping his mouth shut.

"Don't fight it," V said roughly. "Keep it down. You need
to keep it down."

Butch's gut heaved and he choked on the shit that shot up
into his throat. Panicked, nauseated, unable to breathe, he
shoved against the heavy body that straddled him and managed to knock Vishous off to the side. But before he could get
free, V grabbed him from behind and forced his jaw shut
again.

"Keep . . . it . . . down . . ." V groaned as they struggled on
the bed.

Butch felt a thick leg come around and trap his thighs. The
wrestling move worked. He couldn't move. He fought anyway.

The spasms and the nausea intensified until he thought his
eyes were going to burst. Then there was an explosion in his
gut, and sparks started flowing throughout his body . . .
sparks that lit off a tingling . . . now a hum. He fell still, the
fight going out of him as he absorbed the sensations.

V's hold eased up and he took his hand away, though he
kept an arm around Butch's chest. "That's right. . . . Just
breathe through it. You're doing fine."

The hum was rising now, turning into something like sex,
but not really. . . . No, it definitely wasn't anything erotic, but
his body didn't know the difference. He hardened, the erec-

tion pushing against his slacks, his body suddenly raging with heat. He arched back, a moan coming out of his mouth.

"That's right," V said into his ear. "Don't fight it. Let it wash through you."

Butch's hips swiveled of their own accord, and he moaned again. He was hot as the center of the sun, his skin hypersensitive, his vision gone. . . . And then the roaring in his gut shifted up to his heart. In a flash all his veins lit up like they had gasoline in them, the whole inside of him becoming a network of fire, growing hotter and hotter. Sweat poured off him as his body gyrated and jerked, and he threw his head back against Vishous's shoulder. Hoarse sounds broke out of his mouth.

"I'm . . . going . . . to die."

V's voice was right there with him, seeing him through. "You gotta stay with me, my man. Keep breathing. This isn't going to last long."

Just when Butch thought he couldn't handle any more of the inferno, an eighteen-wheeler orgasm overtook him. As the top of his cock blew off, Vishous held him through the convulsions, speaking in the Old Language. And then it was over. A storm passed.

Panting, weak, Butch shuddered in the aftermath as V eased off the bed and covered him with a blanket.

"Why . . ." Butch said like a drunk. "Why, V?"

Vishous's face appeared in front of his. Both of the Brother's diamond eyes glowed . . . until the left one suddenly went all black, the pupil expanding until the iris and the white part became nothing but an infinite hole.

"The *why* of it . . . I don't know. But I saw that you were to drink from me. It was either that or you were going into the ground." V reached out and smoothed Butch's hair back. "Sleep. You'll feel fine by nightfall because you lived through it."

"That could have . . . *killed* me?" *Well, shit, yeah.* He'd assumed he was going to die.

"I wouldn't have given it to you if I weren't sure you'd

make it. Close your eyes, now. Let yourself go, true?" Vishous headed out, but paused in the doorway.

As the Brother looked back, Butch felt the oddest sensation . . . a bond flowing between them, something more tangible than the air between their bodies. Forged in the oven he'd just been in, deep as the blood in his veins . . . a miracle connection.

My brother, Butch thought.

"I'm not going to let anything happen to you, cop."

And Butch knew that was absolutely true, though he really didn't appreciate being blindsided. Then again, if he'd known what was in that glass, he never would have swallowed the shit. No frickin' way.

"What does this make me?" he asked softly.

"Nothing that you weren't before. You're still just a human."

Butch sighed in relief. "Listen, man, do me a favor. Warn me before you pull another stunt like that. I'd rather choose." Then he smiled a little. "And we still ain't dating."

V laughed in a short burst. "Go to sleep, roomie. You can kick my ass for this later."

"I will."

As the Brother's broad back disappeared down the hall, Butch closed his eyes.

Still just a human . . . Just . . . a . . . human.

Sleep claimed him like a prize.

Chapter Forty-eight

The following evening Zsadist pulled a fresh set of leathers over his thighs. He was stiff, but he felt incredibly strong, and he knew it was Bella's blood still nourishing him, giving him his full power, making him whole.

He cleared his throat as he buttoned his fly, trying not to cry over her like a sissy. "Thanks for bringing these, cop."

Butch nodded. "No problem. You going to try and poof it home? Because I got the Escalade if you don't feel up to it."

Z yanked a black turtleneck over his head, shoved his feet into his shitkickers, and stalled out.

"Z? Z, my man?"

He looked over at the cop. Blinked a couple of times. "Sorry, what?"

"You want to ride with me?"

Z focused on Butch for the first time since the male had come into the room ten minutes ago. He was about to answer the human's question when his instincts fired up. Cocking his head, he sniffed a little. Stared at the man. *What the fuck . . . ?*

"Cop, where have you been since I saw you last?"

"Nowhere."

"You smell different."

Butch flushed. "New aftershave."

"No. No, that's not—"

"So do you want a ride?" Butch's hazels hardened as if he wasn't going to go a single inch further on the subject.

Z shrugged. "Okay, yeah. And let's get Phury. We'll both go with you."

Fifteen minutes later they were pulling away from the clinic. On the way to the mansion Z sat in the back of the Escalade and stared at the passing winter landscape. It was snowing again, the flakes streaking horizontally as the SUV sped down Route 22. From the front seats, he could hear Phury and Butch talking in low tones, but they sounded far, far away. Actually, everything felt that way . . . out of focus, out of context. . . .

"Home sweet home, gentlemen," Butch said as they pulled into the compound's courtyard.

Jesus. They were back already?

The three of them got out and headed for the mansion, the fresh snow squeaking under their boots. As soon as they walked into the foyer the females of the house came at them. Or rather, came at Phury. Mary and Beth threw their arms around the Brother, their voices a lovely chorus of welcome.

As Phury wrapped the females up in his arms, Z stepped back into the shadows. He watched covertly, wondering what it would feel like to be in that knot of limbs, wishing there were a welcome-home for him.

There was an awkward pause as Mary and Beth glanced over at him from Phury's embrace. The females quickly looked away, avoiding his eyes.

"So, Wrath is upstairs," Beth said, "waiting for you guys with the Brothers."

"Any word about Tohr?" Phury asked.

"No, and it's killing everyone. John, too."

"I'll go see the kid later."

Mary and Beth gave Phury a final squeeze; then he and Butch headed for the stairs. Z followed.

"Zsadist?"

He looked over his shoulder at the sound of Beth's voice. She was standing with her arms over her chest, and Mary was right by her side, looking similarly tense.

"We're glad you made it back," the queen said.

Z frowned, knowing that couldn't be true. He didn't imagine they liked having him around.

Mary spoke up. "I lit a candle for you. I prayed that you would come home safely."

A candle . . . lit for him? Only for him? As the blood hit his face, he felt pathetic that the kindness meant so much.

"Thank you." He bowed to them and then rushed up the stairs, sure he was the color of a ruby. *God* . . . Maybe he'd get better at the whole relating thing. Someday.

Except when he walked into Wrath's study and felt the eyes of his Brothers all over him, he thought, *Maybe not*. He couldn't stand the scrutiny; it was too much when he was this raw. As his hands started to shake, he shoved them into his pockets and went to his usual corner, far away from the others.

"I don't want anyone going out to fight tonight," Wrath announced. "We're all too much in our heads right now to be effective. And I want you boys back in the house by four A.M. As soon as the sun rises we'll be in mourning for Wellsie all day long, so I want you fed and watered before we get down to that. As for her Fade ceremony, we can't perform it without Tohr, so that's on hold."

"I can't believe no one knows where he's gone," Phury said.

Vishous lit up a hand-rolled. "I go to his house every night, and still there's no sign of him. His *doggen* haven't seen him or heard from him. He left his daggers. His weapons. His clothes. The cars. He could be anywhere."

"What about the training?" Phury asked. "Do we keep it up?"

Wrath shook his head. "I'd like to, but we're damn short-handed, and I don't want to overwork you. Especially because you need time to recover—"

"I can help," Z interjected.

All heads turned in his direction. The disbelief on their faces would have been a laugh riot if it hadn't stung as much as it did.

He cleared his throat. "I mean, Phury would be in charge, and he'd have to do the classroom shit because I can't read. But I'm good with a knife, you know. Fists, too. Guns. Explosives. I could help with the physical training and the weapons parts." When there was no response, he looked down. "Yeah, or maybe not. It's cool. Whatever."

The silence that followed made him itchy as hell. He shuffled his legs around. Eyed the door.

Fuck me, he thought. He should have kept his yap shut.

"I think that would be great," Wrath said slowly. "But are you sure you'd be into it?"

Z shrugged. "I could try."

More quiet. "Okay . . . so be it. And thanks for manning up."

"Sure. Ah, no problem."

When they broke a half hour later, Z was the first to leave the study. He didn't want to talk to the brothers about what he'd volunteered to do or how he was feeling. He knew they were all curious about him, probably looking for signs that he'd been redeemed or some shit.

He went back to his room to arm himself. He had a hard task in front of him, a long, hard task, and he wanted to get it over with.

Except as he went for the weapons cabinet inside his closet, his eyes latched onto the black satin robe Bella had worn so often. Days ago, he'd thrown it in the trash in the bathroom, but Fritz had obviously picked it out and hung it back up. Z leaned forward and touched the thing, then took it off the hanger, draped it over his arm, and stroked the smooth cloth. He brought it to his nose and breathed deep, catching both her scent and the smell of his bonding for her.

He was about to put the thing back when he caught sight of something flashing as it fell onto the floor at his feet. He bent down. Bella's little necklace. Left behind.

He fingered the fragile chain for a while, just watching the diamonds sparkle; then he put it on and got out his weapons. As he stepped back into the bedroom he meant to leave right away, but his eyes caught sight of the Mistress's skull sitting next to his pallet.

Crossing the room, he knelt in front of the thing and stared into the eye sockets.

A moment later he went to the bathroom, grabbed a towel, and headed back for the skull. Draping the thing in terry cloth, he picked it up and moved fast, racewalking and then jogging down the hall of statues. He took the grand staircase to the first floor, cut through the dining room and the butler's pantry, then crossed the kitchen.

The basement stairs were way in the back, and he didn't turn the light on as he took them downward. As he descended, the roaring sound of the mansion's old-fashioned coal-burning furnace got louder.

Approaching the great iron beast he felt its warmth, as if the thing were alive and fevered. He leaned down and looked through the little glass window in the hutch. Orange flames licked and gnawed at the coal they'd been given, always hungry for more food. He flipped the latch, opened the door, and got a blast in the face. Without hesitating he tossed the skull in with the towel.

He didn't wait around to watch it burn, just turned and headed back upstairs.

When he got to the foyer he paused, then walked up to the second floor. At the head of the stairs he took a right, went down the hall, and knocked on one of the doors.

Rhage opened the thing, a towel around his waist. He seemed surprised to see who it was. "Hey, my brother."

"Can I talk to Mary for a minute?"

Hollywood frowned, but said over his shoulder, "Mary, Z wants to see you."

Mary was pulling a silk dressing gown closed and tying it with a sash as she came to the door. "Hi."

"You mind if I do this in private?" Z said, glancing at Rhage.

As the brother's eyebrows got real low, Z thought, Yeah, bonded males didn't like their females alone with anyone else. Especially not him.

He rubbed his skull trim. "It'll just be here in the hall. Won't take long."

Mary stepped between them and nudged her *hellren* back into the room. "It's all right, Rhage. Go finish getting the tub ready."

Rhage's eyes flashed white as his beast checked in with its own bonded reaction. There was a weighty pause; then Mary was kissed soundly on the throat and the door shut.

"What is it?" she asked. Z could smell her fear of him, but she met him in the eye.

He always had liked her, he thought. "I heard you taught autistic kids."

"Ah . . . yes, I did."

"Were they slow at learning things?"

She frowned. "Well, yes. Sometimes."

"Did that . . ." He cleared his throat. "Did that get on your nerves? I mean, did you get frustrated with them?"

"No. If I got disappointed at all, it was with myself for not figuring out the way they needed to learn."

While he nodded, he had to look away from her gray eyes. He focused on the door panel next to her head.

"Why do you ask, Zsadist?"

He took a deep breath and then threw himself off a ledge. When he was finished speaking, he risked a glance at her.

Her hand was over her mouth and her eyes were so kind they were like sunlight on him. "Oh, Zsadist, yes . . . Yes, I will."

Phury shook his head as he got into the Escalade. "It has to be ZeroSum."

He *so* needed to go there tonight.

"Figured as much," V said as he slid behind the wheel and Butch hopped in the back.

As they made the trip into town, the three of them were totally silent. Not even music was banging in the car.

So much death, so much loss, Phury thought. Wellsie. That young female, Sarelle, whose body V had returned to her parents.

And Tohr's disappearance was like a death, too. So was Bella's.

The agony of it all made him think about Z. He wanted to believe that Zsadist was on the road to some kind of recovery or something. But the idea that that male could turn himself around was completely baseless. It was only a matter of time before the brother's need for pain came back and shit started to unravel again.

Phury rubbed his face. He felt a thousand years old tonight, he really did, but he was also wired and twitchy . . . traumatized on the inside, though his skin had healed. He just could not keep it together. He needed help.

Twenty minutes later, Vishous pulled up to the back of ZeroSum and parked the SUV illegally. The bouncers let them in right away, and the three of them went for the VIP section. Phury ordered a martini, and when it came he finished it in one long swallow.

Help. He needed help. He needed double-barreled help . . . or he was going to explode.

"'Scuse me, boys," he murmured. He headed for the back, for the Reverend's office. The two huge Moors nodded to him, and one spoke into his watch. A second later they let him through.

Phury walked into the cave and focused on the Reverend. The male was sitting behind his desk dressed in a pristine pin-striped suit, more businessman than pusher.

The Reverend smirked a little. "Where the hell is all that beautiful hair?"

Phury glanced behind himself, to make sure the outside door was closed. Then he took out three Benjis. "I want some H."

The Reverend's violet eyes narrowed. "What did you say?"

"Heroin."

"You sure about that?"

No, Phury thought. "Yes," he said.

The Reverend ran his hand back and forth over his cropped

mohawk. Then he leaned forward and pressed a button on his intercom.

"Rally, I want three hundred worth of Queen up here. Make sure it's fine-granule." The Reverend eased back in his chair. "Straight up, I don't think you should take that kind of powder home with you. You don't need that shit."

"Not that I'd take any direction from you, but you told me I should go hard-core."

"I retract that comment."

"I thought *symphaths* didn't have a conscience."

"I'm half my mother's boy, too. So I have a little."

"Aren't you lucky."

The Reverend's chin dipped down, and his eyes flashed pure, purple evil for a split second. Then he smiled. "No . . . all the rest of you are fortunate."

Rally arrived moments later, and the transaction didn't take long. The folded packet fit neatly in Phury's inside breast pocket.

As he was leaving the Reverend said, "That stuff is very pure. Dead pure. You can sprinkle it in your blunt or melt it and shoot up. But a word of advice. It will be safer for you to smoke it. You'll have more control over the dose."

"So familiar with your products."

"Oh, I never use any of this toxic waste. It'll kill ya. But I hear from folks about what works. And what'll give you a toe tag."

The reality of what he was doing shimmered across Phury's skin on a nasty little tickle. But by the time he got back to the Brotherhood's table he couldn't wait to go home. He wanted to numb out completely. He wanted the deep nod that he'd heard heroin gave. And he knew he'd bought enough of the drug to take him to heavenly hell a couple of times.

"What's the matter with you?" Butch asked him. "You can't sit still tonight."

"Nothing doing." As he put his hand inside his pocket and felt for what he'd bought, he started tapping his foot under the table.

I am a junkie, he realized.

Except he didn't have enough left in him to care. Death was everywhere around him, the stench of sorrow and failure polluting the air he breathed. He needed off the crazy train for a little while, even if it meant getting on another kind of sick ride.

Fortunately, or maybe unfortunately, Butch and V didn't last long at the club, and they were all home a little after midnight. As they walked into the vestibule Phury was cracking his knuckles, a flush breaking out under his clothes. He couldn't wait to be alone.

"You wanna eat?" Vishous said, yawning.

"Damn straight," Butch said. Then he glanced over as V walked off for the kitchen. "Phury, you with us for some chow?"

"Nah, I'll see you later." As he hit the stairs he could feel the male's eyes on him.

"Yo, Phury," Butch called out.

Phury cursed and looked over his shoulder. A little of his manic drive bled out as the cop's knowing eyes burned up at him.

Butch knew, he thought. Somehow the guy knew what he was up to.

"You sure you don't want to eat with us," the human said in a level voice.

Phury didn't even have to think. Or maybe he refused to let himself. "Yeah. I'm sure."

"Careful, my man. Some things are damn hard to undo."

Phury thought of Z. Of himself. Of the shitty future he had little interest in slogging through.

"Don't I know it," he said, and took off.

When he got to his room he shut the door and dropped his leather coat on a chair. He took the packet out, grabbed some red smoke and a rolling paper, and doctored up a blunt. He didn't even consider shooting up. It was just too close to addict status.

At least for this first time.

He licked the edge of the rolling paper, pressed the joint up tight, then went over to his bed and sat back against the pil-

lows. He picked up his lighter, flicked it so the flame leaped
to life, and leaned into the orange glow, the hand-rolled between his lips.

The knock on his door pissed him off. *Fucking Butch.*

He clicked off the lighter. "What?"

When there was no answer, he kept the dutchy with him
and pounded across the room. He threw open the door.

John stumbled backward.

Phury took a deep breath. Then another. *Chill.* He had to
chill.

"What's doing, son?" he asked, stroking the blunt with his
forefinger.

John brought up his pad, wrote a few lines, and turned the
thing around. *I'm sorry to bother you. I need someone to help
me with my jujitsu positions, and you're so good at them.*

"Oh . . . yeah. Ah, not tonight, John. I'm sorry. I'm . . .
busy."

The kid nodded. After a pause, John waved good-bye.
Turned away.

Phury shut the door, locked it, and went right back for the
bed. He flicked the lighter on again, put the blunt between his
lips—

Just as the flame hit the tip of the hand-rolled, he froze.

He couldn't breathe. He couldn't . . . He started gasping.
As his palms grew wet, sweat broke out above his upper lip
and under his armpits and all down his chest.

What the fuck was he doing? What the fuck was he doing?

*Junkie . . . junkie motherfucker. Low-life junkie . . . moth-
erfucker.* To bring *heroin* into the king's house? To be lighting
the shit up in the *Brotherhood's* compound? To be polluting
himself because he was too weak to fucking deal?

Hell, no, he would not do this. He would not disgrace his
brothers, his king, like this. Bad enough he was addicted to
the red smoke. But H?

Shaking from head to toe, Phury ran for the bureau, picked
up the packet, and bolted for the bathroom. He flushed the
blunt and the heroin down and flushed again. And again.

Stumbling out of his room, he raced over the hallway's runner.

John was halfway down the grand staircase when Phury burst around the corner and all but fell down the steps. He caught up to the boy and dragged him into his arms so hard, those fragile bones must have bent.

Dropping his head onto the kid's shoulder, Phury shuddered. "Oh, God . . . thank you. Thank you, thank you . . ."

Little arms came around him. Little hands patted his back.

When Phury finally pulled away, he had to wipe his eyes. "I think tonight's a great night to work on your stances. Yeah. It's a really good time for me, too. Come on."

As the kid looked at him . . . his eyes suddenly seemed eerily knowing. And then John's mouth worked, moving slowly, forming words that had impact even if they didn't have sound.

You are in a prison with no bars. I worry about you.

Phury blinked, caught in an odd kind of time warp. Someone else had said those very things to him. . . . Just last summer.

The vestibule's door opened, breaking the moment. As Phury and John both jumped at the sound, Zsadist came into the foyer.

The brother looked beat as he glanced up the stairs. "Oh, hey, Phury. John."

Phury rubbed his neck, trying to come back from whatever déjà vu slice of weirdness had just happened with John.

"So, Z, ah, where you coming from?"

"A little trip. A little trip far away. What's doing?"

"We're going to go work on John's positions in the gym."

Z shut the door. "How about I join you? Or . . . maybe I should put it this way. Can I join you?"

Phury could only stare. John seemed likewise surprised, but at least the kid had the good grace to nod his head.

Phury shook himself into focus. "Yeah, of course, my brother. Come with us. You're always . . . welcome."

Zsadist crossed the brilliant mosaic floor. "Thanks. Thanks a lot."

The three of them headed for the underground passageway.

As they walked to the training center Phury glanced at John and thought that sometimes it took only a hairbreadth between cars to avoid a mortal accident.

Sometimes your whole life could hinge on a fraction of an inch. Or the beat of a nanosecond. Or the knock on a door.

Kind of made a male believe in the divine. It really did.

Chapter Forty-nine

Two months later . . .

Bella materialized in the front of the Brotherhood's mansion and looked up at the dour gray facade. She had never expected to return. But fate had other plans for her.

She opened the outer door and stepped into the vestibule. As she hit the intercom and showed her face to the camera, she felt as if she were in some kind of dream.

Fritz opened the doors wide and bowed with a smile. "Madam! How nice to see you."

"Hi." She stepped inside and shook her head when he tried to take her coat. "I won't be long. I'm just here to talk to Zsadist. For a minute."

"But of course. Master is over here. Please to follow me?" Fritz led her across the foyer to a set of double doors, all the while chatting along merrily, updating her on things like what they'd all done for New Year's.

But the *doggen* paused before opening the way into the library. "Begging your pardon, madam, but you seem . . . Would you care to announce yourself? When you are ready?"

"Oh, Fritz, how well you know me. I would love a minute to myself."

He nodded and smiled and disappeared.

She took a deep breath and listened to the voices and footsteps in the house. Some were low enough and loud enough to belong to the Brothers, and she glanced at her watch. Seven o'clock at night. They would be getting ready to go out.

She wondered how Phury was. And whether Tohr had returned yet. And how John was.

Stalling . . . she was stalling.

Now or never, she thought, grabbing onto a brass handle and twisting. One half of the door gave way soundlessly.

Her breath caught as she looked inside the library.

Zsadist was sitting at a table, bent down low over a piece of paper, a thin pencil in his heavy fist. Mary was next to him, and between the two of them there was a book open.

"Remember the hard consonants," Mary said, pointing to the book. "Che*ck*. *C*atch. The *k* and *c* in those words sound close, but aren't the same. Try again."

Zsadist put a hand up to his skull trim. In a low voice he said something that didn't carry. And then his pencil moved on the paper.

"That's good!" Mary put her hand on his bicep. "You've got it."

Zsadist looked up and smiled. Then his head whipped around toward Bella and he lost the expression.

Oh, good Virgin in the Fade, she thought as she drank in the sight of him. She still loved him. She knew it down to her gut—

Wait a minute . . . What the . . . hell? His face was really different. Something had changed. Not the scar, but something was different.

Whatever. Get this over with so you can get going.

"I'm sorry to interrupt," she said. "I was wondering if I could talk to Zsadist."

She was vaguely aware of Mary getting up and coming over, of the two of them hugging, of the female leaving and shutting the door behind her.

"Hi," Zsadist said. Then slowly rose to his feet.

Bella's eyes widened, and she took a step back. "My . . . God. You're *huge*."

He put a hand to his thick pec. "Um . . . yeah. I've put on about eighty pounds. Havers . . . Havers said I'm probably not going to gain much more. But I'm about two-seventy now."

So that was the change in his face. His cheeks were not hollow anymore, his features no longer so stark, his eyes not sunken. He looked . . . almost handsome, actually. And much more like Phury.

He cleared his throat awkwardly. "Yeah, so, Rhage and I . . . we've been eating together."

Jesus . . . They certainly had. Zsadist's body was nothing like she remembered. His shoulders were massive and corded with muscles she could see under the tight black T-shirt he was wearing. His biceps were three times the size they'd been, and his forearms were big enough now to fit the size of his hands. And his stomach . . . his belly was ribbed with strength, and his leathers were stretched over heavy, roped thighs.

"You've been feeding, too," she murmured. And instantly wished she could take the words back. As well as the tone of censure.

It was none of her business whose vein he took, though it hurt to imagine him with one of their kind—and surely that was who he was drinking from. Human blood couldn't possibly have been responsible for this kind of growth.

His hand fell from his chest back to his side. "Rhage has a member of the Chosen he uses because he can't take Mary's vein for sustenance. I've been feeding from her, too." There was a pause. "You look well."

"Thank you."

Another long pause. "Um . . . Bella, why have you come? Not that I mind—"

"I have to talk to you."

He didn't seem to know what to say to that.

"So what are you doing?" she asked, pointing to the papers on the desk. This was also none of her business, but she was hopelessly stalling again. Tongue-tied. Lost.

"I'm learning to read."

Her eyes flared. "Oh . . . wow. How's it going?"

"Good. Slow. But I'm working at it." He glanced down at the papers. "Mary's patient with me."

Silence. Long silence. God, now that she was in front of him, she just couldn't find the words.

"I went to Charleston," he said.

"What?" He'd come to see her there?

"It took a while to find you, but I did. I went the first night I was out of Havers's."

"I never knew."

"I didn't want you to."

"Oh." She took a deep breath, pain doing a quicksilver dance under every inch of her skin. *Time to jump off the cliff,* she thought. "Listen, Zsadist, I came to tell you—"

"I didn't want to see you until I was finished." As his yellow eyes stared at her, something changed in the air between them.

"With what?" she whispered.

He looked down at the pencil in his hand. "Me."

She shook her head. "I'm sorry. I don't understand—"

"I wanted to give you back this." He pulled her necklace out of his pocket. "I was going to leave it with you that first night, but then I thought . . . Well, anyway, I wore it until I couldn't get it around my throat anymore. Now I just carry it around."

Bella's breath left her, just eased out of her mouth until she was empty of air. Meanwhile he started to rub the top of his head, his biceps and chest so big now, they pulled his shirt until it strained at the seams.

"The necklace was a good excuse," he murmured.

"For what?"

"I thought maybe I could go to Charleston and show up at your front door to give this back and maybe . . . you might let me in. Or something. I was worried that another male would court you, so I've been trying to go as fast as I could. I mean, I figured maybe if I could read, and if I took a little better care of myself, and if I tried to stop being such a mean-ass motherfucker . . ." He shook his head. "But don't misunderstand.

It's not like I expected you to be happy to see me. I was just . . . you know, hoping . . . coffee. Tea. Chance to talk. Or some shit. Friends, maybe. Except if you had a male, he wouldn't allow that. So, yeah, that's why I've been hurrying."

His yellow eyes lifted to hers. He was wincing, as if he were afraid of what might be showing on her face.

"Friends?" she said.

"Yeah . . . I mean, I wouldn't disgrace you by asking for more than that. I know that you regret . . . Anyway, I just couldn't let you go without . . . Yeah, so . . . friends."

Holy . . . Moses. He'd come looking for her. With the intent of coming back and reaching out to her.

Man, this was completely outside any scenario she'd imagined as she'd prepared to talk to him.

"I . . . What are you saying, Zsadist?" she stammered, even though she'd heard every word.

He glanced back down at the pencil in his hand and then turned to the table. Flipping the spiral notebook to a new page, he bent way over and labored on top of the paper for quite a while. Then he ripped the sheet free.

His hand was shaking as he held it out. "It's messy."

Bella took the paper. In a child's uneven block letters there were three words:

I LOVE YOU

Her lips flattened tight as her eyes stung. The handwriting got wavy and then disappeared.

"Maybe you can't read it," he said in a small voice. "I can do it over."

She shook her head. "I can read it just fine. It's . . . beautiful."

"I don't expect anything back. I mean . . . I know that you don't . . . feel that for me anymore. But I wanted you to know. It's important that you knew. And if there's any chance we could be together . . . I can't stop my job with the Brotherhood. But I can promise that I'll be so much more careful with myself—" He frowned and stopped talking. "Shit. What am I saying? I promised myself I wouldn't put you in this position—"

She crushed the paper to her heart, then launched herself at him, hitting his chest so hard he stumbled back. As his arms came around her with hesitation, as if he didn't have any idea what she was doing or why, she wept openly.

In all her preparations for this meeting, the one thing she had never considered was that the two of them might have some sort of future.

When he tilted up her chin and looked down at her she tried to smile, but the crazy hope she felt was too heavy and joyous a burden.

"I didn't mean to make you cry—"

"Oh, God . . . Zsadist, I love you."

His eyes flared so wide, his brows nearly hit his hairline. "What . . . ?"

"I love you."

"Say that again."

"I love you."

"Again . . . please," he whispered. "I need to hear it . . . again."

"I love you. . . ."

His response was to start praying to the Scribe Virgin in the Old Language.

Holding Bella tight, burying his face in her hair, he gave thanks with such eloquence she started to weep all over again.

When the last laudation had been murmured he switched back into English. "I was dead until you found me, though I breathed. I was sightless, though I could see. And then you came . . . and I was awakened."

She touched his face. In slow motion he closed the distance between their mouths, pressing the softest of kisses on her lips.

How sweetly he came to her, she thought. Even with his bulk and his power, he came to her . . . sweetly.

Then he pulled back. "But wait, why are you here? I mean, I'm glad you—"

"I'm having your young."

He frowned. Opened his mouth. Shut it and shook his head. "I'm sorry . . . what did you say?"

"I carry your young." This time there was no response from him at all. "You're going to be a father." Still nothing. "I'm pregnant."

Okay, she was running out of ways to tell him. *God*—what if he didn't want this?

Zsadist started to sway in his shitkickers and the blood ran out of his face. "You carry my young within you?"

"Yes. I'm—"

Suddenly he gripped her arms hard. "Are you all right? Did Havers say you're all right?"

"So far. I'm a little young, but maybe that'll work to my advantage when the time to deliver comes. Havers said the baby is well and I'm under no restrictions . . . well, except I'm not allowed to dematerialize after my sixth month. And, ah . . ." Blushing . . . she was seriously blushing now. "I won't be able to have sex or be fed from after the fourteenth one until the birth. Which should be around month eighteen."

When the doctor had given her those warnings, she'd thought she'd never have to worry about either of those things. But maybe now . . .

Zsadist was nodding, but he really didn't look well. "I can take care of you."

"I know you will. And you're going to keep me safe." She said this because she knew he would worry about that.

"You will stay here with me?"

She smiled. "I would love to."

"Will you mate me?"

"Are you asking?"

"Yes."

Except he still looked green. He was literally the color of mint ice cream. And these rote words of his were beginning to freak her out. "Zsadist . . . are you okay about this? Um . . . you don't have to mate me, if you don't—"

"Where is your brother?"

The question startled her. "Rehvenge? Ah . . . home, I guess."

"We go to him. Now." Zsadist took her hand and dragged her out into the foyer.

"Zsadist—"

"We will get his consent and we will be mated this night. And we will go in V's car. I don't want you dematerializing again."

Zsadist was pulling her to the door so fast, she was having to run. "Wait, Havers said I could until month—"

"I don't want to take any chances."

"Zsadist, that's not necessary."

Suddenly he stopped. "Are you sure you want my young?"

"Oh, yes. Oh, dear Virgin, *yes*. Even more now . . ." She smiled up at him. Took his hand. Placed it on her lower belly. "You're going to be a wonderful father."

And that was when he fell over in a dead faint.

Zsadist opened his eyes to find Bella looking down at him with love shining out of her face. All around his periphery there were other members of the household, but she was the only one he saw.

"Hi, there," she said softly.

He reached up and touched her face. He was not going to cry. He was not—

Oh, to hell with it.

He smiled up at her as the tears started rolling. "I hope . . . I hope it's a little girl who looks just like—"

His voice cut out. And then, yeah, like a complete flipping nancy, he broke down totally and wept like an idiot. In front of all the Brothers. And Butch. And Beth. And Mary. He was no doubt horrifying Bella with his weakness, but he couldn't help himself. This was the first time in his whole life that he had ever felt . . . blessed. Fortunate. Lucky. This moment, this perfect, shimmering moment in time, this one, sublime moment where he was flat on his back in the foyer, with his beloved Bella, and the young inside her, and the Brotherhood around him . . . this was his very luckiest day.

When his pathetic sobbing dried up, Rhage knelt down, grinning so wide his perfect cheeks were about to split. "We came running when your noggin cracked into the floor. Put 'er there, daddy-o. Can I teach the little bugger how to fight?"

Hollywood held out his hand, and as Zsadist took hold of it to shake, Wrath got down on his haunches. "Congratulations, my brother. May blessings from the Virgin be upon you and your *shellan* and your young."

By the time Vishous and Butch offered their laudatory words, Z was sitting up. Mopping up. God, he was such a pansy, crying all over himself. *Shit.* Good thing none of them seemed to mind.

As he took a deep breath, he looked around for Phury . . . and there his twin was.

In the two months since Phury's night out with that *lesser*, his hair had already grown down to his jawline, and the scar he'd put on his face was long gone. But his eyes were flat and sad. And they were sadder now, too.

Phury came forward and everyone got quiet.

"I should like to be an uncle," he said quietly. "I'm so happy for you, Z. You too . . . Bella."

Zsadist grabbed for Phury's palm and squeezed so hard he could feel his twin's bones. "You're going to be a fine uncle."

"And perhaps the *ghardian*?" Bella volunteered.

Phury bowed his head. "I would be honored to be the young's *ghardian*."

Fritz bustled in with a silver tray of slender glass flutes. The *doggen* was glowing and all atwitter with happiness. "To toast the occasion."

Voices mixed and mingled and glasses were passed and laughter sounded. Zsadist looked at Bella as someone put a flute in his hand.

I love you, he mouthed. She smiled back at him and pressed something into his hand. Her necklace.

"You keep this on you always," she whispered. "For good luck."

He kissed her hand. "Always."

Abruptly Wrath rose to his towering height, lifted up his champagne, and tilted back his head. In a tremendous, booming voice, he hollered so loud, you could have sworn the walls of the mansion shook.

"To the young!"

Everyone shot to their feet, raised their glasses, and yelled at the top of their lungs, *"To the young!"*

Ah, yes . . . Surely their chorus of voices was bold and deafening enough to carry to the Scribe Virgin's sacred ears. Which was precisely as tradition demanded.

What a true and proper toast, Z thought as he tugged Bella down to kiss her on the mouth.

"To the young!" the household all shouted once more.

"To you," he said against Bella's lips. *"Nalla."*

Chapter Fifty

"**Y**eah, well, I could have done without the passing-out part," Z muttered as he pulled into the driveway of the safe house Bella's family was living in. "And that whole bawling-my-eyes-red routine, too. Definitely could have lost that one. Christ."

"I thought you were very sweet."

With a groan he killed the engine, palmed his SIG Sauer, and went around to help her from the Escalade. *Damn it.* She already had the door open and was stepping out into the snow.

"Wait for me," he barked, grabbing for her arm.

She shot him a level stare. "Zsadist, if you keep treating me like a wineglass, I'm going to go nuts over the next sixteen months."

"Listen, female, I don't want you slipping on this ice. You're wearing high heels."

"Oh, for the love of the Virgin . . ."

He shut her car door, kissed her quickly, then put his arm around her waist and led her up the front walkway of a big, Tudor-style house. He scanned the snow-covered yard, his trigger finger itchy as hell.

"Zsadist, I want you to put the gun away before you meet my brother."

"No problem. We'll be in the house by then."

"We're not going to get jumped here. We're out in the middle of nowhere."

"If you think I'm taking even the slightest chance with you and my young, you are out of your mind."

He knew he was being overbearing as hell, but he couldn't help it. He was a bonded male. With his *pregnant* female. There were few things on the planet more aggressive or dangerous. And those bastards were called hurricanes and tornadoes.

Bella didn't argue with him. Instead she smiled and covered the hard hand on her waist with one of her own. "I guess you should be careful what you ask for."

"What do you mean?" He moved her in front of him as they came up to the door, blocking her with his body. He hated the porch light. It made them too conspicuous.

As he turned the thing off with his mind, she laughed. "I always wanted you for a bonded male."

He kissed the side of her neck. "Well, you got your wish. I'm deep bonded. Way deep bonded. Deep, deep, ultra—"

As he leaned forward and hit the brass knocker, his body came into full contact with hers. She made a little purring sound in the back of her throat and rubbed herself against him. He froze.

Oh, God. Oh . . . no, he was instantly erect. All it had taken was that one little move of hers and he had a big, flipping—

The door swung open. He expected to see a *doggen* on the other side. Instead there was a tall, slender female with white hair, a long black gown, and a whole lot of diamonds.

Crap. Bella's mother. Z hid the gun in the holster at the small of his back and made sure his double-breasted jacket was buttoned all the way down. Then he linked his hands together right in front of his zipper.

He'd dressed as conservatively as possible, in the first suit he'd ever worn. And he was even plugged into a pair of fancy-dancy loafers. He'd wanted to wear a turtleneck to cover up the slave band at his throat, but Bella had nixed that, and he supposed she was right. There was no hiding what he'd been, and there shouldn't be. Besides, no matter what he was dressed like, and even though he was a member of the Brotherhood, the *gly-*

mera would never accept him—not just because he'd been used as a blood slave, but because of what he looked like.

Thing was, though, Bella had no use for them, and neither did he. Although he was going to try to put on a polite show for her family.

Bella went forward. *"Mahmen."*

As she and her mother embraced formally, Z came into the house, shut the door, and looked around. The manse was formal and wealthy, befitting the aristocracy, but he didn't give a shit about the drapes and the wallpaper. What he approved of was the lithium-powered security contacts on all the windows. And the laser receptors in the doorways. And the motion detectors on the ceiling. Huge points for all of that. Huge.

Bella stepped back. She was stiff around her mother, and he could see why. It was clear from the gown and all those sparklers that the female was a hard-core aristocrat. And aristocrats tended to be about as cozy as a snowdrift.

"Mahmen, this is Zsadist. My mate."

Z braced himself as her mother took him in from head to foot. Once. Twice . . . and yeah, a third time.

Oh, man . . . This was going to be a really long evening.

Then he wondered if the female knew he'd gotten her daughter pregnant, too.

Bella's mother came forward and he waited for her to reach a hand out. She didn't offer him a thing. Instead her eyes watered.

Great. Now what did he do?

Her mother fell to his feet, her black gown pooling around those fancy loafers he wore. "Warrior, thank you. Thank you for bringing my Bella home."

Zsadist stared at the female for a heartbeat and a half. Then he leaned down and lifted her gently off the floor. As he held her awkwardly, he looked at Bella . . . who was sporting the kind of expression folks usually reserved for feats of magic. A big *what the hell*, laced with wonderment.

As her mother stepped away and blotted carefully under her eyes, Bella cleared her throat and asked, "Where's Rehvenge?"

"I'm right here."

The deep voice drifted in from a darkened room, and Zsadist glanced to the left as a huge male with a cane—

Shit. Oh . . . shit. This was *so* not happening.

The Reverend. Bella's brother was that mohawked, violet-eyed, hard-ass drug dealer . . . who, according to Phury, was at least half *symphath*.

What a flipping nightmare. Technically the Brotherhood should be running his ass out of town. Instead Z was looking to mate into the guy's family. God, did Bella even know what her brother was? And not just the drug-dealer part . . .

Z glanced at her. *Probably not,* his instincts told him. On both accounts.

"Rehvenge, this is . . . Zsadist," she said.

Z looked at the male again. The pair of deep purples staring back at him were unwavering, but beneath the calm there was a flicker of the same kind of *holy hell* that Z was feeling. *Man . . .* exactly how was all this going to play out?

"Rehv?" Bella murmured. "Um . . . Zsadist?"

The Reverend smiled coolly. "So, are you going to mate my sister now that you've knocked her up? Or is this just a social call?"

The two females let out gasps, and Zsadist felt his eyes flash black. As he pointedly drew Bella to his side, he itched to bare his fangs. He was going to do his best not to embarrass anyone, but if flyboy with the mouth peeled off any more one-liners like that, Z was going to drag Bella's brother outside and beat an apology out of him for upsetting the ladies.

He was damn proud of himself when he only hissed a little. "Yeah, I am going to mate her. You drop the tough act, civilian, and we might invite you to the ceremony. Otherwise you're off the list."

The Reverend's eyes flared. But then he abruptly laughed. "Easy, there, brother. Just want to make sure my sister is taken care of."

The male put his hand out. Zsadist met the big palm halfway.

"That's brother-in-law, to you. And she will be, don't you worry about that."

Epilogue

Twenty months later . . .

Oh . . . the agony. This training was going to kill him. Sure, he wanted to get into the Brotherhood, or at least be one of their soldiers, but how could anyone survive this?

As time was finally called, the new pretransition candidate sagged because the class on hand-to-hand was finally over. But he didn't dare show any more weakness than that.

Like all the trainees he was terrified and in awe of their teacher, a great, scarred warrior, a full member of the Black Dagger Brotherhood. Rumors abounded about the male: that he ate *lessers* after he killed them; that he murdered females for sport; that his scars were his doing just because he liked pain. . . .

That he'd killed recruits for making mistakes.

"Hit the showers," the warrior said, his deep voice filling the gym. "Bus is waiting for you. We start tomorrow, four sharp. So sleep up good tonight."

The trainee ran out with the others and was grateful to hit the showers. *God . . .* At least the rest of his class were just as relieved and sore. They were all like cows at this point, just standing under the spray, barely blinking, stupid from exhaustion.

Thank the good Virgin, he wouldn't have to go back onto those godforsaken blue mats for another sixteen hours.

Except as he went to put on his street clothes, he realized he'd forgotten his sweatshirt. With a cringe he shot down the hall and sneaked back into the gym. . . .

The trainee stopped dead.

The teacher was across the way, shirtless and sparring with a punching bag, his nipple rings flashing as he danced around his target. *Dear Virgin in the Fade* . . . He bore the marks of a blood slave, and scars ran all the way down his back. But, man, he could move. He had incredible strength and agility and power. Deadly. Very deadly. Totally deadly.

The trainee knew he should leave, but he was unable to look away. He'd never seen anything snap out so fast or strike so hard as the male's fists. Obviously, the rumors about the instructor were all true. He was a flat-out killer.

With a metal clank, a door opened at the other end of the gym, and the sound of a newborn's cries echoed up into the high ceiling. The warrior stopped in midpunch and wheeled around as a lovely female carrying a young in a pink blanket came over to him. His face softened, positively melted.

"Sorry to bother you," the female said over the wailing. "But she wants her daddy."

The warrior kissed the female as he took the small young into his heavy arms, cradling the newborn against his bare chest. The baby girl reached her tiny hands up and around his neck, then settled into his skin, calming instantly.

The warrior turned and looked across the mats, pegging the new trainee with a level stare. "Bus is coming soon, son. You better hurry."

Then he winked, and he turned away, putting his hand on the female's waist, pulling her close to him, kissing her again on the mouth.

The recruit stared at the warrior's back, seeing what had been hidden by all that vicious movement. Over some of his scars there were two names in the Old Language in his skin, one on top of the other.

Bella . . . And *Nalla*.

LOVER REVEALED

Butch O'Neal is a fighter by nature. A hard-living ex–homicide cop, he's the only human ever to be allowed into the inner circle of the Black Dagger Brotherhood. And he wants to go even deeper into the vampire world, into the war with the Lessers. If he can't have the female vampire he loves, then at least he can fight side by side with the Brothers. . . .

Fate curses him with the very thing he wants. When Butch sacrifices himself to save a vampire from the slayers, he falls prey to the darkest force in the war. Butch is left for dead, and the Brotherhood calls on Marissa to bring him back, but even her love may not be enough to save him. . . .

P.S. Don't miss the first two books in the series, *Dark Lover* and *Lover Eternal*.

Oh, dear Virgin in the Fade, Marissa thought.

Butch hadn't showed at First Meal. And no one had seen him or Vishous. Two hours . . . he was two hours late for meeting with her.

When she heard someone approach, she turned around.

It was Vishous, not Butch, who came into the room. The Brother was wearing black leathers and heavy black boots, but he had on a fine white shirt. Turnbull & Asser. She recognized the cut. Something told her he'd put it on just to see her.

"Tell me he is alive," she said. "Save my life right here and now, and tell me he is alive."

Vishous nodded. "He's alive."

Her knees buckled in relief. "But he isn't coming, is he?"

"No. Tomorrow night. You'll see him then."

As they stared at each other, Vishous stood in the doorway, overwhelming her even though he was across the room. He was a dangerous male, she thought, and not because of the tattoos beside his eye and the goatee and that warrior body. He was cold to the core, and someone that removed was capable of anything.

In the heavy silence, she feared both him and the news he brought.

"Where is he?" she asked.

"He's okay."

"Then why isn't he here?" She crossed her arms over her chest. "I want you to tell me what's happened."

"Just a quick fight."

A. Quick. Fight. "I want to see him."

"Like I said, he's not here."

"Is he at my brother's?"

"No."

"And you're not going to tell me where, are you?"

"He's going to call you in a little bit."

"Was it with the *lessers*?" All Vishous did was continue to stare at her, and panic kicked her heart into overdrive. She couldn't bear for Butch to be involved in this war. Look what had already been done to him. "Tell me. Goddamn it, tell me, you smug bastard."

Only silence. Which of course answered the question. And also suggested that Vishous didn't care whether she had a good opinion of him.

Marissa gathered up her skirts and marched over to the Brother. She had to crane her neck to meet him in the eye. God, he was so much bigger than Butch. And those eyes, those diamond white eyes with the midnight blue lines around the irises. Cold. So very cold.

"I don't want Butch fighting."

One black eyebrow cocked. "Not your call."

"It's too dangerous for him."

"If he is an asset, and he's willing, he'll be used."

"I don't like the Brotherhood at this moment," she blurted out.

She started to go past him, and his hand shot out, grabbing her arm and jerking her close, holding her though not hurting her. His glittering eyes went over her face and her neck.

"You know, you really are the great beauty of the species, aren't you."

"No . . . no, I am not."

"Yeah, you are." Vishous's voice got lower and lower, softer, until she wasn't sure whether she was hearing it or he was in her mind. "Butch would be a wise choice for you, female. He'd take good care of you, if you'd let him. Will you, Marissa? Or are you just playing him?"

Those diamond eyes hypnotized her, and she felt his thumb go over her wrist. As it stroked back and forth, her heart rate gradually slowed to the lazy rhythm. She swayed.

"Answer my question, Marissa."

"What . . . what did you ask?"

"Will you let him be your mate?" Vishous leaned down, his mouth at her ear. "Will you let him take you?"

"Yes . . ." she breathed, aware that they were talking about sex, but too seduced in the moment not to reply. "I will take him within me."

That hard hand loosened, then stroked her arm, moving over her skin warmly, strongly. He looked down at where he was touching her, an expression of deep concentration on his face. "Good. That's good. The two of you are beautiful together. A fucking inspiration. But I want you to remember something. You hurt him again, and I will consider you my enemy. We clear?"

The male turned on his heel and stalked out of the room.

Butch paced around the mansion's library, feeling caged by the bookcases full of leather-bound classics. They reminded him of all he hadn't read, all that literary culture bullshit he'd never been a part of, all the higher education he hadn't had.

Street smarts were his deal, and he'd always thought that was enough.

Except now he wished he was a fricking Rhodes Scholar.

With a curse, he forced himself to chill by the fireplace. Looking into the flames, he fiddled with the collar of his silk shirt. Smoothed the jacket of his Prada suit. Checked his shoes to make sure there were no scuffs on the Gucci loafers. He wanted to be perfect for his female. After all the misunderstandings and . . . the other thing, he prayed they finally had a shot at a future.

So he wanted to at least *look* as if he were worthy of her.

The smell of an ocean breeze drifted into the room, and Butch closed his eyes, dragging the fragrance down deep into his lungs. He had to brace himself as he turned around.

Oh, Christ, she's beautiful.

Marissa appeared in the doorway like an angel, and his mind momentarily seized up, seeing her not as real, but as a figment of his obsession. Her pale yellow gown and her hip-length blond hair seemed like a divine aura and her body became the apparition of beauty he'd seen in his dreams . . . and his nightmares. As she looked across the room at him, his pathetic, racing heart transformed her into a vision right out of his Catholic childhood: the Madonna of salvation and love. And he, her unworthy servant.

"Hello, Butch." Her voice was soft, gentle. Devastating.

"Marissa." This woman . . . this vampire . . . was everything he'd ever wanted and nothing he'd dared ask for. Too good for him on his very best day.

And so help him God, *he wanted her.*

Yet as she came into the room, he ditched the hearts-and-flowers stuff. Jesus, look at how weak she was. She moved slowly, as if she couldn't feel her legs, and she was terribly pale, nearly transparent from a lack of energy.

Her words, too, were as thin as breath. "Butch . . . we need to talk."

He inhaled as he nodded. "I know what you're going to say."

"You do?"

"Yeah." He started across the room toward her, arms out. "Don't you know I would do anything for—"

"Don't come any closer." She shuffled backward, bouncing up against a panel of matching bloodred volumes. "You've got to stay away from me."

He dropped his hands. "You need to feed, don't you?"

Her eyes widened. "Yes. How did you—"

"It's all right, baby." He smiled a little, aware of a blast of heat flaring in his body. "It's *very* all right."

"So you know what I've got to do? And you do not . . . mind?"

He shook his head. "I'm fine with it. More than fine."

"Oh, thank God." She lurched over to a sofa and sat down as if her knees had given way. "I was so afraid you'd be offended. It'll be hard on me as well, but it's the only safe way. And I can't wait any longer. It has to be tonight."

This time, when he came closer, she let him. He knelt in front of her, taking her hands in his. God, they were cold. He rubbed them back and forth in his palms, warming them.

"Come on," he said, aware of a thick anticipation. "Let's go."

A curious expression crossed her face. "You want to watch?"

He stilled their mingled hands. "Watch?"

"I, ah . . . I'm not sure that's a good idea. You can get a little protective—"

"Wait—watch?" He became aware of a sinking feeling in his gut. Like someone had popped the stoppers on a number of his internal organs. "What are you talking about, *watch*?"

"When I'm with the male who lets me take his vein."

Abruptly, Marissa recoiled, giving him a good idea of what the expression on his face must be like. Yeah, or maybe she was reacting to the fact that he'd started to growl.

Butch jacked up to his feet. "The hell you're using another man. You have *me*."

"Butch, I can't feed from you. I'll take too— Where are you going?"

He stalked across the room, shut the double doors, and locked them in together. As he came back at her, he tossed his jacket onto the floor and ripped open his shirt so that the buttons popped off. Falling to his knees in front of her, he tilted back his head and offered his throat, himself, to her.

"Use me."

There was a long silence as their stares warred. Then her scent, that gorgeous clean fragrance, intensified until it flooded the room. Her body began to shake, her mouth opening. As her fangs unsheathed, he got an instant erection.

"Oh . . . yeah," he said in a dark voice. "Drink from me. I need to feed you."

"No," she moaned, tears glowing in her pale blue eyes.

She made a move to get up, but he launched at her,

taking her by the shoulders, holding her down on the couch. He moved himself between her legs, bringing their bodies together. She trembled against him and pushed at him and he kept her close . . . until suddenly she was gripping the two halves of his shirt. And pulling him in tight.

"That's right, baby," he growled. "You grab on to me. Let me feel those fangs get into me deep. *I want it.*"

He palmed the back of her head and brought her mouth to his throat. An arc of pure sexual power exploded between them, and they both began to pant, her breath and tears hot on his skin.

But then she seemed to come to her senses. She struggled hard, and he did his best to keep her in place, even though he knew he was going to lose the fight against her soon. As he was just a human, she was physically stronger than he, even though he outweighed her.

"Marissa, please, take me," he groaned, his voice hoarse from the struggle and now the begging.

"No . . ."

His heart broke as she sobbed, but he didn't let her go. He couldn't. "Take what's inside of me. I know I'm not good enough, but take me anyway."

"Don't make me do this."

"I have to." God, he felt like crying with her.

"Butch . . ." Her body bucked, strained against his. "I can't hold back . . . for much longer. . . . Let me go . . . before I hurt you."

"Never."

It happened so fast. His name shot out of her on a yell and then he felt a searing blaze of pain at the side of his throat.

Her fangs sinking into his jugular.

"Oh . . . *God* . . . *yes*. . . !" He loosened his grip, cradling her as she latched onto his neck. He called out her name as he felt a powerful, erotic draw on his vein. Pleasure swamped him, sparks flowing all through his body as if he were orgasming.

This was *so* the way it had to be. He needed her to take from him so she could live—

Marissa broke the contact abruptly and dematerialized right out of his arms.

He fell headfirst into the empty air where she'd been, face-planting into the sofa cushions. He shoved himself up and spun around.

"Marissa! *Marissa!*"

He threw himself at the door and clawed at the lock, but couldn't budge it. And then he heard her broken, desperate voice on the other side.

"I'll kill you. . . . God help me, I'll kill you. . . . I want you too much."

He pounded on the door. "Let me out!"

"I'm sorry—" Her voice cracked then grew strong, and he feared her resolve more than anything else. "I'm so sorry. I'll come to you afterwards. After it is done."

"Marissa, don't do this—"

"I love you."

He beat at the wood with his fists. "I don't care if I die!"

The lock sprang free, and he burst into the front hall. The vestibule's door was just easing shut. He ran for it flat-out.

But by the time he got out into the courtyard, she was gone.

J.R. Ward

DARK LOVER

THE DEBUT NOVEL IN THE BLACK DAGGER BROTHERHOOD SERIES

In the shadows of the night in Caldwell, New York, there's a deadly turf war going on between vampires and their slayers. There exists a secret band of brothers like no other—six vampire warriors, defenders of their race. Yet none of them relishes killing more than Wrath, the leader of The Black Dagger Brotherhood.

The only purebred vampire left on earth, Wrath has a score to settle with the slayers who murdered his parents centuries ago. But, when one of his most trusted fighters is killed—leaving his half-breed daughter unaware of his existence or her fate—Wrath must usher her into the world of the undead—a world of sensuality beyond her wildest dreams.

0-451-21695-4

"A midnight whirlwind of dangerous characters and mesmerizing erotic romance. The Black Dagger Brotherhood owns me now."
—LYNN VIEHL, AUTHOR OF *THE DARKYN* NOVELS

All your favorite romance writers are
coming together.

SIGNET ECLIPSE